Promise Me Nothing

Hermosa Beach Series, 1

Welcome to Hermosa Beach

JILLIAN LIOTA

This book is a work of fiction. While reference might be made to actual historical events or existing locations, the names, characters, places and incidents are either the product of the author's imagination or are used fictitiously, and any resemblance to any actual persons, living or dead, business establishments, events, or locales is entirely coincidental.

Copyright © 2019 by Jillian Liota

All rights reserved. In accordance with the U.S. Copyright Act of 1976, the scanning, uploading, and electronic sharing of any part of this book without the permission from the author is unlawful piracy and theft of the author's intellectual property. Thank you for your support of the author's rights.

Love Is A Verb Books

Book Cover Design and Layout by Jillian Liota

Editing and Formatting by Jillian Liota and Daniel Liota

Cover Photo © iStockPhoto.com/Portfolio/JeffBergen

ISBN 978-1-7337638-5-1
ISBN 978-1-7337638-3-7 (eBook)
ISBN 978-1-7337638-4-4 (kindle)

For my dad:

It was always a joke, whether or not I'd end up being your only child, or whether the family would find out about someone else someday.

I feel lucky that I ended up being the only one who got to know you as a daddy.

Thank you for loving me like no one else ever could.

I miss you

<3

HANNAH

It felt like it had to be a mistake this morning when I saw the email in my inbox.

Or maybe *mistake* isn't the right word.

I tap my pen against my half-finished math homework, trying to come up with the word I'm actually trying to…

Warning.

That's the word I'm looking for.

It feels like a warning, the email that sits in my inbox.

It taunts me even now as I choose to ignore it. Try not to think about it. Consider deleting it so I don't have to deal with the whole mess that's surely headed my way once I decide to finally face whatever information it contains.

If I decide to face it.

There's a big part of me that wants to delete it. Like one of those Bed, Bath and Beyond emails letting you know you have a twenty percent off coupon for one item as long as you use it this week.

Just chuck it in the trash. You don't need it.

I scrub my hands over my eyes, feeling like my thoughts aren't making sense.

There's a niggling voice, a little thing in the back of my mind that's telling me this message is... *not* as disposable as a discount coupon email. Even now, ten hours after I received the ping announcing its presence in my inbox, it feels like *for some reason...* this is just, something else entirely.

Something bigger.

Something life-changing.

And being someone who aggressively dislikes change, I saw the email and did what felt right.

Powered down my phone, closed the screen on my rented laptop, and pretended it didn't exist.

The easiest thing to do when you're faced with something difficult is to ignore it. Obviously that's also the stupidest thing to do as well. But easy and stupid tend to go hand-in-hand.

Instead of reading something that I knew could very well change my life in an instant, I tried to distract myself with other *more important* things that needed to be accomplished today.

Like this homework that still sits incomplete in my lap, my pen tap, tap, tapping against it like that will somehow clear my mind and allow me to focus on polynomial functions. Whatever the hell those are.

I stare blankly at it for a moment longer before finally accepting defeat.

Setting my homework to the side, I stretch my long, lean frame diagonally across my full-size bed, focusing my eyes on the cracks in the ceiling. The little bit of water damage in the corner from where the leak upstairs happened last month. The dusty ceiling fan that stopped working last year.

Sometimes I wonder what else life could possibly have in store for me. What *other* land mines and trip wires are stacked along the path ahead? Will my life ever *not* feel like I'm rushing head first into a war zone with every step I take?

I suck in a deep breath, hold it, then let it out. Long. Slow. Trying to release the pent up anger and frustration and disappointment. Because sitting in irritation never solved anyone's problems.

Rolling onto my side, I glance at the alarm clock sitting next to my bed. It's two o'clock on a Friday. That means Sienna is probably sitting uncomfortably on a bar stool at her sunglass kiosk job at the mall.

I briefly consider heading her way. I might not have any money to spend, but I have a monthly bus pass that can get me there, and talking to Sienna is better than sitting around my hot ass apartment.

But when I do the math in my head, I know there isn't enough time to get there and back before I need to pick up my roommate Melanie's daughter from school a little after three o'clock. So I stay laying on my back, just staring at the ceiling, trying to force myself to complete my homework.

I hate going to school, and all of the tedious busywork that comes along with it.

It didn't take me long to realize that I wouldn't be getting the traditional college experience. The one you see in the movies filled with coffee shops and doing homework at the library, Friday night frat parties and Saturday morning walks of shame.

Unfortunately, that is just not the hand that I've been dealt.

Instead, I'm a twenty-one-year-old ex-foster system resident, babysitter and waitress, fitting college courses in where I can manage the time and financial impact.

Of course, I feel guilty even thinking of myself like that. My mother was always saying there are two sides to every story. That just because I see something one way doesn't mean that's the right way to see it.

She had this thing about always countering the negative thoughts with the positive, something she was great at but, unfortunately, a skill I've never learned to apply on any kind of regular basis.

Like right now.

I *could* try to describe myself as a young woman who hasn't let foster care get the best of her, who is busting her ass to create a happy life by taking on two jobs and going to college, while slowly getting the knowledge and experience I need to build up a photography business.

I nearly gag at that description, feeling like it's something out of a Lifetime movie.

I look around my apartment. At the shabby furniture and

cracks and stains and... it just feels like I'd be giving myself too much credit. The reality feels grittier. Dirtier. More riddled with tragedy and failure and fear that still startles me awake some nights.

With my emotions full of upheaval, I know there's really only one way to deal with it. So I drag myself off of my bed and over to my dresser and closet, put on my favorite old top from my Cross Country days in high school, a shirt so worn there are holes in the armpits, and then I lace up my ragged trainers and head for the door.

It was my brother that got me into running, back when I was in junior high. Our parents had recently passed away and the two of us were in separate foster homes in opposite parts of the city and I just didn't know how to deal with my emotions.

They felt so big.

Too big.

Too overwhelming to deal with.

All the time.

Joshua was a sprinter on the Track team at his high school. A senior that year on the Varsity team, with the cool jacket to back it up, he said that running let him focus on something other than the pain he felt at the loss of our parents.

He told me how it made him feel like he was blurring out the world. Gave him a sense of calm that he couldn't find anywhere else. A numbness that eased the pain.

The first day we went jogging together, I knew exactly what he meant. I just ran and ran and ran. When we were done, Joshua was gasping for breath, and I was in a happy place I'd never known existed before. We ran seven miles that day. I hadn't known I could run that much, especially at so young. That I had the stamina or muscles or mental endurance.

I started running all the time, especially when life got harder. And in a tribute to my brother, I managed to get my own Varsity jacket when I made the Cross Country team sophomore year.

It's still one of the nicest things I own and hangs carefully in my closet.

After stretching out my stiff muscles for a few minutes, I hit the pavement with the same end in mind that Joshua introduced me to so many years ago. To let my mind fall away. My mind and everything that I don't feel like dealing with.

Today, I want to fade to nothing.

I start at an easy pace, my feet touching the ground lightly as they propel me forward. And it isn't long before I can feel my body taking over and my mind falling in line. I run like a machine, without emotion or feeling. And that's what I enjoy the most about it. The bit of nothingness that I can find when I run for long enough. Almost like I'm able to disappear.

Going on a run usually helps me pound out the frustration - a byproduct of a life spent running away from my problems.

I almost laugh at that. It's something my brother would have said. But a lance of pain shoots through me at that thought, so I dig my feet in, propelling my body forward, hoping to keep my mind distracted.

And around mile three, everything starts to fade away.

My tuition bill, which is still unpaid even as the end of the semester looms closer and closer; the fact that Paul keeps cutting back my waitressing hours even though I told him I couldn't afford to work any less without picking up a third job; Melanie's face last week when she told me that she and Lissy would be moving to New Mexico to live with her sister; the email that remains unopened, taunting me from my inbox and reminding me that life can change in an instant.

It all becomes a blur.

I don't see faces or hear voices or think about problems or feel pain. I don't allow myself to focus on the uncertainty, the many unanswered questions, the constant unknown.

I don't focus on anything.

I just run.

I'm finishing up mile six when I pass PHX Municipal Bank, my eyes connecting with the time posted on the sign outside. I curse when I realize I've lost track of time and I'm going to be late to pick up Lissy. I pick up the pace, not wanting Lissy left waiting for me out front.

She's a sweet kid. First grade. Mrs. Schumaker's class. She has a retainer and pigtails and glasses that are a little too big for her face. She struggles to make friends, but I think she's pretty amazing.

"I've been waiting for you!" she says when I come running up to where she stands next to the school sign - Randolph Woods Elementary School for the Deaf.

I'd laugh if I thought she wouldn't get mad at me. She's so cute when she's angry, her arms crossed, her backpack flung in a heap next to her feet.

"I'm sorry," I say. "I was on a run and lost track of time."

She rolls her eyes, lugs her backpack up and over her shoulder, then blazes down the pathway towards the parking lot, through the massive fence that divides her small school's property from the public.

The thing about babysitting a deaf child is that when they run - or in this case, storm - away from you, you can't just yell after them. So, I chase her down and bring her to a stop by standing in front of her.

"I didn't drive today. We have to walk."

The look of irritation written on her face could turn me into a pile of ashes. Luckily, I'm pretty familiar with this look, so I just give her a smile and take her backpack.

"I'll hold this. That way you don't have to worry about lugging it up the hill." I sling it over my shoulders, then I crouch down slightly, making sure my face is level with hers, and speak slowly, so she can understand every word. "I really am sorry for not being here on time. You don't deserve to sit out front and wait. I hope you can forgive me."

Her brow pinches together and she stays standing with her arms crossed, the cutest look of frustration still covering her face.

Then, finally, *reluctantly,* her face relaxes and she drops her arms.

"I was worried you forgot me."

My heart twists, and I nod.

It's her greatest fear, being forgotten. And it kills me to know that my own stupid mental games with myself made her feel that way.

"I know, Lis. And that's my fault. Sometimes, adults are imperfect and we run late. And you have every right to be upset." I put a hand on her shoulder. "But I want to make sure you know that no matter what, I will always be here to pick you up. I would never just leave you here."

"Even when we move to Mexico?"

Part of me wants to laugh, though I don't correct her. She's still learning her states. The other part of me is sad that even at her age, she already understands that our remaining time together is limited. I shake my head and she sighs, slipping her hand into mine as we both turn to start the walk home.

She stays quiet for a little while, but eventually she launches in to a story about Cliffton, a douchebag in her class who always says mean things to her. I know I shouldn't call a kid a douchebag, but anyone who has had to interact with this Cliffton dick before would probably take my side.

And I can't help but be fiercely protective of Lissy. I've known this pipsqueak since literally the day she was born. Her mom, my roommate Melanie, was one of the only other kids I developed a real relationship with in foster care.

Even after everything I've been through over the years, all the different places I bounced around, we've always kept a close relationship. And when Melanie's sister moved to New Mexico and I was aging out of the system, becoming her new roommate and helping out with Lissy was just a natural next step.

Discounted rent to help out with a kiddo that I already loved? Yes times ten.

I started learning to sign when Melanie found out Lissy was deaf, and when Mel is around, we use both sign and vocals to communicate. But when it's just Lis and me? She hates the attention that signing brings to her, so she asks me to speak to her instead.

Melanie usually gets mad about it, saying that lip reading as opposed to signing is a form of trying to 'fit in' that will work to Lissy's disadvantage long-term.

But I figure what Melanie doesn't know won't kill her. And having been the kid that stood out, I know that anything to feel like you 'fit in' can make a huge difference.

Once we get home, Lissy forgets all about stupid Cliffton and we spend some time on her homework and practicing new words she's been learning. Melanie gets home around six o' clock and the three of us eat dinner together.

"How was work?" I ask her as I finish putting the rice and beans out on the table. "Did you turn in your notice yet?"

Melanie works as the administrator for a health insurance claims company. She hates her job, but feels like she won the lottery with the benefits she gets. I have to agree with her.

Sometimes, you put up with the mundane, frustrating shit because it gives you what you've never had.

Consistency.

"Yeah, and my boss was really supportive." She sighs. "I wish things were different and I didn't have to leave."

"You know you can stay, right?" I say, feeling a little guilty for trying to get her to change her mind.

But Melanie shakes her head, giving me a sad smile. "And *you* know that I can't."

She's right, though I don't say it.

Melanie and her sister are best friends, and she's had a really hard time adjusting ever since Marissa moved to New Mexico three years ago. So, Melanie and Lissy are going to be packing up and following her out there. They're going to move in with Marissa and her husband, and apparently she has a job already lined up to work for a construction company that needs someone to cover a receptionist going on maternity leave.

It's great for her. Doesn't mean I'm not sad about it, though.

Eventually, we finish dinner, and then I pack up and head out to the bus stop, leaving Lissy and Melanie to their Friday evening routine of renting a movie and splurging on a few sugary treats.

Most Friday nights, I'm working at The Lone Grill, a barbeque restaurant a few miles from where we live. But stupid Paul has been stealthily slicing away hours here and there from my schedule and giving them to this new girl that I think he might be sleeping with.

Part of me wants to file a complaint, though I don't have any real proof and I'm not sure anything would come from it.

And, with mid-terms coming up next week, I decide to just take the night off for what it is: a much-needed opportunity to study and try to pass this pointless class.

Campus is only a fifteen-minute bus ride away, and I just can't afford any distractions. Even though I feel completely lost, and I'm struggling to keep up with everything, I still have to do my best.

My parents always wanted my brother and I to go to college, and there's something inside of me that won't allow myself to give up on their dream. Especially since I'm the only one left to try and live it into reality.

So, instead of calling Sienna or trying to do something interesting with my night off, I trudge my butt onto the next bus that stops at my station, and head to campus.

I truly do have good intentions when I get to the library. It's a weekend, so the building is fairly empty. Only a handful of other students are wandering around or slumped over textbooks, their lives just as pathetic as mine if we're finding ourselves studying on a community college campus on a Friday night.

Knowing I have a reflection paper to write for my Intro to Literature class, I wander over to the textbooks that are available to check out - because I definitely can't afford to buy my own - and grab the one for my class. Then I spend an hour reading a collection of poems. A bunch of flowery shit by Emily Dickinson and Walt Whitman.

When I get to Robert Frost's *The Road Not Taken,* it takes everything in me not to roll my eyes.

I don't despise literature. But I do aggressively dislike shit that's stated as fact without any consideration for what someone else's perspective might be.

Like, why would you encourage people to intentionally take the more difficult road, Robert? Maybe I'm pretty exhausted because my road is full of branches to climb over and I've got scratches from limbs and bruises from tripping and falling.

A well-traveled road that's easy to navigate sounds pretty damn great to me. And who says you get to choose? Sometimes, life gives you one shitty road and that's what you have to walk. The end.

I slam the book closed, maybe a little louder than I should in a space that's supposed to be quiet. Glancing around, I catch one girl's eyes. *Sorry*, I mouth at her, but she just looks away without acknowledging me.

Cool, cool, cool.

I carry my stuff over to one of the computer stations and log myself in to the system, gearing up to write this reflection paper that's due on Tuesday.

And it's then I make my first mistake.

I open my email.

There, sitting towards the top, sandwiched between a reminder to pay my tuition and - I can't make this up - a Bed, Bath & Beyond coupon, is the email I've been avoiding.

I minimize the screen, attempting for just one more minute to pretend that it isn't there. I crack open the literature book again and glare at Robert Frost's name, as if everything about this is his fault.

But all I can think is *just get it over with.*

Choosing to let impulse guide me, I quickly reopen my email browser and click on the message that has dominated so much of my thoughts today.

And it's here, in a quiet library, sitting at a computer, next to a printer that's whirring out what must be someone's entire dissertation, that my world does exactly what I thought it would.

It changes forever.

I barely even hear it when someone sits down at the computer to my right. Hardly notice when someone finally comes to collect the printed pages out of the printer to my left.

Because the words in this email have robbed me of my ability to use my legs. My hands. My mouth. Even my eyes, which have gone blurry and unfocused.

I blink a few times, trying to adjust my vision, the bright light of the computer screen feeling now too aggressive in my face.

But even as I blink, and blink, and try to refocus my eyes, those words never shift, change or disappear.

Your brother has joined MatchLink. Do you want to connect?

It shouldn't make a lick of sense. But it does.

My brother.

My brother.

My *brother.*

No. *Not* my brother.

My brother died when I was twelve. *My* brother's name is Joshua. *My* brother is… *was.* He was everything. He was the man I looked to for support and guidance in a world where we both felt so lost. He was my constant support until he was taken from me. Too soon. Too quickly after our parents.

So *this?* This isn't a way to connect with *my* brother. *My* brother has been gone for years, and I have mourned him and the life I thought we'd have one day.

Whoever this is? On the other side of this screen?

He might share blood with me, but he is *not* my brother.

And he'll never take Joshua's place.

My cursor hovers over a green button with a tiny DNA link on it and a few simple words.

Do you want to connect?

And then, before I can think better of it, before I can question myself, scold myself, feel ashamed about the fact that I might be replacing *my* brother ... I click yes.

Chapter Two

HANNAH

I stay seated as everyone shuffles around, slowly grabbing their things and filing noisily off the bus.

When Sienna found out I was taking a Greyhound, she told me to make sure I carried sanitizer in my hand at all times. I'd actually laughed at her, though the occasion didn't have much room for laughter. We'd been drowning our sorrows in a goodbye cheesecake while crying and saying our goodbyes at the time.

Then, as I rode on the 1353 bus route from Phoenix to Union Station in Los Angeles, I finally understood what she meant. The blue micro suede seats weren't an issue. Neither was the bathroom in the back. Everything about the bus itself was totally fine.

The bus wasn't what Sienna had been referring to.

It was the people.

Specifically, it was the kid in front of me picking his nose and wiping it on the window. And the guy a few seats away who was dipping and spitting noisily into a water bottle.

And then there was the woman sitting next to me that pulled a full-size bucket of KFC out of her bag and proceeded to eat the entire thing as I watched in mortification out of the corner of my eye.

Part of me marveled at her ability to put it all away. She was a tiny little thing, so I couldn't imagine where she stored it all. And the precision with which she went after every last little bit of chicken was nothing short of impressive. But after she was done - two hours later - she never wiped her greasy hands and proceeded to touch everything around her.

I have some mild issues with cleanliness. It doesn't matter what the situation is. My room? Impeccable. My clothes? It's an intentional choice to wait three days between washing things, and that's only because I've never lived somewhere that doesn't charge for laundry and the expense of doing it daily would have been too much.

When you're a kid who isn't in control of the environment you're in, when you're surrounded by dozens of different habits and levels of hygiene and just have to deal with overall dirtiness, having a clean environment to exist in becomes important.

At least to me.

So I'd practically jumped through the window when her hand moved in my direction once or twice on the seven-hour ride.

Now, as I sit in my window seat, my eyes staring through the glass unseeing towards the platform while everyone waddles off this beast of a bus, our bodies tired from having to sit uncomfortably for so long, I'm starting to have second thoughts about my decision.

Fears that I made the wrong choice. That I gave up too easily and took the simple way out.

I gave Frost the middle finger and darted down the path *more* travelled the second I saw an indicator that maybe the branches had been trimmed back and the fallen trees cleared away.

Does that make me weak? That I don't want to be on my own anymore? That carrying around the weight life has handed me is starting to buckle me at the knees?

I close my eyes. Count to ten. Pull in a long breath. Hold it. Let it out slowly.

And then I remember Lucas' voice over the phone.

God, he'd sounded just like my dad. I'd had to mute the damn thing so he didn't hear me trying not to fucking cry. I haven't really cried in – I quickly try to do the math – nine years. Since the day I watched as Joshua's body was lowered in to the ground.

My brother was many things to me. My best friend. My secret keeper. In some ways, he was my guardian, even if not legally. It was just the two of us against the world. After our parents died, we both went in to the system. Being eight years older, he aged out within a year and tried to get custody of me.

It didn't work. He might have seemed so strong and mature to me when I was so young and unsure and filled with grief. But an eighteen-year-old with almost no money was too young to take care of a squirrelly elementary school student, at least in the eyes of any Child Protective Services representative he could get to listen to him.

But that didn't stop Joshua from being involved in my life. He was always kind-hearted, thinking of other people, trying to make our lives better. He helped me with homework and made sure my foster parents were doing right by me.

Which is why his death was so startling. So unfair.

I'd already lost enough, hadn't I? What had I done to deserve this new cruel twist?

Rationally, I know now that life just happens, and you can only control how you react to it. But when you're just about to turn ten and you lose your parents, and then the center of your universe is ripped away less than three years later... it's hard to think the world *doesn't* have it out for you.

I'd lost my breath, nearly keeled over, dry heaved. The woman from CPS that came to tell me about Joshua's death tried to be empathetic, but if I could have killed her in that moment, I would have.

She promised me everything would be okay. But I felt so small. And so lost. I'd just lost the last person in the world that mattered, and it was hard to believe anyone who promised me anything.

It wasn't hard to believe Lucas though, a voice whispers in my mind.

It's been an awkward month and a half, trying to get to know the brother I'd never known about.

Well, I guess that's not entirely honest.

I might not have known about Lucas, but finding out about him allows some of my memories to make a lot more sense.

Like the fact that dad always took a 'business trip' to California every summer, even though he mostly worked at a local hardware store that probably wouldn't have sent him anywhere.

Or that one time when I was seven and he disappeared for a few months. My mother cried at the sink as she did the dishes. Joshua, typically a jovial and friendly teenager, changed into this moody and sullen creature that slammed doors and stayed out past dark with friends even though my mom told him not to.

Eventually he came back. And I guess I just blocked some of those things out, or at least pushed them aside. Because it wasn't until my first email exchange with Lucas that any of that even popped back in to my mind, a written indicator that I'd known something was amiss all along.

And then there's the fear that I've been somehow complicit in covering it up. I wonder how much Joshua knew about Lucas. If he'd known anything more than what I did.

The only real and true thing I know about this whole fucked up situation is that now I have a brother who is two years older than me, but would have been four or five years younger than Joshua. Which means my dad had an affair.

"I'm the bastard child," Lucas joked when we talked on the phone for the first time, sounding way too relaxed when everything inside of me was squirming with discomfort.

We've talked a few times. Well. *He* did most of the talking. I responded awkwardly in fits and stammers and one-word answers. *Are you in college? Yes. Have you ever been to the beach? Never. Do you know what you're doing for the summer? No clue.*

"Come to California," he'd said, surprising the hell out of me the second time we talked on the phone. "You're in between things and there is more than enough space for you here. And I'd love to *really* get to know you. There's only so much you can understand about someone on the phone, you know?"

I'd sat on my bed, legs crossed and head leaning back against the wall, thinking it all over while Lucas rambled on and on. About what his house was like and how I could have my own room and bathroom and he'd help me get a summer job if I needed one. All the ways we could make it work.

I only heard part of it, thinking instead about my own situation. Melanie and Lissy had left the week before for New Mexico, leaving me behind to finish out the lease, which was almost up anyway. School was going to be out for the summer soon and my hostess hours continued to go down thanks to Paul being a disgusting pig.

I could have stuck around in Phoenix and tried to keep things going. Tried to find a new place to live, new roommates, a new job that replaced babysitting Lissy as well as the discounted rent and my declining hours at the restaurant.

I could have done it.

But sometimes, when you've been treading water for so long, it feels easier to slip beneath the surface, even just for a minute, to give yourself a break.

So it felt normal to wonder if that's what I'd done when I agreed to abandon my life in Arizona and spend the summer with my new brother at some beach house in California. If I'd given up. Given in. Accepted that I couldn't make it on my own. That I needed someone else to keep me afloat. Someone else to help me find that easier path.

"You awake?"

My head whips to the side, and I see the bus driver hovering over me, a confused look on his face.

"Sorry," I say, shuffling awkwardly out of my seat and into the aisle. I swing my backpack onto my shoulders. "I was just..." I trail off, shake my head. "Thanks."

He nods at me, steps in between two seats to let me pass, and I walk through the bus and down the steps, out on to the platform. I grab my duffle bag, the only one still sitting on the ground next to the bus, and pull the strap across my shoulder, holding it tightly against my stomach.

Today, everything I thought I knew about life... is going to change.

Time to go meet my new brother.

It doesn't take long for me to realize something's wrong.

I look at my watch, a cheap thing I got when I was eleven. Joshua won it at the arcade near my school the weekend before it shut down. Replaced by a pet shop full of animals desperate for somewhere to belong. Being one of only a few small things I have that remind me of my brother, I haven't ever had the heart to get rid of it.

I've been waiting over two hours for Lucas to get here and pick me up, the hunger in my stomach starting to pinch and pull. Taking another sip from my water, I dig my phone out of my backpack to check *again* that my data is working, that there aren't any missed emails or phone calls.

Nothing.

It's strange that he isn't here, especially since I called him yesterday to make sure that everything was still good-to-go. That he had my bus' arrival time and knew what I'd be wearing. A comfortable pair of jeans and a loose red Diamondbacks t-shirt that I got when Sienna took me to a game for my birthday last year.

I try calling Lucas' number, but it goes straight to voicemail again, and I let out a sigh.

There are plenty of people who would probably call me stupid. Running off to California to live with someone I don't know at all, regardless of how simple he made everything sound on the phone. Having some of the same blood running in our veins doesn't mean I'll be safe.

There's a point of pride I have, though, in still trying to trust people, even though it doesn't come naturally. It would be so easy to give in to the idea that everyone I meet has an ulterior motive. My entire life so far has done nothing but shove that idea in my face. Over and over again.

But that doesn't mean I have to believe it's true. I might not be able to be as bubbly and positive as my mother usually was, always able to see the bright side in every situation, but I can still try to believe that people are worth trusting. And I'm hopeful my time with Lucas will help prove that.

Letting out a sigh, I wander over to the information booth and grab a map of the bus system, resigning myself to the idea that I'm probably going to have to find my own way to Lucas' house. He might not be here to get me, but I literally don't have anywhere else to go, so I'm thankful I was at least smart enough to get his address for mail forwarding so I'm not just stuck here, completely helpless.

I close my eyes and look up, letting the sun wash over me, the air a bit more humid than I'm used to. Arizona has that dry, desert heat, devoid of any kind of moisture. You never feel like you're sweating because it evaporates faster than you notice the dampness on your skin. The humidity of the beach cities in LA is going to be an adjustment.

I take a seat against the building on the patterned brick that stretches across the passenger pickup area, making sure to get in a sliver of shade provided by a handful of palms clustered together, and take a look at the bus routes, trying to figure out a way to get to Lucas' house.

Once I've sorted out a route for myself, I feel a little better, the bit of tightness in my chest that had been forming finally starting to loosen. Maybe by the time I get on the subway, then transfer between a few buses, he'll be able to answer his phone if I call again.

I'm digging around in my wallet to double check the amount of cash I have, cringing as I remember that I spent a few dollars on snacks for the trip, when I hear my name.

I turn my head sharply, surprised, my eyes darting to the curb with the faintest glimmer of hope. Towards a truck parked at the curb and a blond guy rounding the back and looking in my direction.

He lifts a hand to give me a small wave as he steps up the curb and walks towards me. He's all casual beach attire in a pair of trunks and sandals, his shaggy hair making him look exactly like the beach boy I'd pictured him to be.

And then a smile stretches across his face.

A face that looks so much like my dad's that my mouth actually drops open.

I saw a photo of Lucas when we Facebook friend-ed each other, and I knew the instant I saw that picture that he truly was related to my dad.

But seeing him now, in-person, as he walks towards me with an expression that reminds me of the man who used to tuck me in at night when I was a little girl...

It's a hard pill to swallow.

"Hannah?"

He says my name again and I manage to finally give him a little bit of a grin and a half wave from where I sit on the ground, sprawled out with my few belongings.

I must look absolutely ridiculous.

"Ye... Yeah. Yeah, that's me," I say, my throat choking on the words. I scramble to my feet, dusting my hands off on my shorts, then stick a hand out to him. "Lucas, right? Nice to meet you."

He grins at me, an easy smile full of a sincerity that surprises me. And then he does the last thing I expect.

He steps forward and pulls me into a hug.

A tight one. The type of hug you expect to get from people who love you. The type of hug I haven't felt in quite a while. Since the last time I saw Joshua.

Not knowing exactly what to do with myself, I stand there stiffly, finally raising my forearms so I can give him a light tap on the back.

He chuckles, then steps away.

"Not really a hugger, huh?"

I lift a shoulder, giving him a small smile. "It's been a while, I guess."

His face falls slightly. "Since you've been hugged?"

I nod.

His expression stays confused. But I don't offer him any more than that. Besides, I'm sure the last thing he wants to hear when he's first meeting the sister he never knew about is the nitty-gritty of what happens in the system.

It's not even something I want to hear, and I'm the one who lived through it.

I lug my backpack over my shoulder, using it as an excuse to look away from him. This causes him to spring in to action, reaching over to grab the duffle that's resting at my feet.

"So, is this all you brought?" he asks, walking us towards his swanky blue truck, which sits still running at the curb.

"It's all I own."

He chucks my duffle into the back with a little more force than I'm expecting, then plants both hands along the rim of the bed and lets out an exhale, his shoulders tight.

Then he turns and looks back at me, and gives me a smile. "You know, I heard being a minimalist is pretty freeing. Maybe I can learn something from you." Then he pops open the passenger door for me and rounds the front to climb in to the driver's seat.

I don't have the heart to tell him that I've never been a minimalist, so I keep my mouth shut and just get in.

"Sorry I'm so late," he says, giving me that same comfortable smile as we pull out onto the road. "Traffic was horrible."

"Oh, that's okay," I say, not wanting to focus on his tardiness. The last thing I want to do is make him feel bad when he's going out of his way to pick me up. "I wasn't waiting that long."

He makes a light humming sound. Not an agreement, just an acknowledgement.

"So how was the trip? It was like, eight hours or something, right?"

I let out a sigh. "A little over seven. And it was exhausting. I haven't sat in one place for that long before."

"Well, I'll try to get you back to the house as quickly as possible so you aren't sitting for too much longer," he says. Then his eyes drop to my shirt. "And once we get there, I'll see if I have a better shirt for you to wear."

My eyes drop, taking in the Diamondback shirt. "Huh?"

"This is Dodger territory," he says, and I finally pick up on the teasing in his voice. "I'm not sure I can have a D-Bag supporter staying in my house."

I allow myself to smile. "I don't really watch baseball."

"Me neither. But if you're staying with me, I gotta make sure you fit in."

Nodding, I look back out the window and watch as we drive through Downtown Los Angeles. It only takes a few minutes to get onto the freeway, and holy moly was Lucas not joking when he said traffic is bad right now. It's horrendous.

I remember when I was younger there was some big thing on the news about freeways in California. Carmaggedon, I think it was called. Bumper-to-bumper as far as the eye can see. Exactly what things look like right now.

And then I face the realization that I'm tired and starving and facing another long ride before I have a moment to myself.

I've never been particularly good at small talk. Sienna said the girls at our old school used to call me The Cactus because I was so prickly. I struggle with jokey-joke stuff and just kind of... enjoy silence. It works for me, but other people don't seem to get it.

I glance at Lucas out of the corner of my eye. He seems nice enough as he sits there, singing lightly with the music coming from the radio. But I can't think of anything to say. So I sit like a mute, my mind in a jumble, just looking in to the neighboring cars as we bob and weave and pass them, then fall behind. It's an endless crawl.

"Is it always this bad?" I finally ask about fifteen minutes later, having thought about no less than a hundred things I could say to not remain a mute.

Lucas shrugs. "Pretty much. Although, we're about to breeze through it."

My brow furrows in confusion until I see Lucas pull off to the left side, into two lanes that are completely free from traffic. And then suddenly we're going eighty miles per hour and blowing past everyone.

I smile, looking over my shoulder as we leave everyone behind. "This is awesome."

"Yeah it is." He points at a little box that sits on his dashboard. "I don't mind paying extra to drive in the FastPass lanes. There's nothing in the world more satisfying than driving past everyone else stuck in traffic."

"We don't have a lane like this in Phoenix, so when it's time for traffic, you're just sitting in it for *forever*. I mostly rode the bus. But I can't imagine sitting in something like this every day."

At Lucas' silence, I take a peek at him and catch his eyes on me.

"What?"

He shrugs. "I just think that's the most words you've said to me at once since we started talking. I'm glad. I was starting to worry that you were, I don't know, afraid to talk to me or something."

I blush, the heat of my embarrassment rising to the space between my cheeks and my ears. Whenever I'm embarrassed, I blush and then start sweating. It's really unpleasant, but even worse in an environment where the sweat doesn't evaporate into thin air.

"Hey, I just meant I'm glad you feel like you can say something to me. Anything. The last thing I want is for you to get here and feel like your lips have to be zipped."

I nod, give him a tight smile and look back out the window, which is where my eyes stay for the majority of the ride. We change freeways after a little while, get stuck in more traffic, then finally pull off.

I already did a Google street search to make sure I wouldn't be living in an area worse than where I was living in Arizona, so I know he lives in a big ass house right on the water in a town called Hermosa Beach. But really, that's all I know about where he lives.

When we talked on the phone before I agreed to move, he told me a little about his life. Just enough to make me feel like coming to stay with him would be a good thing.

I know his mom is a work-a-holic who manages 'talent' for some big agency and that Lucas is basically on his own even though he still lives at home. I know he has a girlfriend named Remmy that is finishing up college in Santa Barbara.

So, if my assumptions are correct, it will be mostly just the two of us this summer, since his mom and girlfriend aren't around much. Which works for me. I haven't had parents in almost ten years. The last thing I want is a mother-type hovering over me and resenting me because of something my dad did several decades ago.

"You ever been?"

I realize he's been talking as we breeze past all of the traffic and I totally zoned him out.

I shake my head. "Sorry, my mind wandered. What did you say?"

He gives me that charming smile again. "I asked if you've ever been surfing before."

I laugh. "Definitely not. Unless you count boarding sand dunes in Yuma, which I doubt. And really, that was more like sledding, though I wasn't entirely horrible at it."

He nods his head, turning his eyes back out to the mess of cars surrounding us.

"I'm assuming you do? Surf?"

He lifts a shoulder. "You could say that."

"How long have you been doing it?"

"Since I was like, maybe four or five. My dad taught me."

His words are innocent, but we both feel the guilt of the marks they leave behind. Because what isn't said when he shares that *his dad* taught him to surf is that *my dad* taught him how to surf. *My dad* was the one who got into the water with him and showed him what he was doing.

Or I guess... *our dad,* if I want to be technical.

Which I don't.

In our first conversation, we tried to figure out the timeline from way back. From when we were kids and the lives we were living didn't exactly match up to what was actually happening.

At least for me.

But apart from knowing the year it happened and a few of Lucas' scattered memories of the times dad visited him during his childhood, we don't have much else to go on. Joshua never talked about it that I can remember, and Lucas says his mom is like a vault of information unwilling to open.

The only thing I'm certain of is that there was some kind of *affair.* And knowing that my parents didn't have the idyllic relationship that I'd always imagined them having is definitely an adjustment.

How do I look back on the life of the man I idolized and realize it was all a lie?

Chapter Three
HANNAH

I had an idea in my head of what Lucas' house looked like. No, scratch that. I literally looked online to see what it would look like. From the maps view, I'd been able to tell it was big, and figured it was fancy since it has a beach view.

But still, nothing could really prepare me for seeing the real thing, up close and personal.

When we got off the freeway, Lucas had rolled down his windows, drumming his fingers on the steering wheel to an old Foo Fighters song. He's an energetic guy, and really into music, that's for sure.

But it wasn't until we passed Hotel Hermosa, a mammoth of a place that seemed to welcome you to town, that I smelled the ocean for the first time.

There was something familiar about it. Something that stirred an emotion inside of me that I wasn't ready to feel.

Salty and sticky and a little bit fishy. The ocean air wrapped around my throat and squeezed, keeping me from saying much as we cruised down and then up and then down again, over a handful of small hills as we got closer and closer to the water in dips and waves.

And then the road opened and we turned onto the main drag of Hermosa Beach, a long stretch apartments and small houses to my left across the large street, and the large beach-front homes side-by-side to my right.

And then Lucas slowed, clicked something on his visor, and I realized we were here.

And now, I can't stop staring, my mouth slightly ajar as I gape up at the absolutely enormous mammoth that I'll be calling home for the summer.

What the hell did I get myself into?

"It's beautiful," I say, finally managing a few words, though they honestly don't do this place any form of justice.

Glancing over at Lucas, I find him looking at me with a microscopic smile on his face. But he doesn't say anything. He just finishes pulling his truck into the three-car garage, slipping in between a car and SUV. He turns off the engine, leaving his windows down, and slips out.

Before I can even open my door, Lucas has rounded the back and grabbed my duffel bag from the bed of the truck. He taps twice on the frame of the car above where I sit, then tilts his head towards a door in the corner of the garage that I can only assume leads inside.

"Come on, *sis,*" he says with a smirk, then walks off. "Let's get you settled in."

I slide slowly out of the front seat, clutching my backpack against my chest, and follow him inside.

I've never envied wealth. Never felt like I missed out on something as a child because we lived in a rented apartment in a cheaper part of town. I never felt ashamed of the fact we'd lived on food stamps for a few months when I was a kid when my dad lost his job. And when everything in my life imploded, I might never have wished to live in foster homes, but for the most part I was still kept fed and sheltered.

So, looking back, there wasn't anything I wanted that I didn't have, apart from my own family. Because I'd never been taught to desire anything more.

Some of how I felt is probably because I didn't really *know* what wealth looked like when I was a kid. And then I didn't care about it as I grew older. Sure, you see Beyoncé and Jay-Z's family on magazines at the grocery store and wonder what it might be like to have unlimited spending power. But nothing like that feels real, tangible, something you can feel with your own hands.

But this? Right now? The sprawling entry that leads through a home where I can see the sun setting in floor-to-ceiling windows on the other end?

This makes me embarrassed of the food stamps as a kid, the foster care as a teen, the apartment I could barely afford as an adult. Everything about my life screams that I'm lacking in the things that Lucas seems to have in abundance.

Like money. And confidence. Complete comfort in his own skin and a belief that he deserves to take up space in this world.

I hate how it makes me feel.

My host doesn't seem to notice, though, as he walks in and casually chucks his keys onto a small entry table, setting my bag down and heading to the right.

"Want something to drink?" he calls out, and I force myself to close my mouth and follow him in.

"I'm not really thirsty," I say, clutching my backpack tighter against my chest, my eyes flying all over the place, trying to swallow everything I can as if I only have seconds to take it all in.

"Are all the houses in the area this big?" I ask, hating myself for being curious but still unable to keep myself from asking.

"Actually, no. Good catch," he says, leaning against the counter and crossing his legs, his hands braced behind him on the marble. "This house is a double lot, so it really is an obscene amount of space."

I nod, still glancing around.

The kitchen is large and modern, with stainless steel and double ovens, fancy marble and antiqued white cabinets. It opens up to an expansive living room with a flat screen on the wall and multiple overstuffed couches. A glass dining room table separates the kitchen from a wide balcony that looks out to the beach.

"Welcome, officially. Do you want to snoop around on your own, or do you want a real tour?" Lucas asks, chuckling. "We have people here all the time but if you're going to be living here I guess I should make sure you know where everything is."

I manage to nod again, setting down my backpack on the floor near the kitchen island.

"Let's go downstairs first."

"I thought this was the ground floor."

"It's the floor that's at street level, but the house is built in to an incline. So the actual ground level is downstairs and opens out to the beach."

I smile at Lucas and try to push away some of my initial discomfort. "I feel like I'm on *Lifestyles of the Rich and Famous.*"

Lucas laughs, shakes his head and motions for me to follow him downstairs.

When we emerge from the staircase, we enter what looks like a living room, fairly similar to the one upstairs, with a large TV and lots of couches. Though there's also a pool table, a long bar stocked with alcohol and a novelty juke box in the corner.

"Down here is the party room," he says, then turns to point to a few closed doors. "There's also the home theatre, a gym, and the wine cellar. This space gets used a lot when friends come over because it opens out to The Strand."

He walks over to the sliding doors that lead out to a patio, opens one up, and then slides it all the way to the side, effectively taking the indoor living room and making it part of the outside.

And then there's the sand and sea. Right there. Close enough to touch right now if I want to.

"That is so cool," I say, stepping out onto the tiled exterior space and pulling in a deep inhale of salty sea air. "God, I love that smell. It's so weird, there's something familiar about it, but I've never been to the beach before."

Lucas doesn't say anything, surely just watching me be a weirdo.

Once I've got my fill, I open my eyes and turn to look at him. "So, if you have a party room, do you have lots of parties?"

He gives me a smile that I've seen on a lot of my foster siblings. The ones who feel like they've been caught doing something they shouldn't.

"I wouldn't say a lot," he answers, and I know instinctively that he's downplaying the party atmosphere at his house. "But I do host a huge 4th of July event every year. And there are a few others throughout the summer, for sure. But mostly, it's just a hangout room. My friend Paige says it's our MTV room because it's so flashy."

I nod, deciding not to say anything else, then step back in and help Lucas close up the sliding doors.

He quickly shows me the theatre room, which consists of several massive couches and a projector screen. "Any gaming system you could possibly want," Lucas boasts. "And a pretty decent movie collection."

Then the gym, which is floor to ceiling mirrors and filled with workout equipment, yoga mats, exercise balls and weight sets. And the wine cellar, "which isn't really a cellar as much as a massive fridge room."

"You have an entire room of chilled wine?" I ask, raising an eyebrow and holding back a laugh. "Part of me feels like you're not even a wine drinker."

He crosses his arms in what I can only guess is fake displeasure. "You don't know. I could be a connoisseur of wine." But then he winks at me and heads back towards the stairs.

"You saw the main floor. Kitchen and dining over here, living space on the left," he says when we hit the floor we came in on, but he doesn't stop walking, just continuing up to the top floor.

"There are four bedrooms up here. The two masters belong to me and my mom, though, like I told you before, she's almost never here," he says, rolling his eyes. "She's dating this total dick who lives near her office and she stays there a lot. So you won't have to worry about seeing her around much. But feel free to pick from the other two. They're pretty identical. Both have access to a balcony that faces the street, and the rooms share a bathroom."

He leads me into one, filled with white furniture and peach bedding, then walks me through a massive bathroom with a walk in shower and oversized claw foot tub. Then we go to the next guest room. It's basically a mirror of the other one, but with blues and teals instead.

"It doesn't have a beach view from these rooms, but..." Lucas says, leading me out to the small space that overlooks the road. Then he points at a spiral staircase in the corner that leads up. "...it does have roof access. And there's a beach view up there. Plus a Jacuzzi."

My eyebrows lift. "A Jacuzzi on the roof, huh? I think you're not being completely honest when you say you only have a few parties a year."

I'm teasing him, but he actually blushes. It makes me want to laugh since we clearly both got that trait from my dad.

Our. *Our* dad.

"Well, okay. Maybe I have people over a lot." He shrugs. "I'm a people person."

I smile at him. Possibly my first real smile of the day. "I can definitely tell that you're a people person."

He chuckles and leads me back inside and downstairs.

I look around again, hoping to take in more this time as I absorb everything about this place. This new house I'll be calling home for the upcoming few months. Until I figure out what's next.

"Your house is amazing," I say, knowing my words are inadequate. It looks like something out of a magazine. Or something I might see on HGTV. "I can't believe you live like this."

"Oh yeah? What was your house like?"

He's not saying it maliciously. I can see the genuine curiosity on his face. But I'm starting to realize that Lucas could never understand the situation I came out of. What I've been through. How I scraped by, just barely.

I shrug and look away, though my mind thinks about the apartment I just moved out of. The one in the bad neighborhood, with a broken A/C unit and hardly enough room in my bedroom for a twin bed. "Smaller," is what I settle on. "And not as clean. Which I *love* about this place, by the way. I'm a bit of a neat freak."

He groans. "Ugh. Thalia's gonna love you, then. She normally hates when I have guests because they're so messy."

"Who's Thalia?"

"Our maid."

I laugh for a second, then stop abruptly, realizing that he's serious. "You're serious."

He nods. "Yeah. It's pretty common around here, I think."

I nod back. "Cool." I feel thankful that I'll be in a house that's kept clean, but also, I can't help but feel slightly awkward at the idea of someone cleaning up after me.

I'll need to think that one over.

"I'd say let's get you settled, but we should head outside first, enjoy the last little bit of daylight," he says. "Come on."

Lucas leads me to the floor to ceiling windows that overlook the ocean, the sand, and what he referred to earlier as The Strand, a long stretch of path where people are walking and running and riding bikes. Then he opens a sliding door out to the balcony, letting the ocean air rush in.

I step out, lean on the railing and look out at the beach, at the ocean in the distance, so large it could swallow anything whole.

Suddenly, all at once, all of the emotions I've been feeling all day long - a rush of exhaustion and anxiety and stress - hit me in one fell swoop.

"You okay?" he asks.

I should be wary of how quickly he's learning to read me when we've only been around each other for a few hours. But instead, I just nod. "Yeah. Feeling pretty tired. It's been a long day of bus riding and waiting at the station and then traffic here."

Lucas winces, and I feel bad for bringing up my long wait at Union Station. "I'm sorry again for being late. Traffic was bad but I also left a little bit later than I should have." He scratches the back of his neck, clearly uncomfortable.

I shrug it off, trying to seem unaffected even though I'd been anything but. "It's not a big deal."

"It *is* though."

The sincerity in his voice has me looking at him again.

"You're traveling all this way to meet me, to get to know me, and the first thing I do is leave you waiting?" He shakes his head, his hands braced on the railing in front of us. The remorse on his face is palpable. "I am *really* sorry, Hannah."

My mouth ticks up slightly at the side and I bob my head, a silent thank you for his sincerity. I turn away again, looking towards the sun setting beautifully on the horizon, enjoying this strange but lovely moment with the only family I have left in the world.

"Lucas!" a feminine voice calls out, and my eyes look down the way, towards a girl in a pink bikini on a beach cruiser heading in our direction.

"Fuck."

It's barely a whisper that I hear from Lucas, but it has my eyes flicking to him.

"Not someone you want to see?" I ask, a small smile making its way to my face.

He lets out a sigh, but gives the brunette in the tiny bathing suit a wave.

"Hey Lennon. How's it?"

She pulls her bike up to the ground floor outside of Lucas' house, hopping off and putting down the kickstand.

"Pretty good. We missed you at Otto's last night." She rests her palms against the top of the short wall that divides the downstairs patio from The Strand, then gazes adoringly up at where Lucas and I stand a floor above her.

"Yeah, I got caught up."

She pulls her sunglasses up and rests them on the crown of her head. "Can I come in?" she asks, then bites her lip. "I'd love it if *we* could get caught up."

My eyebrows rise up so high I'm certain they blend in with my hair. I've been around a lot of young girls and young women who are pretty overt with their interest in someone. But that response right there has to take the cake.

I glance over at Lucas, then back at Lennon, who seems to be looking between the two of us.

"Sorry," Lucas says, shrugging a shoulder. "My sister just got to town and I'm gonna be pretty busy tonight."

Lennon's head jerks back and her brow furrows. "You don't have a sister," she says, letting out a disbelieving laugh, her eyes coming back to me, assessing.

"Well, she's new in town and we're just getting caught up and relaxing on the patio." His words are a clear dismissal, the implication that he doesn't have time to chat ringing loudly.

"Oh fun!" she says, clearly missing the point, instead giving him a smile. "I love relaxing on your patio and chatting about anything."

There's an awkward pause.

"Well. It was good to see you, Len. I'll see you later."

Her smile falls slightly, but then picks back up. "Okay, yeah. I'll see you soon. Maybe at Otto's this week?"

Lucas bobs his head. "Yeah, maybe."

Lennon hops back onto her bike and gives him a wave again, then heads off, continuing her journey down The Strand.

A few minutes tick by and we stand in silence before I can't help myself. "There's a story there," I say, giving him a smile.

He barks out a laugh. "There's like, ten stories there."

But he doesn't elaborate any further, his expression becoming somewhat distant as he stands next to me, looking out over the beach.

As the sun dips lower in the sky, the temperature takes a sudden dip that has me wishing I had on a sweater.

Lucas turns to me. "So, what do you say we get you settled in one of the rooms and then we grab something for dinner? I know you're tired, but you've gotta be hungry."

I smile just as my stomach gurgles loudly.

We both laugh.

Looking like I don't really have a choice in the matter.

"Count me in."

Chapter Four

HANNAH

A short while later, we're sitting at a place called Bennie's at the Pier, an upscale brewery with a rooftop bar and a view of the ocean and the Hermosa Pier as it stretches out into the water.

We rode here on bikes along The Strand, the sea breeze snagging tendrils of my hair from the unkempt bun I've had up since midway through the bus trip. It took about ten minutes to ride from Lucas' house to the pier, and was actually pretty fun. It's been a long time since I've ridden a bike, my own disappearing when I went in to the system. I love that I'll be able to ride around town on two wheels.

Lucas took me out to this little storage area on the side of his house filled with a handful of bikes, a few surfboards, and other beach equipment, and told me I could use anything I wanted. I picked a light blue and pale pink beach cruiser, one of the ones you see on TV that has a basket and wide handlebars. It will be such a great way to get around Hermosa this summer.

I sip my vodka soda, keeping my eyes on the horizon, the sun having set not too long ago. The glow from it still radiates out from where the earth meets the sky.

"The sky just after sunset is my favorite," Lucas says, drawing my attention over to where he sits, glass of whiskey in-hand. "Most people want to watch the sun dip down, but I prefer how it looks afterwards. Especially when there are just a handful of clouds. It looks different every night."

"It seems like living at the beach would be magical all the time."

He shakes his head. "I don't want to sound like a snob, but it's definitely not. There are a lot of positives, don't get me wrong," he laughs at the disbelieving look on my face. "But there are the negatives, too."

I squint my eyes at him. "Name three."

Lucas rubs his hand across his chin. "Putting me on the spot here." He takes another sip from his drink and then puts it down, leaning forward and considering me before he answers. "Okay. One is that everything is damp all the time. The ocean air is so wet that metal rusts a lot faster. Even paper curls up and gets wrinkly."

I nod. "Okay, I'll accept that. Another one."

He chuckles again. "Alright, everyone sees it as the party spot and not a place where people live, so tourists treat the area like shit and get really loud all the time."

"Don't you do that, too?" I ask. "When you have your parties?"

Lucas lifts a shoulder. "I might annoy my neighbors with the parties *on occasion,*" he emphasizes, "but I definitely don't litter, and people treat the beach like it's a trash can."

I grin. "One more."

He drops his head back, groaning. A beat goes by before his eyes return to mine. "You got me. That's all I can come up with."

"Ha!" I cry out, pointing at him. Then I flush, realizing how loud I was, forgetting myself for a moment.

Lucas just smiles and lifts his menu to peruse.

I lift mine as well, and my stomach bottoms out when I see the prices. What was I thinking, coming here?

My mind starts racing through what I have in the bank and in cash, trying to quickly calculate how much I'll need to get by until I can manage to find a job. But realistically, I know that eating anything other than the ice cubes in my drink isn't in the plans for me tonight.

Time to just suck it up and blurt it out, because the cash in my wallet and the little bit in my bank account just cannot allow me to do anything but head to a grocery store and stock up on PB&J and microwave ramen.

"I probably should have thought of this beforehand," I say, wincing slightly at the embarrassment tugging at my neck, "but I can't afford this place." I point at the menu. "They're charging twenty-five dollars for an appetizer."

Lucas smiles at me. "Don't worry about it. I've got dinner."

I shake my head. "I don't want it to seem like I'm coming here expecting you to..."

"Hannah." He shakes his head. "Welcome to Hermosa. Tonight is my treat. I knew you weren't going to have gobs of cash when you got here, okay? That's why I'm gonna help you find a job."

I let out a sigh. "You're *sure,* sure? Because I can..."

"*Hannah.*" His tone is a mixture of exasperation and amusement. "I'm sure. Now." He lifts his menu and takes a look at it again. "Let's see what's on the menu tonight." He dips the menu slightly so I can see his face again. "Do you like hipster food? Because that's everything they have on the menu."

I can't help the little giggle that escapes my lips, but it gets cut off by a near shriek from the corner.

"Oh my *god*, she wasn't lying!"

I snap my head to the left, to a short blonde standing at the top of the stairs and looking in our direction with wide eyes and an even wider smile.

Wearing a bikini top under a white tank and a pair of jean cutoff shorts, her skin tan with a hint of pink, she looks like she just stepped out of a photo shoot. Her hair is a thick mess of short tendrils tucked back behind a pair of gold sunglasses.

She's gorgeous, with amazing curves on a petite frame, and when she finally moves in our direction, slipping between tables with ease and confidence, never letting her eyes stray from where I'm sitting, I can tell that she knows the type of power her presence commands.

"When Lennon told me you were spending time with your sister, I said she must have taken one too many surfboards to the head but here she is. In the flesh."

She continues to stare at me, her eyes roving over everything she can see on the surface. Though, if I had to guess, I'd say she's trying to find the secrets underneath as well.

"Paige. It's rude to gawk."

Lucas' reprimand is said with a hint of teasing, and it's then that I connect the name with the person standing in front of me.

"Is this the Paige you mentioned earlier?" I ask.

Paige tilts her head to look at Lucas, her eyes narrowing. "Been talking shit about me, Pearson?"

"No, no, no," I say, my eyes widening and worry rolling through my body. "We were talking about the downstairs room in his house and he said you called it... *shit*, now I can't remember."

Lucas starts laughing and Paige follows in his wake, and I just give an awkward smile as I try to follow along and understand the dynamic between them. Are they friends? Dating? I thought his girlfriend's name was Remmy?

"Don't mind this troll," Lucas says, aiming his thumb in her direction. "She just never realizes when she's unwanted."

Okay. Definitely not dating, then.

Ignoring Lucas' words, Paige plops down in the seat next to him, dropping a tiny leather backpack into the one other vacant chair, then gives him a not-so-unnoticeable elbow in the middle of the bicep.

"What he's trying to say is that before he had a real sister," Paige says, pointing at me, "he had me, which was the closest thing he's ever had to a sibling to tease and torture."

Lucas rolls his eyes, but I can see the bit of affection and playfulness that he's trying to hide.

"Ignore her. She always thinks she's more important than she really is."

Now it's Paige's turn to roll her eyes.

"Anyway," she says, dragging the word out and then turning her attention in my direction, "Lucas having a sister is already the only thing anyone can talk about. So, help a girl out and tell me everything about yourself so I can be the insider with all of the information." Then she rests her elbow on the table and her face in her palm, giving me a big grin.

I let out a choked laugh. "The only thing anyone can talk about? I've been here for like, less than two hours."

"Exactly," Paige says, looking at me with disbelieving eyes. "That's plenty of time for the Hermosa Beach gossip machine to begin churning. And if Lennon's the one with the information, you better believe it's moving at a rapid pace."

Then she turns her head and looks to Lucas. "I'll never forgive you for letting her get the inside scoop on this before me," she pouts, poking Lucas in the ribs. "Lennon's number one goal in life is to be the person everyone goes to for the goss."

"No it's not," Lucas says, shaking his head and pursing his lips. "She likes knowing what's going on, but she isn't…" He pauses. "That's ridiculous."

"Excuse me, Mr. Top of the Pyramid. Who is Lennon's bestie? Me. I know what matters to her. You don't."

Lucas scoffs but doesn't add anything else, opting instead to pick up his drink and take a hefty swallow.

Paige leans forward, looking closely at me, her eyes beaming.

"Lennon finding out about you basically means that everyone we know now knows you're here and they're all trying to get as much information as possible."

A bit of fear slices through my body, and I chuckle uncomfortably. I don't want people knowing about me. Knowing my past and my pain and the secrets that still boil beneath my skin.

"Paige, you're scaring her," Lucas says. "Leave the special agent shit at the door, okay?"

"I'm not trying to scare you. Promise," she says, lifting her hand daintily in the air to flag down the waitress. "But if you're going to be living with Lucas this summer, I just feel it's fair for you to know the truth."

There's a pause. Lucas lets out an irritated sigh. Paige sits quietly and watches me. And I feel like she's waiting. Like she wants me to be curious enough to ask her what she's talking about.

And even though I don't want to be the one who gives in to that type of gossip mentality, I feel like I need to know.

Because secrets destroy.

"What truth?" I finally ask, glancing between them.

Paige smirks. "Your brother is as close to beach royalty as it gets, honey. The people here always want to know what's going on with him. And as his sister – a sister nobody knew about – people are going to want information about you, too. So… get ready for a wild summer."

Lucas shakes his head, his expression pinched, but doesn't

add anything.

Before I can ask any questions, the waitress shows up and takes a drink order from Paige. I decline, tapping my vodka soda to indicate I'm still good with my own.

"What does that mean?" I ask once the waitress has taken off to the bar. "That he's beach royalty?"

"It means that everyone cares about what's happening with Lucas Pearson. Where is he partying? Who is he sleeping with? Is he out surfing? Can he get me in to this club?" Paige rolls her eyes, then sits back in her chair, giving Lucas a look I don't quite understand but rings loudly of frustration. "It really is incredibly irritating."

"She's making it sound more intense than it is," Lucas pipes in. "Really. No one cares about me."

"Bullshit!" Paige cries. "I've had two people text me about your sister since I found out about her thirty minutes ago. And that's *after* the handful that checked in to see if you were having another party soon."

Lucas' eyes lock with mine at the mention of partying, and I see a little bit of a smirk.

"I knew you had a party house," I say, though I make sure to keep a smile in my words. "That place is too amazing not to show it off all the time."

"Oh yeah, parties at Lucas' house are like, infamous. Every weekend. The only reason he doesn't get shut down by the cops is because his neighbors want to be invited to join in on the fun."

My stomach tilts slightly. I've lived in a party house before. Maybe not one as fancy as Lucas', but I know what it's like to have people coming and going at all hours. Loud music, drugs, wishing I could lock my bedroom door.

I push that brief thought aside. Things are different now. I'm an adult. I can leave if I'm uncomfortable. I can't dwell only on the negative, shitty things from the past, or I'll never be able to move forward.

Lucas shakes his head, glaring at Paige. "Thanks for giving it all away, P. I was trying to make myself sound like an upstanding citizen."

Paige scoffs and takes her drink from the returning waitress, lifting it to her lips and mumbling, "Like anyone would ever believe that."

"Not to be rude," I say, looking to Lucas, "but why does anyone care what you do with your time?" My question seems stupid. Clearly there's something about him that people want to understand, be near, know. But to me, he's just a random guy I happen to be related to who has a nice house. Surely that can't be the reason.

Paige and Lucas glance at each other, and I get the feeling they're doing some sort of communicating thing that I don't understand.

"You're starting to freak me out," I say.

Paige violently shakes her head, bends forward and places her hand over mine on the table where I am nervously drumming my fingers. "No, there's nothing to freak out about," she says. "Lucas is just... kind of... well known?"

I look back to him where he sits with an expression of extreme irritation.

"Why?"

"Because I'm a surfer," he finally says, glaring at his friend. "Jesus, Paige, quit it with the cloak and dagger shit. It isn't that big of a deal." Looking back at me, his expression smooths out and he repeats himself. "It isn't that big of a deal. I've won a few titles."

"Nine of them," Paige pipes in.

"I don't get noticed often."

"Uh, try *everywhere we go.*"

"Tourists think it's cool, but the locals don't care."

"They *literally* consider you a hometown hero."

My eyes volley back and forth between the two of them. Their relationship, while confusing, kind of reminds me a little bit of what things were like with Joshua. Irritating but familiar. Argumentative but loving.

Joshua might have been eight years older than me, but I used to sass around with him a lot. And he loved it. He always told me never to lose that spirit.

I tried. I tried to stay myself when we went in to the system, but it really is a bitch that chews you up and spits you out. And when you come out, you just don't look the same anymore.

I miss that.

Of course, I miss my brother, too.

Every day I wish I could see him again. Talk to him. Get his opinion on things.

But I also miss the other version of me.

The one that wasn't so afraid of things. The one that didn't have to work so hard to believe promises. That never assumed the worst.

She's buried somewhere. Possibly dead. And I don't know if she'll ever resurface again.

"So don't be surprised if people recognize him," Paige says, bringing me back to the table. She lifts her drink and takes a sip from the tiny black straw. "Most of the time it doesn't matter. They'll just say hi or whatever. Maybe ask for a picture. And the people who live local are mostly just looking for some kind of invite to something, so they're never rude. But every once in a while you get the crazies."

I chuckle, then look at Lucas, who looks particularly uncomfortable. "So, can I Google you?"

He rolls his eyes. "The only things you'll find are lies. Just fair warning if you do it."

He's trying to make it seem like it isn't a big deal, but he's failing. I don't know why I can tell. Maybe it's the new tension in his shoulders or the lack of honesty in the smile stretching tight on thin lips. Or maybe it's simply that the mere idea of people starting to dig through my very lacking online presence has me feeling my own bit of discomfort. Regardless, I know the idea of me looking him up online makes him anxious.

"Oh, I'd rather not," I say, hoping to assuage any fears he might have. "I'd rather let you tell me what I need to know about you."

There's a hint of surprise in his expression, though he wipes it clean as quickly as it appears.

"Well, you're definitely not from around here, then," Paige says, giggling and taking another sip of her drink.

Her words aren't meant to wound. They're flippant, said in the moment. And, honestly? Targeting something about myself that I don't mind. The fact that I'm not a gossipmonger and I'm not obsessed with the internet.

But I can't help that something sour twists inside of me at her words. Because she's pointing out a truth I don't want to accept just yet. That this place, like every other, is just another where I don't belong.

"I'm gonna go to the bathroom," I say, sliding out of my side of the booth. "Can you order me a burger or something when the waitress comes back?"

Lucas nods, though his expression shifts to concerned. "Sure. Anything specific?"

I shake my head. "No. I'm simple. Whatever is fine."

And then I head across the rooftop deck and down the stairs. I'd said I wanted to go to the bathroom so I could have a few moments to myself. But when I spot the exit sign in the corner, leading back out to Pier Ave, I book it in that direction, eager to get out of here, even if just for a few minutes.

It's nearly eight o'clock, but the promenade doesn't look to be slowing down any time soon. I guess that isn't surprising, being a Friday night in a beach city. Looking around, I try to find a place I can go to sit for a minute. And when I spot an open bench about a hundred yards down the Pier, I head in that direction.

Maybe a moment watching the waves will soothe me.

But just as I'm sitting down, someone else steps over to sit as well.

"Oh, I'm sorry, you can sit here," I say, internally kicking myself for always deferring to others.

Especially when I get a look at the guy.

Because, holy fucking wow.

For a split second, all I can feel is my own heartbeat and the cadence of my irregular breathing as a flush stretches from somewhere low and rushes up across my chest and onto my neck and cheeks.

There's this poem I read in high school. I forget who it was written by. Someone famous. Someone forgettable, at least in my eyes. I've never been a big poetry buff.

But I remember this one because it detailed the physical reaction of attraction as if it were a color highlighting different parts of the body. A neon rainbow that travelled from eyes to cheeks to neck, down the chest and lower.

It was one of those things where everyone in class giggled the whole time, including me - *especially me.*

But I remember thinking how embarrassing it would be, to have a physical reaction that spread around like a rash, highlighting how a person feels without their permission.

Exactly the way I feel when our eyes connect.

Like everything I'm feeling and thinking about him is scrolling across my forehead for everyone to see. I know I'm turning bright red and starting to sweat, so I barely hear his response, instead only registering his nod and choice to sit next to me on the bench.

Of course, I leave my brother at a table and escape to a bench to think and sort through things in my mind alone, and the only thing I can focus on is the guy next to me.

I peek over at him and find him looking out at the water. Yanking my eyes away, I do the same, taking quiet, slow breaths to calm myself down a bit.

"You never forget how it smells, you know?"

My whole body tenses when I realize he's probably talking to me. I chance a glance in his direction again, and this time, he's looking at me.

He's talking to me. I need to say something back. What did he ask me? Oh, right. The smell.

I shake my head. "I wouldn't know. Today is the first day I've ever seen the ocean."

He smiles, a slow sexy thing that transforms his face into something so charming and slightly devilish. I can tell almost instantly that he's one of those men who gets away with a lot because of that smile. It's mischievous, like he knows a secret and he just might be willing to share it with me if I play my cards right.

Perfect for me. I suck at games.

"I don't think I've ever met someone who hasn't seen the ocean before," he says.

I shrug. "Well, consider me the first."

Returning my eyes out to the stretch of sea, which is finally resting in darkness now that the sun has well and truly set, I try and think of something to say. But I can't. My mind is blank. Empty.

Normally, my mind is full of thoughts and words and opinions. I just never have the nerve to vocalize them. But right now? It's just white noise.

Luckily, my seat friend fills the void.

"You're not from around here, then."

I shake my head and laugh, trying to even visualize what it would be like to be from here. My skin would be a lot more tan, that's for sure. "Definitely not. I'm just visiting family." Then I muster the courage to look at him again. "You? Are you from here?"

The stranger gives me that smile again. "Yeah. I am."

"Well, it's beautiful. And you're right about the smell. I don't think I'll ever be able to forget it."

He nods, lifts his arm so it rests on the back of the bench, his fingers resting just inches from where I'm sitting, and tilts his body towards mine.

I'm shocked at how my body seems to want to mirror his, tilting just slightly to the side to face him a bit more.

"I've been gone for a few years," he says. "Even lived near the ocean, too. But there's something about the way it smells *here*," he says, shakes his head and looks back at the water. "It's just different."

"It's the smell of home," I say, giving him a soft smile. "You can't ever replace that."

It feels strange to give him an answer like that when I don't have my own smell of home. But instinctively, I know what he's talking about. I just wish I could find it for myself.

We sit in silence for a few minutes, and I realize then that I've totally calmed down, for which I am incredibly thankful. The last thing I want is to be a sweaty, gaping mess right now, especially next to a guy who looks like he should be on a billboard somewhere selling you literally anything.

I would totally buy it, too.

"How long are you in town?" he asks, breaking me from my trance of staring at the water as it crashes against the shore and then rushes back out again.

I shrug. "I'm not sure yet. Not long, though."

"Can I take you out?" he asks.

I look to him so quickly I'm surprised I don't give myself whiplash.

"What?"

"To grab a drink or something," he adds.

I'm already shaking my head. "Oh, that's okay. Thanks for the offer though."

His brows twitch, as if my answer caught him off guard. There's a long pause. "How about a coffee?"

I shake my head again. "Thank you. But I'm just here to spend time with my brother."

At that same moment I feel my phone vibrate in my pocket. Pulling it out, I see Lucas' name, along with a text asking if I'm okay.

"Speak of the devil... look, I have to go." I stand, only half looking at him again. Sometimes it's just too hard to look at someone that gorgeous in the face. "Thanks for the chat, and for sharing the bench."

Then, before he can say anything else, I spin on my heel and power walk my butt back to Bennie's.

"Sorry," I say when I finally slide back in to my seat across from Lucas and Paige. "I just needed some fresh air."

I realize how stupid it sounds. Especially since we are literally sitting on a rooftop deck, sucking in all the fresh air we could want. But it's also true.

"No worries. Just wondered what happened," is all Lucas says, but he looks a little concerned.

Paige, though, is focused on something on her phone. In fact, as her mouth drops open and her eyes grow wider, I wonder just how important it might actually be.

"Holy. Shit," Paige whispers, frantically responding to something. Then she looks at Lucas. "You'll never believe who just got back in town. Even if I give you a thousand guesses, you wouldn't get it."

Lucas rolls his eyes, clearly not as impressed with whatever this newest piece of gossip is.

"The best thing I could possibly do right now is tell you that you're not allowed to let me know who it is."

Paige smacks him in the chest, then returns to her texting, her thumbs flying across her screen without breaking stride. "Not funny."

Lucas rubs his chest, but smiles and reaches for his drink. "Alright, Paige. I'll humor you. Who is back in town?"

"Wyatt. Calloway."

At Paige's admission, Lucas freezes, his glass nearly to his mouth but not there quite yet. Paige is looking at her phone, seemingly getting live updates while Lucas looks... well, I can't really tell. But, definitely not as calm as he looked a moment ago.

"I thought he was backpacking in Europe this summer," Lucas

finally says, then tips his drink back, finishing the last little bit in one swig.

Paige shakes her head. "His dad said he wasn't even coming home, that he'd just be leaving for London from San Francisco."

Lucas' brow furrows. "Why were you talking with Calvin?"

Paige shrugs. "I saw him at Penny's gallery opening." Then she rolls her eyes. "He was there with his child bride."

"Don't call her that."

"Wyatt calls her that."

"Wyatt does a lot of things he shouldn't do."

"Well she's twenty-two years old, Lucas. Mr. Calloway is forty-eight. It's gross."

I lean forward and lower my voice. "I didn't even know there were real people who do that. I always thought the mid-life crisis thing was a myth."

Lucas' nostrils flare, but before he can say anything, Paige pipes in.

"It's not a myth. Actually, it's far too common around here. When you live in a beach town, you keep getting older and the sexy girls on the beach stay the same age." Paige makes a gagging noise. "Krissa, his new wife, is younger than both of his sons. *That's* the part that grosses me out."

The server shows up then and drops off our food. My stomach pulls at me, reminding me that it has been a long day without much to eat. The burger looks amazing, and I don't hesitate to pick it up and chomp right in, moaning at the delicious taste.

"That is a really good burger," I say, once I finally finish my first bite. I set it back on my plate and wipe my hands. "I haven't had something that good in a while."

Lucas smiles. Paige eyes my burger with envy as she cuts up her fancy salad.

"Speaking of the creepy Mr. Calloway, I can't go with you to the Marina tomorrow night," Paige says to Lucas. "But it probably works out, because now you can take Hannah."

Lucas slows his chewing and glances in my direction. "Do you want to go with me to a formal dinner tomorrow night at the Marina? There's a charity auction, too."

I twist in my seat, feeling slightly uncomfortable. "You know, I don't know if I'd really... fit. Fit in with everyone. You know? Besides, you saw my bag of stuff. It's filled with jeans and shirts. I wouldn't have anything to wear."

"I can totally let you borrow something of mine!" Paige says, her smile stretching from ear-to-ear.

I let out an awkward laugh, not knowing how to even begin to react to the idea of that.

"I don't... uhm..." I stammer, not sure what to say. Part of me wants to go, to spend time with my brother. And the other part of me wonders if I'm just setting myself up for a really big fall.

"It'll be fun, Hannah. I promise."

My stomach tightens. I hate promises. Somehow, they never live up to what you're expecting.

But I nod anyway, my lips forming a tight smile.

Paige claps her hands together, her excitement bubbling up like a fountain. "Oh this is going to be so fun!"

I want to laugh at that, but I stay quiet instead. I can't imagine in what world this would be fun, but as Paige goes on and on about what to expect when I go with Lucas to dinner tomorrow night, I can't help but hope she's right.

Chapter Five
WYATT

The smell of home.

The girl on the pier said those words, and I bet when she said them, she thought she was saying something emotionally revealing or romantic.

She couldn't have been more wrong.

I lift my leg over to straddle the seat, pull the clutch, and hit the start, revving the engine a few times before I throttle down the alley and back onto Hermosa Ave.

The smell of the ocean in Hermosa Beach doesn't make me feel like I'm at home.

Not anymore.

Instead, the smell reminds me of all the reasons I left.

I come to a stop at a red light and glance to my left, seeing a convertible full of women singing along to some pop song. They wave and giggle, but I ignore them, turning back and screeching away when the light turns green.

I have to admit, this bike has been quite useful over the past few months. I've always known that women love a man who rides a motorcycle. But there's a certain pitch to this engine that seems to hit the ladies right between their legs.

The motorcycle I've had since I turned twenty is still up in San Francisco, safely tucked away in storage while I travel. This baby is a birthday gift my dad sent me last year. An Indian FTR 1200 Rally.

It didn't even debut until the end of last year. Didn't go on sale until January. But somehow, he managed to figure out exactly what I wanted and have it assembled and sent to me before any of that. It was a surprising gift, primarily because my dad isn't the type to pay attention to anything I say.

So, I suspect Ivy is to blame.

I smile, looking forward to seeing her soon.

But that brief bit of joy gets quickly overshadowed by the truth of why I'm home. Why I'm here instead of drinking a whiskey neat on Otto's dad's company jet, bound for London.

My smile quickly slips away.

I'm only on the road for about ten minutes before I finally pull in to the short driveway at my mom's house. It doesn't take long to get anywhere in Hermosa, unless you're driving from the Tourist End to the Money End.

It might sound conceited or elitist, but I didn't come up with this shit.

I park the FTR and pull my helmet off, irritated that I'm not in a better mood. I thought stopping by the pier would give me time to relax. Help calm my mind before I enter the storm.

But it did neither of those things.

Sure, I'd gotten a brief distraction when the hot blonde and I shared the bench. Her legs were so fucking long. It took everything in me not to tell her how much I'd like to see those babies wrapped around my waist.

I knew nothing was going to happen tonight, though, with anyone, regardless of whether they wanted it to or not. So I'd decided to just play friendly stranger instead, and we had a nice little chat about nothing.

But once she was gone - after turning me down, too - my mind when straight back to the real reason I'm here.

Clenching my hands, I grab my small bag off the back and head inside, banging through the front door, but closing it softly behind me. I set my bag down on the marble-floored entryway and take a deep breath, *the smell of home* hitting me square in the chest.

That must be what Pier Girl was talking about. Because as much as I hate that I have to be here, that familiar scent of green tea that my mom makes on most evenings, and the waft of the gardenia bush that sits out back… they're familiar smells that help calm me just a bit.

Thankfully.

Because the last thing I need is to be upset right now. The last thing I should be is anything other than loving and happy and warm.

"Welcome home, Wyatt," comes a melodious voice from my right.

I turn just my head and give Vicky a smirk. "I thought you were supposed to call me Mr. Calloway."

She rolls her eyes and takes the few final steps until she's right in front of me, her arms wide for a hug. I step in to her embrace, thankful for a positive, familiar face as my first reintroduction to this house.

"There's only one Mr. Calloway, and I won't be saying his name with affection any time soon, okay?"

I let out a small laugh, though it's tinged with the knowledge of what she truly means.

"Yeah, well, my dad won't be coming here any time soon. So don't stress about that too much."

She takes a step back. "Oooooh, boy, you've grown. At least another inch since the last time I saw you." She pokes my chest. "And I'm not talking about your height."

I roll my eyes, ready to tease her right back about the muscle mass I've added on since the last time I was home, when I hear my name called from somewhere else in the house.

"Go on, see your family. I'll grab your bag and get you settled in."

I kiss Vicky on the cheek. "Thanks Vic. Love you." And then I wander off into the house, searching for the voice that called to me.

Vicky has been my mother's everything since I was a kid. Her assistant, her personal shopper, her maid, her closest friend. She's one of the few people that I've known my entire life. That I've loved my entire life. And I'm glad to know that she's one of the people invested in keeping things in order around here.

I head down the hall between the large formal dining room and my mother's office, through the kitchen and out to the patio where I find her lounging by the pool.

One of the smart things my parents did during the years they were trying not to save their marriage was build a house one street off the beach, acknowledging that it provided them with slightly more privacy. They purchased an apartment complex and a house, demolished them both, and created the behemoth known to most Hermosan socialites as the Calloway Estate, though my friends in high school mockingly called it Calloway Castle.

Seven bedrooms, nine bathrooms, a media room, two offices, a game room, gym, swimming pool, three car garage, and two thousand square feet of outdoor patios and grass, plus a completely separate two bedroom guest cottage over another garage, it's an absolutely outrageous property. The only real goal my parents could have had was to irritate all of the neighbors and flaunt their wealth.

Mission accomplished, mom and dad.

I might have seen only a handful of other homes over the years that have a pool this close to the beach. And those people wasted a lot of real estate to have it. But this property would seem almost too big if there wasn't the large almost unearthly blue mammoth sitting on the edge of the property against a tall wall covered in carefully manicured ivy.

The irony is that my dad is the one who insisted on getting the pool, and my parents divorced before he ever had a chance to use it.

"Wyatt. I'm so glad you're home," my mother says as I take a seat next to her on a lounger.

She's wearing sweats and fuzzy socks and reading a book. On a Friday night.

This is the woman who once told me that staying at home any evening was the first step to becoming irrelevant.

Just goes to show how circumstance can play a part in the choices people make.

"Good to see you, mom." I lean over and place a kiss on her cheek. "Though I'm surprised to see you out here reading. I assumed you'd be upstairs."

She sighs. Another indicator that things are taking a turn.

Vivian Calloway doesn't show her true emotions. She used to be made of plastic, and she enjoyed life that way. "If you're made of glass, if you let people see inside, you might shatter at any given moment," she told me once. "Plastic doesn't break as easily."

It was the most honest and heartbreaking thing she's ever said to me.

"Well, sometimes you just have to take a deep breath outside, you know? Breathe in that ocean air. Breathe out all of the fear and helplessness."

I nod, squeezing her hand.

It's weird, this closeness with my mother that seems to have sprung up out of nowhere. Being plastic always made her feel fake. Inaccessible.

Now, in the wake of anxiety and sadness, she's letting that false exterior slip away and I feel like I'm finally getting glimpses of the real Vivian. The mom I might have had if things had been different.

"How was the trip from San Francisco?" she asks, her eyes dropping to my boots. "Tell me you didn't ride that rickety scooter all the way down here." At my silence, she sits forward, her eyes wide. "Wyatt, that's a dangerous ride to take by yourself. You should have just flown. I'm sure Greg Slader would have let you hop on one of his jets. Lord knows he goes back and forth to see that mistress of his enough."

I smile just a little bit. "Mom, it's not a rickety scooter. It's a high performance sport bike. And I was completely fine."

She rolls her eyes, another newer expression I've only seen from her a few times. "I'm your mother. I'll never think you're completely fine."

I'm twenty-five years old, but she still knows how to pull the *I'm your mother* card like I'm still in my teens.

Settling back into the lounge chair, I look up at the sky, both anticipating and dreading the next thing I'm going to ask.

"How's everything going?" Then I turn to look at my mom's face, because with her defenses temporarily down, I know she doesn't have the ability to hide anything from me. "Honestly."

My mom stays silent for a moment, and I can't tell whether she's shoring herself up to tell me something bad, or if she's just struggling to find the right words. But eventually, she confirms what I knew to be true.

"The doctors said we just have to wait and see."

I clench my jaw, shake my head. Bunch of fucking crocs, these doctors. Always with the *wait and see,* as if we aren't sitting around absolutely terrified of what comes next.

"That's bullshit. We're getting another opinion."

She looks at me with sad eyes. "Wyatt..."

"Not about the diagnosis itself. Okay? I just... there has to be a better solution than just doing nothing."

She leans her head back against the lounger, her eyes looking up at the sky. But eventually, she nods.

"Is there anything I can do around here to make things easier?" I ask. "For anyone?"

She tilts her head to look at me, a sweet, gentle, unguardedness in her eyes that is so unlike her. "No. Just be here. That's all we want. That's the only thing that will make any of this feel manageable."

I nod, just once, then lean over and give my mom a kiss on the cheek.

She lifts a hand and places it on my shoulder. "I love you, Wyatt. And I'm glad you came home."

I reach out and squeeze her hand, trying not to focus on the tightness in my chest. Then I stand up and head back inside.

Vicky will have taken my bag out to the guesthouse, knowing I typically prefer privacy and dread the idea of staying in one of the guestrooms in the main house. But before I head out there and get settled in for the evening, I have one more thing to do.

I jog up the staircase to the second floor, then head down the long hallway to the bedroom at the very end.

Cracking the door open, a sliver of light slices through the room, illuminating the tiny body that rests in my mom's bed. She's curled up on her side, totally passed out, dead to the world, and snoring like a fucking chain saw.

I smile to myself, debating for just a minute whether I should wake Ivy or let her sleep and just say hello in the morning.

My sister has her own bedroom, but I know she's been sleeping in here with mom for the past few years. Part of me thinks it's unhealthy, and I've talked to my mom about it before. But another part of me can't help but see what they're both going through right now.

I step into the room, leaving the door cracked, and wander over to the other side of the bed where I can see my little sister's face. She looks so at peace right now, so adorable and fresh-faced the way only a twelve-year-old can. I can't muster up the will to wake her when mom told me she's been having trouble sleeping over the past few weeks.

But before I can even make it back to the door, I hear a small voice mumble in my direction.

"Are you seriously not going to say hello to me?"

I spin around and find Ivy has rolled to her other side and faces me, a sleepy smile on her face.

Sorry, I sign, though my smile is just as big as hers. *I just didn't want to wake you.*

Come give me a hug. And then she lifts her arms out, a silent command.

And, of course, I follow her directions, crawling up onto the bed and wrapping my arms around her, giving her a tight squeeze.

Once we're done hugging, I kick off my boots and lean up against the wall, looking down at her.

When did you get here? she asks, her hands moving quickly with the skill of someone who has been signing her entire life.

Not that long. I talked to mom for a few minutes, then came up here to see you.

My signing is a bit choppier. I didn't start learning until much later, since there's a big gap between our ages. And Ivy is always making fun of me for how poorly I sign.

How did she seem to you?

I sigh. *Honestly? Not good. But I figure that's okay. It's a lot for her to take in. You know.* I smirk. *Now that she isn't a plastic anymore.*

Ivy giggles.

She loves when I talk about mom being a human Barbie. I'm the only person in her life that doesn't see mom as this perfect untouchable thing, and it makes Ivy feel like mom is more relatable somehow.

I'm really glad you came home. I don't like having to deal with this on my own.

I nod, feeling the pang of having been gone too long. *I'm sorry for not coming home sooner. I should have been here more.*

No. No way. You still have a life to live. I'm just glad you're here now. Unlike somebody.

She means our dad, the expression on her face morphing into something unpleasant and resentful.

I roll my eyes, not wanting to get in an argument it right now.

Let's not talk about him, okay? He isn't important. I lean forward and kiss her forehead. *I'm exhausted and need to head to bed. Wanna go get breakfast together in the morning? I'll take you to Mary's.*

She beams. *Yes, please.*

I give her one more hug and then hop out of bed.

"Night," she calls to me, then snuggles back in under mom's fluffy down comforter.

I close the door behind me and make the short trek back down the stairs and out to the guesthouse, kicking my boots off at the entry and tugging my jacket off just as quickly.

A six-hour drive down the center of the state was instead a long ten-hour journey along the coast, and I am shattered from the draining day behind me. Similarly to my decision to visit the pier, I'd hoped to have some sort of calm, some modicum of clarity come over me.

Instead, I'm just sore and achy and tired, and my mind has been in no way relieved.

I strip off the rest of my clothes as I make my way into the master bedroom, foregoing a shower, even though I desperately need one. Instead, I plop right onto the bed, feeling almost dead to the world within just a moment.

But I do have one more thought right before I slip all the way into dreamland.

Even though it's highly unlikely, I wonder if I'll get to see the pretty blonde from the pier again while I'm in town.

Chapter Six
HANNAH

That night I lie in bed and wonder what the hell I got myself into by coming here.

I thought it would be simple. Spend time with my brother. Get to know him a little bit. Learn about his life. Maybe find some sort of common ground or friendship or something that makes me feel like we're connected.

But within only a few hours I'm realizing things are probably going to be a lot more complicated than that. Lucas lives in such a different world with what seems like a completely different set of rules.

I don't know if I'll fit.

Though I guess that's my biggest fear no matter where I am.

Unable to sleep and feeling restless, I crawl out of bed and crack my door open, listening to see if anyone else is awake.

Everything is super quiet in this house, and as I'd trudged to my bed earlier this evening, the sound of my footsteps the only noise I could hear, I'd wondered how Lucas lives here without anyone else. It just seems like it would be... lonely.

When I see no one in the hall, I pad softly on the carpet past the other rooms on the third floor, then tiptoe down the stairs.

The house is quiet, though the living room windows are cracked open, the breeze from the water rushing through and filling the space with damp air and cooler temperatures than I'm able to feel in my bedroom, which faces away from the ocean.

I open one of the sliding doors and step out onto the front-facing balcony, getting a good look at Hermosa Beach at night.

Well, I guess, in the early hours of the morning.

There isn't much to see under the night sky, when the beach is asleep and so much of the view is cast in darkness. I can see the Hermosa Pier to the south with a string of lights leading from The Strand all the way out to the tip. I can see the dim lights on a handful of large boats still out on the water in the distance.

But most of what can be seen is just the concrete path of The Strand, separating homes from the sand, rows of lights illuminating the path as it stretches from the south to the north.

I lean against the railing and cast my gaze back to the water, to the inky blackness in the distance.

What I find so strange is that you assume sight would be the most important sense at the beach, that the view would be the focal point. But in my sneaky evening moments alone, I'm recognizing that my other senses seem to be taking over.

The smell of the ocean, the sound of the waves, the feel of the cool tiles of the patio under my feet, the taste of the salty air.

It's a moment full of sensation, and I feel at once both overwhelmed and incredibly sad.

It's breathtaking to experience something as magnanimous and dominating as the ocean, and I doubt anyone who has grown up near the beach will ever fully understand how it feels to see it for the first time.

But it's also lonely, standing out here on the patio by myself. No friends or family at my side to revel in this newfound understanding of the world together.

Lucas seems like a nice person, and I'm honestly looking forward to getting to know him.

But I can't help but wish Joshua was here with me.

I wonder if he ever saw the ocean. If he ever had this feeling in his chest when he heard the power of the waves.

I guess that's something I'll never know.

Unsure of how long I've been out on the patio, but recognizing that I'm finally starting to get a bit tired, I turn to go back inside.

The house is still dark, since I didn't turn any lights on, which is why it's easy to slip over to a corner when I hear footsteps padding down the stairs.

A girl giggling and a man making shushing noises.

Lucas and...

My eyes widen when I see the woman at his side.

Lennon.

I keep my mouth shut and stay tucked away as the two of them walk together to the front door.

"Thanks for letting me come over," Lennon says when they stop in the entry. She wraps her arms around his waist and tilts her head back to look up at him. "You know I always have a good time with you."

It's hard to tell, but it looks like Lucas smiles at her. Leans down and whispers something in her ear. Goes in for a kiss.

I turn my eyes away, trying to tuck myself further into the corner where I stand, focusing on my fingernails. Lucas seems to be a bit of a playboy, if I'm reading everything correctly. He's got a girlfriend at college, I think. And then there's Paige, because I can't be sure that relationship isn't something. And now Lennon, who I thought he didn't want around.

My earlier thought comes back to mind.

A different world and a different set of rules.

After another minute or two, a few moans and giggles, I finally hear the front door open and shut. Hear the lock being turned back into place.

I let out a quiet breath. Perfect. Now I just need to wait for Lucas to go back up to his room and I can...

The living room lights turn on, and Lucas and I lock eyes.

"I knew it," he said, a smile on his face. "I could just feel it. Like a sibling sixth sense or something."

I chuckle awkwardly, not sure what to do. "I'm so sorry," I blurt out. "I was down here already and looking at the ocean because I was having a hard time going to sleep. I didn't mean to..."

"Hannah." That stern voice again. The one that's a reprimand in just one word. My name. "It's not a big deal. You live here, too.

I'm not gonna have sex on the couch or something, okay? Anything that happens out here I'll assume is public."

My shoulders drop, relief rushing through me that he's not upset. I don't know why I'm so afraid of upsetting him when he's done nothing but make sure I feel welcome since the minute we started emailing.

But the fear of upsetting my host is very real.

Old habits die hard, I guess.

I take a few steps out from my awkward place in the corner, heading to the kitchen to fill a glass of water.

"Thirsty?" I ask, glancing over at him as I search through the cabinets for a glass, finally finding them next to the fridge.

"Yeah. Sure."

I fill up a blue-rimmed glass for him and then one for me. We both take quiet sips from opposite sides of the island.

"So," I finally say, feeling like I should break the silence and only having one thing on my mind. "Lennon, huh?"

I'm feeling confused based on his reaction to her earlier. He'd seemed pretty clear that he wanted her to take a hike.

He laughs, drops his head back and stares at the ceiling. "Yeah, I know."

"I mean, I don't know her at all. And I'm not judging. But you seemed super disinterested earlier today. And I thought you said you have a girlfriend."

He bobs his head, grits his jaw. "Remmy said she wanted an open relationship while she was at school." He shrugs, but I can tell he's irritated. "I don't normally..." he trails off. "I guess the best way to explain it is..." he pauses again, scratches the bit of stubble growing on his chin. Then, a devious smile comes across his face. "Lennon and I are physically compatible."

My face flames red.

He's talking about his sex life.

"Ooooooh, Ms. Morrison. Is someone easily flustered?" he says, his voice teasing.

I cross my arms and narrow my eyes, trying to neutralize my facial expression and failing miserably. "Maybe," I finally say.

"Nobody gave you the uncomfortable sex talk huh?" he says, laughing slightly.

I know he's joking, but I shake my head. "My friend Sienna always had something... interesting to say to me that kept me adequately informed. But I didn't really have anyone to talk to about this stuff at the places I used to live growing up."

His smile drops. "Oh. I guess I didn't really... think about that. That you didn't have someone to talk to. About life."

I lift a shoulder. "It wasn't so bad."

Lucas' jaw tightens again, and a part of me thinks he knows I'm lying. But it's still too early to share those pieces of me, the bits that I try to shove down deep and ignore whenever possible.

That's if I decide to talk to him about it at all.

"I just feel like... I could have done something." He looks at the marble on the island. "So you weren't alone."

I reach across the island and place my hand over his, the move seeming to surprise him.

If I'm honest, it surprises me, too.

But there's something in his expression that makes me feel like this is the only way I can convince him that he isn't to blame for my shitty circumstances.

"It isn't your fault," I say. "Life just happens sometimes. Things aren't fair. And yeah, it sucked to basically be alone and on my own for so long. But I'm okay. Or... I'm at least *mostly* okay. You couldn't have known or done anything different."

Lucas takes a deep breath, something shuddering inside of him. Something painful.

It makes me want to give him a hug – another surprise – but I stay where I am.

Lucas' head drops forward and he rubs his nose, his eyes squinted shut. Then he looks up at me.

"I'm going to make sure you're never alone again, okay? I promise."

I give him a soft smile, appreciating the sentiment. I truly do want to believe what he says. But I can't help that the whisper of doubt stays ever-present, like a bug hovering near my ear that I can't manage to swat away, no matter how hard I try.

"Lucas, I don't expect you to promise me anything, okay? I just want to spend time getting to know you. I haven't had family in a long time. Let's just see how this goes."

He nods, letting out a long breath.

Then he gives me a small smile, takes my hand, and tugs me sharply against his chest, his arms wrapping snuggly around me.

"First thing's first. You need to learn how to accept a hug."

I laugh. "And if I don't want one?"

"Well I'm your brother and I'm bigger and stronger, so tough shit."

"Oh, you gonna give me wet willies now, too?"

"I have a lot of time to make up for. Expect me to use your stuff and steal your toys and eat your snacks from the pantry."

I laugh again, finally letting myself enjoy his hug.

It's easy to forget what unconditional love feels like when you haven't felt it in so long. And this with Lucas might not be there yet, but it feels like we're on our way.

"This is delicious," I say, taking another bite of my pancakes. "I haven't had a breakfast as fantastic as this in a while."

Paige laughs. "Honey, get ready for a whole lot of deliciousness. We do Monday brunch here every week."

"Have you eaten everything on this menu? Because I feel like that would be tempting."

"Unfortunately, no. I stick mostly with the low-carb options." She pats her incredibly flat stomach. "Gotta keep this body in top shape."

I nod, though I don't feel like she has anything to fear. Paige is one of those women who are naturally beautiful. But I guess we all see different things when we look in the mirror.

"I'm sure Lucas will bring you to the next one. You'll get to meet the whole gang. There's a pretty big group, and we call it Monday Mournings. M-O-U-R-N. Because we commiserate about the tragedies from the weekend."

"That's clever," I say, picking up my orange juice. "But I probably won't be able to..."

"Don't say you won't be able to afford it. I'm under strict instructions from Lucas not to let you think or worry about that at all while you're in town."

My eyes widen in shock, then narrow as embarrassment pulses through my body. The last thing I want is to be Lucas' charity case.

"Paige, I don't expect for you guys to pay my way. I'm going to get a job while I'm here. I'll just have to be choosy about what I can afford."

But she's already shaking her head. "Nope! I totally respect where you're coming from, especially when considering that you have a famous brother who not only comes from a lot of money but also earns a lot of money. But you also have to accept that Lucas has a lot of time he wants to make up for. He wants you to have fun, enjoy yourself. And that includes spoiling you and making up for all the years you guys haven't had together."

I let out a sigh. "But..." I pause, looking away, towards the water in the distance. "I don't want him to see me as someone he has to take care of. I already feel bad enough by living in his house without paying for anything."

Paige leans forward and rests her hand on mine. "Honey, you're not mooching. Let the man take care of you." Then she sits back. "You've been on your own for a long time, right?"

I flush from cheeks to neck, wondering if there's something about being near the ocean that causes me to turn bright red all the fucking time. This never used to be an issue.

But I nod anyway.

"You're not on your own anymore, sweetie. You have family now, and family takes care of each other."

God, she makes me want to break into tears, but I grit my teeth and give her a tight smile.

Paige is a conundrum. Both obsessed with gossip and yet I don't doubt she is also a great secret keeper. Focused on looks and the superficial, but kind and welcoming to her core.

When I first met her, I thought she was just a richer version of the mean girls that I went to high school with. The ones who called me The Cactus, or Homeless Hannah. But the more I talk to her, the more I realize she might just be the exact opposite of those girls. She's probably what those girls *wish* they could be, but they're too small-minded and self absorbed to figure it out.

Paige pays the check, glaring at me when I try to grab it, and we clear out from our place on the patio. Having breakfast at Mary's was her idea, a pit stop on the way to her house to pick out something for me to wear to the charity auction at the yacht club tonight.

It's a great little spot, a breakfast and brunch place only a few blocks away from Lucas'. There was quite a crowd waiting when we got here, but Paige walked right up to the host and gave her a hug. We'd gotten a table with a view of the water just a few minutes later.

"Oh, shit, I left my phone on the table," I say just as we get back to Paige's car parked on the curb a block away. Trepidation rolls through my veins. As much as I try not to be phone obsessed, still, I can*not* afford to lose that thing. "I'm gonna run back and grab it."

Paige smiles and nods, already getting her own phone out, likely to catch up on the daily Hermosa Beach gossip.

I jog back to Mary's in record time, letting out a sigh of relief when the hostess holds up my phone.

"Oh my gosh, thank you so much," I say. "I would have died if I'd lost this."

She smiles at me. "No problem."

"You're not one of those girls who is glued to her phone all day, are you?"

I turn to look over my shoulder and can't hide my surprise at seeing the guy from the night before. The pier guy. The super sexy guy. The one I thought about mentioning to Paige at breakfast when she asked about my first day in Hermosa Beach.

I can't hide my surprise, and I also can't hide my smile.

A smile he gives me right back.

"This is quite the coincidence," he adds.

"Hey there, Pier Guy."

He continues to smile at me, his eyes twinkling. "Hey there, Pier Girl."

I rotate my phone in my hands, feeling slightly nervous. "What are you doing here?"

"Stalking you."

My eyes widen.

"I'm getting breakfast," he says, laughing, and I blush, embarrassed to have taken him so literally. "But man, you should have seen your face."

I purse my lips, but there's no heat in my expression. "Funny."

"You know, I think it's fate, you and me, meeting here. Out of all the places you could have gotten breakfast while you're in town, you picked here. My favorite brunch place." He crosses his arms and studies me. "In the movies, they call it kismet."

"I thought the movies call it a meet-cute."

He chuckles. "Us meeting here *is* a meet-cute, but the *fact* we're both here is kismet. Fate. Just like it's fate that you're going to meet me at Harbor's tonight for a drink. They have an excellent view of the ocean."

Now it's my turn to laugh. "You're a little cocky, huh?"

"Confident."

"They're the same. The only difference is how someone else perceives it."

"That's not how words work."

"That's *exactly* how words work. You ask a girl on a date a few times and she keeps saying no. You'd call that pursuit. A girl who likes you and is playing hard-to-get would call it persistence. But a girl who isn't interested would call it harassment."

He hums lightly, but his eyes light up with mischief. "And which girl are you in this scenario?" he asks, stepping closer to me.

My mind freezes, the inability to come up with a response tripping my tongue.

Normally when I'm around men, my natural instinct is immediate suspicion. What are their ulterior motives? Why are they talking to me? What do they *really* want? I have to fight against that instinct. All the time.

But this guy? Pier Guy? I feel like I can believe how he presents himself. Like he doesn't have any reason not to be exactly who he is. This confident, cocky, charming guy who probably always gets what he wants.

So this Hannah that I am right now feels new. She's flirting and smirking and giving back sass to a hot guy. Playing hard-to-get.

Is that what I'm doing? Playing hard-to-get?

It feels like a rush of caffeine after going without for so long.

He's handsome, yes. Undoubtedly. A strong jaw, a little bit of scruff, that smile that makes me weak-kneed, and a muscular frame that hints at quite a rigorous workout schedule.

But I also like talking to him. We've only exchanged a few words today, a few last night, but I already see him as someone who would keep me on my toes.

Spar with me.

And I like that.

Even more? I like that I like it.

Finding someone to spar with for fun is so much better than someone who kicks you when you're down.

"I haven't decided yet," I finally say, sticking with honesty.

He laughs, his head falling back and exposing his neck. "Well, what can I do to convince you one way or another?" he asks, looking back at me with a gleam of laughter in his eyes. "Because one reaction will get me a date. The other will get me a date with a police officer."

I chew on the edge of my lip, a habit I've been unable to break since childhood, but release it immediately when I see his eyes drop to my mouth.

Maybe I will say yes to him, though for another night.

Obviously I'm busy this evening with the yacht club thing with Lucas. But it couldn't really hurt anything to get a drink with an attractive guy.

Right?

Before I can respond, a young girl approaches us and taps his arm.

I told the hostess we were both here. She said it would be a few minutes, she signs.

Then she looks at me, and I can't help but beam at her. Part of me wants to just bust out the sign language, tell her I can sign, too. But that's pretty forward of me, to assume she'll get as excited about talking with me as I would be to talk to her.

Now that I'm not spending regular time with Lissy and Melanie, I realize how big a part of my life sign language was. I kind of miss it.

I thought you were going to spend time with me, she says to Pier Guy, but her eyes glance back at me. *Can't you flirt with tourists some other time?*

I blush, look down.

Well then.

"Ivy, I'm talking to someone. Can you give me a minute?" He both says it and signs it, probably for my benefit.

Ivy smiles at me, then looks up at Pier Guy. *This is me rolling my eyes. Just get her number and put it in your phone with all the others. I'd like to spend time with my brother without him flirting, for once.*

She gives me one more fake grin, then walks off, headed for the row of chairs set up outside of Mary's for waiting customers.

"Sorry about that," he says to me, taking another step closer and crossing his arms, emphasizing his muscles and a tattoo that peeks out from under his right sleeve. He looks me up and down, seduction evident in his eyes. "So. Harbor's? I'd love to take you for drinks."

I smile, though the joy in my expression has diminished slightly. In the last two minutes, something changed. We went from playful banter to... something else entirely. It felt like we were chatting before. Like we were friends who knew each other in some way. And now?

Now it feels like I'm a conquest. And that's not the side of things I want to be on.

"Unfortunately I have plans tonight with my brother."

"Ah, come on," he says, giving me that charming smile that probably gets him out of, or in to, anything. "You were about to say yes just a second ago."

I lift a shoulder. "Sorry. I really do have plans. Have a nice day with your sister."

His smile remains, though I can tell he's legitimately confused, trying to figure out what just happened. My guess is that he doesn't get turned down very often.

"Bye, Pier Guy," I add, then I walk past him and head down the street and towards Paige's car, not looking back even though I really want to.

When I finally get there, I find her sitting in the driver's seat, her eyes glued to her phone.

"Sorry it took so long," I say, opening the passenger door and climbing in to her periwinkle blue Camaro.

Paige glances at me. "Honey, I was so focused on this game I didn't even realize where I was."

We both break into laughter, allowing me to push away how talking with Pier Guy made me feel.

As Paige pulls away from the curb and we roll down Hermosa Ave, I glance towards Mary's. Pier Guy is still standing outside, his sister sitting next to him.

They're laughing, but I see his head come up and look in my direction.

I look away quickly and we continue down the road.

I thought for a second that I'd met a guy who might be worth the time to talk to. Someone who might be interested in chatting with me, too, and not just for the possibility to get into my pants later.

But he turned out to be just like most of the guys I've met before. Flirtatious and focused just on what he can get.

And right now, someone like that just isn't for me.

Chapter Seven
HANNAH

"No one will even notice."

Lucas' words have me wanting to roll my eyes. But I don't. Because that would probably be rude.

We pulled up to the Hermosa Beach Yacht Club earlier, and when I slid out of Lucas' car – a BMW instead of the truck, because apparently it's normal for people to have multiple cars – I swear it was like something out of a James Bond movie. Expensive cars. Women in sexy dresses and men in suits. Valet parking.

And there was a damn red carpet leading inside. Though, thankfully, no photographers. Not that they'd want to catch me on film as I totter into the building on a pair of slightly-too-small heels. But based on the way Paige was going on about Lucas, they might want to get a picture of him for the gossip pages of something.

Paige gave me this really beautiful dress to wear, and I really do love it. It's a deep green with lace sleeves and an open back. The problem is that Paige is at least six inches shorter than I am. At Lucas' house, while I was getting ready, I'd worried the dress was too short, so I put on a pair of nylons that Paige had given me *just in case.*

But of course, because I'm *fucking stretch Armstrong* and have legs a mile long, I tore a hole in them as I was getting out of Lucas' fancy ass car. A long stretch down the back of my left leg.

Even though I'm not typically one to worry about how I look, I know that Lucas matters here, and the last thing I want is for the cogs of the Hermosa Beach gossip machine to start talking about his trashy sister.

I'd pushed back my shoulders and held my head high, determined not to allow myself to feel like I didn't belong. Though I didn't entirely appreciate the looks I was getting from a few of the men who were old enough to be my dad.

It wasn't until we were through the front doors that I tugged Lucas to the side and had a meltdown about the tear.

"Of course people will notice," I hiss at Lucas. Then I feel bad for being snippy. But what does he expect? I come from nothing and now I'm here at this black tie event and I feel like a fucking mess. I sigh and wring my hands together. "I'm gonna go take them off in the bathroom."

Lucas steps forward and rests his hands on each of my biceps. "Hannah," he says, his voice quiet and calm. "Take a deep breath."

I do. A really deep one. And then I hold it, let it out slowly.

"Good. Now, don't freak out about what anyone here thinks about you. It doesn't matter if they like your dress or think you look like trash because of a tear in your leggings."

"Nylons."

"Same thing."

I laugh, a small one, just barely a breath that comes out of my nose, but it's still a much needed break from the tension that filled me a second ago.

"You're my sister, and I'm glad you're here with me." He squeezes my arms. "What other people think doesn't matter."

I glance around the lobby, watching people chit chat in little groups while others head into the main dining room. I let out another long breath, then look back at Lucas.

"I'm okay. I'll come find you once I take this piece of shit off."

Lucas smiles. "Awesome."

Then he turns and heads inside the main dining room.

I head towards the women's bathroom in the corner, hoping to make my way in and out as quickly as possible.

Unfortunately, that just isn't in the plans.

"Are you here with Lucas Pearson?"

I turn my head and spot a tall, lanky brunette heading my way. What is it with everyone around here being so damn beautiful? It's really annoying.

But I smile and nod my head, continuing my movements towards the bathroom. If she wants to talk to me, she can do it through a toilet stall.

"I didn't realize he was dating someone," she says. "I mean, someone other than Remmy."

There's a barb in her words that gives me pause, and I turn to look at her more closely, wondering what kind of point she's trying to make.

But then I realize that it doesn't matter what point she's making. I really shouldn't care.

"We're not dating," I tell her, placing my hand on the door to the restroom and pushing through.

I almost want to laugh when I see it. Of course, the bathroom looks like something you'd see in a Kardashian house. A huge open space with carpet and couches and big mirrors. At least a half dozen women are staring at themselves, making adjustments to their makeup. It's like the high school girls' bathroom, but for adults.

I don't realize the brunette has followed me in until I hear her speak from behind me, her words sharp and loud.

"So you're just fucking him, then?"

At that my back shoots straight and I turn to look at her. She stands with her arms crossed and an eyebrow raised.

"Excuse me?" I feel like I can't have heard her correctly.

Like, who says that? What world does she live in where it's okay to say something like that?

"There's a pretty long line of people who are waiting for a shot at Lucas Pearson," she says. "I don't know who you are, but I'd consider yourself lucky for even being on his arm tonight. Just don't forget that you're as expendable as the rest of them."

A burst of uncomfortable laughter comes barreling out of my mouth. It's something slightly hysterical, since I literally *cannot fucking believe* she just said that.

"I can't even... I don't even know how to respond to that," I finally say, just gaping at her as she continues to give me elevator eyes.

Finally, I spin away and head towards the individual bathrooms, but not before catching side-eye from a few of the women lined up at the mirrors.

Once I make it into a stall, I take a second to brace against the door. I stare at the floor as I try to process what she just said.

What a *bitch*.

I mean, seriously. Who *says* shit like that? I thought I'd watched enough *Gossip Girl* and *The O.C.* to prepare myself for the cattiness of rich people, but holy cow was I wrong.

Finally, I push it aside and slip off my shoes and make quick work of yanking off the stupid nylons that were clearly a mistake to put on in the first place. Then I step back into the high heels that are just barely a size too small, wincing only slightly, and head back to the main bathroom area.

Dropping the nylons in the trash, I don't even glance at anyone else before I return to the lobby. I don't know who those women are, but I feel like it's in my best interest to avoid them if they're going to talk to me like that. Cattiness isn't attractive.

Yuck.

I am beyond glad I get to walk away from whatever the hell *that* was.

I walk through the lobby, which has emptied considerably since I went into the bathroom, as guests make their way to assigned tables. Slipping into the main dining area, I watch for Lucas while allowing my eyes to take in the room.

I've never been in a yacht club before, but something tells me this one is pretty fancy. I always pictured them being more like a dive bar that just happens to be connected to docks with boats on them.

But this place? This looks like a resort. Or at least, what I imagine a resort would look like based on all of the commercials that air in Phoenix about the fancy places to stay in the area.

The room is a large circle with high ceilings and massive windows overlooking the marina outside. There are several dozen round tops covered in fine cloth and set for eight with a million knives and forks that I'm going to need to ask Lucas for help with.

A small jazz band plays to the left of a stage, where a podium is set up in front of the windows.

It almost feels like dining in a fish bowl.

My eyes are still searching for Lucas when they connect with a pair of beautiful browns that I can't believe I'm seeing here.

His mouth drops open, mirroring mine. But where I stand still, shocked, Pier Guy moves quickly, heading in my direction.

"Okay seriously, are you stalking me?" I ask, laughing awkwardly. "Because I thought you were joking earlier."

He shakes his head, that charming smile coming back to play. "I wish I was," he says, his eyes raking me up and down in disbelief, clearly as surprised to see me as I am to see him. "My mother is a member and I'm escorting her and my sister tonight."

The way he says *escorting* makes me take notice of something I hadn't seen before.

When I met him last night, he was wearing a biker jacket and dusty boots. This morning he was in jeans and a Henley. He'd looked like just a regular guy you could meet anywhere.

Standing in front of me now, he's wearing a suit. One that fits his body perfectly. His hair, where it was slightly shaggy this morning, now sits tucked back under product. A flashy watch rests on his left wrist.

Pier Guy is a money guy. Part of the world Lucas inhabits. If I had to wager a guess, I'd bet they might even know each other. And for some reason, that disappoints me.

I nod slowly. "Well, I guess I'll see you around this evening, then."

When I start to walk away, he moves to grasp my wrist.

I spin quickly and yank my hand out of his reach. It always saddens me, how quickly I've learned to side-step a man's touch. The knee-jerk reaction is fairly normal for me. But I guess that just comes with the territory.

He lifts both hands up. "I'm sorry, I didn't mean to..." He lets out an awkward laugh, drops one hand and rubs his face with the other. "I thought you were joking this morning. About the harassment. But were you serious? I'm not trying to bother you, I swear."

I shake my head. "No, I'm sorry. I just..." I glance away, not finishing my sentence. I wring my hands together, my body feeling uncooperative. How do you explain to someone that your reactions are based on something that has nothing to do with them?

"Look," he says, stepping closer. "I don't know you. I don't even know your name. But I do know that since we met yesterday, you've been on my mind constantly. And it felt like seeing you again this morning, and now a third time, here of all places... I don't know." He tucks his hands in his pockets, and the move strikes me as somewhat submissive. Something that Pier Guy isn't used to being. "But if you want me to, I'll leave you alone."

"No, don't..." I clear my throat, embarrassed that I responded so quickly, a flush creeping up my neck. Then, with a soft laugh, I say, "I mean, you don't have to leave me alone."

He smiles at me, and this one is tender. So different than the wolfish ones he's been giving me so far.

Maybe he was right this morning. Maybe it is kismet or a meet-cute or whatever else fate has in store for us.

Pier Guy really is incredibly handsome, and when he looks at me the way he is right now, there's this weird feeling in my chest that I can't quite place. A pulsing, beating thing, like my heart is pumping too quickly.

Maybe I misjudged him earlier.

It's the one thing I don't want anyone here to do with me... *assume*. And I'm guilty of it first.

Before we say anything else, his sister... Ivy? ...approaches us and taps Pier Guy's arm.

It's almost time to sit. You coming? she asks.

He looks at me, then down at her, looking conflicted. Even though I'd like to keep talking to him, I also remember her comment this morning about wanting to spend time with her brother.

I'm heading to my own table, I sign. *I'll see you later.*

His eyebrows raise, but I look away and turn to Ivy.

You look beautiful in that dress, by the way. Blue is a great color on you.

A split second of shock makes way for a smile to break out on her face.

Then I turn to the handsome man to my left. "See you later, Pier Guy." I give them both a wave, and wander off in search of Lucas.

And then, I can't help it. I glance back over my shoulder, and a thrill runs through me when I catch him watching me as I leave, his eyes on me with laser focus. I grin, then turn away, allowing myself to get lost in the crowd.

Hopefully we'll get a chance to talk again soon.

And if that does happen, I'll try not to run off again.

Weaving through the crowd, I finally find Lucas at the bar talking to... I want to laugh. He's talking to the aggressive brunette from the bathroom.

I let out a sigh. It feels like every part of being here so far has been about maneuvering land mines. So fucking exhausting. But I suck in a breath, then let it out slowly, and head in his direction, keeping a smile on my face.

"There she is," he says, reaching out and pulling me closer. "Hannah, I want you to meet Adrina. Her mother is a friend of my mother's."

Adrina lets out a laugh, a nasally thing that sounds a lot different than her voice from earlier. "Oh, Lucas. We're so much closer than that, wouldn't you say?" Then she looks at me. "We've known each other since we were kids. Grew up doing so much together."

I smile, though I'm sure it doesn't reach my eyes. "How fun for you."

"Adrina, this is my sister Hannah. She's living with me for the summer."

Her slightly bitchy expression pales, morphing into one that speaks much more of discomfort.

I feel just a little bit evil watching it happen, unable to help but enjoying her unease. "Adrina and I already met, actually. In the bathroom. She was really sweet. Helped me get rid of those horrible nylons."

Adrina laughs, high pitched and strangled.

"Ready to go sit?" I ask Lucas, giving his thigh a pinch. "Because I'd love to find our table."

Lucas winces and rubs the spot on his leg, but stands, grabbing his drink off the bar. "Adrina, good to see you."

She nods, then scurries off.

A part of me feels bad, knowing that I just did something kind of manipulative and mean. But the other part of me still remembers the way she looked at me like I was pond scum. So I focus on that to assuage my guilt.

When I turn back to glare at Lucas, he chuckles. "I feel like there's a story you should tell me."

I nod. "Don't worry. I will. But let's go sit first. These heels are a bitch."

"It doesn't surprise me."

"Well it surprised me," I reply, spooning the last bit of soup into my mouth. "Who talks like that?"

Lucas rolls his eyes and takes a sip of his whiskey. "Adrina thinks she lives in a soap opera. And I'll be honest, she kind of does. Her mother is friends with a few other Hermosa 'socialites'," he says, using air quotes. "I personally don't put a whole lot of stock in it, but they certainly do."

"So there isn't a long line of women just waiting to jump into your bed?" I tease, giving him a cheeky smile.

Normally, I probably wouldn't ask a question like that. But I'm feeling pretty good after having had two full glasses of the most delicious wine I've ever had. I think Lucas said it was a Syrah.

He chuckles and does a weird little shrug that makes me think it's actually true. "I mean…" he trails off, a smile on his face.

"Oh my *god,* it's *true.* What she said is actually true?" Then I scrunch my face up. "Yuck. I don't wanna know that."

He adjusts the napkin resting on his knee and lifts his drink to his lips again. "Well don't ask questions to which you don't want the answer," he murmurs, then tips the glass back and finishes the last bits of amber liquid.

Having come from a life of financial struggle, I've never been a big drinker. There just isn't really a chance to spend money on stuff like that when I'm trying to make rent and survive on coupon food from the clearance section of the grocery store.

And the few times I *have* had too much to drink, nothing good has ever come from it. So when I do have the chance, I drink slowly. Really try to savor it.

Lucas, on the other hand, is on at least his third glass of whiskey. Clearly he doesn't experience the same feelings about alcohol that I do.

"Do you want another wine, miss?" the server asks me.

I shake my head. "No thanks. I think I'm good for a while."

Lucas lifts his glass and the server nods, heading off to get him a refill.

"Not a big drinker?" Lucas asks.

I shrug. "Just don't like not being able to defend myself."

The words slip out before I can stop them. My eyes widen and I glance at Lucas.

He's sitting with his hands frozen where they were cutting his own food, his eyes on me.

I turn and focus my attention on the new plate of food I was just given. Some sort of chicken. I quickly slice it into pieces and stuff a big one in my mouth, looking around at the other people at our table, desperate for anyone to engage in conversation so I can avoid Lucas' eyes.

"Where did you say you were from?" the woman to my left asks me, and I let out a quiet sigh of relief in my mind.

"Phoenix," I reply. "Arizona."

She nods as she daintily cuts up her own chicken. "I have a cousin who used to live there. In Paradise Valley."

Of course her cousin lived there. I'm pretty sure that's the richest part of the entire state.

"She and her ex-husband had a home on a golf course until he came home and found her screwing her caddy."

I nearly choke on my chicken, but manage to sort myself out. Lucas taps me a few times on the back and I give him a grateful grimace.

"That sounds... unpleasant," I reply.

"From what I heard, it was *very* pleasant for her."

It takes everything in me to just nod my head and take a sip of my water without laughing. And from the look on Lucas' face, I'd guess he's going through the same thing.

We manage some light chatter with the remainder of guests at our table until I see a woman take the stage to my left.

"Ladies and gentleman, thank you so much for joining us tonight at the Annual Charity Auction for the Arts."

Everyone applauds. Once it trails off, she continues.

"Our evening tonight is made possible by the Calloway Foundation, who provide one hundred percent sponsorship for this event year after year, so that each and every dollar raised goes where it belongs. Now if you'll please join me in welcoming the

CEO of the Calloway Foundation to the stage, Calvin Calloway."

We all applaud as a tall man in in a fitted suit heads to the stage. He's handsome for a guy looking to be in his late '50s.

"Remember what Paige said about the guy with the midlife crisis and the twenty-two-year-old wife?" Lucas says, his voice quiet.

I nod. Then gasp. "The child bride?" I whisper.

Lucas grins. "That's him."

I giggle, looking back at the man on the stage, trying to imagine how anyone around my age could ever be interested in someone so much older.

I shrug, then look at Lucas, hoping to rile him up. "I understand what she was going for, now that I've seen him."

Lucas looks shocked and then I burst into laughter.

The applause fades as Mr. Calloway begins speaking, talking about the different charities that the event this evening helps to support. As much as he seems like a decent guy, he also sounds like someone who enjoys listening to himself talk.

Thankfully, I get distracted when I spot Pier Guy at a table on the opposite side of the room. But then I glance to his right and see his sister, bored next to him.

I can see Lissy when I look at her. Know that she's feeling that same thing Lissy used to complain about.

"I always feel like I'm on the outside," she told me once. "Like everyone is a part of something and I'm not invited."

My heart pangs for Ivy.

When the Calloway guy finishes speaking, people begin standing. I glance around, then look to Lucas, confused.

"Wanna go check out the auction?" he asks, folding his napkin and setting it on the table next to his plate.

I nod, realizing that the dinner is over and the auction part is beginning. "Yeah. I'll be there in a minute."

Lucas smiles and then heads off to the gallery that connects to the dining room, a large space that looks to be filled with tables covered in stuff to bid on.

I stand from my own chair, and head in the direction of Ivy and Pier Guy.

I really do need to find out his name.

When Ivy sees me heading in her direction, she lifts up slightly in her chair, her expression morphing into a small smile. I connect eyes with Pier Guy, briefly, but keep my attention focused on his sister.

How are you enjoying dinner? I ask her.

It was okay. I hate coming to these things. But mom says it's important for me to 'get acclimated', or whatever that means. She rolls her eyes.

I smile. *Did you try that liver thing?*

Ivy shudders. *No way. That looked so disgusting.*

Right? You couldn't pay me to eat that. So gross.

We both laugh.

Wanna go with me to check out the auction? I don't even know what I'm getting myself into, and I'd love to have someone who knows what's going on in there to explain things to me.

Ivy pops out of her chair, beaming. *Absolutely. Let's go.*

I catch Pier Guy's eyes for another moment as Ivy leads me away to the gallery room. I give him a little wave.

"I'll see you later," I say, and enjoy the soft smile and nod he gives me in return.

Then I head off with Ivy to the auction.

I'm Hannah, by the way. Your name is Ivy right?

She nods, then loops her arm in mine and leads me into the auction room.

Ivy spends a few minutes explaining everything to me. How the bidding works. How the room is organized, with the smaller items to the right and more expensive items to the left.

Naturally, we walk to the expensive stuff first, and my mind practically explodes when I see it.

Will someone really buy a boat tonight? I ask her.

She laughs. *You'd be amazed what people buy.*

We spend about fifteen minutes rotating around the tables, oohing and aahing at the fancy stuff people are bidding on. I can't help but glance at a few of the amounts listed as minimum bids, my eyes nearly popping out of my head when I see what people are willing to throw towards gifts and tickets and extravagant luxury.

I look to Ivy, about to ask her if she's planning to bid on anything, but pause when I find her staring off into the distance with a sour look on her face.

Everything alright? I ask when she finally looks back at me.

She sighs dramatically. *I have to go talk to my dad for a minute. I'll be back, okay?*

I nod. *Sounds good. I'm gonna go outside for a bit. I need some fresh air. It's a little stuffy in here for me.*

She giggles, picking up on my pun, then nods and races off to find her father.

And that leaves me free to do whatever I want. Which is definitely finding an empty outdoor space so I can get just a minute to myself.

I walk the perimeter of the room, then slip out of an open doorway, taking in a deep breath when I feel the rush of cool sea breeze on my face.

Closing my eyes, I breathe slowly, enjoying the sound of the water moving around the boats in the marina. I step to the edge of the patio area I've found and look over the short hedge to the yachts owned by the millionaires of Hermosa Beach.

There's so much money here. I can't help but feel like I'm breaking some kind of rule. Some sort of poor girl rule. Just by being here.

I'm supposed to just scrape by for the rest of my life. Live in shitty apartments. Work crappy jobs. That's the life the universe has given me.

Mansions that look at the ocean. Fancy dinners. Yacht clubs. I'm not supposed to see these things, let alone be invited to be a part of them.

I take another deep breath, hoping that my moment alone helps me build back up whatever confidence seems to always slip away so easily.

Chapter Eight

WYATT

She doesn't know I'm out here.

It's the only explanation for why she's standing there, her arms wrapped around her middle, eyes closed, taking deep breaths.

When she first walked out, I thought we might get one of those interactions you see in the movies, where I would say hello and she would startle and giggle a little bit. Maybe we'd chat and I could get her to finally agree to grab a drink with me. Or let me take her home.

But then I saw her face. And as beautiful as it was, it was also incredibly sad. As much as I'd like to get to know the girl, even I'm not the monster who tries to pick up on a chick on the verge of tears.

So I sit here in silence, letting her have her moment alone instead of trying to steal it for myself.

She really is absolutely gorgeous. Her long hair is up in a fancy twist, and she's wearing a beautiful dark dress with an open back and long lacy sleeves. It's a little bit short for an evening like tonight, but it shows off her long legs, so I doubt any man in the room would complain.

Maybe a few of the women, but really that would just stem from jealousy.

A few minutes go by where she stands with her eyes closed, her face up to the moon-lit sky, taking deep breaths and letting them out slowly.

Then she does something I don't expect. She takes off her shoes, a pair of black heels, then wiggles her feet around, stretching her toes and ankles.

It's a move I don't see often from the girls around here. The whole 'beauty knows no pain' mantra having been chiseled into their minds early on.

I think back to our first meeting, when she was in shorts and a shirt, her hair up in a messy knot on top of her head. And our second, a pair of ripped jeans and a zip up hoodie. Nothing about her indicates she's from money, from privilege and wealth and comfort. If anything, her every movement indicates her discomfort at being here.

Though I can't help but take in those movements with an appreciative eye, my eyes glued to her legs and that tight ass that fills out her dress so nicely.

Hey, I might let her have her moment, but that doesn't mean I can't admire her from afar. I'm not a monster, but am a man.

Suddenly, she turns around, which is when she spots me, sitting in the corner, scotch in-hand.

I assume she'll be embarrassed that I've been watching her. But instead of blushing or stammering or any of the other reactions I'm expecting, that sadness flees from her face, and she gives me a smile. A brilliant smile that might be the first real one I've seen on her face.

She doesn't seem like the type to smile very often. I'd argue that Botox eliminates laugh lines, like most of the women I know, but I don't see a Botox bunny when I look at her. The reason I don't think she smiles often is because she has that same hint of sadness in her eyes that I see when I look in the mirror.

The eyes of someone who has seen enough in this life.

Much more than any young person should.

So when she does turn and smile at me, I soak it in, because it's important to acknowledge the gifts people give to us. And seeing her smile, I can tell, is a gift.

"I didn't know you were out here," she says, her long legs eating up the concrete pavers as she joins me at my table.

"You looked like you needed a minute to yourself. I didn't want to interrupt."

There's the slight flush. Now that she's closer, I can see the bit of embarrassment on her skin. Even though this patio area is a part of the yacht club, the only light is coming from a handful of tall heaters with flames glowing in the middle.

"Yeah, I'm not... really a people person," she says, taking a seat in the chair across from mine. Then she freezes. "Oh. Is it okay if I sit? With you?"

I laugh. "Of course. I've been stalking you for the past day and a half, remember? You're finally getting with the program."

She smiles again, and I truly enjoy it.

There is something about her that I'm drawn to. Something pure. Almost raw. I know nothing about her, and yet I'd bet my life on the fact that each reaction I get out of her is genuine. It's a breath of fresh air after spending time with so many fake, plastic people for most of my life.

"Thanks for spending time with my sister."

But Pier Girl shakes her head. "I don't need thanks for that. She's pretty amazing."

"She is. But not everyone realizes it." Which is true. For some reason, the Hermosa Beach crowd doesn't seem to want to welcome Ivy Calloway with open arms. She's one of the richest residents, and has a heart the size of the entire fucking city, but being deaf? I guess it's a non-negotiable for some people.

Those people are pricks, but whatever. I've learned that having money can't buy class.

"Can I ask how it happened? I mean, was she born deaf or...?"

"She got a virus when she was a toddler. Crazy high fever. She was hospitalized for weeks while they tried to figure out what was going on." I shrug. "She's been deaf ever since."

She nods. "My friend Melanie's daughter had a similar situation. That's how I learned to sign."

"You're really good at it. Ivy's always telling me I need to get better, that sometimes the things I say don't make sense."

"Well if you need a tutor..." she trails off, giving me a playful smile.

There's a pause when Pier Girl turns her head and looks out at the marina, and I use that brief moment to take in her profile. Her long, graceful neck, soft skin, button nose.

"How was it?" she asks, looking back at me. "Coming home after so long away?"

For a moment, I'm confused. But then I remember what I told her last night, at the pier.

I rub my chin, scratch at the bit of stubble that's growing in that I refused to shave off even though my mother told me she wouldn't let me attend tonight unless I did. I'd called her bluff, since she was the one who was obligating me to go in the first place.

"It was exactly what I expected it to be," I say. "My sister was excited. My mother was a mess of emotions, some of which weren't particularly genuine. My brother probably doesn't know I'm in town yet. And my dad... well, we're not on speaking terms, even though it was likely his idea for me to come tonight."

She purses her lips. "I'm sorry it wasn't the perfect homecoming. But at least your sister was excited. How long were you away before coming back?"

"Three years."

Her brows raise. "That's a long time. What were you doing?"

I sigh. "Is it cliché to say I was finding myself?"

She laughs and shakes her head. "We're always constantly trying to find ourselves, aren't we?" she asks. "It's a process that never ends."

"Well, my process took me to San Francisco."

"And did you find yourself there?"

I pause, wondering the best way to say it. How do I tell her that instead of trying to find myself, I lost myself in someone else? Or, I guess, the plural of that. In the many *someones* of San Francisco.

I left because I wanted to get away from the drama with my family. I stayed because I wanted to piss off my father. And I left because the enjoyment I got out of being there dwindled enough that I knew it was time to try and find something new. But the reason I came home instead of going somewhere new? That's a completely different story.

"I didn't, though I wish I had. I left to escape the drama in my family. It was just supposed to be a vacation. A few months to try something different. But when that time had passed, I realized I'd created a little life for myself that I enjoyed. So I thought I'd stick it out." I shrug, deciding to stay vague about why I've returned. "And then at some point, I just realized it wasn't for me anymore."

"I wish I could have confidence like that," she says.

"What do you mean?"

She shakes her head and a piece of her twisty hairdo falls out. Absentmindedly, she tucks it back behind her ear. "Well, I'm kind of doing that by being here. Though I guess I didn't come to get away from family. I came to find it. I've only been here for two days and I already feel like I should just go back home. But I'm hoping I can just... I don't know, be stronger or happier or more courageous in putting myself out there. I want to belong somewhere and..." she laughs. "Sorry, getting a little too deep there."

I only kind of understand what she means, but I can tell she's emotional about it, regardless.

"What's keeping you from just giving up and going back?" I ask, hoping that her relationship with her family is enough to keep her here, at least long enough for me to spend a little more time with her.

She smiles, though that same sadness sits in the back of her eyes. "Well, there isn't really a home to go back to."

My brow furrows, but before I can say anything else, the door to the patio opens and Ivy comes waltzing out and over to us.

Sorry. Stupid dad was being stupid.

I laugh, and so does Pier Girl.

Ivy looks at me. *Dad wants to talk to you, too. I'm supposed to grab you and take you back.*

I roll my eyes, then look to Pier Girl. *His highness beckons,* I say, my sarcasm evident in my facial expressions. *You wanna come back in or are you going to stay out here?*

I'll come in with you, she signs. Then she looks at Ivy. *Maybe I'll even bid on that boat, huh?*

Ivy giggles as the three of us walk back into the dining area, the rush of conversational noise smacking us squarely in the nose.

Dad's over there, Ivy says, pointing in the direction of the stage where my father is currently holding court, his child bride standing next to him.

I look back at Ivy. *Well, let's go talk to him.*

But Ivy shakes her head. *No way. I already had to talk to him. It's your turn. I'm gonna hang out with Hannah.*

Something registers in my mind when she says that, and my eyes flick up to look at the beautiful woman who is watching us both.

Hannah.

But before the thought can fully form, I hear my name called out. I look over and see my mother giving me a small wave.

I'll find you two in a little bit, I tell the girls.

Then I head over to where my father and Krissa are talking with my mother.

Exactly the situation I want to join in on.

Awesome.

When I reach my mother's side, my father extends a hand, which I ignore, instead crossing my arms.

I only see a flicker of disapproval on his face, but he hides it quickly, dropping his hand and tucking it into his pockets, taking on an easy stance that makes him look like the king of the world.

Or at least of Hermosa Beach.

"You didn't shave." Of course that's the first thing he says. He looks to my mom. "You shouldn't let him show up to events like these without a clean face. It's an embarrassment."

"I'm twenty-fucking-four years old," I bite out, though I'm careful to keep my voice low enough as to not attract attention. "I don't need anyone to tell me how to clean up for an event."

There's a pause from my father, and I can see him assessing me with shrewd eyes.

It's the first time he's seen me since I moved to San Francisco. That's three whole years, during which time my faith in him diminished even more than it already had before I left. Even though I resent him for so many things - the way he treats his children, the dismissive way he treated my mother, his natural inclination to manipulate and control - there is a part of me that wonders what he sees when he looks at me now.

Does he see the same rebellious teen that snuck out? The one who never wanted any involvement with the Calloway Foundation? Or does he see the man I've become on my own? Feel his own resentment that I'm doing something without his help?

"Watch your mouth," he mumbles, that calm exterior staying in place. He lifts a hand and waves at someone behind me, smiling as he keeps talking to me. "You're lucky I even let you and your mother come to these functions anymore."

But I bark out a laugh, a little too loud if Krissa's watchful eyes are any indicator.

"You're a fucking joke if you think anything about my life can be dictated by you."

"Oh, boy, you'd be surprised to know how much control I have over things around here."

I push my shoulders back. "I don't care how much money you have, old man. The only reason I'm here is because it was important for mom and for Ivy." Then I cross my arms. "Clearly there wasn't a better man to escort the Calloway family to this event. So I gladly stepped in where the space was left vacant."

"Wyatt, don't speak like that to your father," my mom says, a pleasant expression on her face that makes me wonder if she popped a Xanax before coming here tonight. "He's done a lot for you and deserves your respect."

I barely manage to muffle my laughter, earning me an expression from my father that looks like he wishes he could melt me into the ground.

"What has he done for me?" I ask, struggling to keep my voice low and feeling thankful that no one is coming over to glad-hand with the man I have to call father. "Cheated on my mother? Left the family? Put his own selfish needs and wants before the people he's supposed to love? A man like that doesn't deserve my respect. He deserves my contempt."

My father's jaw ticks to the side.

Things haven't always been this hateful between us, even if we never had a loving father-son relationship. I'm not even sure that he completely understands why I've so aggressively and angrily turned my back on him.

Gone is any semblance of a resentful but dutiful son. In his place is a man hell-bent on giving Calvin Calloway the middle finger at every opportunity. He knows the true laundry list of his crimes... all the ways he's mistreated the people in his life. It shouldn't be a shock that I've finally decided that enough is enough.

Before I can say anything else, though, I catch sight of my mom's face. I see the hidden embarrassment. The two red patches on the sides of her neck that seem to flourish in these situations.

She can barely handle the life she tries to keep organized for herself. She doesn't need me causing any unnecessary problems or drama. And antagonizing my father is exactly that.

I let out a sigh. "Why do you even insist on talking to me," I say to him. "It's no secret that our family isn't a happily ever after story, regardless of the image you try so carefully to craft. So I don't understand why you could even believe that talking to me in public has any impact on anything."

Because really, that's the only reason he could want to talk to me, right? The only thing he wants is the attention it brings. That the powerful Calvin Calloway *can* have it all.

Endless money. An amazing marriage that ends in friendship. The hot young new wife. And in the face of all of that, the same wonderful, adoring family.

That's all he wants. And I can see the calculating gleam in his eye. The one that's trying to figure out what he can gain or lose in any situation.

But he's a fool if he thinks a single person in this damn town thinks Ivy, Ben and I look at him with anything other than loathing.

Adoring family.

Ha.

Fuck that shit.

"You wouldn't have anything right now if it wasn't for me," he says, his voice menacing, so unlike the charmer that got up on the stage just a short while ago to espouse the virtues of donating to worthy causes. "I think it's about time you remember who gave you what you have."

It's a shallow dig, an easy one to hit and one he likes to bring up whenever he can. Something to put me in my place. Something to remind me of where I *really* come from.

"Call me over like a dog again at the next event we're all at together. We'll see how well that goes over." My words are like venom, and my only hope is that they have their intended effect.

Keeping my father the fuck away from me as often as possible.

I relax my shoulders and step towards my mother, squeezing her hand even if she's upset with my actions. As frustrating as she can be, I hate when the things I say or do cause her stress.

As much as the things she does can irritate me sometimes, I owe my entire life to her. My brother and I were adopted when we were babies. He was one and I was a newborn. A perfect little family for Mr. and Mrs. Calloway.

But my father never lets me forget it.

I'm a charity case to him. A pawn he can try to manipulate in whatever way he thinks works to his advantage. My brother might have been easily played by him back when we were younger and significantly more naïve, but not me.

I always make sure Calvin Calloway knows that his wealth doesn't mean shit to me.

I turn away from them and head back towards the auction, keeping a carefully neutral expression on my face. Part of me hates myself for playing into that. Because as much as I spout at my father, I still don't make a scene, even though it's what he deserves.

Maybe someday, I'll manage to find the nerve to react exactly how I want. Be angry. Yell. Throw something.

And I hope on that day, my father is there to see it.

Chapter Nine

HANNAH

Ivy and I wander into the gallery and peruse some of the cheaper items that are more in a somewhat realistic price range.

Emphasis on *somewhat*.

That's how we find Lucas as we round the back of a table in the far corner of the room.

When he spots Ivy at my side, he gives her a huge smile before turning to me.

"I see you've met Ivy Calloway."

"Yeah, do you two know each other?" I ask. Then my eyes widen, and I turn to look at her.

Your last name is Calloway? You're related to the guy that was on stage?

Ivy rolls her eyes. *Only by blood. Not by choice.*

I laugh, loving her sassiness. Then I look back at Lucas.

"You can sign?" he asks, his face in some expression I don't understand.

I nod. "Yeah. My old roommate's daughter was deaf, so I learned as she learned. As she grew older."

Then I turn to Ivy. *He wants to know why I'm super awesome and can have secret conversations with you.*

Ivy giggles. *That's the one thing that's great about being deaf. I wish my mom didn't know how to do it so I could talk to my brothers without her knowing what we're talking about.*

We both laugh.

"See, I always feel like she's talking about me," he says, then sees my hands are moving. "Are you talking to her while I'm talking?"

"No," I say, continuing to sign. "I'm signing what you're saying so she isn't left out of the conversation."

I look to Ivy, about to ask her if she wants to grab something to drink - wine for me and something nonalcoholic for her - when I see that her eyes have gotten glassy.

Are you okay? I ask, concern racing through my body.

She nods, giving me a watery smile. *Yeah.*

You're sure? Most people don't cry when nothing is wrong.

She smiles and wipes at her face. *I'm okay. Promise.*

"She's just emotional because you care enough to include her when so many others leave her out," I hear from my left.

I turn to see her brother stepping up to us. Pier Guy wraps his arms around Ivy's shoulders from behind, tucking her in against his chest with an affectionate hug.

"Don't tell her I said that. She wouldn't want you to know," he adds, his eyes laser focused on me.

I smile at him.

I can't seem to help it.

The love he has for his sister is pretty beautiful. I'm sure they're just like all other siblings, driving each other crazy on a regular basis. But there's a fierce protection there, a willingness to do anything for her. His affection for her reminds me of how my brother Joshua was with me.

It couldn't hurt if I went out for a drink with him, right? I mean, out of everyone I've spoken with since I've gotten here, Lucas and Paige aside, this guy seems to be the most normal.

He might be a money guy, but I shouldn't hold that against him any more than he should hold my lack of money over me.

"Holy shit, man," I hear from my right, and I look over to see

Lucas' eyes are wide. He breaks into a smile, and my hands fly into motion for Ivy. "Paige told me you were back in town but I wouldn't have believed it if you weren't standing right here in front of me."

Pier Guy steps out from behind Ivy and shakes Lucas' hand, the two of them giving each other a brief hug.

"Wyatt Calloway, in the *fucking* flesh," Lucas adds, stepping back and shaking his head.

I change the f-word as I'm translating to something a little more suitable for Ivy.

Wyatt Calloway. What a name. He sounds like he's going to storm into your western town after robbing a bank and demand a drink.

"I thought you were traveling this summer. Heading to London or something?"

Wyatt shrugs a shoulder, his eyes returning to me. "I changed my mind. Thought a ride down the coast would be enjoyable before I spend the summer at home." Then he looks at Lucas. "I wanted to get in extra time with Ivy, too."

Lucas' expression becomes cautious, and I see him shift from foot-to-foot, something uncharacteristic of him.

Well, at least since I've known him.

Wyatt's eyes travel between Lucas and me. "It looks like you two know each other. Please don't tell me you're dating. I've been trying to get her to agree to go out for drinks with me."

"No, we're not..." I pause. I did it again. Spoke so quickly he must know I'm interested. I don't know how to play hard to get. "We're not dating," I add, letting out an awkward laugh.

Wyatt bites the inside of his cheek, stifling a grin. "Well that's good. Ivy said your name is..." but he doesn't finish the sentence. His voice trails off and he looks at Lucas again.

Then back at me.

"Hannah," I say. "My name is Hannah."

Lucas clears his throat, looks to me. "This is my friend Wyatt Calloway. We've known each other since before we were even old enough to start making memories." Then he looks to Wyatt. "This is Hannah Morrison. My sister."

I give Wyatt a soft smile, glad to finally be given an introduction since I seem to have problems giving him my name on my own.

But Wyatt's expression, while friendly and mischievous when

he first walked up to us, immediately shifts into something neutral. Something bland and unfriendly.

Guarded.

There's an awkward pause as Wyatt's eyes take me in, and my happiness slips slightly, unsure of what's happening.

It feels like I'm looking at a completely different person than the Pier Guy I talked to yesterday and this morning. Even just a few minutes ago.

That guy had been friendly and open. A charmer. Dare I say he had been lowering walls he didn't normally drop to talk to me about... well, I guess we didn't talk about much. But it felt like we did.

This guy... Wyatt... is quickly morphing into someone who looks like he could light this building on fire with his eyes.

It makes me want to shrink back.

But before I can do or say anything, Wyatt turns his focus to Lucas, his nostrils flaring, his jaw tight. "You weren't going to tell me?" he demands, his voice a low rumble that seems to fill the space around us.

Confusion hits me and I also look to Lucas, but I find his eyes focused firmly on Wyatt. Lucas remains silent, instead lifting his whiskey glass to his lips and taking a sip.

Wyatt lets out some sort of groan or grunt of frustration, his eyes looking at me once again before he suddenly turns and storms from the room.

I remain where I stand, my eyes following him as he drags his cloud of anger away. Then I look to Ivy, who is watching him go, a sad expression on her face.

She looks back at me. *I better go,* she says. Then she steps in and gives me a big hug. *It was great meeting you Hannah. I hope we can still be friends even though my brother is the moodiest person I've ever met.*

I nod, though my smile is weak. *Absolutely.*

She gives us both a wave, then heads off in the direction Wyatt just huffed off to.

When I turn to look at Lucas, I find him staring off towards that same doorway.

"What was that?" I ask, still confused. Still shocked. And if I'm honest, possibly a little bit more upset than I should be.

I don't know Wyatt from Adam. We'd just had some playful

banter. Some friendliness. I shouldn't be expecting anything from him.

But I guess, that's my naivety coming out to play. The very reason why I struggle to trust, even though I so desperately want to. I always seem to be left standing confused and wary.

Lucas shakes his head, letting out a long sigh. "It was just Wyatt being a moody asshole," he says. "Come on. Let's go buy something."

Following his lead, I loop my arm with his, and let him walk us around the room, my thoughts feeling more jumbled than ever.

"I'm glad you came tonight."

I look up from the book I'm reading to where Lucas is standing at the door to my bedroom. He's wearing a pair of sweats and a tank top, likely also getting ready to climb in to bed.

"Thanks for inviting me." I tuck a finger in to hold my spot and close the book, turning slightly onto my side where I rest snuggled in to the plush down comforter on my bed. "It was... an adventure."

He huffs out a laugh and shakes his head. "Well, it was great having you there. And I'm sure Ivy enjoyed having someone to chat with."

I nod. "I'm surprised more people aren't receptive to her. I mean, no offense, but if you've known her all her life, why haven't *you* learned to sign?"

Lucas looks away. "I should have. I just... I guess I was too self-absorbed to realize the difference it could make." When he looks back at me, I see regret swimming in his eyes.

"I didn't say that to hurt your feelings."

"I know. I know you didn't. But it still hurt, even if it's my own fault, you know?"

I shift my position and rest my chin on my hand, my elbow pressed in to the cushy mattress topper. "I'd be happy to teach you, if you want to, like, learn a little bit and surprise her? Maybe?"

He smiles at that, crosses his arms and leans on the doorframe. "Something tells me that you're just naturally a person who thinks about others before thinking about herself. That might be my favorite thing about you so far, *sis.*"

I roll my eyes. "I don't know how I feel about this whole *sis* thing. How about *your highness.* I'd even take *Lady Hannah.*"

Lucas laughs.

"What? I was on a *Game of Thrones* kick before I came here. Lady Hannah has a ring to it, don't you think?"

"Well, I have every subscription and streaming service imaginable in this house. You should pick a new show and we can watch it together."

"That sounds awesome. Do you want to start it tomorrow? I was thinking about going to the pier to apply at a few different places for a summer job, but other than that I won't have anything else going on."

"I have plans in the evening with some friends."

I nod, trying to hide my disappointment. The last thing I want to do is become some sort of burden for Lucas. But at the same time, he seems like a guy who might not have as much space in his life for new people as I'd assumed. And my entire reason for coming here was to spend time with him.

"Okay. Well, we can find another night then. Thanks again for inviting me. It was fun spending time with you."

Lucas raps twice on the doorframe with his knuckles. "Night, Hannah."

"Night."

I shift my position back to get comfortable and open my book back up. Sienna was really into fantasy novels, and gave me the first in an apocalyptic series to read. Hopefully I'll be able to borrow Lucas' library card or something to get the next ones, because this baby is *really* good.

But even though I want to spend time enveloped in this story, I realize that the entire chapter I read before Lucas showed up at my door is basically white noise. I retained nothing.

All I'd been able to think about was what happened at the yacht club.

The confusion still sits unsettled on my chest. How did we get from the playful banter about asking me out for drinks, to the relaxed conversation about San Francisco, to Wyatt storming out the door, not looking back?

I feel like I'm missing something.

Something important.

Something you'd only be able to understand if you live here. If you *belong* here. Which I don't.

I sigh, deciding to give up on reading for the night. Reaching over, I set it on the night stand and flick off the lights, hoping that tomorrow is a more fruitful day.

I don't know exactly how I got here.

Okay, that's not entirely true. I can remember the bunny trail of events that led to me sitting here now, at Harbor's, surrounded by people I don't know, and wishing I was somewhere else.

But the truth is, I don't understand why I'm here.

"If you want a job for the summer, you start right now."

That's what Lucas' friend Hamish told me when I showed up at Bennie's at the Pier this morning to ask about waitressing.

I'm pretty sure my eyes about fell out of my head, but I'm smart enough not to look a gift horse in the mouth. I'd grabbed the apron from the counter and wrapped it around my waist.

"Just gimme a shirt and I'm ready."

Hamish had smiled at me. "I'm gonna like you. I can already tell."

And that's how I'd found myself waitressing at Bennie's, learning the menu and POS system on the fly, trying to keep track of which tables were what numbers, and keeping myself from being barreled over as I carried a huge plate of food up the stairs to the rooftop deck.

The place was packed for my entire shift, which wasn't surprising, considering it was a Sunday afternoon, the restaurant sits right on the pier in a beach town, and the menu contains a range of food, along with craft beer and a full bar.

The clientele at Bennie's is eclectic, ranging from couples dressed nicely on a date, to families with whiney kids with sand in their hair, all the way to a handful of surfers who embody beach culture to the extreme.

The one consistent? The food looks damn delicious.

When I'd been a customer on Friday evening with Lucas, I

ordered a burger, just asking for what looked like a cheaper item on the menu. But getting familiar with the dishes served made my mouth start to water.

My day today was incredibly long, and my feet were aching. But as my very first shift came to an end, I'd been invited by a group of servers to go out for a drink.

Which is where I am now.

Harbor's is a bar near the yacht club. Close enough for us to walk from work but far enough away that I quickly regretted my decision to join in when I realized I'd need to walk back to Bennie's to get my bike and then ride back to Lucas' house once we were done.

The place is packed, but our group of seven managed to find a four-top table and a bunch of chairs. So now, we're squished together, chatting about work and life and more work.

Well, *they* are talking about those things. I'm sitting here mute, uncomfortable, as usual.

When I was invited out, I tried to remind myself that I need to make friends. That getting to know people is important. But I always forget how much work is involved in something like that. How exhausted I feel afterwards.

I think back to my conversation with Wyatt. It didn't feel exhausting talking to *him*, I remind myself. Then I roll my eyes and try to focus on something else. Instead of the gorgeous, somewhat broody man that seems to infiltrate my every latent thought.

As my eyes wander around the bar, I see a booth in the corner that looks big enough to seat a large group.

"Hey, why don't we go sit over there. We'll have more room," I say.

Everyone laughs.

I look around confused, wondering if I missed a joke that was told right before I spoke.

"That table's reserved," Loren says, sipping from a pale ale gripped in his right hand, disdain dripping from his voice.

I glance back at the table, not seeing a sign or anything.

"It's for the owner's daughter and her friends." That was Denise. She's worked at Bennie's since it opened seven years ago, a fact she has reminded me of at least a handful of times. When I take a look at her, I catch her glaring at the booth like it did her wrong in a past life.

Or maybe this one.

"I keep forgetting you're not from here. Most of us grew up here or in one of the neighboring cities," Eleanor says, looking up briefly from the phone she's constantly glued to. Then she looks at Denise. "You should tell her about them."

I look between all of the people I'm sitting with. "Who are *them*?"

Denise laughs. "Well, it looks like this might be perfect timing. They're coming right now."

I turn to look over my shoulder and like something out of a movie, I see a group of people about our age walking across the floor and heading towards the booth.

Growing up, you learn pretty quickly that people like to associate with what's familiar. It's why people typically don't date outside of their attractiveness level, and aren't usually friends with people from different backgrounds or socio-economic statuses. It's the reason people so easily flock in gender or ethnic groups. Familiarity and similarity is the most comfortable place to be, because it is a reflection of yourself.

So it makes sense that the group of people that walk through the door all look like they stepped out of a magazine. Tall, fit, attractive. They ooze wealth and confidence.

They're not the type of people to ever wonder if they belong somewhere. They're the type of people who believe that somewhere doesn't exist if they aren't there.

"You'll learn pretty quickly that the Hermosa elite have some sort of exclusive section everywhere in town. Here, it's that booth. At The Wave, it's an entire VIP section. At Bennie's, they have their own table on the rooftop." Denise pounds her drink. "They're so *fucking* annoying."

The noise from the bar is loud, but it fades slightly as I watch them. The 'elite' of Hermosa Beach. A tray of drinks is brought out but I didn't see them order. They laugh and cheers and get out their phones to take pictures.

"Which one is the owner's daughter?" I ask, just trying to make conversation.

"She's not here," Loren says. "She's so hot. I'd love to show her what a real man is like instead of those pansy rich boys she's always hanging out with."

I hold back my disgusted face, but barely. I don't like men who assume women can be manipulated with sex. Like getting fucked by someone strong enough or *man enough* will make them think differently.

I've always wished I was brave enough to confront pigs like Loren. They feel entitled to women's bodies, assuming that because they find someone attractive, they should be able to control that person in some way. And when that woman doesn't respond the *right way,* they're a bitch or a cunt or a whore or any other number or names I've been called throughout my life.

But I've never been willing to stand up for what's right. Hold them to task. Tell them what I really think.

That goes with anything, really. Sexist men, abusive foster families, the mean girls in high school. I don't know how to speak up. When you live in a place where no one listens to you, enough time goes by and you start to believe your voice doesn't exist anymore.

Maybe someday I'll learn to speak up. But today isn't that day.

Instead, I look back at the table of 'rich bitches' and take a sip of my vodka soda, and listen to the people I'm sitting with gossip about them.

I learn something about each person sitting at that table. How the brunette, Rebecka Jane, is an 'influencer' - a term Denise uses with air quotes and another roll of her eyes - and doesn't have a real job. How the Asian girl, Ji-Eun, comes from old money in South Korea. How the blond guy, Aaron Singer, likes to make actual notches in his bedpost after sleeping with tourists.

"They own everything in town, which is why shit is so expensive," Loren groans. "Double lots and pools and gyms."

I bite my cheek, thinking of Lucas' house.

"And that's just the people sitting over there," Eleanor adds. "You should see the rest of them."

Instinctively, I know.

I know that Lucas and Paige are a part of this group that my fellow servers despise so much.

And in what can only be described as an act of God, the moment I come to this realization, I see Paige walk through the front door.

She looks just as beautiful and happy as she did the last time I saw her, strolling into the room with a big smile on her face. I see her eyes connect with that booth and she raises a hand in the air to wave at them.

And then, like it's slow motion, her head pans across the bar, scanning, her eyes connecting with mine, passing, and then darting back.

Her smile grows.

I smile back.

I might not be the best at confronting assholes like the ones at my own table, but I *do* know that, regardless of who I'm friends with, I try to be nice to everyone.

As far as I know, Paige is the same way. Hopefully the people at this table can get over themselves and realize that at some point.

"Oh my God, is she actually coming over here?" Denise hisses at no one in particular.

Eleanor puts her phone down immediately and adjusts herself in her seat. "Do I look okay?" she asks, fixing her hair.

Now it's my turn to roll my eyes as I realize that everything Denise, Loren and Eleanor just told me, everything the rest of our group listened in on with wide ears and big eyes, was a bunch of bullshit.

Sure, it might have been true. There might be a girl who lives of her parents' money and a guy who bangs tourists and another girl who wants social media to pay for her life.

But the people in this group right here who are talking about them like they're the scourges of society? They're fucking jealous. They're outraged because it doesn't feel fair.

Well I have a few opinions on life and what is fucking fair, and I can promise it has nothing to do with what the 'Hermosa elite' do with their time and money.

"Oh my gosh, Hannah!" Paige exclaims as she reaches our table. "This is awesome. I didn't know you'd be here." Then she glances around, her smile remaining. "Hey everyone. Eleanor, your hair looks awesome today. Did you cut it?"

Eleanor looks like she just fell in love when she runs a hand through her hair. "Oh. Uhm. Yeah. Last week."

"I've always thought a bob was a great look on you. Remember that time you put blue highlights in?" Paige says, giggling, and Eleanor joins her. "I was so jealous. My mom *never* would have let me do that."

Eleanor shrugs, her hand playing with the ends of her hair. "It was just wash out stuff you can get at the store. You should totally try it out."

"Maybe," Paige says. "If I do, I'll ask you what brand you got. I'm always worried the color will bleed and ruin the rest of my hair."

"Just let me know," Eleanor says, nodding.

"Hannah, Lucas is going to be here soon if you want to come join us," Paige says, giving me a smile and then glancing around to the group again. "But no pressure if you're making new friends."

I nod, giving Paige my own smile.

"Thanks. I'll probably swing by to say hi when Lucas gets here."

"Sounds good. Bye everyone!"

And then she whisks off, moving confidently across the floor and over to the booth where her friends are waiting.

There's a pregnant pause and I can feel everyone's energy shifting, moving in my direction. Something that's confirmed when I glance around and see every set of eyes at our table trained on me.

"What?" I ask, though I definitely know.

"How do you know Paige Andrews?"

"She's friends with my brother."

"Who is your brother?" Denise asks, one eyebrow raised high enough that it looks like it's gossiping with her hairline.

"Lucas Pearson. Do you guys know him?"

I take a sip of my drink, knowing full well that they know who he is. And of course, my admission is like a bomb dropping in the group.

Eleanor seems excited, her eyes lighting up. Loren looks suspicious, his face pinched in an expression that tells me he thinks I might be full of shit. Denise seems a little pissed, but is trying to hide it. The rest of them seem to only be half listening as they fuck around on their phones.

"I didn't realize Lucas had a sister," Eleanor says, leaning forward on the table, her eyes wide. "I thought he was an only child. He never had siblings when we were in school together."

"We just found out about each other," I say, though I immediately regret it. One of the very first things I learned when I moved here was that the gossip machine is aggressive. I have to be careful what I say, and who I talk to.

Denise looks like she doesn't know how to handle this bit of news. But before she can ask any questions, I cut it off at the knees.

"I'd rather not talk about that, though, since it's so new. I'm gonna grab a drink and then head over there since it looks like Lucas just got here. I'll see you guys at work, okay? And thanks for inviting me out."

I stand quickly and head over to the bar for a new drink, trying to buy myself time before I head over to Paige's table.

The last thing I want is some kind of barrier between me and the people I work with. I mean, I can't control who my brother is. And it would be stupid of them to treat me different just because they can kind of associate me with this group of 'elite' that they seem to despise, or be really jealous of.

But it doesn't seem like the people here handle things with maturity. The pyramid of importance is based on wealth, and gossip is its own unique form of currency.

I'll just have to wait and see how things go during my next shift, I guess. But if I'm completely honest? I don't see myself making great friends with Denise or Loren, so I'm not too upset about it.

After grabbing my vodka soda, I head over to the booth in the corner. Paige and Lucas immediately make room for me, getting everyone to scoot in so I can sit on the end.

"There she is," Lucas says as I approach the table. "Everyone, this is my sister Hannah. Hannah, these are some of my good friends."

I get some friendly smiles and one or two curious glances. The group has grown since the gossip-sesh back at my previous table, and there are at least eight people all seated around the booth.

"Congrats on the job at Bennie's," Lucas says, taking a sip of his drink.

I smile. "I went by this morning around nine o'clock to drop off the application and Hamish hired me on the spot."

Lucas smiles. "I'm glad it all worked out so well."

"Yeah, things tend to work out well when you're friends with Lucas." The guy who says it is sitting next to my brother, and he chuckles and takes a sip of his own drink.

Lucas rolls his eyes. "Ignore Otto. He's just being a dick. We're not actually friends."

Otto laughs again, and I nod and give him smile, but a sense of unease rolls through my body.

I've never been one to take a handout. Just being here already makes me feel like I'm abusing someone's generosity, not to mention the meals he and Paige have paid for, and borrowing some of Paige's clothes for the event last night.

But if Lucas had something to do with me getting that job? I'm not sure I know how to respond to that.

Obviously sensing my discomfort, Lucas leans towards me. "It wasn't a big deal. I just flicked Hame a text letting him know my sister was probably going to swing by to apply for a job. That's it." He bumps me in the shoulder. "I feel like I missed out on a lot of things that being a big brother entails. The least I can do is make sure the people I know can help you get a job if you're qualified for it, right?"

I grin, brushing off that earlier feeling. He's just doing the brotherly thing. The helpful thing. Like what Paige said at breakfast the other day. Family helps each other.

"Thanks for that," I say. "I definitely need extra cash this summer, so I really do appreciate the help."

He bobs his head and takes another sip of his drink.

I continue to sip my own drink slowly, and choose to stay fairly silent for the rest of the evening, just observing Lucas and Paige interact with their friends.

I glance back at the other table a few times. I can see them looking at me as they talk.

This is why I don't gossip. Why I don't like to sit around and talk shit about people. Because it means the second I leave, they're going to keep doing it, but this time, it'll be about me.

People talk shit. I can't control that. But I can control what I say, and what I listen to.

And this is my lesson. This is my one smack over the head to remind me that I don't have to sit and listen to stuff like that. It doesn't feel good. It feels manipulative and aggressive and angry. It feels like it's filled with jealousy and bitchiness.

Those things aren't me. And if I'm going to finally find my own place in this world, I have to stay me, even if that means I stick out here.

Eventually, someday, I'll find the place I fit.

Chapter Ten

WYATT

I wake up to a small hand poking me in the face.

Squinting, I peek open one eye and spot Ivy sitting on the edge of the bed with a smile.

I close my eyes again.

"I know you're awake, weirdo," she says, poking me again.

I pull my hands out from under the comforter. *Then why are you poking me?*

She giggles and I peek an eye open so I can see her. *Because it's after ten in the morning and you're still in bed.*

She sets her hands on my chest and starts shoving and shaking me until I'm flopping around like I'm having a seizure.

"Alright, alright." I open an eye again. *What can I do for you, your highness?* I sign, doing a little wave with my hands.

She laughs again.

I wanna go see Ben. Can we do that and get lunch there today? I'm in the mood for some cheesy pretzels.

I smile. Any day that Ivy is in the mood to see our brother *and* fill up her tiny frame with some food is a good day.

That sounds like something I can definitely make happen.

Yay! Okay, I'll go get ready. And then she's sprinting out of my room and out of the guesthouse, to do god knows what.

I roll over and push my face back against the pillows, wishing I could have gotten just one more precious hour of sleep.

Especially after the last few days.

I should have known when I came back and things with my mother were so easy that first night that it was too good to be true. That her previous promises of a quiet family summer at home were bullshit attempts at something I have no interest in.

As real and open as she was with me when I first got home, the woman just can't help herself. Even in the wake of our family's troubles, even with the very scary shit storm headed our way, she still wants to showboat and schmooze with the socialites of Hermosa Beach.

After I got back Friday night, I woke up Saturday morning to my mother standing over me in bed, that plastic mask back on her face, letting me know I'd be attending a fundraising dinner with her and Ivy at the marina.

She didn't care that I might not want to go.

She didn't care that *Ivy* might not want to go.

All she cared about was the fact that it was a Calloway Foundation event and that dad couldn't be the only one getting the attention for something helping the community.

I roll my eyes just thinking about it. The last thing I'd wanted to do after getting back to town was deal with the insufferable members of the local yacht club.

But I didn't really have a choice. Because there's only one person keeping this family together right now. It's definitely not my brother Ben, who isn't allowed at our house. And it's definitely not my dad, who thinks it's completely acceptable to attend a yacht club function with his ex-wife, his children, and his new twenty-something-year-old child bride.

So it has to be me.

Most of the dinner had been exactly what I thought it would be. Black tie. Stuffy, unbearable conversation with people who don't give a rat's ass about anything but money and status.

That might have been the world I was raised in. It might even be the world I'm the most comfortable in. But that doesn't mean it's the world I envision for myself in the future. It doesn't mean that's what I enjoy.

In San Francisco, I can be a nobody. I throw on a pair of jeans and a graphic t-shirt, and I'm just another hipster trekking through the city. Anywhere else, I don't have to be a Calloway. The second son of one of the wealthiest business moguls in the South Bay. I get to just be me. Wyatt. The guy who enjoys riding motorcycles, spending time in the company of beautiful women, and building up my business portfolio.

But at home, I have a role to play.

Caretaker.

The prodigal son.

I think my dad still assumes that one of us – me or my brother Ben – will finally step up and start working for his company. But I don't see that ever happening. I'm far too independent, and have too much self-respect to ever grovel at the feet of a man who saw our family as inconsequential.

My presence at the Hermosa Beach Yacht Club was strictly for my sister, since it was her first invitation to the annual event. Technically, she didn't need me there. She's been to enough Calloway Foundation functions to know how they work. But after I'd told my mother that I wouldn't be going, Ivy begged me to reconsider.

Imagine my surprise when I saw Pier Girl, her bright eyes just as shocked to see me. I could have sworn something larger was at play. To see each other three times in less than twenty-four hours is... not plausible. In any environment.

This might be a little beach town, but it's also the real world, not a Hallmark movie, and my earlier wonderings if I'd see her again had been followed with a very reluctant acceptance that it was highly unlikely.

And yet... there she was.

She's one of those women who leave an impression. Not in the way she looks, though God knows I was trying to recite baseball stats to myself when she'd bent over to pick up her shoes and I'd caught an accidental peek down the front of her dress. She's a bombshell, and I don't think she has any clue.

No. The impression she left had everything to do with who she is, not just what she looks like.

My heart stutters as I remember her translating for Ivy. Making sure she wasn't left out.

Even Lucas, who loves Ivy to death, would never have thought of something like that. Something so simple. So small.

But then, the floor had fallen out from beneath me.

I grit my teeth at the memory.

She's Hannah fucking Morrison.

How?

How?

I never thought it would actually happen.

That she would be here. In this town.

I should be mad at Lucas.

Fuming.

For his scheming. How he manipulated this. Twisted everything up.

But really, I'm mad at her. She shouldn't be here. Infiltrating the locations we go. Probably making friends with the people I've known since childhood.

I never looked her up. Even after all these years. And there I was, checking her out, wondering – or, worrying, rather – if she was dating Lucas or was free game.

And now she's here. In my face. Making friends with *my* sister. I had to deal with Ivy's incessant pestering yesterday. All Sunday long, she kept asking about Hannah, how I knew her, whether I could call Lucas and see if Hannah wanted to hang out.

Like they could ever be friends.

I force myself to roll out of bed and stumble in the direction of the shower, hoping to find the pick-me-up I need to wake my ass from its severely hungover state.

I don't need to be thinking about how fucking hot Hannah Morrison is. About her wavy blonde hair or how green her eyes were when she looked at me. How red her face flushed when she got embarrassed.

I crank on the shower, chuck off my clothes, and step under the spray before it's even gotten warm, letting the frigid water drench my body and wake me up in my bones.

It heats quickly, and I spin to let it pound against my back, bracing my hands against the shower wall.

This is my favorite shower in the whole property, and one of the reasons I enjoy staying in the guesthouse instead of the main. I smirk, thinking about the fun I've had in this shower. The privacy is definitely appreciated.

I stand in silence for a few minutes, trying to force my mind to turn off. The roving thoughts that seem to keep me up at night and stressed and on edge all day don't seem to want to go away, though. So eventually, without even washing, I just turn the water off and step out.

I'm drying off when I hear a knock on my door. Wrapping the towel around my waist, I head out to the entry, curious about who would be knocking on my door this early on a Monday. Everyone I know is either asleep, hungover, or already at work for the day.

To say I'm surprised when I see Lucas standing on the other side of the door when I open it is an understatement.

Surprised and irate.

He gives me a smile that oozes with arrogance, that self-satisfied look that he so often has that always seems to crawl under my skin.

"You have a lot of fucking nerve coming by here," I bite out, spinning around and heading back to my room, but leaving the front door open.

I slam my bedroom door, though it doesn't actually make me feel any better. Glancing around, I grab my duffle bag and dig around, grabbing a pair of boxers. Then I step over to the closet.

I had a company send down a bunch of my stuff, including most of my clothes, before I got here. It's a mix of things I want for while I'm here, as well as the things I'll be taking with me when I leave for London at the end of the summer.

The good thing about hiring someone else to handle it is that I don't have to deal with everything myself. The shitty part is that it means I never know where anything is for the first few days as I sort through things that have been tucked into the dresser, hung in the closet, or organized onto shelves and around the house.

Once I've picked out some jeans, a dark blue shirt and gotten changed, I take a deep breath, letting the air out slowly, and then emerge from my bedroom.

Lucas stands in my kitchen, his back to me as he mixes himself a drink.

"A little early for that, don't you think?" I say.

He glances over his shoulder to look at me, scoffing. "Coming from you, I can't take that seriously."

I cross my arms. "What are you doing here, Lucas? I can't imagine we have anything to talk about."

He stays quiet, taking a sip of his drink, assessing me from over the top of the glass.

The rage I've been feeling since I saw him at the club with Hannah begins to boil under my skin.

When he continues to stand there, silent, an almost amused expression on his face and sipping from that damn glass, I finally spit something out.

"Lucas, I'm not kidding."

He sets his drink down on the counter. "I'm not here for any specific reason other than to try and convince you to give this a chance."

I clench my fists. "Give *what* a chance?"

He shrugs. "Everything."

I don't know what to say in response, so I stay silent, waiting for him to continue. Lucas always has something else to say. But another minute goes by and he doesn't add anything, so I say what I've been dying to get off my chest since the minute I realized it last night.

"You like her," I say, remembering the easy way they'd interacted, the loving way he'd looked at her.

He shrugs, but continues to stay silent. It reminds me just how much I hate that stupid shrug.

There was one time in junior year of high school when Lucas and I got into a fight. What was it over? His stupid fucking shrug. Well, that and Amie Hanover. But it was mostly the shrug.

I've never met someone who seems so incredibly indifferent to everything. I hate it.

"Time for you to go," I say, picking his drink up off the counter and dumping it into the sink. "We have nothing to talk about."

"Come on, man," he says. "You had to know this day was coming. I tried to talk to you about this, but your stubborn ass wouldn't fucking budge."

"So you just took matters into your own hands? Is that it?"

He sighs. "Wyatt, we've been friends since we were kids..."

"That's where you're wrong, Lucas," I say. "We're not friends. As far as I'm concerned, both you and Hannah do not exist."

He looks away, and I grit my jaw. Then I head over to the front door and open it, standing next to it, glaring at him.

"I hope you feel differently someday," he says. "That you realize nothing is worth throwing away a friendship. A relationship with someone you care about." Then he turns and heads to the door. He stops right in front of me and slips his sunglasses back on. "I'm taking Hannah to Mary's for Monday Mournings with everyone. Any way you'll consider joining?"

"Not a chance in hell."

He nods his head a few times, adjusting the watch on his wrist. "Like I said. I hope you feel different one day. And that you let me know when that day comes."

And then he walks out, leaving me angry and unsatisfied, and the door wide fucking open.

But that's Lucas. He thinks he knows everything. Thinks he controls everything. But he's wrong about this. This isn't some game he can play. Lives aren't a game. And that's what he's doing.

And that includes Hannah.

I run my hand through my hair, tugging on the short, damp strands, enjoying the tiny little bite of pain that hits my scalp.

Then I turn and finish getting ready for the day.

Mondays used to be a sacred day for me and my friends. We'd stumble our hungover asses to Mary's and have Monday Mournings. Commiserate about the weekend. Talk about hookups and hangovers, and the girls would catch up on gossip and family drama.

I grit my teeth.

Well, not me. Not anymore. I have other priorities this summer, and they don't include playing whatever fucking game Lucas is trying to bait me into.

Once I'm done getting ready, I head over to the main house, finding Ivy in pajamas, putting on makeup at a mirror set up on the kitchen counter.

I step in front of her and wait until she glances at me.

Since when do you wear makeup? I ask, certain that she hadn't been wearing any the last time I saw her when she and mom came to visit me late last year.

She rolls her eyes and continues to put on more mascara. Once she's done, she closes the tube and sets it down. *Only since forever. Duh.*

I blink.

Well then.

When I turn to grab an orange juice from the fridge, I see Vicky walk into the kitchen with a rag and spray bottle.

"How long has Ivy been wearing makeup?" I ask her, keeping my back to my sister so she can't try and read my lips. The little runt is good at it and it has bitten me in the ass more than a few times.

"She's been wearing makeup for the past year," Vicky replies, spraying one section of the counter and starting to wipe it down.

That can't be right, but I guess it's more likely that I'm wrong than for Vic to misremember something like that.

"She's only twelve," I say, as if that means anything. "That's too young to be wearing makeup."

"I know you're talking about me," Ivy says from behind me.

I spin to look at her.

Don't talk about me when I'm right here and can't hear you. It's really rude.

I nod. *You're right. I'm sorry.* I pause. *I was saying you're too young to be wearing makeup.*

Mom said it was okay.

Yeah and we both know what mom says is always a good idea.

Ivy glares at me, the cute smile she gave me earlier long gone. But that lightning quickness of emotional change is just what being a pre-teen is all about, if I remember correctly.

I cross my arms. *I'm not saying you can't wear it. I just don't like it, is all. You're growing up too quickly.*

She smirks at me, then looks back at the mirror resting on the counter in front of her.

Well, hurry up with your face, short stuff. We have a brother to see and delicious lunch to enjoy. We're leaving in five minutes.

She whoops and hops off her stool at the counter, leaving her makeup and mirror behind. Then she bolts up the stairs with more energy than I thought she had in her tiny little body.

"You don't actually think that's a good idea, do you?"

I glance over at Vicky. "Well, Ben needs to know I'm in town and Ivy wants to see her brother."

Vicky rolls her eyes. "I'm sure Ben already knows you're in town. If you were riding your motorcycle around, and spending time at the marina, *everyone* knows you're back in town."

I smirk at her. "I'll see you later Vicky."

Heading to the stairs, I lean against the wall with my arms crossed waiting for Ivy. I can hear her upstairs, thundering around like she weighs three hundred pounds, trying to get ready.

I glance at the clock that hangs above the entry table. Sure enough, with just ten seconds to spare, Ivy comes sprinting down, taking the stairs two at a time, coming so fast she nearly crashes into the wall at the base of the stairs.

I reach out to catch her but she braces herself. Then she looks to me with a smile.

Alright, mister, I'm ready. Let's go!

Fifteen minutes later, I pull up behind Bennie's in the loading dock, parking off to the side to allow for delivery trucks to still get in and out.

Ivy looks at me. *You're not supposed to park here.*

Well we get special privileges, I tell her.

She rolls her eyes and opens up her door, slamming it behind her before I've even turned the key.

I sigh.

I love my sister to death. But it really is amazing how much she changes each time I see her. It makes me feel old when I'm barely in my mid-twenties.

Powering off the car, I open my door and step out of my own seat, following in her wake to the entrance.

The Escalade my mom bought last summer, when she was going through a car-buying phase along with her friend Joyce, is my favorite car to drive when I'm in town.

Mostly when I'm visiting, I just stay on my bike. I don't need a car, and if I'm hooking up with someone, they ride bitch.

But when I'm driving my sister around, safety is priority number one.

Of course, driving a behemoth of an SUV around makes parking in Hermosa a bit more difficult. Which is why I take advantage of the fact that no one is going to call HBPD on a Calloway vehicle parked at Bennie's.

When I finally meet Ivy at the entrance, she gives me a smile –

these mood swings are going to drive me up a wall - and loops her arm with mine before I open the door and we head inside.

I pull off my sunglasses, letting my eyes adjust to the interior of Bennie's, tucking them into the neck of my shirt. Glancing around, I spot Hamish in the corner.

I lift a hand, giving him a wave.

He smiles at me and heads over from where he was at the bar.

"Wyatt Calloway, as I live and breath." We clasp hands. "Good to see you, friend."

We're not friends, but I don't say that to him.

I'm not friends with people who treat my sister like she's invisible. I know I might be the one people want to talk to, but she's a person too, and it pisses me the fuck off that I've been in here with Ivy a handful of times, and not once has he even acknowledged her.

You don't have to be able to sign to give someone a fucking smile.

"We're here for lunch and to see Ben," I say, getting to the point. "It would be great if you could let him know we're here."

"Absolutely," he says. Then he flags down a server. Denise, I think. "Can you take Wyatt and Ivy to table two please," he tells her. Then he looks back to me. "Glad you're back in town. This will be a fun summer."

I nod once, then head off behind Denise, Ivy following, her hand laced in mine.

I try not to baby Ivy. She's twelve. In junior high. Has lots of personality and attitude. But when we're in public, interacting with people we know, she turns into this wallflower that just wants to hold my hand and stand halfway behind me, shielding herself from everyone.

And it's in those moments that I can't help it. When I see her being ignored, or when people try to yell at her, as if increasing their volume will make her less deaf. It's maddening. And it makes her feel like people think she's stupid.

My big worry is that it makes her feel like she is, too.

Denise takes us up the stairs and out onto the deck, giving us a seat at table two, which is the only table I sit at when I come here since it has the best view of the ocean, The Strand and Pier Ave.

She leaves us with some menus and then tells me she'll be right back with waters. As soon as she's gone, Ivy stands back up.

I have to go to the bathroom.

Okay. Do you want me to order for you or wait?

Wait, please, she says, giving me a smile, then prancing off to the stairs.

A few minutes go by and Denise returns.

"Can I get you anything yet?" she asks, setting our glasses on the table.

I shake my head. "I'm gonna wait until Ivy gets back from the bathroom."

She nods. "Sounds good. I'll be back in a little bit to check in again." Then she heads off, back inside the building and likely down the stairs to the bar area, where the servers typically congregate.

I like coming to Bennie's this early. Glancing at my watch, I see it's only a little bit after eleven o'clock. Having just opened, Ivy and I will be the only ones on the rooftop, at least for a little while since it looks like an oddly cool day, the morning fog having not been fully burnt away by the sun just yet.

My eyes look off to the distance, down The Strand, in the direction of Mary's, which is a few blocks away. I can't seem to stop myself from wondering if Hannah and Lucas are there, being chummy with my friends.

I fold a cardboard coaster in half, irritated *as fuck*. I can't explain it. This seemingly irrational frustration. This overwhelming anger at the fact that she's here and...

I sigh, remembering how she included Ivy. Thought about her in relation to everyone else. It makes the blood in my body thrum harder as it pumps through me, until I can feel my own pulse in my neck and my fingers.

Chucking the now broken coaster onto the table, I grab my water and take a sip, looking out at the beach. I just have to remind myself that I'm allowed to think she's beautiful, and even that she's capable of being a nice person, and still be suspect of the fact that she's here. Sniffing around our town.

Of course, now that I'm irritated and frustrated, a chair next to mine gets pulled back.

"Morning, Wyatt," Ben says, his face friendly but distant. Just like usual.

"Hey, Ben," I reply, feeling even more on edge. "How're things?"

He bobs his head once. "Could be better. Could be worse."

I take another sip of my water.

My relationship with Ben is a little bit difficult. Tense, some might say. But those people would be the ones in polite circles.

I'd say it's a hot fucking mess with little chance of recovery. But then again, I've always been the pessimist.

I'm not here for me, though. I'm here for Ivy. Because she loves both of her brothers and it's important we both get time with her. Even if he does live only a few blocks from my mom's.

Though it makes sense why he never visits. When you get caught fucking the yacht club owner's wife, and a rumor flies around town that you were accepting money to dick the rich housewives of the South Bay, it's pretty easy to understand why mom isn't too keen on welcoming you into her home.

But that's not why things between us are bad.

Oh no, no.

I don't give a shit who he's fucking, as long as it isn't the same person in my bed. The problems we have are a bit deeper than that. Stem from years of...

Well... that's not what today is about.

The focus today is Ivy. And making sure she gets quality time with the brother she loves but never sees, because he isn't allowed to come home.

"Look," I say, "I'm only home for a few months. There's no reason we need to be anything other than friendly."

He sits quiet, just watching me with that same fucking face of his staring back, making sure not to reveal even a crumb of how he's really feeling.

That's the thing about Ben that drives me insane. Nothing can ever be simple.

Easy.

Straightforward.

You'd never assume we would be these people if you knew us when we were younger. Ben was the good boy. The one who never broke rules, followed directions, listened to our parents.

I was the rebel. The one who skipped class, slept around, partied. I liked to drink and smoke and stay out late. Even more, I liked to talk back, which I think was my greatest enemy. And I guess I still am the rebel.

But I'm definitely not the black sheep anymore.

That title has definitely fallen on Ben.

And I think that's why he harbors so much resentment towards me. Why he can't stand to be around me. His end of the anger between us is because I did everything my entire life that he always wanted to, and he was the one who toed the line. And yet I'm welcome home and he isn't.

"Ivy's birthday is next month," I say.

"I know."

"Well, we're probably gonna have a party at the house, and I just wanna let you know you're invited."

His eyes fly to mine. If I'm judging his expression correctly, I'd say he almost looks surprised.

"I'll work on mom. See what I can do."

His shoulders sag, as if realizing his presence will have to be excused rather than welcomed.

"I'll make sure to stop by and talk to Ivy before you guys leave," he says. Then he stands, without saying anything else, and heads back inside the building, effectively ending our conversation.

When Ben first bought this place, I was jealous. He was my older brother, even if by barely a year, and he seemed larger than life. So sure of himself. Knowing exactly who he wanted to be. He worked hard, got his degree, and then did exactly what he said he wanted to do.

He told me once that his goal was to own the best restaurant in the South Bay. He wanted everyone to want in, and for him to be able to decide who was welcome.

Looking back, I can see now where that desire stemmed from. He might have been the good one who always obeyed our parents. But he was also always on the outside. Never really included in the circles of friends at school that held power and popularity.

I've never understood why he didn't seamlessly slip into those groups like I did. He grew up with the same kids. Went to school together. Played sports together. Went on trips with families together.

But he just never fit.

And I guess, in his mind, the ultimate revenge for never being welcomed into those cliques is somewhere between creating an exclusive place where those very people will have to cater to him to get in, and sleeping with those individuals' moms.

But back then, when he was first talking about creating

Bennie's at the Pier, he represented something I wished I could be.
Certain.
Because money can buy you most things. But being certain of what you want isn't one of them.
So now, he hides behind this place. He's here because he doesn't really have anywhere else to go.
And that makes me sad for my brother.

Chapter Eleven
HANNAH

The next week is a lot of work, which I should be happy about. The operative word being *should* be.

But with most of the servers being bristly at best, and the fact that Lucas is out with friends when I get home most evenings, I can't help but feel a little lonely.

It's not a new feeling. A lot of people assume that being in foster care means you live in basically a kennel full of kids. Loud noise, too many to a bedroom, no personal space and no true belongings. And that's true, to some degree.

The thing that isn't thought about is that not all kids play well with others. Not all foster parents know how to encourage appropriate behavior, or even have the time to start.

So when you're bounced around from home to home - because, let's be honest, who wants to adopt a twelve-year-old kid when they can take home a baby - you learn to handle things in one of two ways.

The first is to be the loud, aggressive one that gets all the attention. The whole 'the squeaky wheel gets the oil' thing.

The second is to be quiet and avoid everyone. Stay unnoticed so you don't become the target for any of the louder ones. Or any of the parents that fall at the abusive end of the scale.

When I was fifteen, I made the mistake of getting on the bad side of one of my foster fathers, though I loathe the idea of ever calling him that. The foster mom, Renee… she was okay. Though she drank a little too much. So did her husband, Rob.

Sienna and I had plans to spend the night at her older sister's place after the Winter Formal dance at Sienna's high school. We'd had a few drinks with some of her friends in the parking lot, and were a little giggly. But her dad was the one who showed up to pick us up, because her sister had gotten into a fight with her boyfriend.

One look at us and he knew we'd been drinking. He did the good dad thing. Gave us a talking to. Expressed his disappointment. Sienna looked like she might cry. But then he told her she was grounded and that he would be taking me home.

I wish it had been a situation like you read about. Where something is so scary, the person instantly sobers up. But that wasn't the case for me.

Sienna's dad dropped me off, making sure I made it inside okay, and then left.

And I'd been left to deal with Rob, finding me stumbling into the downstairs bathroom, drunk, at eleven o'clock at night.

"What do we have here?" Rob asks, leaning against the doorway as I try to pull off my heels.

I startle at the sound of his voice, afraid of getting into trouble if he realizes I've been drinking. But my slow reaction time prohibits me from catching myself when I start to tumble over.

Rob just watches me as I hit the ground with a thud, his eyes dropping to my legs, which are now spread awkwardly as I flounder and try to right myself.

"Is that dress a little short?"

He squats down, examines me as I scramble back, tucking my legs underneath me and away from his wandering eyes.

I might have had a few shots of Jäger in the parking lot with Sienna, enough to make my vision swim and the downside of life seem right-side up. But that doesn't mean I don't see the gleam in his eyes.

He leans forward and puts his knees on the ground, getting more into my space, placing a hand on my knee.

My stomach revolts, though I do my best not to throw up everything I drank earlier.

"Had a few drinks tonight, Hannah?" he asks, shaking his head and making this weird tsk-ing noise. "Such a bad girl."

"I was just hanging out with some friends. I'm sorry." *My words are a jumble, I'm sure. I scoot away a little bit more, my back hitting the wall, and I realize I have nowhere else to go.*

"Sorry isn't enough," he says, his own words coming out slightly slurred, and when his face gets closer to mine, I can smell the liquor on his breath.

"I won't do it again," *I say, shrinking back as much as the wall behind me will allow.*

But that doesn't stop Rob from getting closer, his body bowing over mine, his hands reaching for the hem of my dress and beginning to push it up.

"Stop," *I whisper, trying to push his hands away.*

He pauses. "Did you just say something to me?"

I choke on my own words at the look on his face now, a hint of anger appearing where there wasn't any before.

"I... I said stop."

"Tough shit. You wanted to be a bad girl tonight. You're gonna see exactly how whores like you deserve to get treated." *And then he's shoving the dress up with one hand, his other groping at my breasts.*

I shout out. "No! Rob, stop it. Stop!"

I twist my body. Try to wrench myself away. To use these long ass fucking legs that always have everyone's attention for something useful, like kneeing Rob in the balls.

But he's practically laying on top of me and I can't seem to do anything but shout out. Cry for help.

I know there are other people in this house. Other kids. Ones in bedrooms right around the corner. But no one comes. No one does anything.

He shoves a hand between my legs, makes me cry out in pain, holds me down and calls me a slut and a whore and a cunt. Tells me I deserve it. That I was asking *for it, with how short my dress is.*

When he starts to unbuckle his pants, I'm able to free an arm and I smack him hard, in the face. Hard enough that his nose starts to bleed, the blood dropping quickly onto my chest and my dress.

"Fucking bitch!" he shouts out, pulling back and holding his palms to his nose.

I pull a leg back and kick him right in the stomach, and he goes down on the ground, on his back, a loud oof *noise coming out of his mouth.*

Just as a pair of sneakers comes into view.

I look up and see Renee, my shoulders dropping, relief coursing through my body.

Finally. Someone's here. Renee's home from work.

I burst into tears, shift my clothes around to cover my breasts and pull my dress back down.

"What the hell is going on!?" Renee shouts, her eyes wide as she takes in the scene. Me, sobbing and covered in a slick of blood. Rob, sprawled on his back, one hand wrapped around his stomach, the other clutching his bleeding nose.

"She came home drunk, and when I confronted her about it, she attacked me."

"What?" I say, disbelief heavy in my voice.

"She started pulling her clothes off, begging me not to tell you," Rob says, looking at Renee. "And when I told her no, she punched me in the face and kicked me."

"That's a lie!" I shout, then look at Renee. "Ask anyone else in the house. He attacked me. I've been screaming for help for the past five minutes."

"Obviously, if she'd been screaming, like she said, someone would have come to help. But that's not what really, happened, is it Hannah?" Rob says, shaking his head at me, like I'm a child that's been caught lying.

I can't believe what's happening. And when I look at Renee, I can see it in her eyes. She knows. She knows I'm telling the truth. I can tell because she looks pained. Like it sickens her that Rob would do what I'm accusing him of doing.

But I can also tell that she's going to choose to believe what Rob says instead.

"Go to your room, Hannah," Renee says, and I see her face harden, a glare creeping into place. "We can deal with all of this tomorrow."

I sit in stunned silence for just a second, my mouth open in surprise.

"Go!" she shouts, and I scurry up to standing, even though I'm still slightly drunk. Then I slink off to my room, skirting Rob, his eyes still following me with lust even after what just happened.

It takes me hours to fall asleep that night after I take a shower to clean Rob off my skin, the blood that spattered on my chest making a pink hue as it washes down the drain. I scrub between my legs, along my hips, down my legs, across my breasts. Anywhere that he touched I make sure to clean as well as I can.

Though, try as I might, I can never manage to erase the mark he left on me.

My dress is ruined, though the only reason that actually matters is because I saved up for six months to buy a nicer dress from the mall for this dance. Even if the blood wasn't all over the light green fabric, I still don't think I'll ever want to wear it again. Not after Rob's hands were all over me, pulling at whatever he wanted.

I don't cry though. I cried right after it happened, and it got me nowhere. Renee saw me, sobbing, assaulted, my entire body feeling like a raw open wound. And it did nothing. So I force myself not to cry again about it.

Because no one will care.

The following morning, my caseworker shows up at the door and tells me to pack my things.

She tells me with a disappointed face that I was reported for being violent, lying, and having substance abuse problems.

It only occurs to me for a second to tell her the truth about what happened. But I just can't imagine why she would believe me. Not when the case against me has already been made.

So I just follow along with her instructions. Move to a new foster home. A new place to hate. A new space that never really feels like a place I belong.

I never told Sienna. Never told anyone, actually. Because no one wants to know these things. No one wants to hear that the children in the system are abused, assaulted, neglected, ignored.

It's why I'm going to be a foster mom someday. I want to make sure that the kids who stay with me feel loved and welcomed and cherished, even if they're only with me for a few days. I want them to feel safe. It's the one thing I can promise them and really deliver on.

Because in the world I come from - that they will be coming from - promises don't mean shit.

And maybe my own experience should mean I'm unable to trust anyone. Ever.

But it doesn't.

If anything, it makes me wish even harder to find someone someday that I can believe in. That will love me because they love me. That will prove it to me with their actions, not just their words. Someone that sees me as more than just a paycheck, or a body to fuck, or any other thing that I can be used for.

It's one of the reasons I try not to allow myself to be on my own for too long. I've been a person who has only had herself to rely on for quite a while, now. And I want to push myself to not see that as my only option.

There has to be something better.

Someone better.

I just have to keep believing that.

I look around the dining room after my shift is over, spotting Eleanor on the far side, entering an order into the POS, her hair up in a funky bun held in place with a few pencils.

She's the one person out of the bunch from Sunday evening at Harbor's that has stayed friendly. We've had a few shifts together, and she's always been smiley and willing to chat with me when we're waiting at the bar for drink orders to be filled.

Though if I want to be a pessimist about it, Eleanor is also the one person who seemed like she was beyond excited to talk to Paige. It makes me wonder if she really wants to be friends with me, or if she's staying moderately nice to me because I'm Lucas Pearson's sister.

I hate that I'm even considering that idea, and I try to shake it off. I tuck that thought into the back of my mind, choosing to file it away for examination some other day, choosing instead to believe that Eleanor is a genuine person. And then I head in her direction.

"Hey," she says when I sidle up next to her, giving me a friendly grin as she continues to flick through the system. "You finished for the night?"

"Yeah. Finally. I've been here since one o'clock this afternoon and it's..." I glance at my phone, "almost nine o'clock now."

"That's not so bad. Once, I worked an open through close. But that was back before Hamish started as the manager. He's not so bad when it comes to the scheduling."

"I guess I'm just used to the here-and-there hours I was getting at my last job. My feet are *killing* me."

Eleanor laughs, but keeps entering things onto the screen in front of her.

"Also, uhm... I was just wondering if you were busy tonight."

She pauses and looks my way. "No, actually. It's like, my first Friday night free in months. Why? You wanna go do something?"

My spirit buoys, and I relish what seems like genuine interest in hanging out with me. "Well, my brother is having a party and I was wondering if you wanted to come with me."

Her eyes widen. "You're inviting me to a party at Lucas Pearson's house? Is the sky fucking blue? Hell *yes* I wanna come."

I laugh, enjoying the fact that she's at least being honest about wanting to go to the party. "What time are you off? I can stick around if you're finishing up."

She looks down at her apron and pulls out her little black waitress pad, flips it open. "I'm clocking out after... one, two, three... yeah, I have three tables left and they're all done with main courses. Maybe a half hour?"

"Awesome. You ride your bike to work too, right? I'll just grab a snack and wait, and we can ride there together."

She smiles. "Sounds perfect."

"I've always wanted to see the inside," Eleanor says as we get closer to Lucas' house.

We're rolling along The Strand, weaving slowly in and out of walkers, joggers and people with dogs. I'm always surprised at how many people are out here at any given time of day or night.

"It really is an absolute monster," I reply, glancing back at where she rides just a few feet behind me. "He has a gym. And a movie theatre. And a massive wine cellar and a Jacuzzi on the roof. Who has that? When he gave me a tour I just wandered around with wide eyes the whole time."

Eleanor laughs, her giggle making me feel like she's just as overwhelmed by the concept as I was when I moved in. "I feel like I don't even know what I'm getting myself into."

"You don't. Trust me."

We ride along until we're about three blocks away from Lucas', and that's when I hear the music. It's a deep bass, thumping and loud. And when we finally come to a stop a few houses away, I can't help the surprise that's surely stretched across my face.

Lucas told me he'd be having a party tonight. He said it would be pretty busy at the house. Even suggested I lock my room, telling me he added locks to the bedrooms so personal items could stay secure with so many people coming and going from the house all night.

But I hadn't really... understood, I guess.

Because the absolute raucous happening, the people spilling out from his patio to The Strand, the dozens and dozens of people that I can see inside, outside, up on the deck, laughing and drinking and smoking.

I just, really... I had no clue what to expect.

"Wow," Eleanor whispers from where she stands next to me, sounding just as overwhelmed as I am.

"Right?"

"I heard about the Pearson parties when I was in school with Lucas. Back then, I think they were a little quieter than this. But I was always jealous because I was never invited."

I glance over at Eleanor, see her wide eyes as she looks up at Lucas' mansion.

"Now that I'm here, I'm not even sure I want to go inside."

At that, I laugh, relief coursing through my system that maybe Eleanor and I are more alike than it may have seemed. "I know *exactly* how you feel."

We spend the next few minutes trying to fight our way over to the little storage area where the bikes get parked, then onto the patio and inside the house.

It really is like battling against a stream as we maneuver between people doing shots and shouting over the music and dancing, heading up to the second floor. Thankfully, it's slightly less crowded up here and I spot Lucas right away, standing near the balcony doors, a drink in-hand.

"Hannah!" he shouts, his words lubricated with significantly more to drink than he's had on other evenings since I've been here. He lifts his arms in the air. "Finally! I wondered when you'd get here." He looks at Eleanor. "And you brought a friend. That's awesome. Welcome to the party."

Eleanor smiles as we approach where Lucas stands with Lennon and a few of the other people I met the other night at Harbor's and Mary's earlier this week.

"Lucas, this is my friend from work, Eleanor."

"I know Eleanor," he says, giving her a wink. "We had a few classes together in school."

She blushes. "Oh, yeah, I think so. I don't really remember, though."

I chuckle, but Lucas doesn't notice. Thankfully. Because Eleanor blushes even harder and gives me some eyes that say *zip it, sister.*

My ass, she doesn't remember classes she took with my brother. If I had to guess, she remembers every single one.

"Well, welcome. Grab some drinks. Have a blast. Enjoy yourselves!" And then Lucas wraps his arm around Lennon's shoulders and the two head out onto the patio, surrounded by other people they know.

I glance around. Spot a few people smoking from a bong. See one person snorting something. Lots of drinking, a couple making out in a corner and some hands wandering under clothes.

Then I look at Eleanor. "You're welcome to hang out, but I don't think this party is really for me," I say. "I'm gonna go up to my room. Do you wanna come?"

She waffles for a minute.

"No pressure. You can absolutely stay down here and have fun." I try to make sure I sound convincing, though really, I'd rather have a friend to hang out with upstairs.

"What if we just stay down here for a few minutes? I've just always wanted to see what happens at these parties, and I don't want to miss my chance to really see it."

I laugh. "I guess I could stick around for a few minutes. Let's snoop around, huh?"

Eleanor beams at me.

We each grab a drink, a beer for her and a soda for me, and then we start back down the stairs to the first floor. I let Eleanor lead the way, since she's the one with wide eyes, taking everything in for the first time.

I follow her, trying to keep the grimace off my face as we weave through more bodies, trying to find a place to stand that won't result in one of us getting poked in the eye.

"This is *insane!*" she shouts back at me.

I can only nod in agreement.

We finally make it to a corner, where we stand next to the door to the gym. And then we just watch everyone being rowdy and ridiculous.

It's definitely not a party I want to participate in, but it actually is pretty fun to observe.

There's a group of girls shouting along to the music and guzzling champagne straight from the bottle. Eleanor points out that Aaron guy trying to smooth-talk someone, and we both giggle at the idea that he's trying to add to the mythical notches on his bed post.

Smoke fills the air, the scent of weed becoming stronger, and I wave a hand in front of my face, taking a step back.

And in doing so, I bump open the door to the gym. When I turn to grab the door and pull it closed, I see Lucas' friend Otto having sex with a girl on the rowing machine.

I slam the door closed and look at Eleanor, both of us bursting into a fit of giggles.

"I am totally ready to go upstairs," she shouts at me.

"Oh my god, yes!" I cry out. "Let's get out of here."

"I had no idea what this was going to be like!" she says, giggling again.

I give her a small smile, then take her hand and lead her over to the stairs, then climb all the way up to the bedrooms. Once, we're at the top, I head right for my own room, unlocking the door, pulling us inside and closing it behind me.

The sounds from downstairs are almost non-existent, so different from what it was like when I was younger and there were parties at some of the houses I lived in.

Just goes to show what soundproofing can do.

"I felt like my ears were going to start bleeding," she says, rotating her jaw and pulling at one of her ears. "Is it like this all the time?"

I shake my head. "No, thankfully. This is his first party since

I've been here, but," I shrug. "I can't really say much. It's *his* house."

She nods, her eyes looking around. Then she spots the TV on the wall. "Wanna watch a movie?"

"Thanks for coming over. It was a lot more fun to hang out with you in my room than just barricade myself in here alone."

Eleanor laughs.

We ended up spending the evening catching up on a few episodes of *Outlander,* only venturing out of the room to grab snacks and soda from downstairs, then rushing back up to our quiet little corner.

I felt like I was doing something wrong by hiding away in my room, like a kid who might get a scolding for absconding some of the treats meant for other people. But honestly, it just felt like the only thing I'd like to do tonight.

And having Eleanor here to enjoy it with was great. Especially a little later when we paused *Outlander* because we couldn't stop giggling like kids at having caught Otto having sex in the gym.

"This was fun," she replies. "We should hang out more. I know Denise and Loren are like the bitchy queen and king at Bennie's, but not all of us are like that."

My shoulders drop in relief. "Thanks for saying that. I've been on edge ever since last weekend and I didn't know exactly how to handle it."

She rolls her eyes. "You're a nice person," she says. "Don't let them get to you. I only went that night to Harbor's because you said you were going and I always try to get to know the new people."

I smile, thankful that I was able to muster up the courage to invite Eleanor over tonight. "Thanks."

And then she reaches out and gives me a hug, before swinging her leg over her bike and heading off down The Strand.

When I turn back to the house, I see the crowd has thinned a bit, but only slightly. The noise and raucous behavior is still off the charts, though. So I head up to my room and re-lock the door. Take a long shower to clean off the stink from work earlier, then crawl into bed at around three o'clock in the morning.

The noise from downstairs doesn't really bother me at all, especially with the awesome soundproofing. It's just the knowledge that someone could come in uninvited that makes it difficult to fall asleep.

But eventually, I drift off, feeling the slightest bit uplifted that I might've finally made a friend.

Chapter Twelve
WYATT

The smell of a hospital makes me sick.

I remember one time, having to come to a hospital when I broke my leg when I was six or maybe seven years old. Of course, I probably don't like hospitals because my memories are of a time when I was sobbing, in incredible pain, and I hated my doctor.

Dr. Milson was an asshole. He wasn't a good medical professional for children. But he was a friend of my dad's. So *of course* that's the best person to reset a broken tibia in an upset adolescent.

But now, the smell isn't so much about what has happened here before as much as it is about what's to come.

We're in a waiting room. My mom to my left, my sister on my right. Dad's probably off fucking his child bride, and Ben told me he couldn't make it when I shot him a text earlier.

My sister's hand is threaded in mine, her little grip holding on to me so tightly. I give her a small squeeze and she looks up at me.

It's gonna be okay, I say, signing with my free hand and mustering a smile for her. *I promise.*

She doesn't respond, but rests her head against my shoulder, and I wish I had some mouthwash to rinse out the bitter taste of my words.

I make a habit of not promising anything to anyone. I've had too many promises in life given to me and not followed through on. But I will swallow a razorblade of lies before I'll say something to upset my sister when she's waiting to hear from the doctor.

A much nicer doctor, thankfully, than the one I had as a child. But when your specialty is childhood disease, I'm sure learning bedside manner is important in career advancement.

A door opens to the left and all three of us look up, seeing Doctor Lyons walking through, a clipboard and folder in her hands. When she sees us, she walks straight over, then bends down slightly to look at Ivy, tucking her documents under an arm.

It's good to see you, sweetheart. You ready to come back?

Ivy squeezes my hand again, but nods, slipping off of her chair. She doesn't let go of me, though, and it isn't lost on me that Ivy is looking to me for comfort and support instead of to our mother, who has had on her plastic mask all day.

We follow Dr. Lyons in silence, through a large set of doors and back to a hospital room.

I know what's coming before she tells us, but that doesn't make it any less hard to hear. And after a few pleasantries and checking in with Ivy to see how life has been, how the school semester wrapped up, and what she's been doing with her free time, Dr. Lyons finally gets down to it.

"I'm going to be honest," she says, looking at my mother, but signing for Ivy at the same time. "Ivy needs a bone marrow transplant. The eculizumab is doing its job in building up her red blood cells, so we will continue on that regimen. And we're lucky that her blood isn't showing any signs of clotting, which is usually a big worry with PNH. But her bone marrow function is still incredibly low. And with the regular fatigue and weakness, as well as her propensity for catching colds, a bone marrow transplant is really the best option moving forward."

I grit my jaw. Doctor Lyons has talked about this before. We already did testing on mom and dad to see if they'd be a match, though parents rarely are. Since Ben and I were adopted, the likelihood of us being a match for her is so slight that we had to pay an external provider to do the testing, since the insurance wouldn't cover the tests. And we'll pay for independent testing on any person who could even possibly be a match.

Though, unsurprisingly, nothing came from that testing other than assurances that we would need to look elsewhere.

"None of us are a match, though, for donating," I say, feeling a bit like a dick for telling Dr. Lyons something she already knows. "What are the other options?"

"As I said the last time we spoke, a blood relative is the best option. Usually a sibling. But it isn't the *only* option. We can go through a database to see if others could be a match for her. But it takes time."

"How much time?" my mother asks, her mask firmly in place, but the red splotches on her neck illuminating how the stress of today continues to overwhelm her.

"Right now, Ivy's case isn't life threatening, which is good. But I've seen cases that deteriorate quickly. So I think moving rapidly in finding someone to donate will be to her best advantage."

"What happens if she just stays on the medication?" I ask.

"The side effects aren't aggressively common, but are still a very real risk. Pneumonia, upper respiratory infections, loss of blood cells, and loss of appetite are the most common out of the bunch. Of course, continuing solely on the medication also means Ivy will need to come in regularly for medication administration through an intravenous infusion. And then, of course, there is the fact that a more extreme form of PNH can eventually result in death."

"And if she gets a bone marrow transplant?" I rasp, trying not to get too emotional. The last thing Ivy needs to see is me crying or doing something stupid like storming out of the room in an upset rage. "What does the outcome look like?"

Doctor Lyons looks back to me. "Patients who have a good match for bone marrow have the potential for all symptoms of PNH to disappear. It can cure the disease, and in my other patients, it has done so in the majority of cases."

The rest of the appointment is a blur. More information about transplants and how they'll search the database for a potential match. Ivy gets more blood work done and we schedule her next date for the medication infusion. And then we're back in the car and driving the hour back to our house from the USC Medical Center.

At least we have the one thing you definitely need when you're sick.

Money.

I can't imagine going through something like this and not being able to get the medication you need or see the doctor you want. We will be able to throw money at an independent party to dive into finding a bone marrow match. Pay for Ivy's needs, whether small or large.

It's a welcome relief in the grand scheme of everything weighing down on us right now.

I glance in the back seat and see Ivy, sleeping soundly, her head resting on a soft pillow she brought with her.

She falls asleep pretty easily, now. She has ever since she was diagnosed. I guess it's the fatigue, along with the fact she has trouble eating. When my mom first told me about what was going on with Ivy, it was right before I'd left for San Francisco.

"She just needs some iron supplements," she'd told me. "It's not a big deal."

Turns out it was a fucking blood disease that's going to slowly kill her if she doesn't get this transplant. I'd say that's a pretty big deal.

My mother and I stay silent during most of the drive. She sits in the passenger seat, her eyes staring out of the window, watching as we whiz past traffic in the fast lane.

"It's going to be okay," I tell her, my voice low.

I know Ivy can't hear what I'm saying, but there's something that makes me feel like if I can tell this to my mom without awakening the evils that caused this disease in the first place, maybe the threats facing us won't be able to see where we stand, shaking with fear. Maybe they'll turn around and head a different direction.

"Don't lie to me, Wyatt," she says, her voice sounding fragile and small. "You can say that to Ivy. But not to me."

We go back to being quiet my mother's words weighing heavily on me for the rest of the drive.

Once we get back to the house, my mom heads straight inside, presumably to make herself a stiff drink and pop an anti-anxiety pill. I open the rear door and lift Ivy out, carrying her into the house and upstairs to her room.

I love this kiddo. She came around when I was a bit older, and if I'm honest, I hadn't really wanted any new siblings at the time.

But she's a precious girl and I can't imagine this world without her in it.

"Wyatt," she mumbles as I'm pulling off her shoes. Her eyes open and I'm struck by how young she looks as she curls up and snuggles into her bed. *Am I really going to be okay?* she asks, the fear in her eyes a bit more real today than it has been in the past.

I tuck her under the comforter and give her a soft kiss her on the forehead.

Of course you are, I sign, though I can't help but whisper the words out loud as well, in hopes that some divine being can hear me.

She nods and closes her eyes, and I sit there, watching her fall back asleep.

I have to believe that she's going to be okay.

But in order to believe that, I also have to know that I've done everything possible to ensure that's the truth.

Once I've stepped out of her room, pulling the door shut softly behind me, I dig my phone out of my pocket.

Time to make the last call I thought I'd ever make.

Two days later, I park my bike behind Bennie's and take a second to yank off my helmet.

Technically, you're not allowed to drive motorcycles onto the pier grounds, including the area near the row of restaurants that sit at the base, between the pier and the city. But no one ever checks the back alley that runs behind all of the restaurants sitting along the south side of Pier Avenue.

And because my brother happens to be *the* Ben, of Bennie's at the Pier, no one is going to dare call in my bike to HBPD, just like they wouldn't dare call in my mother's Escalade.

I'm here for multiple reasons today, but also because sometimes, when you have shit going on in your family, you just need to drink a beer with the only person who can understand.

I find Ben at the table I normally sit at on the rooftop, sipping from a dark beer and staring out at the ocean.

"Glenlivet, Single Malt," I say to the approaching waitress before she can even get to the table. I know it's rude of me, but I honestly can't muster up the ability to care.

Then I look at Ben, who is looking at me with that same neutral gaze. Always so careful, now. Because really, it's been years since he's been willing to show me who he really is.

"I don't think I have to tell you how..." I grip my hands into fists and try to find the right word, "...absolutely wrong it was for you to not show up on Tuesday."

Ben looks away, back out to the ocean, taking another sip of his beer.

"She's twelve *fucking* years old, and you couldn't get over yourself for just a few hours? To ride in the damn car with us and sit through a meeting with a doctor?"

"You have no idea..."

"No. *You* have no idea." I jab a finger into his chest, but he doesn't budge an inch. I shake my head, grab one of the coasters off the table and fold it in half. "Doctor Lyons said she needs a transplant."

His head whips in my direction. "I thought the medication was doing okay."

"Yeah, well it does what it's supposed to do, along with a bunch of other shit that can make her really damn sick. A transplant is her only option if she wants a chance at a normal life."

The waitress drops off my scotch, and it takes everything in me not to just tilt my head back and pour it all down the hatch in one go.

"You can't let your ego get in the way anymore."

"*My* ego," he says, then laughs, though it sounds more bitter than anything. "Let me tell you something, Wyatt. The reason I don't attend anything is because I'm not invited. I'm not allowed to be there. Not because I don't want to be or because I'm too embarrassed to show my face."

"So buck the fuck up and show up *anyway*," I grit out. "You think a twelve-year-old cares that you aren't *allowed* to come to the hospital? Or to the house? No. She wants you to show up for her. And that's what she deserves. Because she's your sister."

We sit in silence for a moment, glaring at each other.

He makes me so angry sometimes.

We were never that close as children, since I was always so loud and intense while he was more the rule-follower who didn't want anyone to look his way. But I like to think I understood him to some degree.

Over the past few years, though, we've continued to drift further and further apart. It feels like the brother I loved, even though we were so different, isn't even really in there anymore.

I realize some of the rage I feel at Ben might be slightly misplaced. That some of this is the pain from finding out that Ivy really is sick-sick and not just I-need-meds sick.

When I found out last year about the diagnosis, I hadn't known how to feel. I drank too much. Tried to bury my fears with the false assurances of the first doctor Ivy had seen. It wasn't until two months ago that they said she needed to go onto a drug regimen that they pump into her at the hospital once a week.

That's not a life for a twelve-year-old kid, going to and from the hospital on a regular basis. Ivy's been through enough. She doesn't need something like this hanging over her head as well.

Which is why finding her a bone marrow transplant donor is my new number one priority. It should be the most important next step for *all* of us.

Eventually, Ben finishes his beer, setting it right back in the ring of sweat it had been in before. He stays at the table instead of bolting down to his office like he normally does, and I assume it's because he has something else on his mind.

"I talked with Lucas today," he finally says a few minutes later.

My surprised eyes lift to meet his.

Lucas and Ben have always been friendly, but it never occurred to me that they'd have any reason to talk about... well, anything, really. I guess I just assume my brother doesn't talk to anyone anymore.

"Whatever it is you two are planning..." he shakes his head and trails off. "Well, I just hope you're thinking everything through, is all." He knocks his fist twice on the table and stands up. "Let me know when the next meeting with Dr. Lyons is."

At that, he gives me a tight smile and finally leaves, heading back inside, down to his dungeon of an office.

He'll stay in there for the rest of the day, managing his

business even though some parts of it run without him or are the responsibilities of others he has hired. But it's what he does to avoid the real problems in his life.

And to be honest, running away and hiding sounds like a much better option than anything else right now.

But - I flip my phone over, seeing that the time has finally hit five o'clock - I have to stay. So I send off a few messages. One to my mom, letting her know that I've invited Ben to Ivy's thirteenth birthday next month. One to my friend Derek in San Francisco, since he's been bugging me about a girl he likes that I know.

The last one goes to Lucas, though it takes me a few minutes, and a few more sips of my scotch, before I finally send it off.

Me: Here

He responds in almost no time at all.

Lucas: Got it

And then, I just sit and wait. Order another drink. Watch the sun begin to dip slowly behind a dusting of clouds on the horizon in the South Bay. I've done quite a bit of travel in my short twenty-four years, and there just aren't any sunsets in the world that compare to this one.

I'd bet my bike on it. And I don't say that lightly.

About twenty minutes goes by before I get another text from Lucas.

Lucas: Outside

I take one more look at the sunset, letting the glare singe my eyes just a bit before I toss back the rest of my drink, chuck a few twenties on the table, and head inside and down the stairs.

I give a nod to Hamish as I walk through the main dining room, then push through the exit and head towards the back. Lucas' voice carries as I round the corner to the loading bay where I've parked my FTR.

"Don't worry about it," he says. "It happens here all the time."

"I am so, *so* sorry," Hannah replies, and I can hear the true anguish in her voice. "I swear I thought I locked it up."

"Everything alright?"

My question causes Hannah to look my direction, and I'm hit again with just how damn beautiful she is.

She's in her Bennie's uniform. A maroon polo shirt and tight black pants. Her hair is down and loose around her shoulders, a slight kink lining the middle from where she'd likely had it up when she was working.

She just got off work, a fact I knew before I got here. Something Lucas told me when we planned out the fact that I would be here right now.

"Hannah's bike got stolen," I hear from Lucas, but I keep my eyes on her, since I already knew that was going to happen as well.

She crosses her arms and looks like she's on the verge of tears. Part of me feels like shit, knowing that she feels so guilty about it.

"It happens all the time. It's probably those guys that go around with bolt cutters in a backpack."

Hannah looks at me. "Really?"

I nod. "Yeah."

"Let's just head back to the house and get another bike."

Hannah looks to Lucas.

"I have a few more. Don't worry about this one. It isn't a big deal. Really."

Then Lucas looks to me. "Wyatt, would you give Hannah a ride back to the house? I was meeting her here so we could ride home together after her shift, but now..."

"No, I can walk," she says, and her cute face purses.

Lucas laughs. "Come on, Hannah. No reason to punish yourself when you didn't do anything wrong. If you ride with Wyatt, it'll just take a few minutes." Then he looks at me. "If you have a few minutes, of course."

"Yeah, no problem. I'd be happy to give you a ride." It's the whole reason I'm here.

Hannah looks at me and seems to consider it for a minute, nibbling at the inside of her cheek before nodding.

"Awesome. See you back at the house, Hannah."

And then Lucas takes off down towards The Strand and back to his house, moving quickly, before Hannah can change her mind.

"I'm sorry if I'm ruining any of your plans," she says as she walks towards me, swinging her backpack onto her shoulders.

"Not at all," I say, heading over to my bike and swinging over a leg.

"Wait. You're taking me home on that?" Her eyes are massive and it makes me want to laugh.

But then I realize it's real fear that I'm seeing take over her face.

"Have you never ridden a motorcycle before?"

She shakes her head. "I just learned to ride a bicycle last year. Of *course* I've never ridden a motorcycle."

"Well the good news is that you have a helmet," I point to the bike helmet in her hands. "Plus, it only takes a few minutes to get to Lucas' house. And you won't be steering, so really, it's just like sitting on your bike, but with someone else in charge."

She eyes it warily for a minute before finally putting her helmet on her head. The look of determination when she clips the two straps together has me fighting to hide my grin.

Then she looks at me. "If you fall over on this and smoosh me into the ground, I will be incredibly unhappy."

I laugh and instead take her hand in mine as she prepares to get on behind me. It's an awkward shuffle as she figures it out, but once she's sitting snug against my back, and her arms come around my middle, I realize it's never felt more right to have someone on a bike with me.

"Hold on, sweetheart."

And then I take off, down the alley and out to Hermosa Ave. Hannah squeals a little bit, a cute noise that conveys her surprise, and then she giggles and holds on to me tighter.

I'd give anything to see her face right now, but I'll gladly settle for her arms wrapped around me.

I quickly push that thought aside, reminding myself that I can't let my mind wander in that direction.

Friends.

Friends with Hannah.

That's the focus.

When we finally get to Lucas' house, I come to a stop in his driveway and glance behind me.

The smile on Hannah's face could dwarf the sun.

"Wow," she whispers.

I chuckle, then give her my hand to help her step off.

"Thank you so much for giving me a ride," she says. And then her mouth opens, like she's going to say something else. But she doesn't. She just closes it and gives me a small, lopsided grin.

"Look, Hannah, I want to apologize for how I left things at the auction. I..." I sigh. "I was upset with Lucas about... well, it doesn't matter what. And I'm sorry if I seemed angry or upset."

She twists her hands together. "I was a little confused," she says, her voice sounding small as she looks down at the ground. Something pinches inside of me when I see her like that. "But I also realize life is complicated so... hopefully you and Lucas were able to sort things out." She ends her statement as if it's a question, finally looking back at me.

I nod. "We did, yeah. And now that we have, I hope it's okay if I tell you I'd like to get your number. So we can hang out sometime."

Her face flushes but I can see the beginnings of a smile.

"I know you're new in town and are looking to make friends," I continue, making sure I word myself carefully. "I'd like to be a friend, and I know Ivy would like to spend time with you, too."

The spark in her eyes dulls slightly.

It's intentional, telling her I want to be friends. As beautiful as she is, standing there in her work uniform and her bike helmet sitting slightly askew on her head... as much as I'd love nothing more than to... I let out a sigh.

It just can't happen.

"Yeah, sure. I can give you my number," she says.

I get out my phone and hand it over, giving her a minute to punch in her digits.

"Thanks," I say, taking it back when she's done. "I'll shoot you a message soon. Maybe we can get together. You, me and Ivy."

Hannah nods. "Sounds good. Thanks again for the ride, Wyatt." And then she turns and heads for the side door that leads to the little courtyard off Lucas' entryway.

I watch her go, appreciating her long stride and the sway of her hips, allowing myself - just for a moment - to imagine things were different.

But they're not. And I can't ever let myself forget that. So eventually, I put my helmet back on my head, rev my engine, and ride home.

Chapter Thirteen
HANNAH

When I finally get off of my lunch shift on Friday afternoon, I make slow work of riding back to Lucas' house, enjoying the late afternoon sun as it hangs low in the sky.

The walking and running path is mostly straight, but curves slightly here and there as it winds in front of the million dollar homes facing the water, stretching for miles into the distance. I perk up, even in the face of my exhaustion, at the idea of lacing up my shoes and giving it a go.

I've been in Hermosa Beach for two weeks and have spent most of my time working, so the idea of finally getting out and going on a run makes my heart sing. Even though I've been busy, I know I should make the time to hit the pavement, at least a few times a week. Excuses be damned.

Joshua always used to tell me that you make time for the things in life that are a priority. Clearly I need to work on bumping running back up the list.

When I finally wheel into the front patio at Lucas', though, I know doing anything physical will be too much for me tonight, and I make a promise to myself to run this weekend.

I dig my keys out of my backpack and head in, hoofing up the first flight of stairs and into the kitchen to grab some water. I'm only home for a few minutes when my cell phone rings. Pulling it out of my back pocket, I do a happy dance when I see it's Sienna.

"Girl, the fact you've been there for two whole weeks and you haven't called your *best friend*, is absolutely ridiculous," are the words that blast at me as soon as I put the phone to my ear.

"Oh my gosh it is so good to hear your voice," I say, stepping back out onto the patio and sinking into one of the comfortable loungers, relishing in the familiarity and warmth of the voice of my friend.

Sienna and I have known each other since we were munchkins. We went to the same elementary school and lived next door to each other in the same apartment complex until the year my parents died. She always made sure to keep inviting me to things even though my new foster home at the time was on the other side of Phoenix and it was hard to find a way to get there.

Joshua was helpful for a few years in keeping my relationship with Sienna alive. He was older, had a car, and was able to take the two of us out for ice cream or movies on weekends or after school.

But when he passed, it was just our own resolve. Our own desire not to see our friendship fail just because of circumstance. I used to ride the bus for an hour in junior high to go to her house, never inviting her over to see the places I was bouncing between.

For lots of reasons.

When I finally left the system, and we both graduated high school, it was a lot easier to keep the connection going. But I've always been thankful that she cared about me and loved me even when things were working against us.

"So, how's Richville?" she asks.

I roll my eyes, but she can't see me. "It's not Richville."

"Don't give me that," she says. "I want the full low down on everything. Everyone. All of it. Including the cars and the clothes and everyone's hotness level."

I laugh. "Okay, okay. I guess… it's just different than I thought it would be."

"How so?"

"Well, for one thing, Lucas is really nice."

There's a pause. "How is that different than you expected? I thought you guys talked on the phone a few times before heading out there."

"Yeah well, I'm just surprised he ended up being exactly who he said he would be. The money and the house and the beach is whatever. I'm just glad he's a nice guy." Though I wish he was around more, even though I don't say that to Sienna.

"Girl, I wanna hear about the rich people. *Please!*"

I giggle. "When we pulled up to his house, I about fell through the floor of his fancy ass truck, because it is this crazy mansion right on the water."

"I knew it!" she cries out. "I knew he was going to live in a *Real Housewives* mansion."

I smile at her reaction. "I've met a bunch of his friends so far, and they're all just really beautiful. Like they belong in magazines. Which I guess I can understand if you spend all of your time at the beach."

"Right?" Sienna sighs. "Ugh, you're gonna be living some kind of fancy rich bitch dream this summer, aren't you? And I'm just gonna be stuck in boring ass Phoenix working at the sunglass kiosk and wishing I could visit."

"I'm sure you'd be welcome if you wanted to come out," I say, though I instantly regret it. As much as I love Sienna, I also know that I definitely should have talked to Lucas about it first.

"Yeah, I can't afford that, lady, but thanks anyway."

I let out a quiet but slightly relieved sigh. Bullet dodged.

"So have you met his mom yet?"

"No. Lucas said I probably wouldn't even meet her this summer since she's a workaholic and mostly stays at her boyfriend's place near her office. But there's a little part of me that's morbidly curious."

"Like you wanna see the woman that your dad had an affair with, but at the same time you want to light her on fire?"

"Yes!" I say, laughing slightly. "Exactly that."

"I know this is gonna be hard to hear, but just make sure you don't blame someone else for what your dad did, Hannah. He was an adult. And it doesn't matter what the circumstances are. He had an affair. You can't blame Lucas' mom." She pauses and I let out a frustrated sigh. "Well, I take that back. The only circumstance that would make it okay is if your parents were in an open relationship or were swingers."

"Oh my gosh!" I shout into the phone. "Oh my god, Sienna, that is so disgusting. Like, I can't even *think* about that." I slap my hands over my eyes, as if that will cleanse my mind of the sudden image of my parents agreeing to sleep with other people.

"Hey girl, don't knock it if you haven't tried it."

I sit up straight. "Excuse me?" I can't believe what I'm hearing. "What did you just say?"

Sienna dives into a story about her boyfriend Jerome and a sex party they went to a few weeks before I left town. I'm a little blown away, since Sienna hasn't ever struck me as a particularly kinky type. But I guess you can think you know someone as well as possible and they can still surprise you.

We talk for a while longer about life in Phoenix, about her mom's new job. We talk about my own job at Bennie's and she gives me suggestions on ways to make money this summer with my mediocre photography skills, something I hadn't even considered.

"Alright, sexy lady. I have to head over to Jerome's. He just got off work and mama is in desperate need of something thick between her legs."

I burst into laughter, that same squeamish discomfort running through me at the mention of sex.

Of the two of us, Sienna was always the one more comfortable talking about sex and sexuality. Like I told Lucas the other night, it just wasn't something that was discussed in the houses I lived in. So now I'm left with this kind of awkward bumbling and lack of certainty, just giggling at what other people say.

"Have fun tonight," she says. "Get out and take some photos of that gorgeous beach, girl. And then send them my way!"

We say goodbye and then I hang up the phone, resting my head back against the cushion on the lounger.

She might have been joking, but Sienna hit on something real. Something I've already had on my mind once or twice. It just goes to show how close we are that she was able to pick up on it without me even saying anything to her.

Lucas lives in this grandiose house all by himself. And while I'm sure that's great for partying and having freedom, it seems like it would also be really easy to struggle with feeling lonely.

I lived for eight years in small houses packed with people, oftentimes sharing bedrooms with multiple bunk beds and three or four other young girls. Before that, we had a tiny two-bedroom apartment as a family and Joshua and I shared a bedroom even though I was so much younger than him.

So a large empty house might sound great in theory. But I've only been here two weeks, and sitting here by myself, watching the sun as it begins to dip in the sky… I can feel that sense of loneliness begin to creep in at the edges. *Have* been feeling it moving towards me as I spend the majority of my free time on my own.

Forcing myself not to focus on that feeling, I hop up and head inside, taking the stairs two at a time all the way up to the top floor, down the hall to my room. I dig into my duffle bag and pull out my camera.

It isn't particularly nice. I got it for sale at a pawnshop and then took it to the photography teacher at my high school to ask for help with repairing it. It's pretty old, definitely not digital, and the F-stop sticks and decides not to work of its own will.

But I've been able to figure out how to take pretty good photos with it anyway. The hardest part about having an older camera like this is that I have to use film, which is expensive and doesn't provide me with the instant results I want in order to teach myself to be better.

And if I want to try and grow my amateur photography into any type of business in the future, I'll *have* to get better. I mean, who wants to hire a photographer with a broken camera?

I wander out onto the patio, turning my lens down the length of The Strand to snag photos of three guys skateboarding while holding surfboards.

I capture a big group of birds rising as a flock into the air to escape a toddler on the sand racing towards them.

A pair of friends playing volleyball.

Then I head further out into the sand, closer to the water, the end-of-day sand feeling cool on my feet.

I tilt my camera up to the lifeguard tower, snapping a shot of a leggy blonde in red shorts and a white sweatshirt sitting on a chair and looking out at the water.

Taking the photos buoys my spirits a bit, and I spend the next while trying to capture the slice of beach directly in front of Lucas' house.

Finally, as the sun dips lower in the sky, the last of the beach goers begin to pack up their belongings, and I head back to the patio and plop down on one of the loungers.

A part of me wants to keep taking pictures to see if I can get a good shot of the sun. But another part of me knows I should take a moment to sit and enjoy it. Even if I do have to enjoy it alone.

The photography would only be so distracting. Eventually I'd feel this loneliness again anyways. Might as well learn to get past it instead of avoiding it by hiding behind a lens.

I wonder if I made a mistake coming here all by myself. If trying to meet Lucas should have been done on different terms. Maybe coming out for a few weekends this summer instead of moving.

Because it feels like I might have made a mistake. No one really cares about me, how I'm doing, whether I've been happy or sad. My whole life has basically been like that, so it *shouldn't* be that hard to deal with.

But it is.

I guess that's what happens when you build up expectations that aren't met.

The only thing I can do is remind myself of the people who *do* love me.

Sienna, who I just talked to.

And Melanie and Lissy, who I haven't connected with since after her first message letting me know she and Lis made it to New Mexico safely a few weeks ago.

Thinking about them makes me smile, and I pull out my phone to send off a text.

Me: Hey Melanie. I miss you. I hope you and Lissy are settling in at your mom's place. Give her a hug and a kiss from me. Love you. Call me soon.

And then I put my phone down, intent on watching the sun as it sets in the distance.

A noise behind me has me looking back over my shoulder, a bit startled. But when I see it's just Lucas coming down the stairs, I let out a relieved breath.

"Hey," I say as he steps out onto the patio, surprised to see him since he told me earlier that he and Otto were going out tonight. "I thought you were going out with your friend."

He nods his head and gives me a soft smile before he steps over and sits down on the lounger next to mine. "That was the plan. But then I realized I had something more important I wanted to do."

"Oh. What's that?"

"Spend time with my sister."

The surprise of his statement slams into my chest, nearly knocking the wind out of me.

I turn away and look back at the sun, feeling like looking right at it will give me an excuse as to why my eyes are starting to burn.

Maybe it's because I'm already emotional. Maybe it's because I'd *just* been thinking about being lonely, or that coming here might have been a mistake. Or maybe it's just because hearing someone tell me that I'm a priority is something I've needed to hear for so, so, *so* damn long.

Regardless, it's a welcome feeling.

"Is that okay?" he asks, and I can hear a hint of hesitancy in his voice.

As if I might fucking turn him away. I almost laugh at the idea. I turn back to look up at him and give him a small grin. "That's more than okay. That sounds great."

Lucas' smile returns, and then he crosses his legs as he stretches them out on the lounger next to mine.

And then, on a quiet and cool evening, my brother and I watch a sunset together.

That evening, Lucas and I do what you do when you try to get to know someone. We order pizza and watch *Planet Earth*.

It's amazing what you can learn about someone based on how they watch TV. Especially when you choose to watch something as phenomenal and sometimes savage as nature shows.

In between joking with each other and stuffing our faces, as well as making awkward commentary about birds doing mating dances, we actually talk.

When we first started talking to each other a few months ago, we sent a few emails back and forth, which eventually graduated to phone calls. But it was very surface level. Mostly just to make sure he wasn't some crazy person before I decided to meet him.

We'd talked about his mom, his girlfriend, his house. I'd told him a little bit about school and photography, and we *barely* veered into a conversation about dad. But we didn't hit anything below the surface.

It feels like, now, we're starting to dip below that. Maybe not *super* far below. But enough to know that we're trying to get deeper.

He asks me about what school was like at the community college I went to, about photography and how I got into it. He asks a few questions about Joshua, what he was like. On a different day, I might have been more uncomfortable talking about my dead brother with my new and alive half-brother. But it feels normal.

Especially when I think about the fact that Lucas and Joshua would have been brothers, too.

So I tell him about my brother. About Joshua being a really funny guy, a hard worker, an amazing runner. And it feels good, relishing in the positive memories about a brother that I loved so much.

Love so much.

Because I will always love him. And always miss him.

I talk to him about balancing work and babysitting and school. I tell him about Melanie and Lissy, and about Sienna.

And then he asks me about my parents. About my dad.

Our dad.

I feel a little lost for words when we finally hit that topic. So I just go for honesty.

"I don't really know how to talk about him with you," I say, snuggling deeper into the couch cushions and pulling my knees up to wrap my arms around them. "Dad was... he was this superhero in my mind. Because I only knew him as a kid. By the time I found out about..." I wave in Lucas' general direction, "everything, he had already been given sainthood. He was this great dad who loved us and took us to the park and built crafts with us and taught us to ride bikes." I lift a shoulder. "That's the man I knew."

Then I ask the hard question. The one I don't want to ask, but that I have to, just to satisfy the morbid curiosity that I can't seem to get rid of. "What did *you* know about him?"

He clears his throat and kind of looks off to the side. "Well, Henry was always the guy who came to visit me once a year." He looks back at me. "Every summer, he'd show up for a few weeks. Spend some time with me, with my mom."

My stomach pulls uncomfortably, but I don't ask him to stop.

"He did a lot of the things he did for you and Joshua. Taught me to ride a bike. Took me out to play at parks." He sighs. "And he taught me to surf. One of the few things I learned from my mom was that Henry was a great surfer."

"Really?" I ask, unable to help myself.

He nods. "Yeah. Is that not something he ever mentioned to you?"

I shake my head. "No. I mean, I didn't know he'd ever even seen the ocean, let alone that he could surf it."

There's a pause.

"So I'm assuming he never talked to you guys about the trips to the beach then? I thought maybe you guys all did a vacation together out here or something."

I shake my head. "Definitely not. I've never been to the beach before coming here this summer."

Lucas nods slowly, his eyes watching me.

"Do you know if…" I stop. "Do you know if he loved your mom?"

I jump a little at Lucas' laugh. "Definitely not. The thing with my mom was a brief affair, according to her. There was no love involved. Ever."

I nod, feeling oddly relieved. I know now that my parents didn't have a perfect relationship. But I don't know how I would feel if I were to find out he was in love with someone else while he was married. I guess it's easier to believe he was a weak-willed man who let his baser instincts get the best of him.

"Do you know why the affair started?" I ask. "Like… what made him want to cheat on his wife?"

Lucas shakes his head. "I don't have that answer, Hannah. I'm sorry. I wish I did. But I don't know that having that information would make it any easier."

My eyes well up a little bit. "We never had a lot of money, you know? We had periods of time when things weren't perfect. But both of them were amazing parents, even through all the hard stuff." I wipe at my eyes. "And now, knowing what I do, I don't really know how I feel about him anymore."

I stop talking, feeling the well of emotion surging up in my chest. But before I can try to say anything else, Lucas begins to talk.

"I think the important thing to remember," he says, "is that you can have memories of your dad that are accurate, even if he was a different person to someone else."

"What do you mean?"

"Well, the dad you knew taught you to ride bikes. He may not have had a lot of money, but it sounds like he was loving and affectionate and kind. Just because he wasn't faithful to your mom..."

I wince, hating how that sounds.

"... just because he was imperfect, doesn't mean he loved you any less than what you remember. And it doesn't invalidate the memories you have."

My gratitude towards Lucas' perspective feels overwhelming. It's the first time since I found out about what happened that I feel like it's okay for me to feel confused. That it's okay for me to be conflicted about my emotions and try to reconcile my memories with the truth.

"Thank you for saying that. I guess I just feel like I'm betraying him or something. Like learning new things about him might change how I see him. But I also know that *you* are my only remaining family. And this, with you, needs to be protected and nurtured, too. I can't do that if I'm unwilling to accept these other pieces of who my dad was, as broken as those pieces may be."

He nods. "Totally. One hundred percent. And I'll never expect you to pick someone. Like your loyalty to me can only come if you say your dad is a dick, or something."

I laugh.

But then his expression sobers. "But I also hope you can see that he *wasn't* that dad to me. He might have done some fun stuff when I was a kid, taking me surfing and whatever, but he never called during the year. Never checked in. Didn't send a card on my birthday. So the guy I knew? He was just a man. A man that stopped coming around when..."

Lucas pauses, and I wait patiently for him to finish.

"Well... he just stopped coming around."

I feel like he's not telling me something, but with our

emotions on high, I don't want to push.

"So my only feelings about him have always been a little... different than yours," he says, picking a piece of his crust up off of his plate and taking a bite, then glancing at the TV.

I've seen this episode before, and it's one of my favorites. Hearing David Attenborough talk about nature is one of the most heartwarming things that exists.

We sit in silence for a few minutes, just listening to the Brit and allowing quite a large chunk of the next episode to play with only a few pieces of funny commentary from either of us.

Though, I can barely call what I'm doing *listening*. All I can think about is that my dad was a very different man than I knew him to be.

But I guess you can be a different type of dad than you are as a type of man. You can treat your children better, or worse, than your spouse.

Clearly I'll need to sort through some of my memories of him and my mother. Though I'm not sure if tonight is the night for that.

"I appreciate you being willing to talk about him. To share, even if it makes you uncomfortable," Lucas adds. Then he looks back to me. "My memories of Henry are minimal, and I'll never get to know Joshua. So my only way to understand them is through you."

I nod, though my throat is tight and I don't add much more after that. Hopefully there will be another time for us to have a chat. A time when my memories of my dad won't feel so fragile.

Because that's how they feel right now. Like they might shatter and break at any moment.

And I know that's not Lucas' fault. It's not anyone's fault, really. Except for my dad.

And that's a big and uncomfortable pill to swallow.

Chapter Fourteen
WYATT

My parents told us we were adopted when I was really young. Probably around kindergarten, if I had to guess. It's a hard concept for a child that young to understand. When you're little, the idea that a parent wouldn't want their child, so they gave him or her to someone else… it's pretty startling.

But it wasn't until I was in junior high and my mom got pregnant with Ivy that it started to consume my mind. I had to know who my *real* parents were. Because it felt like I didn't really know who I was if I didn't know where I came from.

The P.I. was surprised to get hired by a child, I think, but when a person gives you a job and waves a Black AmEx, it doesn't matter how old they are.

It took him thirteen months to find my parents. He came by my house with a file of paperwork, a fairly thin stack, and let me know he'd found everything he could.

I waited almost a month before I had the courage to open that file. To look through the pieces of my past that I worried would change me forever.

Ultimately, the entire thing was exactly what I expected. A too young couple in high school tried to raise Ben. But when they became pregnant again with me a year later, they decided adoption for both of us would give everyone the best chance at a happier, more successful life.

At thirteen years old, I hired a driver to take me out to where they lived in Terra Bella, California, a town of about three thousand that's an hour from Bakersfield. My parents were out of town at some function on the east coast, so I figured it was the perfect time for me to go meet Theo Marshall and Marie King. My birth parents.

We drove all the way there, into the mobile home park facility, and then parked outside for over an hour.

And then we left.

I never managed to muster up the courage to go introduce myself to Marie when I saw her leave her house, smoke a cigarette on the patio, then get in her car and drive away. She was leaving for work. I could tell because she had on a green polo shirt with a symbol for a local gas station.

After that, I had the driver take me home. I knew there was no reason to go by Theo's house a few minutes away, where he still lived with his parents, my grandparents, at thirty years old.

It was at only thirteen years old that I realized something incredibly important, something most people don't learn until much later in life.

No one else could be in charge of whether or not I felt like I belonged. I either decided to know myself, believe in myself, and carve out my place in this world... or I didn't. And I couldn't place blame on anyone else for that, ever.

So I went home, tucked that file into a drawer, and didn't think much about it. I had a happy life. A weird older brother that I loved as much as young brothers who are always at odds can love each other. A mom and dad who loved me. And a new baby sister. "A happy accident," my mom had called Ivy.

It was only two years later that Lucas asked me for the name of my P.I. so he could go in search of his own dad. A man who had spent some time with him when he was a kid, but who suddenly stopped coming around without explanation.

Within two weeks he came to me, his emotions in turmoil.

"He had another family," he says, then takes a hit off the joint I bought from Otto's dealer last week. I'd planned to save it for a special occasion, but it seems like Lucas needs it more than I do. "I mean, I guess I knew that already. I think I remember meeting his kids once. He brought them out here. Joshua and Hannah."

He takes another hit, holding the smoke in as he passes it over to me. I take my own hit, deciding not to say anything until Lucas gets it all out. The level of drama in this town never ceases to amaze me.

"Really? Shit. That seems stupid if you're trying to have a secret family."

He shakes his head. "It wasn't a secret. Well, I guess I was the secret. I mean, I never expected that he'd like, come back and be a real dad. But I didn't expect that he'd be... gone."

And that's the real kicker. Finding out that the guy passed away a few years ago. Dying in a car accident along with his wife.

"What happened to his kids?" I ask.

Lucas' expression pinches, true sadness crossing his face. "Joshua died recently, too. Some kind of accident at work."

"Jesus," I say, shaking my head. "Talk about bad luck in the family. Shit."

"I just... I always thought I'd be able to talk to him again. You know? Like, I thought I'd be able to grow up and then maybe know him. And now... that's just gone."

I don't know how to handle Lucas' level of emotion about his dad, not feeling the same emotional connection to my own birth parents, so I pass the joint back, hoping he'll take another hit and it'll help him let it go.

"And now I have a sister," he says. "I don't even know how to handle this. Or what I should do."

"Sisters aren't all they're cracked up to be," I joke, hoping to alleviate some of the tension.

But Lucas only gives me a half smile.

"Should I reach out to her? I mean, she has to be like... so alone, you know? Her parents and then her brother died."

"Look. Don't stress about it now. You've got plenty of time. You

don't have to make a decision today. Give it some time."

He nods, looks back out to the ocean from where we're seated on his balcony, taking a break from the party he's throwing after the sophomore year Homecoming dance.

"What was your dad's name?" I ask, holding my glass of scotch up in the air. I'm still trying to decide if I like the stuff, but it's slowly growing on me.

Maybe, if we toast to the guy, we can try and salvage Lucas' evening with an uplifting speech. Some shit about staying positive and living for the now.

For all I know, the guy was a useless piece of shit, but he was a man who had died, and maybe it will make Lucas feel better.

"Henry Morrison."

At the name, a strange sensation runs the length of my spine, an uncomfortable feeling sounding an alarm throughout my body. An angry, banging, red light alarm in my mind.

I know that name.

How do I know that name?

I still toast the man. Give Lucas a small smile as we lift our drinks to the setting sun in his memory.

But the minute I get home, having left Lucas' party early, I go straight to my mom's room. I call it that because my dad is never here. Always off with some woman, though my mother always claims he's at work.

She sleeps off her vodka hangover while I open her cell phone and scroll through her contacts list. And there, sandwiched between Joanne Mabel and Patricia Murphy, is Henry Morrison.

I click over to messages, searching for the name in the endless mass of texts to friends planning pedicures and salon visits and trips to the Galleria.

I miss you, I finally read. You need to come meet Ivy. She looks so much like you.

It's a text from years ago, sent only a few months after Ivy was born. And his response is about what I would expect from a man having an affair when he had a family somewhere else.

Telling my mom he couldn't come visit. That he had a family and he'd made that clear when she'd decided to keep the baby.

My head starts to pound, everything beginning to feel like a tangled web of lies and affairs and death and I can't keep it all straight.

So I go straight back to Lucas.

The party is still going, and I can't find Lucas anywhere. So I go to his bedroom and bang on the door enough times that he quits banging his girlfriend and lets me in. Remmy waves at me with a sneaky little smile from the bed, tucked under a sheet.

But I storm past her, out to the same balcony where we had just toasted his father.

"What's going on?" *he asks, coming up beside me as I stare out at the ocean.* "Is something wrong?"

I laugh, though there's absolutely no humor to be found anywhere in this fucked up situation.

So I tell him what I know. Which isn't much, but it's enough.

That Henry Morrison, his father, had also had an affair with my mom. That he was Ivy's dad.

Lucas' face says exactly what I feel.

That it's too much information.

Too many secrets.

Too much to keep straight in the wake of everything else.

"So... that means Ivy's... my sister, too?"

That hadn't even occurred to me, and the reality of it pinches something inside of me, knowing he's her real brother and I'm not.

I nod. "Probably."

"So that means Hannah is also related to her."

My brow furrows. "Who?"

"Hannah is Henry's daughter. My half-sister. So, Ivy's half-sister, too."

I shake my head. "No. I don't know what you're thinking in your head, but Ivy is not going to get wrapped up in whatever ideas you have about meeting this... Hannah girl. I don't want Ivy to ever know. She's going to have enough struggles in life," *I say, referencing her how sick she got just last year, how she'd gone deaf.* "She doesn't also need to have strange half relationships with people who don't fucking matter."

Lucas shakes his head. "I can't lie to Hannah."

"So you've already decided you're going to meet her?"

He looks unsure, so I play off that lack of certainty.

Because I don't need any new shit in my life right now. There's enough going on.

"I think it's a mistake, Lucas. You're inviting a host of problems. You think someone like her, who comes from a dad like yours, a guy *who had affairs with any number of rich women in the South Bay, is going to be anything other than money hungry? If she just lost her parents, she's probably living with an aunt or a grandparent. They'll want some of the money that doesn't belong to any of them. They'll just* use *you, Lucas. We don't need people like them in our lives."*

It was a low blow. Something I've never regretted saying but still wonder about.

Lucas' biggest fear in life has always been that he will just be a vessel for other people's desires. That the only thing people care about is his money, and not him.

He brushes it off. Pretends that isn't the case.

But I've known him since we were tykes. And I knew that's where I could hit him that would make him reconsider. Make him turn his head.

And he did.

I promised him back then that I would keep an eye on things. Watch over what was happening with Hannah. Let him know if he needed to know anything.

And I did. For the most part.

I got yearly updates on Hannah, her path in foster care. I saw how she was noted as being aggressive, sometimes violent. That she had substance abuse issues and lied.

I've always felt like seeing those reports has validated the choice I made to encourage Lucas not to reach out to her.

It wasn't until Ivy got sick and I confided in him that she needed a bone marrow transplant that Lucas started making suggestions. Coming up with ways to help Ivy, the sister he's watched grow up from afar. Suggestions that he might have the bone marrow match for Ivy.

Or that Hannah might.

I couldn't do it, though, and I told Lucas not to, either. "Ivy will be fine," I'd barked at him, as I sat in San Francisco and assumed the first doctor's assurances were worth their weight.

But then he brought Hannah here anyway.

Against my wishes. But apparently with perfect timing. Because Ivy might need her.

I never expected to have the reaction I did.

To like her.

To want her to be around.

To think she's beautiful.

She must take after her mom with that hair and her long, lean frame.

So I face two dilemmas, now.

One of conscience.

One of heart.

Do I continue to befriend her? Knowing I'll keep falling for her? Do I use my own interest to push her close to Ivy, hoping for her to feel compelled to help?

Because that's what the original plan was. What Lucas suggested to me. Back before he started to see Hannah as his sister, too. Back before she started to matter to him as a person and not just a conduit for saving Ivy.

I look down at my phone, at the text I'm preparing to send off to Lucas.

Me: Tonight. Bonfire at the dunes. Time to welcome Hannah officially into the group.

I wonder if I'll ever recover from how this feels. This intentional attempt to make someone feel like they belong so we can manipulate her into giving us something we want.

But I also wonder if I'll ever recover from the way she makes me feel when she looks at me. From those soft eyes that are both so world-weary and so trusting at the same time.

Because I know that everything I'm doing will scar her deeply, prey on the most intimate of fears she has.

Instead of thinking about it any longer, I hit send and tuck away my phone.

I'm going to hell. But as long as I go down by helping Ivy, I'll take whatever I deserve.

Chapter Fifteen
HANNAH

I find Lucas waiting in the loading bay with a super smiley Paige, and a bike basket full of beer.

"Get ready for a fun Friday night, girl! We're going to Sand Dune Park!" And then she tips back her beer and finishes it before chucking the bottle into one of the recycling bins behind Bennie's.

I look back at Lucas. "Where?"

"It's this huge mountain of sand in Manhattan Beach. It's usually closed at night, but Wyatt's mom is friends with someone in City Council and blah blah blah," he rolls his eyes. "We can stay as long as we want."

I feel a little ridiculous that my attitude about this sand mountain changes slightly when I hear Wyatt's name mentioned. I mean, he might not even be there tonight. Right? Right. Besides, he just wants to be friends anyway.

"And what do we do there?"

Lucas shrugs. "Drink. Set up a bonfire. Sled down the

mountain."

"It's really fun, and you're going to *love* it," Paige enthuses.

I laugh at how excited she is. "Alright, when do we leave?"

"As soon as Wyatt gets here."

My neck flushes.

"He should be here in about…" Lucas looks at his phone. "Less than five minutes. Want a drink while we wait?"

He stands from where he's seated on a bench near the bike rack, then pulls a beer out of the basket attached to the back of his bike.

I take it, twist off the top, and tilt it back.

Vodka is more my jam if I'm going to drink. Truthfully, I'm not really a beer fan. But the cool ale feels good as it rushes down my throat. And I just know I'm going to need a little liquid courage to get through this evening without feeling like a bumbling mess.

"You started without me?"

I choke. Spray some of my beer out of my mouth, luckily not hitting anyone since they're standing to my right. I cough a few times, then glance over at Lucas, Paige and Wyatt through watery eyes.

Paige is giggling, Lucas looks concerned, and Wyatt has a grin on his face.

"Someone's thirsty."

Paige continues her giggle fit, though she smacks Wyatt in the chest.

"Sorry," I wheeze, coughing one more time and tapping my chest. "I guess I got a little overzealous."

"No kidding." Wyatt walks over to where I'm standing and takes the bottle out of my hand. "If you wanna get into a chugging contest with us, be prepared to lose, Pier Girl."

He winks at me, then chucks my bottle into recycling. "We doing this?" he asks, clapping his hands and then rubbing them together. "Because I've invited a few people and have someone dropping off supplies as we speak."

"Yes! Does that mean s'mores?"

Wyatt gives Paige a nod.

"Let's go!" she cries, her excitement pouring from her like a tidal wave, and then she rolls away on her bike.

Lucas and Wyatt laugh. "Wrong way, Paige!" Lucas calls after her, and she loops her bike around to come back to us.

"Oopsie!" She giggles and heads off towards The Strand.

"You're watching that one tonight," Wyatt says.

Lucas rolls his eyes. "Yeah, yeah, yeah."

I unlock my bike, which now has an *incredibly* sturdy bike lock after what happened two nights ago. I shake my head. I hate when stuff like that happens, especially since the bike didn't even belong to me.

Bouncing from home to home, I became very protective of my stuff. But that didn't stop things from going missing. Eventually, I just whittled things down to only a handful of items that really mattered. And then I protected those things with my teeth bared.

Once I aged out and finally got my own place with Melanie, it was easier to keep my belongings to myself. But I never started 'acquiring' things, sticking mostly with a small amount of clothes, some sundries, and my camera.

And a picture book of photos with my mom and dad and Joshua.

Maybe that's why it's so mind-blowing that Lucas and his friends have just so... much. *So* much. Just tons of stuff. Huge houses and endless sets of shows and movies and books, multiple cars, closets packed full of clothes and shoes. Drawers full of shit like tools and super glue and batteries.

And bikes.

Lucas has five of them, all looking like they're in pristine condition, barely ridden. Well, I guess he has four of them now that I got one of them stolen.

I apologized to him like, eleven times yesterday and today. He keeps reassuring me that it isn't a big deal, that it happens all the time.

"What's with the face?"

I look at Paige, who is riding next to me down The Strand, beer bottle in a little drink holder on her handlebars.

"Huh?"

"You look upset about something."

"Oh, just..." I shake my head. "Sorry, I zoned out."

"Fifty bucks says she was thinking about the bike that got stolen."

I turn my head back and glare at Lucas, who is riding behind me with Wyatt at his side.

He just laughs. "Come on, H. Let it go. Like the song."

And then he and Paige start singing the song from *Frozen*, badly, and at the top of their lungs.

To say I'm mortified at being next to them, completely overcome with embarrassment and prepared to veer off to the side to disassociate is an understatement.

"Just ignore them," Wyatt says, as he and I fall back and let Paige and Lucas gain a significant lead on us. "They get a kick out of getting everyone's attention."

"Do you ever get used to it?"

He chuckles. "Not really. You just learn to ignore it and remember that people are laughing at *them,* not you."

I hum in agreement.

We ride for a few minutes in silence. Well, *relative* silence, since I can still hear Paige and Lucas singing like assholes up ahead.

"So how are you adjusting?" Wyatt asks. "You're from Phoenix right? It's gotta be a lot different here."

I bark out a laugh. "You're not kidding. Night and day, practically. Phoenix is all orange and concrete and sun so hot you think your skin will fry right off. And Hermosa Beach is more... I don't know... breezy?"

Wyatt smiles. "That's a great way to describe this town. In a number of ways. The wind. The attitudes of the residents. The tourists. Things are just ever-changing. Everything blows away and new things come in. Water. Tourists. Businesses."

"I think I was going a little more literal than that, but sure. We'll go with your answer."

He laughs.

"How's Ivy doing?"

He swerves to avoid a young girl on rollerblades. "Why?"

"Oh just, I don't know... because I like her? Haven't seen her since that night at the yacht club. You mentioned she has a hard time fitting in."

"She's fine." But that's all he says and there's something in the way he says it that makes me feel like I shouldn't believe him.

I don't know Wyatt, though, so I drop it, choosing to just ride along in silence. I can still see Paige and Lucas about a football field in front of us, swerving around like idiots, their voices carrying on the beach breeze.

We get to what I assume is the end of The Strand, but

everyone turns right, climbing up a small set of stairs, and then continuing on the same path.

Wyatt comes to a stop at the foot of the steps and dismounts, then lifts his bike with one arm. "I've got that," he says, stepping closer and taking my own bike out of my hands.

Then I watch as he climbs up towards the top, carrying both of our bikes like they weigh nothing, his muscles pronounced.

I've never been one to gawk at attractive men. I never liked the attention myself, not to mention the fact that the male body hasn't ever been something I felt like swooning over.

Wyatt makes all of that go out the window.

I watch him for a moment, the trim line of his hips, the strength in his chest and arms, the muscles that ripple and hint at a man who spends time taking care of his body. He is... mmmmm. I don't even have a word. I just know I like it.

Realizing that I've been standing at the bottom of the steps staring for far too long, I scramble to catch up.

"This is Manhattan Beach," Wyatt offers once I've finally gotten to the top. "It's a pretty cool place. Their high school football team sucks, though."

I take my bike from where he's holding it balanced for me, then give him a slightly playful smile. "It doesn't surprise me that you know that."

"Oh? And why's that?"

I swallow something slightly sour, realizing I'm kind of stuck in a hard place if I answer this question.

Ultimately, I realize I have to tell him I admire his body.

Awesome.

Just what a *friend* would do.

It takes everything in me not to roll my eyes when I remember that conversation from a few nights ago. How embarrassing was that?

Oh, would you like my number? How about a nice little trip between my legs? Oh. No? You just wanna be friends? Cool, cool, cool. That's what I wanted too.

Ugh. I was never very popular with the boys when I was younger, mainly because of the whole Hannah The Cactus and Homeless Hannah thing. And honestly, I'm not sure I've ever *wanted* to be 'popular with the boys.'

I've always associated that moniker with the blonde girl on all those teenage pregnancy posters at my high school.

But there's something about my interactions with Wyatt that makes me feel...

I don't know. There's a warmth in my soul that doesn't just come from the sun. So to have him ask me out, then get so cool so quickly left me slightly chilled to the bone.

"You just look like a guy who likes sports," is what I finally settle on.

There.

That's safe.

I don't need to tell him that he's got nice muscles that pop out at the edge of his shirt sleeves, or that I could see when he stretched earlier before we took off and I caught sight of the tan skin between his jeans and his shirt.

Nah. He just looks sporty. Perfect.

But he's giving me a smile that makes me think he knows where my mind is, so I just choose to focus forward as we climb back onto our bikes and try to catch up with Paige and Lucas.

"How much farther are we going?" I ask.

"We're about halfway there. You tired?"

I scoff. "Not even. I'm a runner. Biking this is a breeze."

He makes a noise of acknowledgement, and when I glance back at him I see his eyes on my ass. His eyes connect with mine and then he winks at me.

I turn back to face front, my cheeks flushing and not just from the bike ride.

"You guys are taking for*ever*," Paige calls back to us. She's pulled off to the side, standing with her bike between her legs. "Hurry up! I wanna get shitfaced tonight."

I start to laugh but when I look over at Wyatt, I see his brow furrowed. "Is something wrong?"

He shakes his head. "No, I just... Paige isn't a big drinker. It's just a weird thing for her to say."

"Yeah, I'm not a big drinker either."

"How come?"

I'm silent, trying to decide if I want to use my normal answer or my honest one.

"Did you have a bad experience? Get a little too drunk and do something you regret?" he asks, a hint of teasing in his voice.

I breathe out a half laugh. "I guess you could say that." And there's something inside of me that wants to knock this rich boy on his ass.

I can't say why, exactly. Maybe it's because his opinion shouldn't matter. Or because so many guys think the way he does. But I can't help it when I just blurt it out.

"I got drunk once when I was fifteen and my foster dad physically and sexually assaulted me. So yeah, I got a little too drunk, and I regret it. Because I wasn't able to defend myself."

When I look back, I see he's not even pedaling. Just coasting next to me, his face having dropped the teasing and instead looks like he's been socked in the chest.

"Hannah, I..." He pauses. "Hey, would you stop a second?"

I squeeze the brakes, slowing down and pulling off to the side. Wyatt does the same, sidling up next to me.

"I'm sorry," he says, his voice and face completely sincere. So sincere I can't look at him, instead opting to look off at the water. "I didn't mean to imply anything by what I said. You didn't deserve what happened to you. And I didn't mean to hurt your feelings."

"You didn't hurt my feelings," I say, though I'd be lying if I tried to tell him it didn't bother me at all. "I just think you should be more mindful of what you say."

He nods. "You're right."

I sit back on my bike seat, ready to take off down The Strand when Wyatt's hand comes out to my wrist.

I quickly shake it off.

Embarrassment overwhelms me. He doesn't say anything, but I'm sure he's remembering the last time I yanked my hand away from him.

Part of me regrets even mentioning it. There's a look people give you when they know you've been assaulted. Usually full of pity. And I hate it. But I also can't stand the idea that he might think I don't want *him* to touch me.

Because that's definitely not the case.

"It's not you," I finally say, managing to look back at him. For some reason I want him to know that I'm not shaking of *his* touch. I'm just wary in general. "It's where I'm at, so... sorry."

"You don't have to apologize," he says. "I was just going to say... I was going to *ask.* Are we okay?"

I nod. "Yeah." I let out a sigh and turn my head away. "We're fine."

And then I push forward on my pedals, propelling me towards where Paige and Lucas are probably singing some hit song from *Trolls* or something.

But I can feel Wyatt riding behind me for the rest of the way.

The night turns out to be really fun, the weird interaction with Wyatt aside. We kind of kept our distance from each other for a little bit, which isn't surprising to me.

I basically flipped out on him because he wanted to apologize for making a joke. I roll my eyes at myself and shake my head.

Sienna told me once that I'm allowed to have real reactions when it comes to men, even if it makes them uncomfortable.

"You don't owe them anything," she told me.

And for a while, I heeded that advice. Yanking back and glaring and making myself untouchable worked for me.

But I'm not so sure it does anymore, though I wouldn't even know where to begin to stop it. To change what feels like a very base instinct

"Come on, Hannah! You have to do it, at least once!"

I glance over from where I'm seated in a camping chair next to a bonfire. Paige and Lucas and most of the group are at the bottom of the monstrous hill, waving me over.

Reluctantly, I get out of my chair and head in their direction, laughing when they start to cheer. I'm going to safely assume they've had a smidge too much to drink.

Paige, Lucas, Lennon, Wyatt, and Otto, as well as a handful of people I was briefly introduced to but definitely don't remember their names, have been going up and sledding down for the past hour. They're all sweaty, sticky, sandy and a little bit sloshed.

So far, I'm the only one who hasn't gone. But as the daylight disappears and the chance to board down starts to fade with it, I know that if I'm going to do it, I need to go now.

Once I'm standing before them, the same beer I've been nursing for the past hour clutched in my hand, Lucas gives me instructions.

"Alright, so you carry this up the right side and then you

board down the left," he says, grinning from behind his board, Burton tagged in bold down the center of it.

My eyes widen. Burton is expensive stuff. I'm surprised Lucas is willing to ride it down the dunes and get it all scuffed. But I guess that's just what it's like having everything you want. And really, cost and value aren't the same thing.

"It's not like I haven't been watching for the past hour," I say, adding a laugh so he knows I'm teasing. "Why can I only board down the left, though?"

He turns slightly to the side so I can see the sign denoting that the left is the children's recreational area and the right is the adult exercise area.

"Will I get in trouble tonight if I board down the other side?"

I might not have an extensive history behind me of vacations to fancy ski resorts, but what I *do* have is six years of summer vacations to Yuma with Sienna's family. And boarding down the dunes? That was my favorite.

The sand on the sledding side is packed in tight. To board down confidently on this baby, I need the loose stuff, like on the adult side.

Lucas lifts a shoulder. "I guess not. Why? You planning on doing some tricks for us?"

I shrug right back at him. "Maybe."

And then I pull the snowboard out of his hands and head off towards the hill, with everyone 'ooooooh'-ing behind me.

It takes me about ten minutes to get to the top, the first half passing quickly and the second half proving to be a real pain in the ass. I'm heaving in breaths by the time I finally get all the way up.

Cardio like this is so different than long distance running, although I'm sure it doesn't help that I haven't really been running since I first got to town, the one or two morning jogs in the one mile loop near Lucas' house barely enough to make me feel anything.

When I finally stand at the top, I get a little bit of vertigo, though it passes quickly. It's amazing how high this little mountain feels at the top as opposed to when you're at the bottom. And now that I'm up here, I'm getting a tiny bit of stage fright.

What if I totally fall on my ass and embarrass myself?

I'm standing there for a few minutes, staring down the dune, when I hear someone walking up behind me.

"Where did you come from?" I ask Wyatt as he steps up next to me and bends over with his hands on his knees, catching his breath.

"There's a bunch of stairs on a path around the backside," he says between pants. "We used to have a designated driver who would drive us around to the top end. It was a lot easier than climbing up every time. God, I always forget what a bitch cardio is."

"I knew you were a gym rat," I say.

Wyatt barks out a laugh, still panting. "Well, at least I know now what you were getting at earlier about my being 'athletic,'" he says with a smirk.

I blush, looking back down the hill.

We're both silent for a second as we get our breathing under control and I try to build up the nerve to drop down.

"It feels bigger up here."

He nods. "Yeah. That's normal."

"How many times have you done this?"

"Today? Three times. In general? A few dozen, but that was before I moved away."

"Does it get easier?"

He shakes his head. "I don't think doing something hard ever gets easier. You just get more brave once you believe you can accomplish what you want."

"What if I fall and everyone laughs." I ask.

It's a rare moment for me, this kind of vulnerability not normally something I put on display. But there's something about Wyatt that I can't put my finger on. Something inside me wants to trust him. That he's the type of man who would catch me if I fell. Believes that he won't make me feel stupid if I say the wrong thing.

Sure, our interactions have been a bit strange so far. But maybe strange is what I need right now.

"Then they laugh," he says, and my head whips over to look at him. He shrugs at my reaction. "If you fall and they laugh, then you've fallen and they've laughed. It doesn't mean you can't laugh too. That you can't join in and be a part of the group."

But I've never been invited to be a part of the group. That little nugget I *don't* say out loud. The last thing I want to tell the equivalent of the hot popular jock is that I'm the stinky kid no one likes to talk to.

How do you find the courage to be yourself when the you

you've always been was never accepted before?

I sigh, look at Wyatt. "Do you think I can do it?"

He tilts his head back and looks up at the sky. "Knowing nothing about your skills and capabilities? Yes. If there was ever going to be a person that could totally blow my mind right now riding down the dune? I don't doubt it would be you."

I smile. "I like that."

"What?"

"The way you see me."

His eyes search mine for a minute before he clears his throat and takes a step away from me.

It isn't until then that I realize how close we'd been standing.

I shake it off and take a seat strapping the board on to my shoes.

Then I stand and give one last look at Wyatt.

"Here goes."

Tipping the end of the board over the edge, I slice down the hill, curving wide and then cutting back, drawing a big, flowing zigzag down the dune.

It feels like forever, but in reality I know it passes in seconds, and as I make it down to the bottom, sliding to a stop in front of Lucas and Paige and everyone else, the blood pumping in my ears eases just enough for me to hear everyone cheering.

For me.

I hear a round of *so fucking dope* and *holy shit, woman,* and even *how the hell did you learn to do that.*

The smile on my face is wide, and I turn to look up to the top, where Wyatt is slowly making his way down the side of the hill by foot, a small smile on his face.

It's a bittersweet pill when I realize in that moment that the only congratulations I want right now is from him.

Chapter Sixteen
WYATT

I feel like a crazy person.

Like one of those guys you see on TV. There was some show on Netflix recently about a stalker, and the girls I knew in San Francisco were always swooning over it.

I thought they were crazy.

Now I'm the crazy one.

I was in the garage. The one connected to the guesthouse, which faces the path heading down to the beach. I had put on my workout gear. Nothing fancy. A pair of trainers. A cutoff tee. A pair of basketball shorts.

I'd been planning on strapping a pair of gloves on so I could get a workout on the bag I had installed right after I got here. Gotta keep up my workouts even when I'm not near my home gym.

But just as I pulled my gloves out, something caught my eye.

Or I guess, some*one*.

It was Hannah, jogging along the bicycle path that sits below the main drag. Heading to the path that would take her down to the beach, probably to run in the opposite direction. Back to Lucas' house.

A nice little one-mile loop, if I'd done the math correctly.

Before I even knew what I was doing, I'd dropped my gloves on a workbench, grabbed my phone, and took off after her.

I can't explain why. What compelled me. The force that implored me to keep her in my sights.

But I did it. I followed her.

Tried to come up with a way I could 'bump' into her on accident. Strike up a conversation. Because she'd been on my mind constantly, and seeing her run by felt like fate.

Only, at the end of the path, she didn't make a left to jog along The Strand back to Lucas'. She turned right. Away from Hermosa. Into Manhattan Beach. Along the northern stretch of The Strand where we rode our bikes on Friday.

And now, I've been running behind her for close to three miles, something I did not prepare myself for, and I'll still have to run back to my house.

Which is why I feel like a crazy person.

My feet hurt. My back hurts. My lungs ache. The sweat is burning my eyes.

But I keep going.

And I don't know fucking why.

Okay, so maybe that's a lie.

There was a moment on Friday night. Some kind of something between us that was… unlike anything I've felt before. And now that three days have passed and I haven't seen her, I feel the need to take advantage of the limited time I'll have with her. Because I know it will come to an end.

Suddenly, this has become bigger. She's become more than just Lucas' long-lost sister. More than just Ivy's potential donor.

She's someone I want to know.

When we'd been standing at the top of the dune and she couldn't find the courage to drop down, her biggest fear had been the group at the bottom. Not getting hurt. Not eating shit. Just the people at the bottom that might laugh.

Makes me wonder what else she's endured in life that the physical pain isn't the main threat.

You hear stories about kids in foster care. What they endure.

And when I first found out about Hannah, I just... didn't know. I was too young to really understand and I didn't think everything through.

Now I'm wishing I had.

Maybe a lot of things could be different.

But there's another part of me that will not be ignored. And that's the one that knows too much.

There is a very real part of me that sees her as the problem, not the solution.

So what do I do when my brain feels like a fucking mess? When I can't seem to make up my mind about what I'm supposed to do?

Apparently I stalk people.

That's a great thing to learn about myself.

I can see in the distance that we're nearing the end of The Strand. Beyond Manhattan, a bike trail continues for miles and miles, stretching up into Playa Del Rey before crossing Ballona Creek and continuing into Venice and Santa Monica.

I've ridden that distance a few times in my life. On a bike. The idea of potentially running it is mortifying.

But I can tell Hannah is slowing as we near 45th Street. Hopefully she's gearing up to turn around, because I can't keep going. And if she does continue, I'll have to admit defeat and hobble home.

I glance around, wondering where would be a good place for me to step off the trail so she can turn around and just keep...

But before I can do that, Hannah comes to a complete stop and spins around, putting her hands behind her head and stretching, taking deep breaths.

Her eyes connect with mine.

She blinks. I blink.

And it feels like my only choice is to keep running so I don't look like the crazy person who just followed her for almost four miles.

But she grins at me, a soft, sweet thing that splits my chest wide open.

Not at all what I'm expecting.

She drops her arms and rests her hands on her hips.

"Hey," she says, still panting as I slow down and approach her.

"Hi." It's all I can manage since I can barely catch my own

breath.

"Are you still stalking me?"

I'm fairly certain that I stop breathing for a few seconds before Hannah starts to laugh. Wheeze really, since she's still trying to suck oxygen into her lungs.

And that's when I remember. We had the stalker joke from the night we met and Mary's and the yacht club.

A perfect distraction since I don't know what else to say.

"Always," is what I manage in response.

It's a flirty thing to say, and the part of me that sees Hannah as a problem wants to kick myself. But something deeper inside of me likes the way her cheeks pink even more than they already are after her run.

"I didn't think you were a runner," she says. "I mean, I don't really know anything about you, so it makes sense I wouldn't know that, I guess. But when you were practically dying the other day at the dunes, I just assumed that you weren't a cardio person. Though, in complete honesty, I was dying by the time I got to the top, too."

I chuckle, though I'm still trying to catch my breath. "It's a new thing," I lie. "Trying to get into it."

"Well that was a pretty amazing run for someone just starting to get into it," she praises, and I can't help it when my feathers fluff up at her attention. "Do you want to run back together?"

My mind races through all of the things that could go wrong with this run back, but ultimately, I nod.

Because the part of me that can't seem to get enough of her? He's been winning since the moment we met.

We take off, running at a steady pace, side-by-side. And I want to laugh at the irony of this situation.

That I'm running on The Strand with Hannah Morrison. Wanting her attention. Smiling at her jokes. Barely able to catch my breath.

Well, that's probably because of the running, but still. It's true whether I'm running or not.

"This beach is so gorgeous," she says, breaking the silence a few minutes later. "I never would have imagined that I'd be here, in a place like this."

"You miss Phoenix at all?" I ask.

"Not really," she says, her voice surprisingly steady for

someone running at least a half dozen miles today.

"Sounds like a great place to live."

My sarcasm isn't lost on her and she laughs, glances my way. "I hated Phoenix. I lived in this beat up little apartment with a childhood friend and her daughter."

Even if I *hadn't* already known that, the Hermosa gossip trail has already burned strong with information about Lucas' secret sister.

At minimum, the machine has dug up the information on her parents' deaths, her background in foster care, her brother's death, her enrollment at the community college in Phoenix, and the fact that she lived with a girl with a deaf daughter.

I know more information than they do, but no one needs to know that.

Some secrets are better kept secret.

"I loved them," she continues, "but I've always felt like my life has been this one giant attempt at trying to climb out of a hole, and I think Melanie felt the same. It's probably better that we parted ways so we didn't start dragging each other down."

"What was life like there?" I ask, trying to keep my voice from revealing how badly I want to collapse on the ground.

This running shit is no joke.

She sighs, and when I look over, I see a look of frustration on her face.

"Well, I worked as much as I could. Babysitting and waitressing. Tried to get photography gigs. Took classes at the community college. That's really it."

"So, you came here to get away from that?"

She pants a few times, takes some deep breaths and glances my way. "I guess. My lease was coming to an end. School was out for the summer." She pauses. "But mostly, I think I'm here trying to figure things out."

"Like what?"

Hannah slows slightly, wrapping her arms around her stomach awkwardly as we jog. And then she laughs. Hard. Almost forcefully, belying her discomfort.

"God, if only it were that easy, that I could just give you a list. But honestly, I don't know yet. But I think being here is a part of the process."

I don't like her answer. I don't like that it sounds vague and indecisive, like she's a feather in the wind just waiting to be pushed in whatever direction is decided for her.

She doesn't seem like that girl to me. That woman. I think she sees herself as weak, but the more I start to reveal the little bits and pieces of Hannah that make up her whole, the more I realize she's made out of something real and twisted and strong.

We stay silent for most of the run back into Hermosa. When my body starts to revolt against the long run and lack of conditioning for this much cardio, I find myself focusing on Hannah's soft breaths panting next to me.

"You mentioned photography?" I ask, trying to find a way to keep her talking.

She snorts, an adorable little thing that reflects how she feels about this portion of her life. "I hope to be a photographer one day. But I'm still trying to figure everything out, so… it's been a work in progress."

I smile even through my pain at the thought of Hannah behind a camera's lens. I've been observing her closely since we first met, and she has incredibly watchful eyes. She's very aware of the people around her, picks up on mood and feeling and can see beauty in so many things.

It suits her.

"I hope it works out for you," is the lame ass thing I manage to come up with to say in response.

I swear I feel on the verge of weeping when we round a light curve and I can see the path that leads to my house in the distance.

"This is where I'll split off," I say.

Hannah's eyes connect with mine. "Can I come by and say hello to Ivy?"

Something trips over in my chest when she asks that. And I know in the depth of my soul that it's a bad idea. But I can't seem to verbalize that. Can't make the words come off my tongue. Which is a good thing. Because in the same thought, I'm reminded of what I'm supposed to be doing.

Making sure Hannah feels welcome.

And time spent with Ivy can only help the cause, right?

The only thing I can seem to manage to say is, "Sure."

So we jog up the path and back towards my house, turning right on Hermosa Ave and down a few properties before I come to an exhausted stop in front of the guesthouse garage door, which I see I forgot to close.

"Wow," she says, her chest heaving up and down as I lean up against a wall and try to catch my breath.

"Yeah. I feel like shit."

Hannah laughs, the sound funny and slightly adorable as it leaves her body between her own pants of breath. "I meant your house, not the run."

I smile, though I literally feel like I'm dying while she looks like she barely took a light jog around the block.

"This place is so cute. You live here?" her eyes are taking in the guesthouse, which sits atop a small secondary garage that serves mostly as a workout space if I don't feel like heading to the gym at my mom's.

"This is my mother's house," I say, the words coming out slowly and surrounded by hard breathing. "I'm just in town visiting for a bit, so when I stay here, I stay in the guesthouse."

She nods.

I tip my head in the direction of the main house, and Hannah follows me as I lead her through the garage and out a side door that leads to the main courtyard and the entrance to the main house.

As I'm pushing open the front door, I glance back and see Hannah frozen near the doorway leading out from the garage. Her eyes are wide as she stares at everything. The grass, the trees, the path, the house, over to the guesthouse, then back into the garage she just came out of.

"You coming?" I call over to her.

Her eyes clash with mine. "You didn't tell me you lived in a castle," she says.

I chuckle. "Calloway Castle is pretty well-known in the area." I lean against the doorway and cross my arms.

"You Hermosa Beach boys and all your money and fancy houses," she teases, and I can't help but smile back at her.

"You gonna stand out here all day or do you want to see Ivy?"

At that, she lights up, and her feet begin to move her in my direction. Up the few stairs leading into the entry and then inside.

Hannah Morrison is inside my house.

I never thought I'd see the day.

Grabbing my phone out of my pocket I flick off a text.

Me: I have a present downstairs. Come and get it. Hurry!

Within thirty seconds, I hear feet thundering around upstairs and then clomping aggressively down towards us. When Ivy rounds the top section of stairs and sees Hannah standing next to me, she has a fat fucking meltdown of happiness.

"Oh my gosh!" she cries out, her words having that same muted quality that most deaf people have, since she can't hear what she's saying.

I've seen a few people stare at her because of the way she sounds when she speaks. They gawk, like she's from the circus. And it makes me want to throw them up against a wall, grab their neck and squeeze.

But of course, I don't do that. Often. Might have once or twice to a few dicks when we were younger. But I've tried to be a bit more mature about things now that I'm nearing twenty-five.

Ivy sprints towards Hannah, the two embracing in a sweet hug once she reaches the bottom of the stairs.

What are you doing here?

Your brother was stalking me, so I told him he had to let me hang out with you if he didn't want me to call the cops.

Ivy turns and glares at me, like I did something wrong. She doesn't get that Hannah's joking, *or* that technically Hannah isn't actually joking.

I hold my hands up. "What?" I say, knowing she can read my lips with how intensely she's looking at me.

Apologize to Hannah.

I laugh as I watch Ivy continue to light me on fire with her eyes, her arms crossed. Then I give Hannah a smirk and a wink. *Sorry, Hannah.* Looking to Ivy, I narrow my eyes. *Better?*

Ivy huffs, takes Hannah by the hand, and drags her away.

I watch as the two of them walk past the living room and out to the backyard, out to sit by the pool, ignoring the living room and the over-sized couches that face a TV that almost never gets used and takes up half of a wall.

I know for a fact that my mom spent over fifty thousand dollars to get that thing and have it set up. It's top of the line, 4K, with absolutely amazing resolution.

It's also going to be outdated in the next few months.

Normally, I'm not one to think about circumstances outside of my own. It might make be a bit of a dick, but it's just my life. We donate to charities and we do the best we can. But we also have a lot of money, and we use it on what we want to use it on.

Things like TVs, private flights, yachts, and living for years without a job.

Those are normal.

Not once have I reconsidered those things. Not once have I felt guilty about having them.

Until the moment Hannah's eyes widened at the size of my house. That's the second I started to notice everything, like blinders had suddenly been peeled away from my eyes.

The huge fucking TV, the wine room that probably has a cool million in aged wine that might never get drunk, the painting on the wall my mom bought at auction for six figures that will be replaced by a new piece next season.

I think about what I know of Hannah's life before coming here. The file I have in the office from years ago, detailing as much of her life as could be found at that time. Her report cards and statements from her foster care families.

She'd been a reckless teen in those reports. Now, having met her, I struggle with believing that's the real story. Now, I see a woman who never felt comfortable enough in her skin when she was younger. Like she never belonged. A woman who was once a girl that had a hard time making friends and felt uncomfortable around men.

I clench my fists.

A girl who was assaulted and taken advantage of.

And I wonder if that money might have made her life better. Different.

Not so full of turmoil.

I know that there's a storm coming our way. Something intense and painful and... I feel helpless to stop it.

Because I want her here. In my house. Spending time with Ivy. Sitting at the pool. Laughing and signing and drinking disgusting vodka sodas.

But I also know that wanting her here is probably the last thing I should be doing.

I can make out some of what they're saying from here, their hands moving in flurries as they giggle and share. Stuff about the house and how their days have been so far. But I turn away from them and head into the kitchen to make the three of us some drinks.

I'm just finishing putting together a vodka soda, Shirley Temple, and three fingers of scotch when Ivy comes barreling into the kitchen, nearly knocking me over.

Can we grab a bathing suit for Hannah from the guesthouse? I invited Hannah to go swimming.

"It's okay if it doesn't work out," I hear Hannah say from behind me.

I turn to look at her.

"A dip in the pool after a run like that sounds awesome, but I don't want to impose."

I'll go get her a swimsuit, Ivy says, then darts out of the room.

Hannah walks over to where I'm standing and gives me a soft smile. "If it's trouble, I swear, it's really not a big deal. I can totally go home."

"No, no. You should go in the pool."

"That sounds like a wonderful idea!" Vicky comes waltzing into the kitchen with a basket of laundry. "That pool doesn't get enough use. I'll go help Ivy pick out a suit for you."

I smile. "Hannah, this is Vicky. She's everything to us. Like another mother. Vicky, this is Hannah."

Vicky grins and continues bustling through towards the door out to the courtyard. "Nice to meet you Hannah! Gimme five minutes and you'll be dipping into that cool pool water."

"She's friendly," Hannah says, giggling. "Is she your... nanny? Or maid?"

"Yes," I say, and we both laugh. "She's been around since my brother Ben and I were babies. She's housekeeper, nanny, assistant to my mother, and a bunch of other things rolled into one. She's family, though."

Hannah smiles. "I like that." Then she pulls her phone out of her pocket. "I'm gonna let Lucas know I won't be home for a while."

"Invite him over, if you want."

She nods. "Sounds good."

Then she wanders off, her phone pressed to her ear.

I shake my head.

Never did I ever think Hannah Morrison would be in my house,

hanging out with Ivy, and dipping into our pool.
Life is fucking crazy.

A little while later, I'm dropping a stack of towels out on a lounge chair when Hannah walks outside in the bathing suit she borrowed from the sets we keep in the guest house.

It wouldn't matter what else was happening right now... a parade, a drum banging in my face, literal fireworks... I can't tear my eyes away.

She's in a white bikini, the triangles at the top fitting her breasts perfectly, the bows tied at her hips enticing. I don't think I've ever seen a woman in a bathing suit before and felt like someone was choking me. But that's how I feel right now.

Because she is absolutely breathtaking.

And when her eyes find mine, she stops moving. They dip down, over my bare chest and down my swim trunks to my feet before coming back up to gaze at my chest and arms. Over the tattoo on my bicep that I got while I was in college.

And then when she realizes she's been gawking, she flushes and turns away, reaching for her drink that's been sitting on the patio table and probably melting in the hot sun of this May afternoon.

"I'm glad the suit fits," I say, wandering in her direction, wanting a closer look at her curves. And that's when I notice a tattoo on her left side. "Is that a tattoo?"

Hannah turns, moves her arm out of the way and glances down. "Yeah. I got it on my eighteenth birthday. It was a gift from my friend Sienna."

I reach out and trace the tattoo slightly. It says 'free' in script, and has a feather underneath. Suddenly, I realize what I'm doing and I yank my hand back.

"Sorry, I shouldn't have..." But I pause when I see the heated look in her eyes. That her breathing has picked up, her chest rising and falling with more effort than our earlier run had produced.

"It's okay," she says, her eyes locked with mine.

We stand there for a moment, just watching each other.

If she were a girl I'd invited over to party, I'd step into her space right now. Bring my mouth an inch from hers. Watch her lips part as I place a hand on her hip.

Then wait for her to step into me.

And I'd do what I've been imagining doing. Press all my hardness against her soft.

I've done it in the past, and it usually works. Whether it's the seduction, the flirting, or just chemistry, I've never had an issue with getting a woman's attention.

And I'm tempted. Especially when I see her eyes drop to my mouth, her tiny tongue peeking out to wet her lips, probably without her even realizing what she's doing.

"Alright, who wants a margarita!"

Vicky's voice has us both stepping apart and looking in her direction. Ivy comes running out behind her, a smile on her face.

I love seeing my sister's energy up, when she's overwhelmed with happiness because life is so good in the moment that she doesn't think to care about the drama that her own circumstances is causing.

She's a much younger twelve-year-old than I was.

When I was her age, I'd already had my first drink. Already made out with a few girls and got a handy from Rita Sholes at an overnight trip we went to as an eighth grade class. I was broody, rebellious and determined and always out doing something.

Ivy only has a handful of friends, a group of girls who are just as sheltered and protected as she is. She's tutored privately and rarely goes anywhere without a family member present.

I've wondered a few times which one of us had it better. If the freedom to be a mess and fuck around and make mistakes is a better life than being protected from everything.

"I'll take a margarita," Hannah says, giving Vicky a smile and accepting a bottle of sunscreen handed to her by Ivy.

Your skin is pretty white like mine. Make sure to cover up or you'll burn.

Hannah glances to me with a small smile, then looks back to Ivy. *Thank you. I'll make sure to do that.*

I make a beeline for the kitchen, intent on helping Vicky with the drinks and avoiding the opportunity to watch Hannah rub her body in lotion.

Vicky eyes me when I come up behind her. "What's up?"

"Just helping."

She raises a brow, then pulls two margarita glasses out of the cabinet. When she turns back to look at me, I see skepticism.

"Since when?"

I roll my eyes. "You act like I never help with things."

"That's because you don't."

"Well, maybe I've changed since I moved to San Francisco."

Vicky snorts. "Whatever, pumpkin. Go get the tequila."

I spend a few minutes helping her make our drinks in silence, refusing to let myself peek out to the pool.

"So, who's the girl?"

"Her name's Hannah. She's Lucas' sister."

Vicky hums as she drops a lime into each drink. But then, out of the corner of my eye, I see her pause. Look up at me.

"Hannah... Morrison?"

I run my tongue over my teeth, fuming at myself for not realizing that my mother talks to Vicky about everything.

I made the mistake once. Just once. In an argument with my mother about dad and money and a bunch of bullshit, I told her.

About Henry's remaining family.

About Hannah.

"Wyatt," she whispers, her eyes wide. "What are you doing?"

I push my shoulders back. "None of your business, Vicky." And then I take a drink in each hand and turn to head out to the patio, guilt tugging wildly at my throat as I leave her in my wake.

"Drink time," I call out, and Hannah turns my way, tapping Ivy on the shoulder.

I put your Shirley Temple in the fridge earlier, I tell Ivy once I've set the margaritas down on the small table between two pool loungers.

She scampers inside.

"This is delicious," Hannah says, taking a second sip of her margarita, then licking her lips.

I'm not even the slightest bit embarrassed to say it gets me a little bit hard. Though I'm also not a creep, so I take a seat on a lounger, discretely adjusting my shorts.

"So, what does your tattoo mean?" I ask. "I meant to ask before."

"It's going to sound stupid, so just remember that I was eighteen when I got it."

"Like you're that much older now," I joke.

She smiles. "I'm almost twenty-two. I'm definitely older now." Hannah sets her drink down next to mine and heads over to the steps to the pool, dipping a toe in, before walking slowly down into the water. "Free is exactly what it sounds like. I always felt like I was... I don't know, imprisoned in these foster homes where no one ever really gave a shit about me. And around that time, I'd started to forgive myself for my own mistakes. It just felt like the right word."

She lifts her arms and tugs out her ponytail, her long hair tumbling down over her shoulders. "And the feather was how I felt at the time. Like I was just being blown all over the place with no clear... anything. No family, nowhere to go, nothing that mattered." She shrugs. "I decided to embrace it. See it as being free rather than being lost. Otherwise I never would have moved on."

She lowers into the water, floating for a second, dipping her head back into the pool then rising out.

"I know it sounds ridiculous..."

"It doesn't." I shake my head, the wonder I feel when I look at her continuing to grow. The coincidence that I'd used almost that exact same analogy when thinking about her spirit while we were on the run earlier. "It's anything but ridiculous, Hannah."

She gives me a little smile, then dips back into the water so only her eyes and the top of her head can be seen.

I turn and grab my drink just as Ivy joins us outside, a Shirley Temple in her hand.

Look who's here! she says, a big smile on her face.

Lucas appears from behind her, swim trunks on, towel in-hand.

He gives me a grin and a wink. "Time for a dip."

Chapter Seventeen
HANNAH

I grin as I count my tips for the evening. Four hundred and eighty-seven buckaroos. In one shift. I can't ever remember making that much money in one evening before, let alone on a Wednesday.

I tuck it away and finish cashing out with Hamish.

"Don't forget, this weekend is Memorial Day weekend. Everyone gets scheduled, no exceptions," he says, giving me a glare that lets me know he means business. "Holiday weekends are smashed around here. The schedule has been up for two weeks, so unless you're in the hospital, no calling in sick."

I nod. "No problem. I'll be here."

Hamish grins, his face relaxing slightly. Then he hands me my receipt for the day, and heads off to do whatever managers do to close everything down. Once I finish tipping the bussers and hosts, I'm still pocketing over four hundred bucks.

Smiling, I swing through the kitchen and staff room to grab my backpack, then venture out the side door, towards the loading area.

But before I even unlock my bike, I hear my name.

I look over my shoulder and grin when I see Paige strutting my way. "Tell me you're not going home right now."

"Uhmmmmmm..." I look at my phone, seeing that it's nearly twelve o'clock. "Yeah, I'm going home right now."

Paige laughs, but continues walking in my direction. She looks amazing, as usual. Her short hair is styled and teased, and she's wearing a red dress that leaves little to the imagination paired with some sky-high heels, though she's still shorter than me when she finally reaches where I'm standing.

"Well, it's time to change your plans, lady. We're going out!"

I shake my head. "I have to work tomorrow morning and then I have a double on Friday and night shifts all weekend. I need to go home and crawl in bed."

Paige pouts. "Oh, come on."

"It's a Wednesday."

"Yeah, it's Wave Wednesday during summer. Half-price drinks!"

I purse my lips and Paige's shoulders slump. "*Pleeeeeease.* It's no fun going out with just the guys, and Lennon went on a trip to visit her grandpa in Boston." She twists her fingers together like she's praying, tucks her hands under her chin. "*Please, please, please,*" Paige whispers. "If you come, I won't tell everyone that you went on a run with Wyatt."

My eyebrows fly off my face. "How do you know about that?"

She lifts a single shoulder, her expression mischievous. "I have my sources."

I rest a hand on my hip and give her a saucy grin right back. "First of all, I don't care if people know Wyatt and I went on a run. We're friends. And second, if your sources know, then it isn't a secret worth bartering with."

Paige sticks a lip out. "You're no fun. I only know because I saw you together. Nobody else knows." She looks side-to-side. "But between you and me? That boy is *sooooooo* into you."

I laugh. "What? No. No, no, no. He's not..." I shake my head. "Nah."

Paige claps her hands and jumps up and down. Impressive, considering those shoes. "Ohmygawwww and you like him tooooooo!"

I continue to laugh in a painfully awkward way, shaking my head. "You could not be further from the truth, Paige. Really. Nope, nope, nope."

She twirls her hips back and forth, still giving me a ridiculous smile. "You know you wanna come with meeeeeee. Besides." She leans forward and whispers. "Wyatt's coming tonight."

I take a deep breath.

Clearly a mistake.

"Knew it!" she says, pointing at me. "Ugh, you guys need to bone, ASAP."

My whole body flushes red. Like, head-to-toe, lobster red. Just the idea of sex with Wyatt... I can't even finish that thought. And honestly, I'm a little embarrassed that it came to mind at all.

Paige giggles, but then steps closer and bumps me with her hip. "Come on, pretty girl. Lucas was the one who told me you'd be here. Come out with us. It'll be so fun!"

Part of me wants to go with her. But part of me *also* wants to climb into the shower and wash away the smell of working in a restaurant, then curl into my jammies and call it a night.

"Let's go back inside and doll you up a little bit, huh?"

I let out a sigh.

"Yes! I knew you'd give in eventually. Being annoying is my best trait."

At that, I can't help but laugh.

Paige leads me through The Wave a little while later, weaving in and out of bodies and heading towards the back wall.

I felt like I was learning something important as I watched her work me over in the bathroom at Bennie's once we'd gone back inside.

She pulled my hair down and used water to give it a styled look. Made me take off my work shirt so I'm wearing tight black pants and a black tank top, then sprayed me with something that smells really, *really* amazing. Then she gave me a little bit of darkness, some black eyeliner and plum colored lipstick.

I might not be my best version of me, but it's a definite step up from what I normally feel like at the end of a shift.

"It's just a spritz of sexy," she'd said.

I'm not a person who laughs a lot, but the shit Paige says always has me trying not to giggle. Though, I'm learning there's a lot to Paige that I don't know.

When we got here, she walked straight up to the bouncer, bypassing the long line, kissed his cheek and waltzed right in, only looking back long enough to wave me along.

And now we're in what Paige told me is the number one club in Hermosa, stepping past another bouncer into a VIP section behind those ropes you see at movie premieres on TV.

"You got her to come!"

I spot Lucas, sitting along the back wall in between a group of people I don't recognize. He has a big smile on his face and his eyes are glassy.

"I didn't think you'd come if I invited you," he says to me, then looks to his friend. "Good job, Paige."

She gives him a salute, then takes a seat in the booth next to his, leaving me to decide whether I want to sit at Paige's table or Lucas'.

All I can wonder is which table Wyatt's going to sit at.

"I'm gonna go grab a drink," I announce to no one in particular, then spin around and head back out of the VIP section and away from the fancy people.

It takes a few minutes at the regular bar, but I finally manage to shimmy my way up to the front.

"Vodka soda," I say, once I've gotten a bartender's attention.

He nods, moving down the bar and throwing it together quickly. Once he's handed it over, he tells me it's twelve dollars.

I laugh. "Are you serious? I thought drinks were half off tonight"

He just looks at me, so I dig into my bag for my wallet.

"I've got it."

The voice has my hand freezing and my head flying up, finding the brown eyes that I've been so enjoying looking into ever since I saw them for the first time a few weeks ago.

"Gotcha. I'll add it to your tab," the bartender says, then he's gone before I can even try to pay for it myself.

Wyatt steps closer to me, leans down to whisper in my ear. "Drinks are on me tonight. We're celebrating."

"What are we celebrating," I ask, loving the way it feels to have him standing so close to me.

He shrugs. "Every day is a reason to celebrate, Hannah. And right now, I'm celebrating that Paige was able to get you to come out tonight."

I can't help but grin, my traitorous face surely revealing how much I enjoy his flirtation.

Because it *is* flirting. Even his speech about friendship last week couldn't mask the way his eyes are looking at me right now.

And I'm reveling in it.

"Done any more running recently?" I ask, taking a sip of my drink as we move along the edge of the crowded dance floor until we've found a place against a wall with a tall table to set our drinks.

It's been two days since our impromptu buddy run back from the end of The Strand, and I'd be lying if I said I hadn't thought about running past his house again to see if he wanted to try it a second time.

Or to see if we could go swimming in his pool again.

God, he'd look so hot without his shirt on. With the water rushing in drops down his chest when he climbed out. That sexy tattoo of a lion and a shield that covers bicep.

Monday had been a fun afternoon. Mostly because the more Wyatt and I interact, the more it feels like we're circling something. Or if I try to use a sports analogy, two hockey players waiting for the puck to drop before we crash into each other.

Though I envision the crashing part looking a lot sexier, a lot less violent and with a lot less clothing.

He kept finding ways to touch me. Little things. Things I always made sure to smile about, to make sure he knew I was okay with it. Especially after I freaked out the first few times.

Wyatt is slowly making his way into the zone of permission, with only a handful of other people. The people I trust, that I allow to see me without any kind of guard up.

And I'm glad. Because in this new place, I need someone else on this side of that wall. Otherwise, I'm sure it'll just get super lonely.

Wyatt laughs, and I'm again reminded that seeing happiness on his face is one of the most beautiful things I've ever seen.

He's normally so broody, his expressions so serious. This

smile and happiness and relaxation is so startlingly different that I can't help but join in, giggling alongside him.

"Definitely no more running for me yesterday or today," he says. "My legs were killing me and this morning I could barely roll out of bed."

"Bummer. I was hoping you'd wanna go with me again."

He leans towards me. "Just tell me the time and where to meet you. I'll go with you anytime."

I smile at his words, pleased in some odd way that he'd be willing to suffer through physical pain again to go running with me.

Then I see the underlying heat in his eyes and I flush, recognizing the latent sexual undertone in his words.

Did he mean running? Or something else?

Taking another sip of my drink, I let my eyes glance around. "I'm assuming if you have a tab here that you come here pretty regularly?"

He nods, his eyes staying focused on me, completely unconcerned with what's happening around us.

"Paige's family owns The Wave," he says.

"Of *course* they do." I laugh. "Because no one here can just have a normal job and live in an apartment."

His brow furrows. "Does it bother you?"

I sigh, not wanting to seem like a Debbie Downer. "Sorry, I wasn't trying to... I just... I'm not upset that Lucas and all of you guys have a lot. I just feel like an outsider sometimes. Like it's hard to relate when life has just been so different for me. I felt that way all growing up and I guess I'd just hoped to feel differently here."

Wyatt's eyes flit between mine, and I see him clench his jaw before he turns and looks out at the dance floor. "Are you happy here?" he asks, not looking at me. "In Hermosa, with Lucas and at your job?"

I chuckle quietly. "That's the question, right? That's always the question. Are you happy?" I chew on my straw for a second. "I mean, I'm not *un*happy. I'm spending some time with a brother I didn't know about and I have a roof over my head and a job that pays me pretty decently." I shrug, watching a couple near us spin and dip together with the music. "What's there not to be happy about?"

Wyatt scoots closer to me, his hip pressed against mine as we both gaze out at the dance floor.

This feels like a much more serious conversation than should be had in a club. But somehow we've found ourselves in this corner, huddled together, talking about things that are deeper than gossip and drama and who did what with who.

"Do you ever wonder if you might not allow yourself to be happy?"

His question startles me, and I look up into his eyes. They're darker than normal, filled with something I don't understand. It feels like he's looking inside of me, that he can see my deepest fears and emotions and the pain that I can't ever really, *truly* seem to get rid of.

"You deserve it, you know. Happiness." His eyes search mine, probe for answers to questions he's never asked me. "And I think you might have told yourself somewhere along the line that you don't."

I can't help the shuddered breath that I take, the wave of emotion rushing into my chest and pushing goose bumps up along the skin on my arms.

Wyatt reaches up and tucks a strand of hair behind my right ear, his fingers trailing lightly down the side of my neck, leaving a ripple of goose bumps in their wake.

"And if I know anything about you," he adds, his hand holding me lightly at the side of my neck, his fingers singeing my skin, "it's that you're probably deserving of an amazingly happy life more than most people I know."

Wyatt steps closer to me and I can't help when my eyes drop to his mouth. To the soft lips that I'd love nothing more than to feel pressed to mine.

He pulls me into him, the length of his tall, strong frame pressed against me, and he wraps me in his arms. A full body hug, one like I've never felt before.

His face tucks into the space between my cheek and my shoulder, and he slowly brushes his stubble along my neck.

My body shivers, and then I feel him press a light kiss against my skin. Hear him inhale. Hold back a moan when his hand squeezes my hip.

He stays like that for longer than should seem normal, not doing anything else, not moving. Just existing in my space, me existing in his, our bodies pressed deliciously together to the point that I can feel his muscles flexing and giving as I remain in his arms.

But it doesn't feel anything *but* normal. My body wants him close, in my space, smelling my neck, licking my skin. As close to me as possible.

And I've never had that before. Never wanted to invite a man into my personal space. Never felt this desire to have someone so close to me.

Sure, there have been the men who disregard how I feel and do what they want. But Wyatt is the first that has been welcomed. That I *want* to stay near me.

He smells really good, a sort of woody cinnamon cologne that screams *expensive* and *man* and *lust*.

That's the only thing I can assume this feeling is. This sudden burst of something racing around my body, hardening my nipples and making me feel slick between my legs.

Gone are the previous emotions, the small ripple of sadness I'd felt at our conversation. In its place is an aching desire to be held, to be pulled closer, if that's even possible.

Which is why I nearly moan the loss when he pulls back, steps away. I have to tell myself to let go from where my hands were gripping the cotton of his shirt.

"Let's dance," he says, and I nod, following him almost blindly out to the dance floor, leaving my twelve dollar drink behind without a care.

Once we get to the middle, I feel awkward, like I don't know what to do with my hands or how to stand and I suddenly can't remember how to dance at all.

But Wyatt just gives me a smile and pulls me close, his hands at my hips and my arms wrapped loosely at his neck. We sway a little, and he takes the lead as the music thrums and pulses around us, a popular R&B song with a deep bass.

We dance like that for a little bit, eye-to-eye, hip to hip. And then at some point, I gain my confidence back. Remember all the times I've wanted to go out and dance with a boy that I like, imagined what I'd do to drive him crazy.

And I take hold of that girl I wish I could be, sometimes, and I allow the sips of alcohol to fuel that little bit of confidence.

My hands stroke along his shoulders, down his arms, my hips rotating and rolling, and then I grip Wyatt tightly at the hips and press into him, feeling a thrill of satisfaction when his eyes drop to half-mast and a small groan comes from his lips.

I bite my lip and do it again, and Wyatt follows my lead, our bodies finding a rhythm that's overtly sexual, feels slightly deviant, but feeds a fire inside of me that I need stoked.

When the song changes, I turn around, press my back into him, feel his strong arms pulling me closer as I grind us together.

I can feel his length pressed against me from behind. He's hard, and I set my hands on his knees and drop slightly, then slide my body up against his waist, pushing my ass into him, enjoying the way his hands tighten on me, the puff of air that hits my neck, a moan I can't hear.

Before I can do it again, before I can continue this bit of seduction that has me feeling sultry and sexy even in my slight cluelessness, he throws a wrench in my game.

Wyatt spins me around, both of his hands coming to either side of my face, and then he presses his lips to mine.

I need no coaxing, my mouth opening to tangle my tongue with his, to invite him in. We're both covered in a sheen of sweat, the dance floor hot and filled with bodies, and I love the way it feels when his hand drops to my lower back and under my shirt, pressing against my damp skin. Stroking lightly, a soft, teasing caress, that sends goose bumps up my back.

He wants me closer, and it's all I want, too.

But as he continues to kiss me, the only thing I can focus on is wanting to touch and taste and pull him into my skin. Under my skin. Inside of my body.

Even over the loud music I can feel him moan, hear it in the pant of his breath.

I feel lost in him, unable to focus on anything but the way his body feels under my hands, the firm body, the ridges of muscle, the sweaty skin, warm and soft and hard at the same time.

He pulls away and grabs my hand, dragging me off the dance floor and back over to the corner we were in before. Presses me up against a wall and leans in, his lips coming to mine again.

It feels like I can't get enough air, but it's the best way to lose my breath, and I gasp slightly when his face moves down to my neck and his hand travels down to grip my thigh.

He lifts my leg just slightly, pressing himself against me, and I moan, loving the way he feels, the sensations in my body growing, feeling too big.

Too overwhelming.

Like he might be able to set me off just from the erotic feel of him rubbing against me.

I grab onto him, desperate to find something to ground me because with each kiss and roll of his hips I feel like I'm being launched into the air and don't know when I'll come back down.

And in an uncharacteristically forward move, I bite his lip, my teeth sinking into the soft skin.

He jerks back slightly, looking stunned.

And I almost apologize, my own expression surely mimicking his.

Until I see a dirty smile stretch across his face.

"Fuck, Hannah."

It's all he says before he dives into my mouth again, his own teeth pulling slightly, a hand moving between us and up to a breast, giving soft squeezes and tracing over a spot that makes me ache at my very center.

I feel so lost in Wyatt, so focused on how it feels to be pressed against him, that I don't realize at first that someone has said my name.

It's only when Wyatt pulls back and looks over his shoulder that I start to come out of the spell I've been put under. That's when I see Paige standing behind him with a huge grin on her face.

"Lucas is looking for you," she says. Then she winks and scurries off.

I can't help it. I laugh. I giggle because I have all of this pent up sexual tension in my body and it has nowhere to go except outward.

Wyatt grins at me, clears his throat, slides his hand along the area on my neck that's slick from where he'd been kissing and sucking.

"We might've gotten a little carried away, huh?" I ask, unable to hide the joy that feels like it's bubbling under my skin, dying to be released into the wild. "That was a little wild."

But Wyatt shakes his head as I tuck my hair behind my ears, then steps into me one more time to whisper, "If you think that was wild, I can't wait to see what you think when I have you beneath me."

My stomach bottoms out, my chest feeling like a cave of

nerves as he pulls back to look me in the eyes. It's amazing how he can make me feel by only uttering a few words.

I giggle slightly, then press a soft kiss to his lips. "I'm going to the bathroom and then to find Lucas. I'll see you back at the table?"

My words seem to be a douse of cold water. His expression loses some of the heat and he nods, pressing his lips to mine once more before we wander through the crowd, parting ways when I head into the bathroom.

As I'm washing my hands, I look at myself in the mirror.

The flush in my cheeks, the sparkle in my eye, the smile on my face. I look like a woman who is truly enjoying herself. Enjoying her life.

I love seeing her smiling back at me.

But as I approach the VIP section and our few tables come into view, my smile falls when I see Wyatt and Lucas.

They're in an argument, and I can't hear what they're saying, but I see my name form on Lucas' lips a few times. He stops when he sees me approaching, but it does nothing to lessen his frustration.

Over what, I can only guess.

"Everything okay?" I ask, sliding next to them and trying to give an unaffected smile, but surely failing.

They eye each other for a minute, and I feel some sort of alpha male aggressiveness brooding between them. A tension that radiates outward from Lucas.

"Wyatt and I were just talking about his sister," Lucas bites out.

I look back and forth between them.

"Is everything okay with Ivy?" I ask, still feeling confused, but also concerned that something's wrong with the adorable girl that I'm quickly becoming a fan of.

Finally, Wyatt takes a step back, his shoulders dropping.

He looks at me. "She's fine. But I need to head home. I forgot I have some plans tomorrow."

I nod. "Okay."

Wyatt rests a hand on Lucas' shoulder. "We're on the same team," he says. "I *promise* you."

He grabs his jacket from one of the chairs, then steps over to me.

"I'll call you soon," he says, leaning in to kiss me on the cheek, before heading through the crowd and out the door.

I don't realize my eyes track him the entire way until Lucas says my name.

I look back in his direction, still feeling a little lost when I see the tight smile on his face.

"Let's have a drink," he says.

I nod and walk with him back to the table, wondering what I'm missing.

And whether I'll ever find out.

Chapter Eighteen

HANNAH

I wake to a knock at my bedroom door.

Stretching my sore muscles, I roll over and glance at the clock on the wall, seeing that it's still pretty early.

"Come in," I say, my voice sleepy and slightly muffled by the pillow my face is still pressed into.

I didn't realize how exhausted I would be. Working a double shift, staying at The Wave until almost two o'clock, and then walking and biking home? I didn't fall into bed until way past my normal bed time, and it is *far* too early for me to be getting up.

But I'm pretty sure it's Lucas on the other side of that door. And if he's knocking this early, something's going on.

"Morning," he says, holding two cups of coffee.

Of course he stayed out way later than I did and he looks like he got ten hours of sleep.

Asshole.

"Hey," I say, sitting up slowly and pulling my rat's nest of hair up into a messy knot at the top of my head. "What's up?"

"Just checking in. Thought you might like some coffee." He hands me a cup, then takes a seat on the edge of my bed.

Not a big coffee person, I just hold the mug in my hands in silence while Lucas takes a sip from his.

"Did you have fun last night?' he asks.

I nod. "Yeah."

"You left pretty quickly."

To be honest, I'm surprised he noticed I left at all.

After he and Wyatt argued, Lucas returned to his table and started doing shots. Within a half hour, he was pretty hammered, so I left.

"I'm surprised you noticed," I mumble, then cringe, instantly regretting it. "I'm sorry. I shouldn't have said that. I..."

"Hannah, it's okay. I deserve that." He sighs, sets his mug down on my nightstand and rubs the stubble growing on his face. "I wanted you to come out last night and then I got into it with Wyatt and got drunk. I should have paid more attention to you."

I shake my head. "You don't have to coddle me, okay? I really was just tired and I figured if you were going to be busy, it would just be better if I went home."

"Well, I'm glad you got home okay. You took an Uber or something?"

I reach over and set my mug of untouched coffee on the nightstand. "No. I walked back to the pier and got my bike and then rode home."

Lucas' expression morphs into a scowl. "You did what?"

Reading his sudden anger, I stay silent.

"Don't *ever* do that again. The pier is not safe after midnight. Anyone still lurking around is either plastered at one of the bars or homeless."

Then it's my turn to glower. "You know, homeless people aren't usually dangerous, and saying stuff like that doesn't help."

His expression softens. "Hannah..."

"Did I tell you that I lived in a homeless shelter for a year?"

Lucas grits his jaw and looks down at his hands.

"When I was fifteen, I was assaulted by one of my foster dads. When I got relocated to a new home, one of the girls there made my life a living hell, so I alternated between sleeping at a shelter, crashing on the back porch at my friend Sienna's and using the hammocks at the YMCA. That's the year everyone started calling me Homeless Hannah."

When he looks up at me, I can't read his expression. But I *can* tell that he's pained by what he hears. This isn't simple empathy, or commiserating about a troubled past.

Lucas is upset.

"You never know what someone's circumstances are, and assuming the worst won't ever get you anywhere you want to be."

He lets out a sigh and twists his hands together. "I'm sorry you went through that."

"It's not your fault, Lucas. It's just life."

He gives a small shake of his head, though he stays silent.

I feel bad for continuing to share little bits of my life with Lucas. It clearly upsets him on a much deeper level than I was expecting. Sometimes I wonder if I should lie about my past. Make it sound fluffier, more filled with fun times and not so riddled with pain.

But then I think about the girl who had to go through those experiences, the younger me, who felt like she never had a voice, and I just can't give in to society's expectation that she stays silent.

So if a moment comes up where something painful needs to be talked about? I need to do it.

For her.

"I have to work today. But do you want to come meet me after my shift? We could do another bike ride or something."

Lucas wrinkles his nose. "I'm surfing in a charity event for the holiday weekend," he says. "That's what I was coming to tell you. I have to drive up to Malibu with Otto. I'm leaving at around noon and I'll be back Tuesday morning."

"Oh," I say, my shoulders dropping even as I try to hide my disappointment. "Okay."

"Do you want to come with?"

But I'm already shaking my head. "I can't. I have to work all weekend. Hamish said there are no exceptions."

"You don't need that job, you know."

I glare at him and he gives me a soft smile.

"God, you're so stubborn. And *so* independent."

"I'm glad you're finally grasping that."

He laughs, nods his head, then stands and heads for the door, but turns and looks at the mug on my nightstand.

"Do you not like coffee?" he asks.

I give him a small smile and scrunch up my nose. "Not really."

"What's your morning drink, then?"

I lift a shoulder. "Juice. Or tea."

"Ah, so *that's* why I keep finding tea bags in the trash. I thought maybe Thalia was sneaking into my Earl Grey, but it's you."

I smile. "Definitely me."

Lucas takes one more sip of his coffee. "I'll drive you to work today. That way I can say bye before I go." He pauses. "You sure you're going to be okay here by yourself this weekend."

"Yeah. I'm a big girl, you know. I've handled worse things than what will probably be a bunch of loud drunk people on The Strand."

He smiles, but it doesn't meet his eyes. "When I get back, we'll spend more time together. I know you said you don't want to be coddled, and I promise that's not what I'm doing. I just... sometimes I get distracted. I really have been meaning to spend more time with you."

"Lucas, you have a life," I say, lifting a shoulder in a shrug. It's the one thing I've been reminding myself whenever I've felt a little hurt at how little time we've actually spent together in the handful of weeks that I've been living here. "I wasn't expecting you to be available to me 24/7. I love that I've been invited to hang out with your friends a few times."

He gives me a nod. "Well, I'm going to make sure I have a different kind of schedule when I come back, okay?" He steps forward and gives me a brotherly kiss on the crown of my head, a new gesture of affection that has me smiling in its wake.

"Let me know when you're ready to leave for work," he says, then leaves the room, shutting the door softly as he goes.

I stare after him, my eyes still focused on the door long after he's gone.

Sometimes, Lucas can be these two completely different people. Like last night. He'd seemed so distant. Drunk, which is one of my least favorite things.

And then there are other times when he seems like this really genuine guy with all these emotions he doesn't know how to deal with. Like he was never taught how to process and feel and that it's okay to be upset and cry and be disappointed.

Not everything has to be a party.
Not everything has to be a great time.
That's not how life works.

I snuggle back into my bed, staring at the ceiling. Maybe another hour of sleep will help me deal with whatever else is going on in my brain.

Lucas drops me off at work with a hug and a promise to check in with me over the weekend, wanting to make sure I'm okay being in the house alone.

Part of me delights in the fact that he's being protective. It's a component of my soul that didn't get nurtured as I grew older and had a good amount of freedom because no one was paying attention.

However, the pieces of me that are very much an almost twenty-two-year-old adult is *not* a fan of his nosiness.

So I shoo him off on his trip with assurances that I'll text him if there are any problems.

Then I get to work. A long, grueling shift that's proving Hamish's predictions about an overwhelmingly busy holiday weekend to be true.

And it's only Thursday. I can only imagine what the rest of the weekend will look like. And I'll definitely know at some point since I've been scheduled to work shifts on Friday, Saturday, Sunday *and* Monday.

I'm just hopeful that the tips will make up for the exhaustion I'm surely going to be feeling soon.

It isn't until I get off that I realize I have a text from Wyatt.

And I also can't help the stupid smile on my face when I remember what it was like to press against him, to want him closer.

Wyatt: How's your day going?

It's simple and short. And I'm sure a teenage me would have obsessed over it for hours before responding to make sure just the right thing was said.

But this version of me is tired of bullshit and doesn't play games the way most girls do.

So I flick off a quick reply.

Me: Long. Split shift. Just got off. You?

Heading out to the back, I reach my bike just as I hear a motorcycle coming up behind me. I look over, smiling as Wyatt's very fancy, very loud bike rolls up next to where I stand.

Then he cuts the engine, drops the kickstand, and pulls off his helmet.

If I could swoon, I would. Because seeing him yank off his helmet, then toss his head and run a hand through his hair? It's the stuff you see in movies.

And then he gives me that grin. The heart-stopping one. The heart-pounding one.

The thrill of being near him rushes through my body.

"I texted you a few hours ago, you know," he says, his voice teasing and playful. "Should I take offense that you haven't gotten back to me yet?"

"No, don't, I didn't see it," I reply, then flush. "I mean, I just responded to you."

He nods. Sets his helmet on his leg and rests an arm on top of it. "You free tonight?"

I grin.

"That's why I was checking in. I wanna take you on a night ride." And then he reaches back and unclips a second helmet from the back of his bike with the ease of someone who knows what he's doing. "You in?"

"Absolutely," I reply, no hesitation as I take the helmet from his hands. I push it on my head, tuck my plastic bike helmet into my backpack, and climb on behind Wyatt, this time with a bit more grace than last time he gave me a ride.

I might seem overly eager. But I'm not entirely sure that I care. At least not enough to change how I respond to him.

I snuggle in close, my hands holding him tight on his stomach, and press my body flush against his. I love feeling the warmth of him, that feeling of body heat that no blanket or pillow or heater can replicate.

He turns the engine on, or whatever he does, and then we roll slowly down the alley, out towards the main street.

"Hold on, sweetheart," he calls back to me, giving my hands around his waist a light tap. And then he revs the engine and pulls onto Hermosa Ave, beginning our journey to wherever he's planning to take us.

We spend a while driving along the water, a long stretch of road that takes us up the coast, under the planes leaving from and landing at LAX. When we hit a dead end, we turn and head down new stretch of road, though this one is much busier.

I know I should be watching as we ride, taking in the scenes, the Los Angeles nightlife. But I can't help it when I rest my head against his back and close my eyes, just enjoying the feeling of being pressed together.

Eventually, we come to a final stop and I'm forced to open my eyes and look around.

I laugh, pulling off my helmet.

"Donuts."

"Yup."

"We drove for thirty minutes so you could take me to get donuts."

"The best donuts."

"Ah, well... see, you should have led with the word 'best' and I would have nodded in understanding," I tease.

He smiles and helps me climb off his bike.

"So where are we, anyway?"

"Santa Monica. We drove through Venice Beach on our way here."

"Oh yeah, I've heard of Venice," I say as we get closer to the pretty pink building that looks to be filled with an absolutely obscene amount of sugar. "That's the place with all the crazies, right?"

He chuckles. "Yes, though it really is a fun place to spend a day. The big cities along the coast are Hermosa, Marina Del Rey, Venice, Santa Monica, and then there's a bit of a stretch until you hit Malibu."

"Hey, that's where Lucas is."

Wyatt pauses. "What?"

"Lucas went to Malibu this weekend. He's surfing in a charity event."

He nods and opens the door for me, and I'm assaulted by the

delicious smell. Our conversation halts as we bend over and peruse the offerings. I'm tempted to buy a dozen, but I know I'll have no way of taking any of them home, and eating them all tonight just isn't an option. So I settle on two. A long, twisty maple bar, and a round chocolate covered in coconut. Wyatt grabs a huge bear claw and a coffee.

Then we head to the tables in the back, a little courtyard with overhead fairy lights and wooden benches. It's a quirky little place, and I love it.

"So what's your plan for the weekend?" Wyatt asks, ripping the paper bag open so our donuts have a makeshift plate. "With Lucas gone, I mean."

I lift a shoulder and pick up the maple bar. "It doesn't really matter. I work the entire weekend, so I wouldn't have been able to do anything fun anyways."

Then I take a bite of my donut, the tasty maple and sugary sweetness hitting my tongue in a burst. I close my eyes on a moan. "Oh god, Wyatt. This is amazing."

I open my eyes again and find him frozen, his eyes heated as he watches me.

"Sorry. I'm a loud eater."

He smirks, then bites into his own pastry. He nods as he chews, letting out his own noise of appreciation, then sets it down and reaches over to take a sip of his coffee.

"So what do you do, Wyatt?" I say, pulling another piece of donut off and popping it into my mouth. "Where do you work?"

He holds his cup loosely between his fingers. "Well, I used to work for a startup business in San Francisco. But recently, I've actually started working for Otto's company."

I shake my head. "I didn't know he had a company."

Wyatt's eyebrows lift. "Oh really? He and Lucas are business partners. I just thought you would have known."

I laugh. "Lucas and I have been trying to get to know each other, but there's still a lot we haven't gotten to yet."

He nods.

"So what is it?" I stretch my legs out below the table. "The company, I mean."

"It's called Elite X. It's a social club."

I laugh. "I have no idea what that even means."

Wyatt smiles over the brim of his coffee cup. "It just means we get people together to do stuff that they're all interested in doing. Otto calls it 'curated experiences'. That's what the X stands for. But I guess the best way to explain it is that people pay us to give them an awesome time. We do group functions, like whiskey tasting at an exclusive club. Or small gatherings with celebrities. But we're looking into expanding into travel experiences, because that's what the market is looking like right now. And that's where I come in."

"What's a travel experience?"

He takes another bite of his bear claw, then licks his lips, my eyes drawn to the motion. "So, an example of something we might offer is a Wine at Night Tour through Italy. People who go on our tours will visit places that are normally crowded with tourists during the day, but they will get an exclusive tour and wine tasting at night."

My mouth drops open. "Oh my gosh, Wyatt. That is *so* cool. So what do *you* actually do?"

"I just started working with them, even though I've been involved with it since it was a start up. I'm moving to London at the end of the summer to find partners. Basically, I'll be setting up the international part. Hiring people, finding the locations and special experiences people will want." He shrugs, like that doesn't sound like one of the coolest jobs ever.

"And you know how to do all that? God, I can't even imagine where to begin."

Wyatt smiles. "I have a business degree from UC Berkeley. It's one of the reasons I decided to head up to San Francisco recently. It was a bit of a vacation, but also an opportunity to work for my friend's company, get a little bit of the experience I needed for this next step, which Otto has been planning for a while."

"That's amazing."

Instead of acknowledging my compliment, he takes another sip of his coffee, then offers it to me. "Want some?"

I shake my head. "No, I'm not really a coffee person. It tastes like dirt to me."

He laughs, his head falling back, his deep chuckle echoing in the quiet area behind the donut shop. "Of course you're not into coffee."

"Is that a bad thing?"

He shakes his head. "No. But you're definitely not like other girls."

My smile slips just a smidge. I can't help it. I wonder if there will ever be a time when something like that doesn't bother me. When someone saying that I'm not like everyone else will sound like the compliment it probably is.

But instead, all I can hear is *you don't fit in, again.*

"Hey, what did I say?" he asks, his expression concerned.

I shake my head. "Nothing."

He rests his hand over mine on the table. "Hannah."

I sigh. "It really isn't anything. It's just... when you say that. About me not being like other girls. I just have a complex about it. I'm trying not to, because I know you probably meant it as a compliment or something, just like Paige and Lucas have when they've said things like that, but..." I shrug. "I spent my entire life not fitting in and I'm just ready for that not to be the case anymore."

Wyatt watches me as I share this with him, his eyes unreadable.

I tilt my head back and look up at the sky through the fairy lights. "Sorry. I didn't mean to be a Debbie Downer about..."

"Hannah."

I drop back to look at him.

"You're not being a downer. You're being real. And I appreciate that. I really do." He pauses, looks down at his half-eaten bear claw. "I used to feel like I didn't belong either. Has Lucas told you that Ben and I were adopted?"

My mouth opens a little bit in surprise.

Wyatt laughs. "I'll take that as a no. Yeah, we were babies, given to my parents by two high school teenagers that weren't in love and were just too young. I've always known. It was never a secret. But for years, I wondered if I would fit anywhere without understanding where I come from."

He picks his coffee back up, probably to do something with his hands more than anything else, because he doesn't drink from it.

"So when I was thirteen, I went in search of them. Wanted to see them through my own eyes. Ask the questions every adopted kid wants to ask. But when I got there, I chickened out. Came straight back home."

"That's not chickening out, Wyatt," I say, reaching forward and resting a hand on his wrist. "You were a kid. It was so brave of you to try and get answers. To want to understand a past you might have had if things had been different."

He swallows, and his nose flares. The emotion he's feeling right now is so deep, so strong. "Is that how you feel about your own past?" he asks. "What things would have been like if life hadn't been so... unfair?"

I puff air out of my nose, an awkward non-laugh at such a serious question. "I try not to think about what life would have been like if my parents had lived. But I do wonder about Joshua. I had an older brother, and he died when I was twelve." I swallow, something thick and tasting sourly of guilt making the next words hard to voice. "He died in an accident at work, one of three jobs he had because he was trying to make enough money to get custody of me."

The final words I voice come out slightly choked. "And I feel all this guilt," I add, closing my eyes and trying to hold back the flood of tears at voicing it like this for the first time. "Because if it hadn't been for me, maybe he would have gone to college or met a girl and gotten married, and then I'd have nieces and nephews and my brother..."

A tear falls then. A streak of wetness trailing a path of pain down my cheek.

"And now I have this *new* brother and I really like him and I'm afraid that I'm diminishing Joshua's memory, or that I'm replacing him in some way."

And then I burst into tears, the wave of emotions that I've been feeling for weeks as I've adjusted to this new life in a new town with new people coming forward in a rush.

I haven't had anyone to talk to about this. About all of this newness that makes my life feel so different.

That makes me feel so small.

"I'm sorry," I whisper, my eyes still closed as I try to wipe away the wetness on my cheeks.

I'm so embarrassed. I don't know if this is a date or not, but I'm pretty sure bursting into tears isn't something most men want to see from the girl they're spending time with.

Suddenly I feel a warm body settle in next to me on the bench, arms pulling me into the warmth, wrapping me snug and holding me close.

"You have nothing to be sorry for," he whispers into my ear, his words holding their own thread of emotions. "Nothing at all."

I take advantage of his nearness, tuck my body firmly into his where he offers it, enjoy the feeling of being embraced by someone who wants to ease my fears, lessen my pain, soften my suffering.

His hands rest softly against me, one lightly at the nape of my neck, the other caressing up and down my spine in soothing repetition.

It's a beautiful thing when you learn to accept love in its varying forms. And while I wouldn't say Wyatt loves me, I would say that he cares enough to want to make sure I feel loved in this moment.

Loved and not alone.

"I'm so embarrassed," I whisper as he slowly rocks us both, the movement soothing. "I keep wanting to cry around you."

He chuckles. "As long as I'm not the one who makes you cry, it's fine, sweetheart." He just continues to hold me, rubbing my back occasionally. And then he adds, barely loud enough for me to hear, "I promise, I never want to make you cry."

Eventually, my tears subside. I pull back and look at Wyatt, surprised to find a host of pain in his eyes. He reaches forward and rests and hand on my jaw, his thumb stroking across my cheek.

"I'm sorry I dumped everything on you," I say, my voice soft and still tinged with embarrassment. "I haven't really had anyone to talk to since I got here, and..."

"You don't have to apologize," he says. "I'm sure holding all of that in was exhausting."

I nod.

"Sometimes, when you're tired, getting it all out means your body can finally rest."

I nod again. "That's so true. I feel like I could take a two-day power nap right now."

He smiles, his eyes flitting over my face as his hand tucks hair behind my ears. "Then let's get you home, sweetheart."

We collect our uneaten goodies and wrap them up in the mangled paper bag, then put it into my backpack.

Wyatt takes my hand as we head through the donut shop and back out to the front. I like the feel of my hand in his. Warm. Safe. It's not a feeling I'm overly familiar with, but I'll take as much of it as I can get.

When we pull up out front of Lucas' a little while later, I

expect to just hop off and head inside. But Wyatt parks his bike, turns off the engine, and takes my hand, then walks me to the door.

It's a sweet gesture, something that reminds me of the dates I might have had in high school.

"I really like spending time with you," he says, looking down at where his hand is holding mine.

I smile. "Me too."

He looks at me with affection, a sweet expression that makes me feel so adored in this moment. "You work a lunch shift tomorrow, right?"

I nod.

"Can I take you to dinner tomorrow night? I want to spend more time with you."

I chew on the inside of my cheek, trying not to show how much I enjoy hearing those words. "Definitely."

But then he gives me a big smile, one similar to how I feel inside, and it eases something in my chest. Something that feels slightly embarrassed at how quickly he has become someone of significant importance in my life.

Wyatt lifts his hands and places them on either side of my face, his thumbs softly caressing my cheeks.

It makes me feel small, but not in the way I usually feel in the hands of someone else. He makes me feel precious, treasured, like I'm something priceless that he needs to protect.

And it's one of the most beautiful things I've ever felt.

Chapter Nineteen
WYATT

I park the Escalade outside of Lucas' house and shut off the engine. Then I take a moment to sit in silence.

Hannah and I are going out to dinner tonight. I made reservations at a place called Papa Louis', a little Italian place one town over that only has a dozen tables but makes the most delicious garlic bread I've ever had.

I know I'm doing exactly what Lucas warned me about a few days ago at The Wave. He'd gotten right in my face, reminded me what was at stake, told me I was thinking with my dick and that Hannah deserved better than that.

At first, I'd thought he meant that I was using her in the wrong way, and it pissed me off. But then I realized he just didn't want me to use her more than I need to. That Lucas is starting to care deeply about her, is starting to feel that protective big brother emotion that doesn't want some guy - any guy - sniffing around his sister.

So, feeling that little niggling bit of guilt at his words, I left.

But I can't help myself when it comes to Hannah. I feel drawn to her, on a visceral level. I love when she smiles. I love *making* her smile.

And that's my plan tonight. Get her to enjoy herself as much as possible.

Because the Hannah I experienced last night? The one who feels partly responsible for Joshua's death? The one who has guilt in her heart about caring about her new brother, and struggles with feeing lost in this town?

I want to help make sure she doesn't feel those things.

Somewhere between meeting her at the Pier and holding her while she cried, this thing with Hannah became less about persuading *her* to give something and more about *showing* her what she deserves.

The promise of happiness and a place she belongs.

Maybe I can confirm that for her.

Though I can't help but battle with the constant reminder looming in the back of my mind of what's to come.

A storm.

And I wonder if we'll make it through the aftermath.

When I finally head to the front and punch in the code at the gate to enter into the enclosed courtyard, I start to feel date nerves, something I haven't had in a really fucking long time.

Then, I knock at the door. Watch through the frosted glass as Hannah's form moves closer and closer to where I stand waiting.

She pulls the door open and my smile falls.

My eyes eat up everything I can see, because *damn*.

"Is this too fancy?" she asks, turning once. "Paige helped me get ready and I borrowed this from her because I definitely don't have any date clothes. She said this was good for anything."

I nod, feeling a bit stunted for words.

Because, again.

Damn.

Hannah is beautiful. Breathtaking. One of the sexiest sights my eyes have ever laid on.

"You look..." I trail off, trying to decide what word to use. Amazing seems too small. Beautiful, too basic. "... stunning," I finally say. Because the truth is, I'm stunned.

She looks like a dream in her black work pants and maroon

polo, sweaty with her hair up in a ponytail.

Tonight?

Her long hair is down, falling softly in waves and curls until it hits below her breasts. She has on just a hint of makeup, the deep red on her lips popping out and grabbing my attention. Her outfit is a similar color, layers of lace on a haltered dress that cuts off mid-thigh, showing off her long legs. And then a heel that pushes her up several inches.

I step forward, realizing I've been silent too long as I've just stared at her. And when I'm inches from her, I can see that those heels put her much closer to my height, making it that much easier to dip down and press a kiss to her lips.

Which I do.

Because how could I not?

My intent is for a light peck, maybe a long one. But what starts that way twists into some deeper, more lustful, and my body responds as she opens her mouth and invites me in, moans softly, her soft tongue pressing wet and warm against mine until I can feel my dick press angrily against her thigh.

I pull back and enjoy a feeling of satisfaction when she looks bereft at the loss of my mouth on hers. Because I feel the same way.

"So you like the dress?" she asks.

I laugh, look at her for a second, just enjoying her. "Yes. It's amazing."

She blushes, and I take her by the hand, twisting my fingers into hers and leading her out to my car.

"I wasn't sure where we were going so..."

"It's perfect."

Fifteen minutes later, I've parked down the street from Papa Louis' and the two of us are walking hand-in-hand past the little shops and restaurants that line Manhattan Ave.

"I have to say, I love how cute these beach cities are," she says, stopping in front of a little coffee shop that's open, comfortable seating spread throughout, with people working on their computers and talking in groups. "Phoenix isn't like this. It's just so big and everything feels spread out and metropolitan." She looks up at me. "Things feel personal here. Like you could know the people who work at the place around the corner or the people that live next door."

I nod as we keep walking. "It's kind of like that, if you take the time to get to know people. It's the same with neighbors, too."

"You know all your neighbors?"

I shake my head. "Not anymore. But that's because I haven't lived here for a while. But when I was a kid, we lived on The Strand. Before my parents bought the land for our current house. We knew all of our neighbors back then. We used to live next to this guy who had a bunch of huge white dogs. They were like polar bears. And he threw parties that were more insane than the ones Lucas has."

She laughs. "No way. That's not possible. I saw one of those a few weeks ago, and I can't imagine anything bigger than that."

"I'm serious. He doesn't do them as much anymore since he's gotten older, but we still see him walking those dogs up and down The Strand every day."

"I knew some of my neighbors once," she says. "When I moved into my first foster home. It was the one I was at the longest, and the neighbors used to do bar-b-ques all the time and all the kids on the block would hang out and do fun stuff together. I loved it, as much as I could. How normal it felt."

We come to a stop in front of Papa Louis' and greet the hostess, then are shown quickly to our table.

"How was work today?" I ask, picking up my napkin and setting it across my knee.

She rolls her eyes but gives a little smile. I love seeing those lighthearted expressions on her face.

"It was fine. Busy. I was actually worried I wouldn't get off in time to get home and get ready for tonight. But everything worked out perfectly." She takes a sip of her water. "What did you get up to today?"

I lift a shoulder. "Just did a little bit of work to prepare for the trip to London. There are a lot of things that have to be set up before I leave, so..."

"When *do* you leave?"

"It's up to me. Otto has a timeline for Elite X's expansion, so as long as I leave by the end of the summer I'll able to meet it."

"That's so exciting. I've never been out of the country, but I've always dreamed of going somewhere beautiful, like Paris or Dublin, to live for a while."

"You definitely should. It's really amazing."

But she's already shaking her head. "Nah. It's probably not in the cards for me. Maybe one day I'll be able to take a trip."

"How come you didn't do a semester abroad in college?"

There's a pause, and she flushes slightly, though this time isn't as satisfying as it seems to be more from embarrassment.

"I've only been able to take some classes here and there. Mostly I just had a waitressing job. Nothing important. But I'm hoping to eventually get my AA."

I adjust my napkin on my knee, realizing in an awkward moment that I've had all of this information about Hannah Morrison's entire life, and I've never thought to look at it more in-depth since she got here.

Though, I guess, it makes our conversations more natural than if I'd known everything about her recent life. And significantly less creepy. I make a promise to myself that I'll leave that folder in my office drawer and not look at it again.

But somehow, even with having looked at it even as recently as a few years ago, I missed the fact that she went to college in pieces. I guess I'd just assumed when I saw her enrolled at a college after she graduated high school that she got a degree.

"What are you getting your AA in?" I ask, trying to redirect the conversation to something more uplifting.

"Photography."

I smile, remembering what she said on our run the other day. "That's right. You mentioned you want to have your own business. What type of photography do you wanna do?"

"I'm waffling between portraits and weddings, though going the wedding route really seems to be on my mind a lot over the past few months. I had the chance to be a secondary photographer for a really big wedding in Phoenix in January and it was amazing."

I like that look of wistfulness on her face. The softness of her dreams. It gives me hope that she sees something bigger in her future than the life she has been handed.

Our waitress comes over, interrupting for a moment. We each order a drink, Syrah for her and scotch for me, along with the garlic bread I love so much.

And then Hannah asks me a million questions about my life growing up. I tell her about playing for the soccer team in high school. About Ben and I always being at odds. What it was like to have a baby sister born when I was already in junior high.

We laugh a lot, which feels good. Because the world doesn't

have enough laughter, and my life *definitely* doesn't. And if I'm guessing, I'd wager that Hannah's doesn't either.

When I realize I've talked all through dinner, I flip it around during our shared dessert, asking her to tell me about her childhood, about anything that she enjoyed growing up, about her friend Melanie and her daughter.

And then I watch Hannah light up as she shares with me the positive memories she has from her past. The moments that were beacons of light shining in such a dark space.

She tells me about her relationship with Joshua, how close they were and how he was always her protector. About how she felt when she got her first tattoo, lived on her own for the first time, fell in love with photography.

I'm astounded by who she is, and I know without a shadow of a doubt that the fears I'd had before I met her, the things I'd said to Lucas to get him *not* to reach out to Hannah, are completely unfounded.

Hannah might be introverted, and a little quieter with people she doesn't know. She might have nerves about new people and have some issues from her past that make her slightly untrusting.

But I am enraptured by her, by her voice and her mind and her lips that speak beauty about life and a painful past.

When we finally call it a night, hours have gone by. I can't remember the last time I went on an actual date, let alone one that was so full I lost track of time.

We pull up in Lucas' driveway at close to midnight, and I walk Hannah to the door.

"I have plans for us on Monday," I say, turning to face her when we're standing at her front door, the single light in the courtyard just enough for me to see those beautiful green eyes as they sparkle. "Be ready for me by noon."

She shakes her head. "I work the rest of the weekend. Double shift tomorrow and an evening shift on Monday."

I take her hand in mine. "I talked to Ben. He cleared you from Monday's schedule."

Her eyes widen. "What?"

My stomach falls at her expression, and I realize I didn't even think about the fact that she's been trying to save money.

I stammer out an apology. "I'm sorry. In the moment, it felt like a sweet gesture. But now, I realize I didn't even ask you."

But then she smiles. "You know? I really do appreciate that apology. But I was just surprised, not upset."

"Don't scare me like that," I laugh. "I thought you'd be mad that I didn't ask."

She scrunches up her nose. "Next time? Ask. But this time is totally okay. I will happily take a day off."

I laugh, and she loops her fingers into mine.

"Thanks for taking me out. I had a really good time."

I nod. "Me too."

We look at each other for a minute, our eyes searching each other, like there might be secrets hidden that we can find if we look hard enough.

But then she steps forward, into me, and I realize she's been waiting for me to kiss her when all I felt capable of doing was looking at her.

She slides her hands along my ribs and to my back, the tips of her fingers gripping me just slightly as I dip my head to meet hers.

I love the way she tastes. Like the peppermint she ate after dinner, and a little bit like the wine she had a few glasses of. And when she moans into my mouth, a breathy thing that has me pulling her closer, I can't help but envision what it would be like to hear that noise as I slide inside of her.

My hands slip down over her back, then lower to grip her ass, the firmness, probably from years of running long distances, giving me visions of what she might look like naked, stretched out on my bed.

Before I know it, I've pressed her up against the door and my hand is rubbing small circles up her thigh, higher and higher, as we taste and take and grind together.

"Wyatt," she whispers when my mouth drops to her neck and I suck on her skin. "Do you want to come inside?"

"Inside?" I say, my mind still focused on where my thumb is now stroking along the crease between her thigh and her center, the easy access of her dress too hard to resist. For a brief moment, I envision her asking me to come inside of her, and I groan out loud, my dick pressing firmly against the inside of my slacks at the idea of fucking her right here.

"Upstairs."

And that's when I realize she wants me to *come up*. The sign for sex. The thing every guy wants on a date. The invitation.

As much as I would love that, my mind won't allow it. I can't knowingly go upstairs when there are things she doesn't know.

But I push that thought aside, deciding to focus instead on not wanting to leave her unsatisfied.

"Right here is fine," I say, and then I drop to my knees, lifting one of her legs up onto my shoulder.

When I look up at her, I see a glazed over, hazy expression. The lust in her eyes is unmistakable, and when I lean in and nuzzle my face against her panties, she uses her hands to hike her dress up slightly, giving me better access.

Her underwear are plain. Basic black cotton. I think too many people assume that sexy underwear is a turn on. That a lover needs to see a pretty package in order to appreciate what's inside.

But that's not the case for me. I wouldn't care if she was wearing a paper sack under her dress if it was as easy to slide to the side as her underwear are now, the tiny scrap of cotton pushed away to reveal her pussy.

She's so wet. I can see it gleaming in the low light in the courtyard. I glance up at her one more time as I lean forward and press my tongue to the center of her, stroke it firmly once from core to clit, then fan out to make sure I don't miss a single spot.

Hannah pants out an impassioned gasp, her eyes following me, her mouth slightly open. And as I move my tongue against her, she starts to roll her hips, a hand coming to rest against the top of my hair.

I want her to grip my hair and press me against her. I've always been dominant in bed, wanting control for the most part. But something in me wants her to take the control right now. Wants her to tell me what she wants and how to give it to her.

My tongue continues to lap at her pussy. I raise a hand to part her lower lips, then focus my attention on her tiny little clit, tracing around and around, then sucking lightly. Her head falls back, tapping against the glass of her door and a soft cry of pleasure escapes from between her lips.

"Wyatt," she whispers. "Shit, what are you doing to me?"

I groan, loving how she's responding, loving the way she tastes, that bit of muskiness mixing with a peachy smell from the lotion I've been smelling on her all night. It's heaven, and I'll happily spend more time on my knees worshipping her if she'll let me.

Sometimes sex can be hit or miss with a new person. Seeing her body light on fire, feeling the goosebumps covering her thighs that are exposed to the cool, damp, night air, watching her eyes glow and her expression morphing as she experiences the pleasure I can bring her... it satisfies something inside of me.

Something primal. Something dirty.

"Oh my god, Wyatt." She cries out, her voice echoing off the walls and bouncing around the courtyard. I wonder if she realizes we're outside, if she likes the idea that someone might hear her pleas. "Oh my *god.* Don't stop.*"*

I continue to lathe her with my tongue, stroke slightly against her core with my middle finger before I slip it firmly inside of her. She cries out, her mouth opening and her eyes wide. I feel a bite of pain as her hands grip at my hair. I savor the surprise on her face, contrasting so beautifully with pleasure. Almost like... it hits me like a bat to the face... almost like she's never felt like this before.

I start to slow, my own emotions and fears coming into play as my mind races through the things she has told me about her past.

"Don't stop, please, Wyatt," she says, pulling me tighter against her. "Please. I'm so close."

Shoving my wandering mind aside, I refocus my attention on getting her off, suddenly overcome with a desperate need to make sure she experiences bliss like she never has before.

My finger slides in and out of her, and she rocks against my hand, against my mouth, searching for the top of the peak as I continue to build her up. And then I feel it. That soft space inside of her body that she probably hasn't ever been able to find on her own.

And when I find it, I press against it, stroke it over and over again, loving the words that are spilling from her mouth, almost against her will.

"God, Wyatt, please. *Please.* Fuck Right... right... oh God. I *can't... I...* please."

She's almost mindless as I continue to torture that sweet spot, bring her to that highest peak, her hands dropping to my shoulders and her nails digging into me enough to leave marks.

But I don't stop, and when I stroke her in just the right way, suck her just hard enough, she breaks apart. Cries out. Closes her eyes and soars over the top.

I groan, enjoying the look on her face, my fingers feeling the pulse of how she comes, my mind imagining what it would be like to have her squeeze against my dick like that.

I continue sucking on her softly as she comes down. Only once her breathing has slowed do I pull my finger out, kiss her on the thigh, wipe my hand discreetly on the back of her underwear, and let her panties slide back into place.

Then I stand, her dress falling back into place as she stays slumped lazily against her front door.

That satisfied look on her face, like she's high on something, her pupils blown out and the tiniest smile... I delight in that look on her face.

Though I worry.

I can't help but worry that I've done something I shouldn't have. That I moved too far, too quickly.

"Was that okay?" I whisper.

This is a different version of me. A softer me. The me I was before Hannah would have assumed the woman enjoyed herself. Would have taken the nonverbals as the only necessary cues that she wanted what I was offering.

But with Hannah, I want that confirmation from her mouth. Want to know I didn't push her too far, something I hadn't even considered before I was already on my knees before her.

Instead of saying anything, she presses her head forward, her lips finding mine, her tongue dipping into my mouth. Searching. And fuck if it doesn't taste so good.

My cock throbs.

We kiss for a while longer, a drunk kind of kiss, the kind you can only have after an intense orgasm.

It's the most amazing kiss I've ever had.

"I can taste me on you," she whispers, her head dropping as she nuzzles into my neck. "That was so amazing."

I smile and wrap my arms around her, holding her tight against me. "For me, too."

I feel her giggle.

"I'm serious," I say, my hands coming up to hold her face, so I can look her right in the eyes. "Seeing you like that?" I groan. "God, I'm so hard."

And that's when the wariness comes. I can see it form on her face, though it's like a light gray cloud. Just a hint that a storm might be coming in the future, even if it's not here yet.

She tries to hide it, though, so I leave it alone. Instead, kissing her softly on the cheek.

"So, Monday. I'll pick you up at noon?"

And just like that, whatever flitted across her expression is gone, replaced with a soft, almost disbelieving smile.

She wraps her arms around my back and kisses me again, her tongue making just a small entrance into my mouth.

"Sounds perfect. What should I wear?"

"Duh. A bathing suit."

She laughs. Gives me another peck.

And then she lets me go.

I give her a wave and a "see you tomorrow," before heading out of the courtyard and to my car, which waits in the driveway.

Then I make the short drive home.

Tonight felt like a game changer.

For a number of reasons.

And I can't help but feel like Hannah Morrison might be a more important piece to my life than I'd originally assumed.

Chapter Twenty

HANNAH

The Sunday double kills me. Slays me. Runs me ragged and buries me deep under the exhaustion that's been building with so many back-to-back shifts with no break.

But I wake up on Monday with a surge of energy. Enough so that I go for a five-mile run up and down The Strand when I roll out of bed at nine o'clock.

I'm surprised by how many people are already out on the sand, setting up their tents and large umbrellas for a long day at the beach. A large group surrounds the volleyball net that's a permanent fixture just a few blocks from Lucas', and a house a few doors down has their music banging loud and dozens of people spilling out of the downstairs patio when I get home just an hour later.

Part of me is bummed that I'll miss out on everything that will be happening around here today. But it's only a small part. The bigger part of me is thrumming with excitement about spending the day with Wyatt.

I step into my bathroom and flick on the shower, letting the water heat while I strip out of my sweaty running gear and chuck it into the small laundry basket in the corner.

My phone beeps before I step in, so I grab it and take a look.

Lucas: Enjoying your holiday weekend so far? Hope things aren't too crazy.

Accompanying the text is a photo of him, Otto and a girl that I think might be Remmy at a beach in Malibu, giving me the shaka.

I shake my head on a laugh and set my phone aside, planning to respond once I finish rinsing off.

Stepping under the heat, I allow my sore muscles to soak for a while, doing nothing except giving my mind a moment to wander.

To think back to my date with Wyatt on Saturday night.

I've only been on a handful of dates in my life. There were only a few boys in high school brave enough to poke at The Cactus and not hurt themselves. And when I got older, I just kept up with the same prickly vibe, enjoying the space it created between me and unwanted male attention.

Wyatt's attention, though? Definitely not unwanted.

It is wanted with a capital W.

When he'd dropped to his knees in front of me, I felt like I was starring in one of the hottest fantasies I could ever possibly imagine. My body gets hot now, just thinking about it, and it takes a concerted effort to push those thoughts aside instead of letting my hand slip between my soapy thighs.

I focus on giving my body a rinse and wash. Shaving my legs. Trimming my bikini line.

I'd been willing to invite him inside. The words popped out without me even realizing it.

Even more startling than the fact that I *said* those words is the fact I'd *meant* them. I wanted him to come inside, both the house and me. Be my first.

There are all of these things out there trying to convince young people that it's strange to be a virgin at twenty-one. But I disagree with all of those things. If the average age for cherry popping is seventeen, that means there are tons of people who lose it much older, even older than I am.

And the last thing I needed when I was in high school was to get accidentally pregnant when I could barely envision a future for myself.

I never really think about sex, though, having never really felt like it was something I wanted or needed. After what happened with Rob, it always felt like something violent, something aggressive. Like something was going to be taken from me when I've always felt like too much had already been stolen away.

But now, with Wyatt, I feel different. Like this could be the right time. The right man.

His mouth and his hands and the way that he looks at me... it makes me feel like he sees sex as a time to give, not take. Give pleasure, give emotion, give connection.

It's a beautiful feeling.

I shake my head, trying to redirect my thoughts.

He'll be leaving at the end of the summer. And even if he wasn't, I probably will be. There aren't any expectations of long-time love, a future, a forever.

There isn't anywhere for a broken promise to fall.

And that suits me perfectly.

I just wonder if I'll have the courage to talk to him about it, or if I'll just try to hide it. Though even thinking that feels stupid.

I finish cleaning up and step out of the shower. Once I've dried and slipped on something cute to wear - the white bikini from Wyatt's that he insisted I keep, with a pair of jean shorts and a deep blue tank top - I grab my phone and head downstairs.

Stepping out onto the balcony, I take a picture of the growing craziness on The Strand and send it off to Lucas with a message.

Me: Things here are great. Parties already happening down the way. Can't wait to see what things are like today!

It only takes a few minutes for him to respond.

Lucas: Just be careful and smart. Memorial Day is pretty chill, though. It's 4th of July that's lit. Can't wait for you to see it!

I smile, staying out on the balcony for a few more minutes and watching the people go by, the noise level rising as time passes.

Someone has set up some speakers out front on The Strand, blasting some R&B music. A group of guys jump up onto the patio wall at the neighboring house, dancing with their shirts off and red solo cups in their hands.

I laugh at their antics and one of them glances up my way, singing along to some ridiculous song I've never heard of.

I push myself to enjoy the attention instead of shy away from it, giving them a wave. Then I head back inside, jogging upstairs to finish getting ready.

There's only one person's attention I want today, and he's going to be here soon.

"This is so cool," I say, smiling at Wyatt as we lay out our towels.

When he picked me up a little while ago, he pulled up on his bike with a cooler resting on a small wagon he was towing, wearing a backpack full of beach stuff. I grabbed my own bike, then we rode down The Strand, half-way between Lucas' place and the pier.

We locked our bikes up and carried the cooler out to a volleyball net, my eyes lighting up when I saw Paige and a few familiar faces.

Including Eleanor.

Now that we've said hello to everyone and added our cooler to the stack of coolers filled with beers and pre-mixed drinks, it's apparently time to watch a few of the guys make fools of themselves by playing volleyball.

"Yeah. Spending time with these guys on holidays is definitely something I miss about living here," he says, taking a seat next to me.

I reach over and grab two beers out of our cooler "I don't understand sand sports, though." I twist one open. "I'm not coordinated at all. Running is as athletic as I get, so this?" I swirl my hand in a circle, indicating the four guys bouncing the ball back and forth before their game starts. "Looks like the most miserable thing I could ever imagine."

Wyatt laughs. "My soccer coach in high school used to make

us jog in the sand, and it was always the most horrible thing I'd ever experienced. Always. It never got any better. So playing a sport designed to be in the sand? Ridiculous."

He twists open his own beer and we clink them together, each taking a sip. Then I take a moment to glance around, spotting Eleanor sitting next to Paige and Rebecka.

"Thanks for inviting Eleanor."

"I'd like to take credit, but it was Paige's idea. She said you guys were friends, and I just wanted you to enjoy the day," he says on a shrug.

My smile is wide.

We spend the afternoon just like that, side-by-side, flirting. But also chatting and laughing with our friends. Well, *his* friends. Mostly.

Plus Eleanor.

Who is really enjoying the fact that Hamish called and told her she didn't need to come in for her lunch shift today.

Wyatt may have given me a devious little smirk when he heard us talking about that. Makes me wonder how impromptu that decision actually was.

"Are you and Wyatt Calloway dating?" she asks me later in the afternoon, her voice a whisper as she stretches out on the towel next to me that Wyatt left vacant when he decided to play volleyball.

I glance at her. "I'm not sure. Why?"

Her eyes widen, a sweet expression coming over her face. "Because you guys are so cute together. Seriously, you would make an adorable couple."

I shake my head, though I can't hide the smile that wants to bloom onto my face. "He's great. I don't know entirely what's going on." Then I have a thought. "But don't tell anyone, okay? I know this town is all about gossip, and we need some time to just get to know each other."

She nods, her eyes wide. "No problem." Then she adds, "And thanks for trusting me with something like this."

I look at her and decide I want her to be someone I can talk to. About life. So I lean closer to her and whisper, "We went on a date on Saturday night, and he went down on me."

Her smile is huge. "Oh shit, tell me everything."

I share most of what happened, though I keep a few of the

dirtier details to myself, Eleanor smiling and nodding and making commentary at all the right moments. And then we move on to other topics, like work and her life. She tells me all about Travis, the new guy that moved into her apartment complex that she has a crush on.

"I saw his penis," she says, and I spit out some of the beer I just sipped. "It was an accident. It's not my fault he decided to stand naked with a massive erection in front of his window."

I break into a fit of laughter and Eleanor tumbles behind me, the two of us unable to control ourselves.

Eventually, she wanders off to chat with Paige and Rebecka, and Wyatt makes his way back over to me. He lathers me in another layer of sunscreen, flirtatiously letting his fingers stroke under the straps of my suit.

"I told you this bathing suit looks amazing on you," he says into my ear as he finishes lotioning under the strap at the base of my neck. "I'm glad you kept it."

I spin in his hold, coming face-to-face with him, and allowing the alcohol in my system to make me brave.

"If you play your cards right, you just might be able to see me out of it, too."

His lips part and his eyes fall to my mouth. Before he can say anything, I give him a wink and then head over to the huge blanket Ji-Eun laid out, stretching out next to the girls.

When I look up at Wyatt, he's biting his lip, but then he looks away, out to the ocean.

A small part of me wonders if I might have been a bit too forward. But I shove that aside. It's okay for me to flirt with him, tell him what's on my mind. And if it doesn't work for him, well... that's not something I can control.

Eventually, the sun dips lower in the sky and people start packing up.

"I don't want today to end," I say as we lug our items back to the bikes.

"It's not ending yet." I perk up at Wyatt's words. "Well, the friend portion of the day is ending. But the date part is just starting."

Then he winks, and something exciting surges through my veins knowing that I'm going to get more time with Wyatt tonight.

It really is amazing how quickly you can fall for someone. In just a short period of time, he's started to slip under my skin, down to the root of me, and he's dug a little hole for himself that feels empty when he's not around.

I hurriedly say goodbye to everyone, then ride off with Wyatt back to the house.

"So what's the plan?" I ask, unloading everything on the patio.

"Tonight are the Memorial Day fireworks," he says, his voice straining slightly as he lifts the cooler and sets it just inside the doorway to the patio. Then he looks at me. "I thought it would be fun to spend some time in the Jacuzzi. Then watch them on the roof."

My mouth dries up at the idea, and I nod, maybe a little too excited. Shit. The last thing I need is to make a fool of myself. Especially if I want to have sex with Wyatt tonight.

Which I do.

I think.

Yeah. Yes. Definitely.

We stop off in the kitchen and munch on some fruit and a veggie tray, then grab towels and head up to the roof.

I'm actually surprised that I haven't been up there before now. We head out my bedroom to the small balcony, then climb the spiral staircase to the top, stepping off on a landing that takes up a small space on the roof of Lucas' house.

And my mouth opens in surprise.

I glance at Wyatt, who has a small but slightly unsure grin on his face.

The rooftop has a large Jacuzzi built into it, as well as a small space for a table and a few chairs. But it isn't the furniture that has me so shocked.

Covering the table is a white table cloth, with a box of donuts and some hot chocolate. A handful of flickering candles are scattered strategically on the table and the edge of the Jacuzzi.

"They're LED candles," Wyatt says, as if that's what's on my mind. "With the breeze at the beach, real candles would have been impossible. And I wasn't trying to light Lucas' house on fire."

I smile at him, step over to where he stands a few feet away from me, and press a kiss to his jaw. Then I raise up on my tiptoes and kiss him on the lips.

"This is so sweet," I say. "And so thoughtful. When did you do this?"

"I may have had Thalia set it up while we were gone."

I grin. I met Lucas' maid, Thalia, last week and I think she's amazing. Not only does she keep Lucas' house completely spotless, which soothes the clean freak in my soul, but she also has the best attention to detail. She does Lucas' grocery shopping, and without even asking, she started stocking up on extra Earl Grey tea and veggie trays because she saw my grocery list on the fridge.

It *is* kind of weird having someone clean up after me, though, so I'm careful not to leave anything too messy.

Wyatt climbs into the Jacuzzi, then takes my hand and helps me over the edge. When I first heard Lucas say he had a hot tub, it seemed a little strange in the warm beach weather. But now, as the temperature cools with the setting sun, the warm water and quiet privacy of a rooftop is the thing dreams are made of.

"Did you enjoy the day?" he asks, taking a sip from his glass of scotch before setting it on the ledge.

I nod, settling in to the corner seat and enjoying the feel of the pulsing jet against my back. "It was really fun."

"Good. I'm glad."

We sit in silence for a few minutes, and I look up into the sky. "It seems like you should be able to see stars here. But it isn't that much better than Phoenix," I say, only spotting a few that burn the brightest and are visible over the glare from the city. "Have you ever seen that app on your phone? You hold it up and it shows you where the constellations are?"

He shakes his head. "No, but we should head up into the mountains soon. The stargazing up there really is phenomenal. And in August, there's a pretty amazing meteor shower that happens every year."

"That sounds so fun. Maybe we could do a camping trip? Like with the whole group?"

Wyatt grins at me. "You know, when you first got here, there's no way you would have thought about our big group doing a trip together. You would have assumed you didn't belong or that they wouldn't want you to come."

I blush, feeling a little embarrassed at how obvious I am with my fears.

"Hey, I'm just glad you're starting to feel like you fit, you know? That we want you here. Because we do." He pauses. "*I* do." His hand slides into mine, our fingers twisting together. "I'm glad you're here, Hannah."

The feeling I get when he says that is a rush into my body. A surge of emotion that starts at my heart and pumps into my fingers and toes, my soul feeling filled and happy in a way it never has before.

Maybe I was wrong when I first got here a month ago. Maybe I assumed I wouldn't belong here, that I wouldn't fit, because I believed the people here wouldn't accept me. But Wyatt is proving that theory wrong.

So is Paige. And Lucas. And Eleanor and Otto and the host of the lovely people I've met and spent time with since moving here.

Wyatt moves forward, his face hovering near mine, and I watch his eyes as they peruse my face. Take in my skin and my stringy damp hair and my lips.

Oh, the way he focuses on my lips.

When he moves the slightest bit more, his mouth meets mine. And I can't even play coy. I can't pretend that having his tongue slipping between my lips, pulsing and twisting with mine, isn't everything I want and need right now. That having him pull me closer in the heated water so that I'm straddling him where he sits isn't the picture of what I hoped would happen tonight.

So when it does, when he pulls me into his body and wraps his arms around me, our skin slick as we press together, I throw myself into it, refusing to care how he feels about my enthusiasm.

He grips my thighs as we kiss, just that bit of pressure bringing my focus away from where his lips meet mine, dropping it lower, to the place where I ache.

His fingers slide up and down my legs in a teasing caress that sends a fire racing through my veins. I shift forward, wanting no space between us, and when I feel the hardest part of him pressed against my center, I shift slightly, lining up with him and rotating my hips, the pressure of him feeling so good that I can't help but pant out his name.

"Wyatt," I whisper. "You're so hard."

He groans, his strong hands spanning my waist, gripping my hips and grinding me against where he waits, hard and ready and throbbing.

"It's because I can't get enough of you," he says back, looking at my eyes as he rocks me against him. "Shit, Hannah. Fuck, you have no idea what you do to me."

His head falls back slightly as I continue to grind against him, his eyes slipping to half mast. I lean forward and latch my mouth to his neck, giving him a soft suck, loving the taste of the salt and sweat on his skin.

I nip at him, give him a gentle bite as he begins to trace the soft patch of skin just above my bikini bottoms, and it takes everything inside of me not to just yank them off or beg him to do it. The scrap of material feels like nothing, and yet it's in the way of what I want.

And that's for Wyatt to slip his fingers inside of me again, to give me that pleasure that I've never been able to fully achieve on my own.

But instead, I slip my hands against his wet skin, stroking over the firm muscle, lightly brushing over his pecs and nipples, through the valleys of his abdomen until I reach his board shorts. When I slip my fingers just barely under the material, one of his hands grabs mine.

"You don't have to do anything you don't want to," he tells me, and something inside of my chest cracks open, spills out, fills the space around us.

"I know," I say back, wiggling my fingers until he lets go, and then I begin to untie his shorts. "I want to see you." I lean forward and put my mouth against his neck again, that sweet spot that had him groaning is calling to me. I suck gently. "Let me touch you."

His moan is a grumble that I can feel in the vibrations of his throat, and he helps me pull down his shorts, freeing his cock beneath the water.

I can't really see it underneath the jets and bubbles of the hot tub, but I reach out and take him in hand, getting another sound from Wyatt's lips, this one a choked noise that I can't help but kiss off his mouth.

And then I start to pump him between my fist, not squeezing hard but just stroking him, up and down, his skin soft but hard at the same time.

So fucking hard.

Wyatt reaches out and unties my bikini top, his eyes watching mine. And I love that I can see him paying attention to my reaction. Making sure I'm okay with his every move. It takes me back to that feeling I knew I felt before.

Safe. Warm. Cared for.

And when the triangles fall away, he brings his hands up, cupping my breasts, his thumbs tracing my nipples in a way that streaks pleasure through my body, the muscles between my legs throbbing with need.

It's almost frustrating, this delicate trace he's doing. Around and around, then a stroke across the tip. I grit my teeth, both loving and hating what he's doing. Loving because it feels so good and hating because it's not fucking enough. I want him to pinch and pull and...

God, when he does. When his hands finally begin to grab and tease and he dips down, sucking one into his...

My head falls back, loving the pulsing pleasure of his lips on my skin, his tongue stroking that point that seems to still need so much more.

"I'm close," he says, bringing me out of my own haze. I look back at him and see his eyes are glazed, that his neck is flushed, and goose bumps pebble his shoulders. He breathes out a puff of air as I squeeze him just a bit tighter. "Fuck, I'm so close."

I let go of him, my sudden desire to see him overwhelming my mind. His eyes widen as I pull back, his expression uncertain as I pull him up so he's standing, then nudge him so he leans back on the edge of the hot tub.

My eyes look away from his, drop to the hard shaft that looks like it's throbbing between his legs. I reach out and take it in my hand, stroking him up and down.

"Hannah, what are you..."

But before he can finish, I press my face forward and wrap my mouth around him.

"Fuck," he cries out, and I know a neighbor had to have heard him. "Shit, Hannah."

His words spur me on as I explore, doing something I'd never really thought about before, my mouth and lips sucking and licking, my tongue tracing along the ridges of his dick.

I feel a hand rest against the top of my head, fingers slipping between my locks of hair and pulling tight.

"Just like that," he says, his eyes locked on mine as I bob against him. "Use your hand, too."

I grip the part of him that I can't fit in my mouth, squeeze and stroke, trying to keep a good rhythm. My only indicator of whether or not he's enjoying it is the expression on his face, his mouth slightly open, his eyes closed, then open, then closed again, like it feels so good he can't hold them open.

I'm mesmerized as his head falls back, a deep groan emerging from between his lips that I hope to spend hours upon hours recreating for as long as possible.

"I'm coming," he pants out, and I pull back, continuing to stroke him as he pumps in spurts onto my chest.

I can't help but smile at his expression, somewhere between dazed and surprised and grateful. A beautiful mix of satisfaction that I was able to put on his face.

When he finishes pulsing into my hand, he drops down into the water and pulls me into him, my bare chest against his, and wraps his arms around me, ignoring the stickiness between us. He presses his face into the crook of my neck, kissing and sucking on the skin, almost like it's soothing to him to lap at my body.

Eventually, he takes a deep breath and shudders, the last of his orgasm leaving his body in a final wave.

I lean back slightly, loving the look on his face. The most blissed out expression I've ever seen from him, a man who normally has such tense features. Except, it seems, when he's around me.

"That was amazing," he says, kissing me softly on the lips, and I preen under his praise.

His hand drifts down between us, but I grip his fingers, shaking my head.

"That was just for you," I say. "I don't believe in tit for tat with sex. We do things because we want to. Not because we think we should."

His brow furrows. "That's not what I was doing, Hannah. Seeing you come on Saturday night?" He leans forward so our mouths are just a breath away from each other. "God, it was the hottest fucking thing I've ever seen in my life. And your pussy..."

I giggle.

Wyatt smirks. "What?"

But I shake my head. "It's just a funny word. Sorry."

He chuckles and tucks me in against him. "Your vagina? Should I call it your vagina and be super anatomically correct?"

I continue to laugh in his arms. "No. I just... wasn't expecting you to talk about going down on me."

"Going down on your love rug?"

"Ewwwww, no! No, no, absolutely not. I'll take pussy over love rug. Who says that?"

Wyatt lifts a shoulder. "I saw it on a YouTube video when I was in high school. Haven't actually thought about that in a while."

Both of us sink into the water, Wyatt tucking himself back into his shorts, and then we sit back against the jets again.

"You'd be *shocked* at some of the words people use."

"Like what?"

He thinks for a second. "Well, there's the c-word."

"Nope."

He nods. "Yeah. And there's like, beaver, love button, poon, coochie, snatch, front butt. But I think my favorite was the Republic of Labia."

I burst into laughter, unable to contain myself, the sound echoing off the concrete walls of the rooftop deck. Wyatt just smiles at me as my laugh finally starts to taper off.

"You have a great laugh," he says.

I grin. Most people compliment my legs, so having a compliment on something he can't see, something he has to hear and feel in his soul?

It feels good.

We finish up in the Jacuzzi, stepping out and drying off with the towels in the small cabinet filled with sunscreen, towels and - oh good lord, Lucas - condoms and lube.

I look at Wyatt with a pinched expression but he shakes his head. "Lucas has this thing cleaned twice a month ever since an issue a few years ago when someone threw up in it and he didn't know. Remmy about had a fucking meltdown."

I laugh again, my shoulders relaxing, and we head back down the stairs and into the house to shower and change.

Wyatt showers first, emerging from the bathroom in nothing but a towel. My mouth drops open and he chuckles, leans in and gives me a kiss. "Your turn."

Shaking my head, I jump into the shower, making quick work of cleaning the sand, salt and chlorine off of my body. When I get out, I put on this amazing peachy lotion that Paige gave me for my date with Wyatt the other night. Then I slip into a pair of yoga pants and a light sweater, since the temperature has cooled significantly.

Then I wander down to the living room, calling out his name

when I don't see him anywhere.

He comes out of the garage holding a blanket. "Fireworks start in about thirty minutes. Do you want to watch them on the rooftop or on Lucas' balcony?"

I think about the layouts, ultimately deciding that sitting on the balcony with the better view of the pier would be best. So we head back to the very top again, each of us grabbing a hot chocolate and a donut before we curl into two of the loungers spread along the top.

"This has been such a great day," I say out loud, though I don't know if I'm telling Wyatt, reminding myself, or informing the universe.

He smiles at me, takes my hand and brings it to his mouth, pressing a kiss against my wrist.

After we're done with our donuts, he tugs me closer, eventually pulling me off of my lounger with a laugh and drawing me over to sit between his legs.

I snuggle back into him, enjoying the feel of his arms around me. We sit in silence for a while, Wyatt's hands resting softly on my stomach.

"How much longer until the fireworks?" I ask.

"They start at eight o'clock, so about ten minutes I think."

I nod, shifting slightly. I pause when I feel Wyatt pressed hard against my back. I glance back at him and he smirks.

"It happens when you're around," he murmurs, and I flush.

I've seen him mostly naked, touched him, come with his mouth against me, and yet the idea of him getting hard just because I'm around? That's what makes me blush?

I shake it off, smiling that I can make him feel such a surge of emotion, such a big physical response.

His fingers, which have been resting calmly on my stomach, do a light sweep, his thumbs rubbing lightly against my soft top, just below my breasts. And then it happens again, and again, and I picture him raising his hands and cupping them again, like he did in the Jacuzzi earlier.

I rest my hands on his knees, tracing the soft skin on the outside of his thighs, unable to help myself when I squirm a little bit against him.

His fingers stop, and I feel his soft pants of breath against my neck behind me. I feel overwhelmed, like a wire pulled taught, like I might snap at any moment. Which is the only reason I can explain how my hands lift and rest on top if his, urge them upwards, pressing his hands against my chest. My breathing picks up as he takes my lead, his fingers stroking my nipples softly through the fabric.

I moan, my body still so primed, so on edge after our moments in the hot tub earlier.

Wyatt's hands continue to rove, caressing me lightly over my sweater, then sweeping down along the tops of my thighs. Then the insides of my thighs. He does this over and over again, until I can barely take it.

His nose presses into my neck and I hear him inhale. "I love that smell," he says. "That peachy lotion. You wearing it again?"

I nod, loving that he likes it, but unable to form any words to respond.

Then, finally, one hand slips over my aching core, cupping me softly and stroking lightly over my cotton pants. It eases something inside of me, and I just want to moan out *yes, finally, thank you.*

But within just a few seconds, I realize his movements haven't eased my need. He's only turned up the heat, raised the bar, stoked the fire to grow bigger and bigger.

His other hand slips under my sweater, reaching for my breasts.

"Are you not wearing a bra?" he asks, feather light kisses peppering my neck.

I can't manage any words, his hands so distracting that I think I might collapse if I wasn't already held so close to him.

"Are you a bad girl, Hannah? You like to taunt me?"

I nod. "Maybe a little."

He groans, then pinches my nipple, pulling it just enough that the bite of pain has my own fingers gripping his thighs.

Wyatt slips his hand under my pants, the stretchy material giving him plenty of room to make his way down to where I'm wet and achy, a pulsing, needy thing that's writhing under his touch.

"Please," I whisper, the only word that comes to mind.

He sucks on my neck, his tongue coming out to lap at me, just as his fingers slip between my lower lips.

"You're so wet," he whispers, continuing to rotate his attention between my breasts and my legs. "Is this for me?"

I nod, though I'm shocked I can do that much.

He rubs the wetness, trails his finger down to my center and slips it inside, then pulls it up to the little bead that's throbbing for him. And then he circles my clit, careful not to touch.

I feel like I could cry out in frustration and desperation and anger and need, like I might burst into pieces at any moment if he doesn't just touch me and give me what I need from him.

"Wyatt, please."

He nibbles on my earlobe. Groans in my ear. "Wait."

It's all he says, continuing to tease and torture, his fingers dropping down and sliding inside of me, then coming back up to circle me. Again and again, but never allowing me to surge to the top.

"God, you need it so bad, don't you?" he whispers, his own voice sounding strained. "Fuck, Hannah, you need it?"

I nod my head, a whimper escaping from between my lips.

A loud pop has my eyes flying open, and I see the fireworks show has begun on the pier.

But at that exact moment, Wyatt brings his other hand down, uses two fingers to spread my lips wide, then uses his other hand to stroke me right on the center of my clit.

I cry out, something loud and painful and pleasured and frantic. The surge of need hits a new level as he strokes right over me, again and again and again, until I'm in near tears.

"I love the noises you make when you're about to come," he groans in my ear. "Like you might die if I don't give you what you need."

"I will," I pant out, my hips writhing, my body unable to sit still.

Then a finger dips inside of me again and he strokes me in just the right way, groaning in my ear, telling me to come, promising me how good it's going to feel.

I shatter.

My bones and muscles and tendons and every atom in my body flies apart, the wave of euphoria pushing out all sensation so I can only feel where he's touching me.

My knees try to slam together but Wyatt's arms hold me open to him, allowing his fingers to continue to rub and slide, stretching out my orgasm until I literally can't breathe.

I can't breathe.

When he finally relaxes his fingers, I gasp for breath, my

entire body going lax against him, like I'm melting into where he sits behind me.

He pulls his hands out, and presses them back into my stomach, making sure my body is as close to him as possible. I turn slightly to my side, nuzzling into him like a cat desperate for attention.

Because that's exactly what I am.

A needy, desirous thing that just wants Wyatt as close to me as possible.

And then, as I pant and try to catch my breath, my body lying sluggish in his arms, the tiny flickers still popping along my nerves, we watch the fireworks show together.

Chapter Twenty One
WYATT

"Shit. Shit, shit, shit."

Hannah's voice has my eyes cracking open. She's running around her room, stopping for a second to peer out the window to the street.

"Wyatt," she hisses. "Wyatt, wake up."

I roll over, reaching my arms above my head, a small smile stretching lazily across my face when I see Hannah in a pair of little panties and a tank top, her skin a little pink from our day in the sun yesterday.

"You have to get up," she says, right before a shirt lands on my face.

I chuckle and push it away, reaching for Hannah's hand as she walks past me and tugging her back into the bed.

It seems like she's stressed about something, but I can't seem to care right in this moment. This might be the first time I've ever woken up with a girl and felt this kind of groggy, morning, joyfulness that comes with sexual release and an amazing woman.

Normally, I'm tugging my clothes on and slipping out the door. But this morning, I can only focus on Hannah's skin and her smell and the idea of bringing her back into this bed so we can do more of what we did last night.

Jesus, we didn't even have sex and I feel almost lovesick. Like I've been drugged on something.

But this is apparently what Hannah Morrison does to me.

Makes me want to drag her beneath me and kiss her in the places that make her blush.

"Wyatt," she says, her voice firm even though she's trying not to giggle as I pull her against my chest, kissing her neck and biting her shoulder. "Wyatt, Lucas just got home."

I lift my head back and give her a smile. "So. Is he going to ground you for having a boy spend the night?" I joke, giving her a grin.

Her expression pinches, and something inside of me tilts just slightly. It's a new feeling. One I don't think I've ever experienced before.

"I'm just not ready for him to know anything is happening between us," she says.

I nod, my eyes searching hers.

She looks apologetic. Like this isn't what she *wants* to say, but it's what she should say anyway.

And she doesn't take it back.

So I climb off the bed, trying to leave this unpleasant feeling tangled in her sheets, and start slipping my clothes on.

Last night, after the fireworks, Hannah and I made out for a while on the deck. Then we packed up the donuts and made our way down to her bedroom. We crawled into bed, spooning together, my need to have her near me almost overwhelming.

It was perfect.

One of the best nights of sleep I've gotten in years. I feel rested, relaxed, happy.

Except for this whole Lucas thing.

There's a knock on Hannah's door and her eyes widen. I shake my head and step backwards into the bathroom, then into the shower so I'm out of the line of sight.

"Come in," she says, her voice slightly off.

"Hey." I can hear the smile in his voice. "Did I wake you?"

"No. No you didn't. I was just... about to get some laundry together."

There's a pause.

"Welcome back. I missed you."

"Thanks. You know, I missed you, too." He chuckles. "It's weird, right? Like, I didn't know you a few weeks ago and now I go out of town and I have a person to miss."

Hannah laughs as well. "I know what you mean."

"We left really early this morning to get back to town, and I'm *starving*. Wanna grab breakfast?"

"Yes, please! Can we go to Mary's?"

"Sure. I'm gonna go shower and change first, that okay?"

"Sounds good."

A few seconds pass and then I hear her door close.

I step out of the shower and stand in the doorway between her bedroom and bathroom. "Can I ask you a question?" I say, before I can think better of it.

She nods.

"Why don't you want Lucas to know I'm here right now."

It isn't a fair question to ask, but can't seem to help myself. The idea that she wants to keep it a secret twists something inside of my chest.

Hannah looks away, crosses her arms. "Joshua was already gone by the time I was finally old enough to date," she says, her voice soft, her expression slightly pained. "He was never able to have the awkward sex conversation. To harass the boy."

She lifts a shoulder, and my heart slumps. I read this situation all wrong.

"I'm still getting used to having family. And if I let Lucas know about us, it means Joshua won't ever get to be the one who does those things." Her eyes close. "I know that sounds *so* stupid, because he's gone. I get that. But I just..."

"Hey," I say, my voice soft. I put hands on each of her biceps, rubbing up and down on her arms. "You don't have to explain. I understand. I'm sorry I pressed."

She nods.

"I just... thought maybe you were embarrassed of me. That's why I asked."

Her head flies up, her eyes wide. "Absolutely not. No way." The vehemence in her voice puts my fears to rest. Fears that came

out of nowhere and that I didn't even know I could feel.
Especially this soon.
"Wyatt, you're one of my favorite parts of life right now."
My heart thumps, and I grin at her.
"Now, will you hate me if I ask you to sneak out while he's in the shower?"
I laugh, press a kiss to her forehead. "Not even a little bit."
Hannah helps me collect the last of my things, then walks me out, down to The Strand where my bike is parked in storage.
"I'll text you soon," I say, taking her face in both of my hands and looking into those gorgeous green eyes of hers. "Last night was amazing. Be prepared for me to annoy the shit out of you this summer."
Her expression is soft but her eyes are bright as I lean down, kissing her on the lips. She kisses me back, her hands resting lightly on my hips. Then she smiles, kisses my nose.
"Bye."
I swing a leg over to sit on my bicycle and head down The Strand, turning back to give Hannah a wave.
But as I'm turning my head to focus on where I'm going, my eyes catch on a figure on the rooftop.
It's Lucas, standing on his third floor balcony, watching me with a flat expression as I ride away.

Hannah: Lucas is having a party on Friday night. I work until 10, but I'll be home after. Are you going to come?

Me: Well, that's up to you isn't it?

Hannah: Is that a jizz joke?

Me: Ha! Yup. Yes it is.

I put my phone down, laughing at Hannah's ability to take a sexual innuendo and make *me* laugh as if it were *her* joke.
She's starting to come out of her shell, and it makes me happy

for her. And I feel like that's a big difference between her and other girls I've spent time with.

I'm happy for *her,* not for me because I get to enjoy the changes I'm seeing. I mean, yes, I'm happy I get to see her changing and coming out of her shell. But my primary interest is in how it affects her, changes her relationships, bolsters her own confidence.

The Hannah that showed up in Hermosa Beach a month ago was shy and insecure. Beautiful, yes. Caring, absolutely. And I loved how she treated Ivy, though it was quite the kick to the gut to find out the truth. That she was Ivy's sister, the one I'd fought hard for Lucas to keep away from our town.

Now, she's making her own relationships, planning for things she wants to happen in the future, smiling and laughing more.

It makes me happy for her, knowing she's enjoying her life here. Hoping that a part of that happiness is because of me.

I shake my head, wondering when I turned into this heartsick fool that gets sentimental about a girl. A woman. I grit my jaw as I remember her coming apart in my hands as we watched the fireworks on Monday evening.

My guess, if I had to make one, is that she's a virgin.

From the way she's talked about men since I've known her, the stories she's shared about her life, I wouldn't be surprised to learn she doesn't let anyone with a penis get close to her.

It only occurred to me at the worst possible time. When I was going down on her after our date. I'd seen her face, the absolute surprise and awe rippling through her expression, and I'd had a moment of concern.

Was I pushing her?

Was it too fast?

But she'd gripped me hard and pulled me in, and I was lost in her again.

During college, and then when I was in San Fran, I was quite the busy body. Literally. And normally, virginity is a deal breaker. I ascribed to the belief that virgins fall in love after their first time, and that was just never something I saw in the cards for myself. So the best thing I could do was steer clear of the cherries.

I thought about it a bit between Saturday and Monday, and for some reason, with Hannah, it isn't something that matters.

If anything, it's a bit intimidating. Knowing I might be her first time. There's a lot of pressure in that. Expectation. The possibility for disappointment.

And again, another reason why things with Hannah are so different. In the past, it was always about avoiding the girls who would put expectations on me that I didn't want.

With Hannah, it's about wanting to live up to the expectations I assume she might have. Especially knowing that she's had some... bad experiences in the past. Times when people took advantage or hurt her.

That's the last thing I want.

So I'm going to let her set the pace. She's a strong person, a sexual being with desires and needs, and I'll just need to pay really close attention to make sure I'm reading her correctly. Giving her what she wants.

My phone beeps again and I look down at where it's sitting on my coffee table.

Hannah: If you come, I think we'll both have a good night ;)

I bite my lip. God, does she get under my skin in the best way.

Me: I'll be there.

I drop my phone on the bench and get back to my workout.

I like to spend most mornings exercising, if I'm not too hungover from the night before. When I was younger, exercise was almost all cardio. Runs with my teammates, playing on the field.

But once I got to college, I wanted a slightly bulkier frame. Nothing monstrous. Just something that looked filled out and strong. So I do a modified CrossFit. Jumping rope, lifting weights, medicine balls, short sprints, and then I add in some swimming in the pool.

This morning, I'm only half into it, though, with my mind scattered on so many different things. So eventually, I give it a rest and just head upstairs to shower.

On my way back to the guesthouse, my phone begins to vibrate in my hand.

Calvin Calling...

I roll my eyes and hit ignore. The last person I feel like talking to right now is my dad. Not with how he treated me the last time I saw him.

It's been almost a month since that night at the yacht club, and I haven't seen or heard from him the entire time. Not even when I let his secretary know when Ivy's doctor's appointment was in case he wanted to come.

Of course he hadn't been there. I don't know why the things he does are both so surprising and so expected at the same time.

I slam the medicine ball into the padded ground. Pick it up. Do it again.

My dad hasn't always been this person I can't stand. I remember being a kid, spending time on the beach with him and Ben, going on family vacations.

But somewhere along the way, something changed.

I'm self-aware enough to know that it's possible *he* hasn't changed but that *I* have. That I've grown up and now understand who he *really* is.

A self-centered, money-hungry, over-indulgent, obnoxious jackass who doesn't care if he has to kick his own family out of the way to get what he wants.

The hard part with my father is that what he wants can change on a dime. So it doesn't matter what you do, how you ebb and flow around his whims... you'll never be enough because what he wants can never be measured.

I remember hearing my mom crying when I was a kid, maybe five or six years old at the time. Being the angry and somewhat rebellious child I was, I asked her what was wrong. Like I might be able to fix the problem if I just knew who was responsible for hurting her so I could go hurt them.

But of course, being the woman she is, my mother looked me square in the eyes and said, "I'm crying because your father doesn't think I'm beautiful anymore."

That's what it was always about for her. How she looked. It couldn't have been because he's just an asshole who cheats. It had to be her fault. She wasn't as young and pretty as she was when they first got married, and that was her only value.

Having gotten older, her worth was gone.

That's when she started to change. When her outer shell became a hard plastic. Cosmetic surgery. Expensive clothes. Luxury cars. Fancy parties. If she couldn't keep my dad's attention, she sure as hell wanted everyone else's.

Eventually, she managed to grab the attention of someone who could make her feel beautiful. A man who could give her what she wanted. Something even my father couldn't give her, with all of his money and resources.

A daughter. A precious baby girl.

That man used her, and she used him in return.

I'll never understand what led my mother to sleep with a married man, let alone one that had also been sleeping with other women. That had already fathered one child within the elite of Hermosa Beach.

But I guess it's easy to excuse your behavior when you're in pain. When you're searching for something that you think could possibly solve your problems.

I push away my thoughts, not wanting to spend any time dealing with the knowledge I hold of what's transpired between Hannah's dad the rich wives of Hermosa Beach.

He might have done something nefarious, something shady and underhanded, committing a betrayal against his vows and his family.

But the girl that I'm rapidly falling for has nothing to do with any of that. She's pure. A beautiful, enchanting ray of sunshine breaking through the cracks of the tangled web that we live in. And like a moth, I am drawn to her, unable to see anything but that light.

Instead of continuing my fruitless workout, I shower, change, make myself a quick breakfast smoothie, and then head into the main house, pushing open the door to the office I use when I'm in town.

I've been dicking around enough since I've been back. Time to start planning for London.

Something squeezes inside of me at that thought, but I carry on, knowing that there's plenty of work to get done over the next few months before the summer ends.

When Otto approached me about stepping out of solely an investor role and into something that would be much more involved with the evolution of Elite X, I'd shrugged it off. It didn't feel like it would be a good fit, considering the small-scale of events he hosts in the local area.

But being a long-time friend, I'd sat with him and helped him brainstorm additional ideas, pushing buttons that would help him formulate longer-term plans. That's when this whole international travel thing sparked up.

Now, he wants me to be the director for the international branch, building up the department in London to create a self-sustaining business that manages partnerships and hotels and airfare. The whole shebang.

It's a pretty big task, and if I'm honest, I'm not sure I want to be the one to do it.

I mean, I think I *could* do it. I'm just not sure I *want* to.

I used to be a big traveller, which is why I think Otto wanted me in on this part of Elite X. And I do love seeing the world. I spent a semester in New Zealand when I was in college. Probably the best few months of my life.

But I also don't see myself living abroad permanently. And this London thing? Even though Otto claims it's only for a few months, it feels long-term. Like I'd be moving to the UK for years. And as much as I want to carve a path for myself in a business like this one, I don't want to have to move away to do it.

Being here, back in Hermosa, is making me realize that I might want to stay. Maybe not in this city, specifically. But at least nearby. The list of important things in my life is starting to shift around, and I'm starting to see the value in staying close, so I can be around for Ivy as she grows up. Maybe try to patch up my relationship with Ben.

And now, I can't even believe I'm thinking this, but Hannah is starting to become a factor. The idea of leaving in August, even though that's two months away… it turns something painfully in my chest. Like my heart, which was so jaded and jagged and rough around the edges, is finally starting to pulse again, and just the idea of going back to how I was before is like catching one of those unsmoothed corners.

"Knock, knock," a voice says, and my head jerks to the doorway, where I see Lucas leaning against the doorjamb. "Hope I'm not intruding. Vicky let me in."

I grit my jaw. Lucas showing up here unannounced isn't surprising. But it *is* grating, especially since I can see in his facial expression that his smile is all for show.

He's not pleased with me, and he's here to share what's on his mind.

"Come in," I say. "Though I feel like you would have come in whether I invited you or not."

Lucas tucks his sunglasses into the collar of his shirt, then takes a seat in one of the two chairs that face my desk, crossing his legs, his ankle propped against his knee and his hands resting casually in his lap.

At least I have the upper hand. When this room was getting designed - by my father - he told me that every office he worked in was made specifically to make sure the other person recognized the power of the person behind the desk. Dark colors, brass, uneven chair heights, and special lighting. Do I buy into that stuff? Not really. But I'll take any leverage I can get.

Because as casual as Lucas is trying to be right now, I can feel him bristling beneath the surface.

"I saw you and Hannah this morning, though I've been hearing all weekend about the two of you together. Riding up to Santa Monica, a date at Papa Louis', getting her the day off and taking her to the beach, spending the night in my house." He cracks his knuckles, though it seems more in stress than intimidation. "I saw your shit on her nightstand this morning."

"It's interesting that you have people keeping tabs on your sister."

"They're not. But that doesn't mean the people in this town aren't loyal enough to tell me when something is going on."

My nostrils flare, and I realize that I have no idea where this conversation is going.

"The minute I realized something was going on between the two of you, it became my business. I brought her here for a reason, and the guilt I feel about it is too much." He shakes his head. "I won't have you using her for anything on top of that."

"I'm not using her," I say.

Lucas rolls his eyes. "Don't blow smoke up my ass, okay? I know you, Wyatt. I know who you are and how you are with women. Hannah is a quick pit stop before you take off, and she doesn't need you as a complication when there's a lot of other shit going on."

I stand up, my chair shooting out behind me. Then I lean forward, one hand on my desk, the other with a finger pointed at Lucas. "You have no idea what's going on between me and Hannah, or how I feel about her. So you have no business getting involved."

Lucas stands, too. "You expect me to believe you actually feel *anything* for her? What, are you in love with her?"

I freeze.

Because in truth, the words form on my tongue but I can't get them to come out of my mouth.

It's too soon, too swift, too sharp.

So I say nothing.

"That's what I thought," he says, heading to the door while I stand mute, unable to say anything worthwhile.

He turns back to look at me before he leaves.

"Stay the *fuck* away from my sister," he spits out.

And then he's out the door.

Chapter Twenty Two
HANNAH

When I hit the brakes outside of the house on Friday evening, I'm not surprised to see dozens of people spilling out onto The Strand.

I could hear the music from blocks away, but I guess that's just the type of good time Lucas enjoys.

I lock up my bike and slip through the crowd, then jog up the stairs from the bottom floor all the way to the top.

I have no interest in getting stopped by anyone for anything, my only focus on heading straight for my room to shower and get ready, since Wyatt's supposed to be here and I want to smell much better than this.

When I open my bedroom door, I see a wrapped package on my bed.

I smile. I don't know how Lucas knew it was my birthday, but I can see his handwriting spelling out my name on the card.

Pushing myself to have patience, I quickly jump into the

shower, scrub the smell of grease and meat off my skin and out of my hair, then make sure to put on that lotion that Wyatt loves.

Finally, after I've gotten fully ready, I open up the card.

Hannah,
Hopefully this helps get you to where you want to be
Lucas

I carefully unwrap the package, having no idea what could possibly be inside. But when I see a familiar logo, I stop unwrapping. My butt hits my bed and I cover my mouth with my hand.

There's no way...

I finish pulling off the pretty blue paper and hold the box in my hands, spinning it around to look at the photos on the outside. And that's when I see another note, taped to the box itself.

Opening the flap, I almost want to laugh when I see the same handwriting.

Hannah,
I know you'll say I shouldn't do this. And I know you'll assume I think you're mooching off of me. But that's not the case. Just consider this a replacement birthday gift for all of the ones I missed in the past.
Happy Birthday,
Lucas

It shocks me how quickly he already seems to know me. But it also warms something in my chest. Something that had frozen over a long time ago.

I take a deep breath and let it out slowly, still struggling to understand how he managed to figure out such a special birthday gift. Something I can really use. Something that has the potential to change my life.

Deciding to accept Lucas' amazing gift without complaint, I slowly open the box, pulling out the Nikon D850.

It fits perfectly in my hands, not too heavy but not so light that I don't realize how expensive this must be.

A camera like this will be a game changer. I might even be able to build up an actual, legitimate photography business now.

Eventually, I force myself to walk away from my gift, heading downstairs to find my brother.

When I find him in the kitchen, chatting with Otto, I bump everyone out of the way and wrap my arms around him. "Thank you so much," I say. Then I pull back and see the pleased smile on his face. "Seriously. And yes, I do think it is too much. But it's also amazing and could possibly completely change everything. So I'm not going to tell you I won't take it."

"I'm glad," he says, his smile matching mine. "Now, let's celebrate."

I look over my shoulder, my eyes widening when I see Paige pulling a cake out of the fridge.

"Sorry, I was supposed to get this ready once I saw you come home and I lost track of time," she says, digging candles out of a box. "Gimme thirty seconds."

The last time I had a birthday cake with candles was my ninth birthday. It was Cinderella themed, though the idea of becoming an orphan and dealing with wicked family drama wasn't even on my radar at the time.

So when Paige gets all of the candles lit, someone turns off the music, and everyone in the area starts singing happy birthday to me?

The rush of emotion is almost too high.

Too much.

I close my eyes before I blow out my candles, not wanting to waste my wish even though I know it's bullshit. Then I lean forward and blow out the candles as everyone claps for me.

"How did you know?" I ask Lucas, stepping to the side as Paige whisks away the cake to pluck the candles and start slicing for our little group. "I didn't tell anyone it was my birthday today."

He shrugs. "I saw it on your MatchLink profile when we first started talking."

"And you remembered?"

He blushes.

Like taking the time to file away information about me is something he should be embarrassed about, or like I might judge him for remembering something like this.

But I embrace him, wrapping my arms around him tight.

"Thank you," I whisper.

He nods, gives the top of my hair a kiss and steps back.

"You're welcome."

My phone beeps in my pocket and I step away, pulling it out, hoping it's Wyatt. I smile when I see it's him.

Wyatt: Can you meet me outside?

Me: Sure. Gimme a second.

I glance around, making sure no one needs me, then head out to the courtyard where I find Wyatt sitting on the steps.

"Hey, why didn't you come inside? You just missed it."

"Missed what?" he asks, giving me a tight smile, his face looking tired and distracted.

I furrow my brow. "What's wrong?"

He shakes his head. "I'm just tired. What did I miss?"

I wrap my arms around his stomach and lift up on my toes. "It's my birthday."

I press my lips to his but I feel Wyatt freeze against me, so I pull back.

"Don't feel bad for not knowing, okay? I'm surprised Lucas remembered. But there's cake. Do you want to come inside and eat some with me?"

He lets out a sigh and presses his forehead to mine. "Happy birthday, Hannah. Sure, I'd love some cake."

I don't know what has him in a weird mood, but I press a kiss to his cheek and lead us inside, dropping his hand as we get into the kitchen.

"Look who I found outside!" I say, with a big smile.

Wyatt gets a chorus of hellos from everyone. He does the rounds, hugs, hand shakes. And just as Paige hands me a piece of cake, he gets to Lucas, who looks at him with a hard glare that I don't understand before stalking out of the room.

Wyatt scratches the back of his neck, his expression uncomfortable.

But no one else notices. Everyone's too busy eating cake and dispersing back into the living room to dance and drink and talk with other people.

I sidle up next to Wyatt. "Everything okay?"

The last thing I want to do is tell him I saw what was clearly an strained interaction between him and Lucas, but I still want him to feel like he can talk to me about it.

But he shakes his head. "Nothing," he says, then steps away and grabs a beer from the fridge.

My heart sinks just a little bit.

This isn't how I pictured tonight.

I thought we'd be flirty, sneak up to my room and fool around while the party raged downstairs. Not that there would be lots of awkward tension and discomfort that I don't understand.

He stands next to me for the next half hour as we listen to Otto and that Aaron Singer guy from Harbor's as they tell us about a trip they took to Iceland last year.

But I can see the writing on the wall when he turns to me not long after and tells me he has to leave.

"Really?" I ask, though I feel guilty even saying that. He clearly isn't having a good evening, and I should want him to get rest or whatever he needs to make sure he feels better.

He nods. "Yeah, I'm just... my head is in a weird space right now. But I'll text you tomorrow, okay?"

"Sure."

We head to the front door and step out to the courtyard, and I can't help myself when I place a soft kiss on his lips. He squeezes my hand, then gives me a tight smile. "Happy birthday, Hannah. I'll make it up to you, okay?"

And then he turns and heads home, leaving me wondering what's really going on.

When I wake up early the next morning, I do the first thing that comes to mind.

I pull out the manual to my amazing new camera and get to reading.

There are so many things to learn, so many differences between my old, crappy piece of shit and this new, very expensive, work of craftsmanship.

And that's where Lucas finds me two hours later. My back against my bed, all of the camera parts spread out around me, with the manual open to one of the last pages. And a huge, nerdy smile on my face

"You know, I feel like there's no way we can be related."

My cheeks pink slightly.

"No one I'm related to would take all of the time to read the manual first."

"Well, my patience is definitely something I got from my mom," I reply, crawling to my feet, cringing when I realize my right foot has fallen asleep.

"Have you fiddled around with it enough yet so we can take it out and shoot some photos?"

I nod, my face covered in nothing but happiness.

"Let's walk down to Mary's to get some morning drinks, and you can take pictures of everything we see."

"That sounds so fantastic."

We wander down The Strand as I test out the camera. I play around with the digital settings and try new exposures. There's an expression I've heard before, being like a kid in a candy store. I've always understood the concept, but having never been a child in a candy store, I never felt like I *really* got it.

Until today.

This feels like the first moment I've really understood what that meant. There's just so many things I want to do and try with this camera, that I don't even know where to start.

"You work tonight, right?" he asks, taking a sip of his coffee as he follows me down The Strand.

I nod.

"Tomorrow, I need to head up to Downtown LA to handle some stuff with my mom and our lawyer." He shrugs, like it's an everyday occurrence that most people would understand. "Do you want me to invite her here after? We could all have dinner."

My eyes widen, behind my lens as I'm attempting to capture a shot of a bird on the wall that divides The Strand from the beach.

Lucas laughs at my reaction.

I step over next to where he stands, leaning against the half wall dividing the pathway from the beach.

He hands me my tea and I take a sip, thinking it over.

"Is it okay if I tell you I'm not ready?" I ask, not wanting to be rude, but also not sure if it's the right timing yet.

He rubs his face, though I can tell he's hiding a smile.

"I do want to meet her, I swear. But I just need a little more time." I sigh. "I have to get over a few things before I can *not* see her a certain way. And she's your mom. I want to care about her the way *you* care about her."

Something soft comes across Lucas' face but he turns away before I can really understand what it means. "Not a problem."

He takes back my tea and we walk for a few more minutes, the sound of my camera shutter clicking softly as I continue to take photos.

"I'll just make sure to tell her you don't want to meet her yet."

I turn and glare at him, seeing his teasing smile. "Stop it, or I'll chuck this at your face right now."

―――――――

When I get off work that night, I have a text waiting for me from Wyatt.

A little happy fairy does a dance in my mind.

After our weird interaction last night, I was worried. I couldn't shake off this strange feeling and I wasn't sure what to expect. So hearing from him is exactly what I need.

Hopefully he was just in a funk and everything is back to normal.

Wyatt: Hey. Plans today and tomorrow?

I grin, shooting off something small in reply.

Me: Nothing. What's up?

A few seconds later, my phone lights up, showing that Wyatt's calling me.

"Hey," I say, excited to hear from him.

"Hi," he replies, his voice warm. Much more like the Wyatt I have gotten to know and am starting to fall for.

I almost laugh at myself.

There's no *starting*. I've fallen. Hard.

And he's totally worth it.

"Hi."

He chuckles. "Hey."

Then I start laughing, too. "You know, it's been one day since I've seen you, and I miss you," I say. "I don't know if that's a thing I should say. But it's the truth."

There's a pause. "I miss you, too. Want me to come pick you up?"

I grin. "Absolutely."

"Good, because I was planning on coming to get you anyway, so I'm pulling in to the alley now."

I turn and see a pair of headlights coming towards me, and I laugh into the phone.

"That was a bit presumptuous of you," I reply as Wyatt parks the car and gets out, his phone still to his ear.

"Confident of me," he corrects, rounding the front of his still running car. He pockets his phone and steps into my space, his hands coming to either side of my face. "But I think you might be just as crazy about me as I am about you. So I took the risk."

I beam at him until his lips drop down to mine, and he gives me a kiss.

A deep one, much more than I'm expecting in a back alley behind my work on a random night of the week.

But it does what every kiss from Wyatt does.

Makes me feel love drunk.

He steps back, grabbing my bike and sliding it into the back of his SUV with the efficacy of a man on a mission. "Let's go."

Ten minutes later, we're walking in the front door of his house. Well, the guesthouse at his mother's. I haven't been up here before, though I've definitely seen the interior of the main, so I feel pleasantly surprised at how homey it is.

Warm colors and soft furnishings. More of a rustic feel than the modern woods and metals across the courtyard.

"This is beautiful," I say, kicking my shoes off at the door and wandering into the living room. "I'll be honest, this isn't at all what I was expecting of the place you live."

Wyatt chuckles as he heads into the kitchen and grabs two wine glasses from an upper cabinet.

"What did you expect?"

"I don't know," I answer. "Something more sterile, maybe. More bachelor-ish. This is like... a home."

"Well, that's definitely Vicky's doing. This guesthouse isn't used often anymore, but she told me she wanted me to have somewhere comfortable to stay when I finally came home." He shrugs as he uncorks a bottle of red. "But this place has never really felt like home to me."

"Where was the last place that felt like home?"

"I mostly grew up in a house on The Strand. My parents bought this property when I was ten, but it wasn't done until I was almost fourteen. So I only lived here for a few years before leaving for college. And I lived in the main house."

"It took *four years* to build this property?"

Wyatt rolls his eyes, carrying our two glasses over to where I stand on the other side of the counter. "Yeah. That's what happens when you want custom everything imported from a million different countries."

I shake my head. "Wow. Well, the main house *is* beautiful."

"Beautiful. And sterile. It's more like a museum than a home." Then he shakes his head. "But let's not talk about that. How was your day today?"

He hands me my glass, then leads me over to take a seat on the couch, a big soft plush thing that you sink right into and never want to get up from.

My expression perks, and I launch into the story of my new camera, so excited to share with him that I now get to take pictures of birds pooping on a wall in really high quality.

He laughs. "That's amazing. I'm so happy for you. So what's your plan, then. Now that you have the camera you need, will you start a business?"

I lift my shoulders, an uncomfortable expression coming across my face, though I try to laugh through it. "Oh, I just… I don't know. I don't think I'm ready for that. You know? Like, I just have so much more to learn first."

He shakes his head. "That's always going to be true. There will always be new things to learn. But that doesn't mean you shouldn't start now. Dive in and grab your dream, Hannah."

I wish it was as simple as that. But a business requires startup capital. Websites, marketing, even *more* tech and resources that I still need to save up and buy.

"I have some things I'm thinking about," I finally say, taking a large sip. "We'll see how it goes."

"I believe you can do whatever you set your mind to, Hannah,"

Wyatt says, and something inside of me wants to weep at how earnest he sounds. "You've gotten through so much in your life. This is one of the last hurdles to get you where you want to go. And I wish you could believe in yourself as much as I do."

I give him a smile, shake my head almost in disbelief.

I've never had someone say things like that before, never had someone speak such beautiful words, try to build up confidence in me so unconditionally.

It scratches something in my throat, wells something up in my chest.

"You look like you have something on your mind," he says, taking my free hand in his and tracing his fingers along my palm.

I shiver, the tiniest movement from him causing big reactions inside of me.

"I'm just glad to be here with you, is all." I gaze into his eyes, enjoying the way he looks right back at me.

Wyatt looks at me like he can really see me. Like I belong here. Like I matter.

There's something inside of me that wants him to be the one I sleep with for the first time. The one who teaches me what it's like to experience that type of pleasure and bite of pain.

I might have been a little irrational with my thought process that first night, when I invited him upstairs on our first date. Now, though, it feels right.

But I'm unpracticed with seduction, even if I do manage to get brave every so often. So I don't even know where to begin.

"You're so beautiful," he says, setting his wine glass down. Then his hand comes up to tuck a loose end from my ponytail behind my ear. "Do you know that? Do you know how it makes me feel when you look at me like you do?"

"How do I look at you?"

"Like you never want to look away." He shakes his head, like he wants to say something else. But instead he leans forward, presses his lips against mine.

I sink into his kiss, allowing myself to be devoured by something that looks so small but feels so big.

So much.

Too much.

No, not too much.

Not enough.

I set down my wine glass and stretch my length on the couch, pulling Wyatt on top of me. The weight of him something warm and comforting as he settles between my legs.

My hands go into his hair, twirling through his strands as our tongues dance and thrust and our bodies move. He makes me feel so sexy, and my body heat level rises as we continue to kiss and moan and touch.

But eventually, I feel like something's wrong.

When I reach my hand down between us, he twists his fingers through mine. When I press against him, he shifts his hips slightly away. It feels like he's subtly rebuking my inexperienced attempts to move us further, and it starts to whittle away at my confidence.

Maybe he's just appeasing me. Maybe he doesn't feel the same about my body as I do his.

The choking feeling it creates inside of me becomes almost overwhelming, until I can't continue to kiss him for fear that I'll cry into his mouth.

"What's wrong?" he asks, pulling back, the concern on his face so intense. "Are you okay?"

I nod. "Yeah, I'm just…" I roll out from under him. "I think I'm gonna go home." I walk over to the door, picking up my shoes and preparing to tug them back on.

"Hannah…" His voice trails off, and when I look over, I see him sitting on the couch, his elbows resting on his knees and his head hanging forward.

"It's okay, Wyatt. You don't have to explain." I shoulder my backpack. "Can you unlock your car so I can get out my bike?"

"Don't go," he says. "Please. I want you here."

My shoulders drop, but I stay silent.

I don't know how I feel right now. Confused, I guess. Because after our previous encounters, tonight feels like he's trying to push me away. So I don't understand how he can really mean that.

He stands and makes his way over to me, taking my backpack off and dropping it to the floor. Then he takes my face in his hands. It's a move that normally makes me feel so treasured. But in this moment? I don't know.

"I want you here, with me. More than you could possibly imagine."

"Then… what was wrong?" I whisper, my eyes unable to look directly in his for fear of what I'll see. I know rejection all too well, and I'm not ready to see it from him.

He dips his head so his eyes are in line with mine. "I just have something on my mind, is all. And..." he pauses. "And I worry that we're moving to fast for you."

My cheeks flush. "Is it that obvious?"

He grins, kisses my nose. "It's not a bad thing to have these things be new, Hannah. It's a little intimidating, but it isn't bad."

I scrunch my brows together as his hands drop from my face, his fingers linking with mine.

"Why is it intimidating for *you*? You know what you're doing."

Wyatt laughs, and while my first reaction is to feel like he's laughing at me, the clear affection shining in his eyes allows that thought to drift away just as quickly as it came.

"Do you have any idea what I feel when I look at you? How enraptured I am with you? I'm afraid I won't be able to give you that perfect first time. That you'll regret me someday." He lifts a shoulder. "It's a lot of pressure, and I don't want to disappoint you."

It blows my mind that he was thinking something like that. That he would even wonder how I felt. My entire experience with men and sex has been them taking what they want without question. Grabbing, groping, touching, shouting.

The idea that he's thinking so much about me?

It brings in a new emotion I think I'm not ready to name. Something I've never said to anyone. An emotion meant only for the closest people in life. Something I haven't put a word to since Joshua died eleven years ago.

"The fact you care enough to... even think about that..." I trail off, shaking my head. "It means everything to me."

He leans down and presses his lips to mine. "And you mean everything to me," he whispers. "There's no rush for something this important."

I feel so much better, having gotten this conversation out of the way. Now, I don't have to worry about some secret that I'm keeping from him.

So I nod, lifting up to kiss him again.

And then he does the gentlemanly thing and goes down on me before he takes me home.

Chapter Twenty Three
WYATT

"Who was that girl?"

My mother's question sends an uncomfortable thread of unease down my spine.

I turn to look in her direction, finding her standing at the door to my office, leaning against the doorjamb, a glass of clear liquid in her hands.

My shoulders droop slightly. If my mother's drunk, this conversation will be a lot easier to handle.

"What girl?"

She waves her hand around, the one holding the glass, spilling a drop onto the carpet. "The one that was talking so much to Ivy today."

I can't help the little bit of joy that shoots through my chest, remembering Hannah and Ivy together today.

It was Ivy's thirteenth birthday party.

Originally, we'd planned on having a party at the house.

Something big and fun to make sure my little sister feels overwhelmed with affection and love.

But as the day got closer and closer, I realized that a big party is what my mother wanted for her, not what Ivy wanted.

So I changed it.

Of course, Vivian Calloway was *not* pleased when she started to get phone calls asking her why the 'event' was cancelled. She gave me quite a bit of shit about it, actually. But I was quick to remind her that Ivy's medications make her tired, and that being *too* overwhelmed wouldn't be good for her health.

She begrudgingly gave in.

So today, we did what Ivy wanted to do.

We had dinner at Bennie's at the Pier.

Hannah was supposed to be a guest at the table, of course, instead of a waitress. I'd offered to call in a favor to get her the Saturday night off, with her permission. But she said she needed to keep working, assuring me that she would be the one to serve our table.

And there she was, with a big smile and so much attention for the birthday girl.

My mother sat at the opposite end from where I sat with Ivy and Ben, who left the dinner table as soon as he could come up with an excuse for why he needed to head to the kitchen for some non-existent emergency.

Lucas came too, though he steered clear of me the entire evening, offering just a hello and a handshake when he arrived.

I assumed that Lucas' presence would distract my mother. She, of course, knows that Lucas and Ivy share a father. And she knows that Lucas knows.

There's a bit of fear, I think, in my mother that Lucas will tell Ivy, even though he already assured my mother that he has no plans to do so.

So she watched him like a hawk.

Which I thought would mean she didn't really *see* the girl that kept talking in sign language with Ivy.

Apparently, that isn't the case.

A little bit of anxiety creeps under my shirt as I consider how to answer my mother's question.

"She's my girlfriend," I say, knowing full well that I haven't said as much to Hannah. "She loves chatting with Ivy since she knows how to sign."

I watch my mother's eyes widen. She's never heard me call someone a girlfriend before.

I mean, she's *seen* the girls, obviously. The parade of women that have been on my arm at every Calloway Foundation function, the ones that did the walk of shame out of my bedroom in high school.

But this is probably a first.

No, it's definitely a first.

For me, and my mother.

She considers me for a minute, like she has something to say.

But ultimately, she just points a finger at me, wavering slightly on her feet.

"Calloway men don't know how to commit to anything but their own self-interest," she finally says, her expression looking bitter and angry. "Don't do something stupid."

And then she stalks off, leaving behind only the scent of her perfume and the bit of vodka she dropped on the floor.

I shake my head, feeling a little confused and a whole lot frustrated at her words since they do nothing but highlight the true conflict that lies in the way of anything serious happening with the girl that's slowly changing my life.

I lie to myself, pretending like it isn't a big deal that I'm dating Lucas' sister behind his back. But it's something that claws at me. Forces me to keep things from getting further physically.

What I said to Hannah that night at my house last weekend was true. I *do* worry that we're moving too fast for her. The last thing I want is to get too hot and burn out quickly. Or for her to want something I'm willing to give her, and then regret her decision later.

I want her to know, for certain, that moving things forward between us is really what she wants. Hannah knows herself well enough to make that decision on her own. So I guess the true *in*decision between us comes from me.

We continue to fool around, though we don't do anything as public as our date a few weeks ago at Papa Louis'.

Instead, we spend time in the guesthouse, just the two of us. Over the past week, we've ordered take out, watched TV, gone on another motorcycle ride. One night, we just read in front of the fireplace, then laid out on the deck and did some stargazing with that app Hannah mentioned to me before.

Spending time with her is magical. And I find myself wanting to promise her the world.

"Promise me nothing," she'd said to me one night as we snuggled in my bed, our mostly naked bodies wrapped together, our skin warm and flushed from recent orgasms.

"What?"

"I know you're leaving for London soon," she'd continued. "I don't want you to feel like you have to make me any grand promises or… I mean, I don't know where this is going, between us. And I…"

She'd paused, and I could hear her trying to steer clear of being too emotional.

Hannah had mentioned once to me that she had to try really hard to take people at their word, that too many people used to let her down, would make promises that they couldn't keep.

So even though I hadn't liked the idea of her thinking we were going to end any time soon, I knew her request was said as a way to protect herself.

"Hannah, I won't make any promises to you that I can't keep, okay?" I'd said.

She hadn't responded, only snuggling closer into me, pressing her face to my chest.

Now, as I sit at my desk in an office that contains a file with all of her personal information, I think about that night, and wonder if I'll be able to keep that promise.

Because Hannah is a secret I want to keep just for myself. Someone I want to hold on to, and I can't seem to get enough of.

But with the news I got a few days ago from Ivy's doctor that they haven't found a match yet from the bone marrow registry, I'm feeling a heightened pressure. This intense feeling that we're just living on borrowed time.

"Are you even listening to me?"

I glance over from where I've been watching Hannah walk around the dining room.

I'm at dinner with Ben at his restaurant, one of the first times I've come in to eat since things between Hannah and I started to escalate.

Hannah suggested this, actually. We've been talking about siblings, the importance of working things out. And I couldn't help but take her advice.

After coming out of such tragedy and loss, I feel like I owe it to her to try and patch things up with my brother.

Though, really, I don't even know where to begin.

"Sorry, I was just…"

"Ogling my waitress."

I finally really look at Ben, grimacing when I see his smirk.

"You know, I wondered why you wanted to sit inside, downstairs, instead of at your precious rooftop table." He waves out a hand in Hannah's direction. "Now I know. It's because of the girl."

I roll my eyes, irritated that he caught me.

That it was so easy to see.

"Don't roll your eyes at me," he says, though I can hear the bit of teasing in his voice.

It gives me pause, because normally, Ben and I aren't teasers. We don't *play* with each other. At least we haven't in years. A decade, probably. Maybe longer.

But I stay silent, feeling awfully broody for a man who is supposed to be trying to patch things up. I should be saying something important. About family and relationships.

All I can manage to do, though, is watch Hannah smile at patrons and move lithely between tables carrying a heavy tray of food, her figure looking just as sexy in her uniform as it does in a pair of panties and a bra.

"Why are we here, Wyatt?" Ben finally asks. "I can count on one hand the number of times in my entire life that you've wanted to get dinner with me for the fuck of it. So there has to be a reason."

I sigh, looking over at him. Seeing the focus of his attention directed at me.

Sack up, I tell myself.

I'm here for a reason. A good one. An altruistic one. It's time for me to just say what have to say.

"We should spend more time together. That's what I wanted

to say."

Ben freezes, a fry half-way to his mouth.

"I know things are awkward and tense and there are probably things I've done to bother you, because there are definitely things you've done to bother me." I shake my head. "But we can't keep going with this hatred anymore. This resentment. With what's happening with Ivy, we can't let this rift be here anymore."

He drops his fry back to his plate and leans against the booth behind him, his expression solemn.

"You could have bet me a million dollars and I never would have guessed something like that would have come out of your mouth."

I furrow my brow.

"Something is different. With you." He leans forward, folding his hands together on the table. "And I can't figure out what it is. But I like this version of you. So don't stop whatever is going on."

I swallow thickly and can't help it when my eyes stray to Hannah.

Ben laughs, a sound I haven't heard from him in a while. Not with any real joy behind it.

"Of *course* it's because of the girl." He glances back at Hannah. "She's beautiful, I'll give you that. But you know who she is, just like I do. And I think you're gambling with something, here. Something bigger, with more risk than you have the ability to bet."

He's right. I'm taking a huge risk. My feelings for Hannah continue to develop. My desire to see her happy growing by leaps and bounds.

But Hannah's happiness isn't the only one I have to consider. And when I take all of the lives I care about and balance them out, it becomes pretty clear that one wrong move will tip everything over.

"Can I give you some advice?" he asks, and I nod. "Be honest with her. About everything."

"That worked out so well for you," I say, drily, remembering what happened to him a few years back.

"It did work out," he says, surprising me. "It wasn't easy. And there were a lot of consequences along the way, things I had to atone for, ask forgiveness for... but it all turned out okay in the end."

He picks up his beer and takes a sip, then lifts his hand up to flag Hannah to come over and give us the check.

She smiles and nods at him, and my heart pitches over.

Because when I look back out at the girl I'm falling for, when I consider all of the intricacies and the delicate relationships and problems moving forward, I just know.

I'm not able to see a future where things turn out okay.

For either of us.

That evening, when Hannah shows up at my door, I can tell something's different.

She went home after her shift.

Showered.

Changed.

She smells amazing when she walks past me into the house, her hair damp and loose around her shoulders, that peachy lotion wafting around her and making me eager to press my face into her smooth skin.

We don't open any alcohol, don't turn on the TV, or focus on anything other than each other.

She just takes me by the hand and leads me into my room.

I follow her wordlessly, mesmerized with her sudden shift in confidence. Enamored by the way her eyes connect with mine.

"I've been thinking about this a lot," she says, pushing me lightly so I'm sitting on the edge of my bed. "And I think you were right. Sex isn't something that we need to rush into. It should be something that happens when I'm ready."

I nod, though a part of me wants to pop that earlier version of me in the face.

"Well, see, the thing is…" she pauses, takes a deep breath and lets it out. "I can't imagine my first time being with anyone other than you." She steps forward so she's standing between my legs, brings her hands up to my neck, leans just slightly into me. "You've been so thoughtful, and caring, so intent on protecting me from making a premature decision about something that feels bigger than I can really imagine. And thank you. Thank you for caring enough that you didn't just take because something was possibly available to you."

She leans in and kisses me, just a soft kiss on the jaw. "But I know this is what I want. I know that if I were to ever have a man be with me in the most intimate way possible... that it wouldn't be right if it wasn't the man I was falling in love with."

Her eyes search mine for just a second, but then she kisses me before I even have the capacity to respond. Her mouth opens against mine, her tongue tangling, tasting lightly of citrus and chocolate.

Before I can think about anything, I'm overwhelmed by her smell, by her taste, by everything she wants to give to me in this moment.

And like the selfish man I am, I decide to take.

I pull her into me, my hands on her ass, lifting her so she straddles me, and then I turn and lay her on the bed against the stack of pillows against the wall.

Taking a moment to look at her, I see flushed cheeks and pouty lips and eyes looking at me, wide and filled with desire.

And then I press my lips to hers, and our kisses are frantic. Like we've been so starved for so long and we're finally being given some sort of sustenance in an unlimited supply. I can't help but take and take and take, hoping to fill me to the brim when I've been living on empty for so long.

We pull off our clothes quickly, having gotten used to being partially naked with each other from all of the other times we've fooled around. But this time, as I hover above her in just my boxers, and she reaches behind her back to unclasp her bra, a lacy black thing that I've never seen her wear before, it feels supremely different.

Infinitely more important.

Like she's offering herself to me as a gift, and it's my job to accept it with incredible gratitude. With the slow reverence she deserves.

I hold her in place, stopping her from removing it herself, and she gives me a questioning look, probably worried that I'm going to stop us from moving forward. But that couldn't be further from the truth. I only want us to slow it down. Savor every breath and sigh and moan and peek of skin.

My hands rise to pull her straps over her shoulders, and I bend my head so I can kiss the areas being revealed.

She smiles, sighs, rests her hands in my hair, relinquishing control to me so I can lead us where we need to go.

"You smell so good," I say, tracing my nose up the crook of her neck and up to her ear.

She giggles softly when I nibble her there, but it turns into a moan when I drop my mouth to her neck and suck, my hands moving to finish taking her bra off.

I peel back the lacy cups, pulling back to watch as I reveal her pert nipples, a dark pink that always makes me salivate.

Sliding further down the bed, I take her breasts in my hands and mouth, lathering her in the attention I know she wants. That she deserves.

I've never been a breast guy, always preferring hips and ass over the top heavy look so many women seem to prefer nowadays. But Hannah could convert me. She doesn't have anything crazy going on, just the perfect handful. But it's enough to grip and touch and play.

I suck one nipple into my mouth, keeping my eyes on her face, twirling my tongue around the tip until I can see her squirm. I love when she gets to that place, when just the light stroking and gentle sucking tugs threads down and starts tugging on her core, makes her start to beg for it, pant with need.

Her hands run affectionately over my body, her fingernails pressing in just enough to raise the hairs on my neck and cover my body in goose bumps.

I continue mapping her body, slipping my fingers into the hip of her underwear and sliding them off, her legs lifting to help me. And then I waste no time putting my mouth between those long stems, licking her over and over, sucking hard and soft and fast and slow, trying to make sure she feels everything I feel when my mouth is pressed against her.

Everything I'm too afraid to voice out loud.

I kiss my way back up and refocus my mouth on hers, but allow my fingers to dip into the well between her thighs, tracing over the spaces that I know make her mindless and flustered and flushed with pleasure.

I slide in a second finger and she cried out my name.

"Wyatt," she says, "oh please, Wyatt."

I strum over her clit, suck on her neck, search for that spot, the one deep inside of her that makes her fly over that peak at the top.

And when she falls apart, her body going rigid then sinking lax back into the mattress, I reach over to my nightstand and get out a condom.

She looks at me with so much love as I slide it on and then hover above her.

"I'm sorry if I hurt you," I say, and I'm almost overwhelmed by how much I mean it.

Because the idea of bringing her any kind of pain is too much for me to process. But there's a place inside of me that know I mean more than just right now, more than just the physical pain.

Instead of responding, she brings her hands to my face and looks in my eyes, kissing me softly as I begin to slide inside of her.

She looks into my soul as she gives me everything.

It's so different like this, the depth of emotion surging through me as she welcomes me in, her arms wrapped around me, her face so close to mine.

She winces as I slide deeper, whimpers slightly, but her eyes stay focused, those greens so beautiful she's all I can see.

When I'm all the way in, our bodies already covered in sweat, I hold myself still, wanting to give her some of the control.

"Are you okay?" I ask, wondering what she's feeling, if her heart is pulsing with the same amount of emotion that's thundering around inside of me.

"I feel so full," she whispers.

I smile and press my lips to hers. "I think you're trying to say 'you're so big.'"

She laughs, and her walls squeeze around me. I can't help the moan, and how my hips pull back just slightly and then go forward again on their own.

She feels so good. That slick heat enveloping me, pulsing around me as she continues to adjust to this new sensation.

Her hands rest on my ribs, lightly tracing my skin. So delicately.

I slide a hand down and lift her left leg, pressing my fingers against the back of her knee and changing the angle as I pull out and then go back in.

Her mouth drops open, something like wonder on her face.

"I love having you inside me," she whispers, and then she tilts her head back and closes her eyes, bliss on her face.

I work hard to keep my movements slow, even though every muscle protests, directs me to take and pound and chase the orgasm I know is at the end of this.

But I don't want it to be over. And I don't want it to be just about me, and what I can get.

I want this to be everything she's ever thought it could be.

I press my mouth against hers, kissing her deeply, my tongue mimicking the plunges of my cock into her depths. And when I shift my hips just slightly, she lets out a gasp.

"Fuck, Wyatt. Can you go faster?"

I grin. "Absolutely. Just tell me what you want okay?"

She nods, and I revel in the awe apparent on her face.

I move, then. Faster. Pulling out and then sinking back in, over and over again, Hannah's moans and sighs and little noises getting louder and louder.

"Harder," she says, and my nostrils flare as I begin to pound into her warmth, the sound of our hips slapping together, the primal drive to bring us both pleasure guiding my movements.

Hannah's breasts bounce when I thrust, her nails digging in, that delicate touch long gone as her desire grows.

And then I feel that tingle at the base of my spine, the warm glow that tells me I'm getting close.

"I'm going to come soon," I say, dropping her leg and bracing over her. "I want you there with me."

She shakes her head. "Can I come again?"

I smirk. "Oh, baby. You have no idea."

My fingers move to her clit, and I begin to rub that tiny spot as I continue to thrust in and out.

Hannah cries out, an almost feral call, her fingernails dragging down my back. She looks like she wants to crawl out of her skin, like she might explode out of it any minute.

And then the flutter happens, the pulsing inside of her that I can feel on my dick, that tells me she's almost there.

Almost. Almost. So close.

Her eyes fly open again. "Wyatt," she whispers.

And then she explodes, her chest bowing off the bed as her orgasm streaks through her body, her inner walls clamping down around my dick.

Two more hard thrusts and I'm falling after her, my body splitting wide at the force of pleasure racing through me.

I call out her name, hold my body still.

We're like needy cats, after that, petting and kissing and caressing each other. Pulling each other close and touching each other everywhere that we can. Any skin-to-skin contact we can manage.

Eventually, I have to chuck the condom, but when I crawl back into bed, Hannah is laying on her side, facing me, a tiny smile on her face.

I crawl in next to her, tuck her in close so we're looking at each other.

Then I run a hand through her hair.

"Was it everything you hoped it would be?" I ask.

She smiles, presses her lips to mine.

"Better."

We wake once during the night and reach for each other again. This time when we come together, she's above me, straddling my hips, tossing her hair back like a goddess, giving me one of the most powerful orgasms I've ever experienced.

She's the most beautiful thing I've ever seen.

That night, I hold her close, my body spooning hers, wanting her near.

Almost like it knows I won't get to hold her ever again.

Chapter Twenty Four
WYATT

We're eating a hearty breakfast of frosted flakes when Eleanor calls and asks if Hannah can pick up her opening shift since she's sick in bed. As much as I want her to stay, I also know she cares about her friend and wants to make the extra money.

So when she grabs all her stuff, kisses me goodbye and heads out the door, promising me a repeat of last night when she comes back this evening, I don't complain.

Too much.

I also don't complain that I'm naked and about to turn on the shower when I hear a knock on the door.

Smiling, I wrap a towel around my waist and head out to the living room, wondering if something changed and she doesn't have to work.

"You don't have to… knock," I say, my voice cutting off and my smile falling when I open the door and see Lucas standing there.

He barges past me into the house, going straight for the liquor on the caddy in the kitchen.

"I told you to stay away from her," he spits, pouring himself a few fingers of his favorite whiskey. The guy really is becoming a bit of a lush. "And I come by this morning to talk to you about Ivy and I see her leaving?"

He takes a sip and glares at me.

"It's not what you think," I say, though as soon as the words are out of my mouth I realize they don't sound right.

What I *meant* to say is that it's different than what he fears. Because I know he assumes I'm just screwing around with her, that I don't really care.

But that couldn't be further from the truth.

If anything, she's becoming someone I care about *too* much.

"Oh really? So you're going to tell me you're not fucking my sister?"

I grit my jaw, hating the way he makes it sound. But I won't lie to him. So I shake my head.

And he laughs, something bitter and angry. Then he tips back his whiskey and downs a third of it.

"I can't believe you would use her like that."

His words are angry, his finger pointing in my direction, and I can't help myself when I say, "Oh, you have no idea the ways I've used her."

It's a nasty thing to say, and I regret it the minute I allow my baser instincts to control my mouth, but it does the intended job.

Lucas clenches his fists, rage overtaking his features, and I can tell we're just a few well-placed barbs away from coming to blows. We've only fought one other time. Back in high school. And that was over something stupid. Teenage hormones.

This, though... I know he means well. That he doesn't want me to mess up his sister's already fragile heart, especially when considering why he brought her here in the first place.

But I can't help how I feel about her. Can't make myself stop this endless plummet into something deep and beautiful. That's what loving her feels like.

I nearly choke when I think the words in my head, bring my hands up to rub at my face, the uncertainty and fear surging through me. I've never said that to anyone before, outside of my family. And even though it *should* scare the shit out of me, it doesn't. If anything, it raises my spirits.

And I know I have to convince Lucas that he needs to let this drop. That his fears about me and Hannah are unfounded.

Or at least, aren't as bad as he's imagining.

"I brought her here for a *reason*," he spits. "There was a plan. I can promise that it didn't include you getting your dick wet. And when you run off to London at the end of summer, guess who gets stuck cleaning up your mess."

At the callousness of his words, I see red, my logical mind flying out the window.

"Fuck you, Lucas!" I shout, jamming a finger into his chest. He bats my hand away, his nostrils flaring. "I was against this from the very beginning. So don't try to rest the blame on me. It was *you* that made up the excuses so I'd bump into her. It was *you* that said I needed to be the one to spend the most time with her."

"That's not how it was."

"That's *exactly* how it was. *You* brought Hannah here. *You* were the one who was so sure that if she met Ivy, felt welcomed, thought she had a family here, that she'd be that much more likely to help. And then what did you do as soon as she got to town? You bailed. You spent all your time with Otto or Lennon or who-the-fuck-ever, going off to surfing competitions and disappearing. And you left me to handle your stupid fucking *plan*. So I handled it."

He just shakes his head, the anger rolling off of him in waves.

"Nothing else to say?" I taunt.

We stand in silence for a second, just glaring at each other, our chests heaving like we've been running for miles.

And that's when I realize what I'm seeing on Lucas isn't anger.

Well. It is.

But it's different.

Because mixed in with that anger is pain. And if I know him at all... regret.

"Look," I say, dropping my arms and resting my hands on my hips, trying to sort out what to say to deescalate this. "We all have feelings involved in this. Much more than I ever would have thought if you'd told me this was going to happen. But this is where we're at."

Lucas continues to glare at me, and I can tell he's trying to hide how he feels. But I can see the pain of guilt around the edges. The emotions he feels because we both care about someone who was supposed to be a means to an end.

A way to possibly change Ivy's life forever.

We just never really thought through the fact that bringing her here would change all of our lives, too.

"When you told me about Hannah and Joshua…" I shake my head. "I mean… that was years ago. Almost a decade. We were just kids ourselves, okay? I think we both wish things had worked out differently. And I'm truly sorry that I talked you out of contacting her back then. But that doesn't mean you can't have a good relationship with her *now*. It doesn't mean the only reason Hannah is here is because we need her to help Ivy. Not anymore."

He sighs, downs the rest of his drink, sets it on the counter.

But before I can say anything else, make my final plea, I see something.

Out of the corner of my eye, I see movement. The front door slowly being pushed open. The blare of sunlight illuminating the room and the outline of someone standing in the doorway.

Hannah.

Hannah is standing in the doorway.

Why is Hannah standing in the doorway?

All I can see is the expression on her face.

The pain and disbelief in her eyes.

Her almost ashen skin.

"I forgot my phone."

It's the only thing she says, her eyes connecting with mine for only a brief second, then flitting to Lucas, a hint of fear and sadness mangled in with rock bottom devastation.

And like an idiot, I'm so stunned by her presence that I just stand there, my mouth gaping, surprise etched in my every atom of being.

She's here.

Right now.

Listening to everything I just said.

How is she here? She's supposed to be gone.

Then suddenly, she is. Her figure disappears, the sound of her tennis shoes plunking rapidly down the wooden stairs outside as she races away from us.

Finally getting the movement of my body back under control, I rush out behind her, nearly tripping down the stairs as I try to hold my towel in place around my waist.

"Hannah!" I shout as I come flying out of my gate.

When I look to the left, I can see her figure pedaling away in the distance.

I kick my garage door. "Fuck!" I yell, startling a woman walking her dog.

I don't even apologize, just race up the stairs two at a time.

Heading into my bedroom, I grab my phone and call her, cursing again when her phone starts to ring on her side of the bed.

Her side.

I could fucking cry right now.

I sit on the edge of my bed and put my head in my hands, wondering if I should do just that.

How did this happen?

"I'm assuming she heard everything we said," comes Lucas' voice from the door to my bedroom.

"No shit," I grit between clenched teeth.

We're both silent. There isn't really anything to say. I don't even know the first thing to do.

"Fuck," I whisper.

"Yeah."

I look over at Lucas and see his expression looks just as crestfallen as mine. He looks like someone died.

And to be honest, I'm pretty sure that whatever she heard? It killed something inside of her.

Because the way she looked at me? It killed something inside of me.

"I thought we'd have more time, that I'd be able to tell her..." I trail off and look at Lucas.

He sighs. Comes and sits next to me.

And then we sit in silence.

I don't know what Lucas is thinking about, but I'm replaying our conversation, trying to remember what I said. What might have wounded her the most.

My comment about using her?

The fact she was only brought here to help Ivy?

"Where do we even go from here?" Lucas asks, clearly feeling as helpless as I do.

I shake my head. "No fucking clue."

I get dressed quickly, grab both of our phones, and leave my house with one purpose in mind.

Find Hannah and make her listen to me.

Convince her to forgive me for all of the ways that I've clearly fucked this up.

My first stop is Bennie's, but I'm not surprised to learn that she got another server to pick up the shift she had picked up from Eleanor.

Lucas calls and says she's not at home, though her bike is there, which means she couldn't have gotten far.

"Unless she took a cab somewhere," Lucas interjects.

"Where the fuck would she go?" I say over the phone.

"Uh, I don't know," he says, sarcasm dripping from his voice. "The airport? The bus station? A hotel? Back to Phoenix? The last thing she wants right now is to talk to either of us. So one of us should probably wait here for her."

My stomach plummets at the idea that she might have left. For good. I can't imagine she would do that though. Hannah isn't impulsive. She's measured. Thoughtful. Careful. A decision like that would take time to make.

Though I can understand how overhearing your brother and your boyfriend talking about all the ways they lied to you might cause some uncharacteristically irrational behavior.

"You stay at your house. I have to keep looking. But call me if you hear from her or see her, okay?"

He agrees, and we hang up.

And then I go on a completely fruitless search, knowing I'm not going to find her on my own.

The Wave.

Harbor's.

Mary's.

I check the sand dune.

Even the yacht club.

I call all of my friends, let them know we're looking for her.

As the hours continue to pass with no sign of her, I head back to Bennie's at the Pier, my mind resigned to the fact that I won't be able to fix this just by trying to track her down.

But my trip back to Bennie's isn't in search of Hannah.

It's to talk to Ben.

He meets me in the loading bay and hands me a beer, clinks his bottle against mine before taking a seat next to me on the grimy steps leading up to the dock.

It's amazing how quickly and desperately I feel in need of my brother's advice.

The one man that I've considered a coward for years.

The man who seemed to be afraid and alone all the time.

Knowing how affected Hannah is probably going to be by what she heard, I need the wise words of a man who has had to deal with painful and bitter issues in relationships. The advice of a man who has truly hit rock bottom before, and seems to have found his own unique way to recover.

Because really, as Ivy's other brother, he might be the only one who will understand both my love for Ivy, *and* how much I love Hannah.

"That is… quite an unfortunate turn of events," he says to me after I finish relaying to him the entirety of the morning.

"So now, I don't know what to do. I don't even know where she is. Do I just wait? Sit around while she might be out there, hurting?"

"Do you really have any other choice?"

I sigh. "That's not what I wanted you to say."

"What did you want me to say, Wyatt? You came to me for a reason, and it isn't because I'm someone who sprays bullshit and rainbows when things are horrible. You came to me because you know I'll tell you the truth."

When I look at him, he must see the pain on my face, because he flinches.

"So tell me the truth," I say, dangling the mostly empty bottle between my fingers. "How do you see this turning out? Do you think she'll forgive us or…"

"Honestly? I don't know how *you* can come back from this. Lucas? Probably. He's her brother. They're blood. He's literally the only family she has right now. But you?" He shakes his head, tilts his bottle back and takes another swig. "You're one of the reasons she was stuck in foster care. Can you imagine what her life might have been like if she and Lucas had hit it off when she was younger?"

My stomach turns over and an iron fist squeezes my lungs.

"You're not to blame for what happened to her parents or her brother," Ben adds. "But I can see how she'll have a hard time getting over the rest. Because shit."

"So that's it?" I ask, shaking my head in disbelief. "Those are your wise words?"

My brother pauses, seeming to go off into his own mind for a moment, a small and painful smile coming across his face.

"You want wise words? Here they are. You will never know what might happen if you don't give everything you have to convincing her that you love her, and that you're worth forgiving. And I mean *everything*."

Chapter Twenty Five
HANNAH

My legs have never felt like this.
Like anchors.
Like chains.
My lungs are throbbing, my head aching as I continue to plow forward.
I don't even know how long I've been running. But I'd have to guess I've been out here for at least a few hours.
And I know I'm probably doing actual harm to my body.
That my muscles are going to rebel against this absolute wreckage I'm putting them through.
I didn't stretch.
I didn't warm up.
I haven't prepared.
And yet I've run longer than I've ever been able to in my life. My best guess would be that I've finally achieved my goal of running a half marathon. Though this isn't how I ever envisioned it

happening.

Because I've been running to find the bliss. The nothing. The absolute blankness that I can usually get to when I'm in pain or hurt or sad or just stressed.

But I can't find it.

I've been pushing and searching and I just... can't find it.

I slow myself down to a walk, my chest heaving, my muscles protesting as I shake them out.

Running the full length of The Strand that leads from Hermosa up to Playa del Rey, the road Wyatt took when we went on his motorcycle... I drop down to a squat and brace my head in my hands.

There's an empty place in my chest, something hollow and sticky and painful that didn't used to be there a few hours ago.

Or maybe it had. But it was much smaller.

Until the bomb that exploded and left a much larger wound behind.

I keep playing it over and over in my mind, as if somehow I can rehear it, not hear it, change what was said. But I know that's not the case.

Because how do you change the words *you have no idea the ways I've used her.* What else could that mean other than exactly what I heard.

"You brought Hannah here," he'd said. *"You were the one who was so sure that if she met Ivy, felt welcomed, thought she had a family, that she'd be that much more likely to help."*

It makes me feel like everything I've ever learned about Lucas, about Wyatt, about this town, this place that I started to feel like I might be able to find a place in...

Was it all a lie?

Was it all some big promise that was meant to fall through in the end?

I feel like I can barely breathe as I collapse in the grass at a small park at the end of the pathway, but it isn't just from the running. It's from this undeniable sense of having been a pawn in someone's endgame. My only role here was to be used.

The tears rush forward, sobs gasping from between my lips.

And the thing that kills me the most is that I probably would have helped anyway.

Whatever is wrong with Ivy? I might have been able to help

without the secrecy. Without the lying.

Without what happened with Wyatt.

I clutch my stomach, feeling like I might heave up everything inside of me.

Was that all a game too?

Was everything he told me just another part of this lie?

I don't know how this happened. How everything fell apart like this.

It feels like the world is closing in. Like, as much as I try to hold everything together, everything I thought about my life is like dry sand spilling between my fingers too quickly for me to recover. And the more I try to keep things going, the faster it falls apart.

How can they do something like this. Lie. Manipulate. Steal.

Because that's what Wyatt did. He stole something from me. And I don't just mean my heart or my virginity or even my first love.

He stole away my already fragile belief that anyone could ever promise me anything and actually mean it.

I finally get home a few hours later, my body feeling broken and battered, possibly even bruised.

Lucas comes flying off the couch when he sees me.

"Where have you been?" he asks, his face etched in concern, though I'm too tired to muster up even a fraction of interest. "We've been looking for you everywhere."

I ignore him, walking straight past where he stands and heading up the stairs, slowly, one step at a time.

He hovers behind me as I crawl up the stairs, finally speaking when I stand in the open doorway to my bedroom, his voice sounding broken and strained. Though I really don't care.

"Hannah, please let me explain."

"Don't," is the only thing I say, my voice rippling with exhaustion and my body fighting off a new wave of tears.

And then I close the door, sliding to the ground with my back against it.

The good thing about the pain I've put my body through with

this run is that most of my attention is focused on where I ache. I know I'm going to be feeling this for a while.

It's slow-going as I try to peel off all my clothes, my socks, my shoes. Every muscles protests, my brain barely able to take control enough to get me up and into the shower.

I soak there for a long time. A really long time. Lay on the tiled floor under cold water, under hot water, pull myself up onto the bench and examine my poor, battered feet. It looks like I might lose a toenail, a bruise forming underneath one already.

Once I've cleaned, soaked, dried and changed, I crawl straight into bed, not worrying about anyone but myself. I don't care if Lucas is right outside my door, worrying and waiting.

He can wait forever.

I'm gonna take a fucking nap.

When I wake, it's dark outside. I don't know how long I've been asleep, but I know it isn't long enough.

My stomach revolts, though, promising evil retribution if I don't put something inside of it. So I reluctantly attempt to get up, wincing and nearly crying with how tired I am.

I make slow work of heading down to the kitchen, intent on grabbing some leftovers. But I'm stopped dead in my tracks when I see Lucas and Wyatt sitting at the dining room table, their eyes zipping to mine as I round a corner and come into their line of sight.

"Hannah, please..." Wyatt starts, standing quickly, his chair scraping the floor.

I put a hand up. "I can't today. Whatever you have to say..." I shudder, a sob making its way through my body.

But I tamp that bitch down.

I will *not* be crying in front of these... assholes, who betrayed me in a way that I doubt can ever be undone.

Surprisingly, they listen. Allow me to head into the kitchen and pull a leftover helping of chicken and rice out of the fridge to warm up in the microwave.

But not saying anything isn't the same as leaving me alone,

and when I turn around, I see Wyatt hovering on the other side of the island.

If I were more mature, I might pay attention to the worry on his face, the concern in his eyes, how pained he looks or even the fact that this is a moment when he looks so entirely unsure when he has always been a man of decisive action since the moment we met.

That's not where I am, though.

I'm *not* more mature, and while I might notice those things, they don't matter to me.

Not right now.

Not when I'm still trying to figure out how I feel, where I stand in all of this.

"Tell me something," I say to Wyatt, holding my plate of food.

He perks up, like a dog desperate for any bit of attention.

"What's wrong with Ivy?"

His head falls forward, his eyes searching the marble countertops as if they hold the answer to my question.

"She has PNH. Paroxysmal Nocturnal Hemoglobinuria. It's a disease in her blood. She needs a bone marrow transplant."

My heart pains for the sweet girl I know. To be so young and have so much at risk. She has her whole life ahead of her, a life that could contain so much pain or be shortened far too quickly.

"Why do you want it from me?"

He pauses, glances off to the side, almost as if he isn't sure he wants to tell me. But then he swallows, looks back at me. "Bone marrow is more likely to be a match from siblings."

Another pause, while I'm trying to figure out how I would be involved. I feel like there's something I'm not understanding. Something that...

"Ivy's dad is Henry Morrison."

My shoulders drop at Lucas' words. My hands set my plate on the counter, and my eyes well with tears.

I shake my head, though it isn't in denial.

It's in disbelief.

How can this be the reality of the world I live in?

My parents die.

My brother dies.

I live in foster care.

And then I find out that my dad had an affair that produced a half-brother.

That's enough. That's all I can take.

Because if that's all there is, it means I can believe that my dad made a mistake one time.

That he hurt my mom but they worked through it.

Now, my dad is in question *again.* He had *another* affair. With Vivian Calloway. *Years* after the one that produced Lucas.

I let out a long breath.

"I know it's hard to believe…"

"I believe you." I shake my head, the broken pieces inside of me accepting exactly what they are. I run a hand across my face, wiping away the tears that have traitorously broken free. "Did you get tested?" I ask, looking at Lucas. "To see if you were a match."

His shoulders drop and he nods, a sad expression on his face. "Yeah. Wyatt paid a private company to test me since Ivy doesn't know about me."

There's a beat of silence, a moment where all I want to do is curl into a ball and cry my eyes out.

For me.

For Ivy.

For this stupid fucked up situation.

"I know it's a lot to take in," Lucas says, stepping forward. "We've had a lot more time to absorb it than you have. It's totally understandable if you need some time…"

"I'll do it," I say, cutting off his little speech. I'm not interested in what Lucas has to say. I'm not interested in words that are meant to soothe when I feel like just a single touch will light up my every nerve with pain. "Whatever Ivy needs. Just tell me where to go."

When I look at Wyatt, I see he's on the verge of tears himself, a small smile on his face. He takes a step towards me. Then another. And like the weak girl I am right now, I do nothing to dissuade him.

He steps into me. Wraps his arms around me. Pulls me into his body.

I can't help but soak it in.

One more time.

Because I know this will be the last time I feel that safety that I once believed was possible. That bit of trust I now know isn't true. The last time I'll smell that bit of woodsy cologne he likes so much.

"Thank you," he whispers, his arms tightening around me. "Thank you so much."

My hands come up between our bodies and I slowly push away, taking a step back, putting necessary distance between us.

"I'm not doing it for you," I say, my words caustic and bitter. "I'm doing it for Ivy."

He nods a few times, his face slightly confused. "Of course."

"And I want to make this clear right now, so there won't be any misunderstandings later…"

He freezes, then starts shaking his head.

"… I don't care what you have to say to me. What excuses you could possibly come up with for why…" my voice cracks. I bat away the tears on my cheeks. "… why you had to *use* me like that, to get what you want. I will *never* care. So I'm only going to say this once. And you better listen."

I pause, grit my teeth and let every ounce of pain pour out in my words, so he understands exactly how I feel. "I never, *ever* want to see you again."

His hand reaches out and grips the island, like he has to hold himself up.

And then I pick up my plate and leave the room, never looking his way, or Lucas', again.

Wyatt surprisingly respects my wishes. I don't know if I like it or hate it or some distorted amalgamation of both.

If he leaves me alone, does that mean he didn't ever really care for me as much as I did him?

I alternate between feeling this uncomfortable, painful lance straight through my chest, and missing him.

Missing what we were.

No.

Not missing what we were.

Missing what I *thought* we were.

Lucas, on the other hand, has become an annoying gnat I can't seem to get rid of. A gnat with big puppy dog eyes that seems to follow me everywhere.

He gets drinks and sits in my section at Bennie's. He's *always* home, which is new. And he even started going on runs with me, even though I never invite him and he always poops out after the first two miles, stopping at a bench to take a break while I continue down The Strand.

I've always been the one to talk about things, as awkward as they may be. But there's something about this that still feels too raw for me to really pull apart and dissect.

So the silent treatment has worked best for me, my only responses to things monosyllabic. Yes. No. Thanks. Hi. Bye.

Maybe it's childish.

But that's okay with me.

Part of me feels like I should just leave. Right now. Go back to Phoenix.

The cruelest part about all of this is that I literally have nowhere else to go.

I have no life anywhere.

I know Sienna would welcome me in an instant if I needed somewhere to stay for a few weeks while I get back on my feet. But I also know she and Jerome are finally moving in together and the last thing you need is a homeless best friend when you're just shacking up together.

And I haven't heard from Melanie in a while, though I'm not sure I would ever want to move out to New Mexico just so I have a couch to sleep on.

So I plug along, picking up every shift that I can, socking away as much money as possible.

The plan hasn't changed, just the circumstances.

But what I don't understand is what Lucas gets out of all of this. And finally, ten days after I found out that I'd been manipulated to come to California for a reason, I ask him.

Kind of.

"Why do you keep following me around?" I ask him as I eat my free meal from Bennie's in a to-go container at the kitchen table.

Lucas is reading on the couch. Which is weird enough, since I never see him read.

"That's what I don't understand. You did what you needed to do. You got me here. Pretended to be my friend and had all your friends do the same."

His face contorts into a grimace.

"Why not just let it go, now? You got what you wanted. There's no need to keep up the charade that you care about me *at all.*"

There's a pause.

Maybe he's absorbing my words because it's the most I've said to him at one time in over a week. Maybe he's figuring out what to say. Maybe he doesn't really know.

When he just continues to look at me, a pained look on his face, I shake my head. "Forget I asked," I say, my words laced with bitterness.

No longer hungry, I close my to-go container, pop it in the fridge, and head upstairs to my room. I close and lock my bedroom door and grab a blanket, then head out to the balcony, and up the stairs to the rooftop.

I've been coming up here a lot in my free time, but not to float in the Jacuzzi, or to sit on the loungers. Both of those things are tainted.

Instead, I crawl up on to the actual roof, tiptoe to the edge, and then sit down with my blanket wrapped around me.

This spot is my favorite because I can see the ocean, the entire beach stretched out in front of me, all of the bikers and skaters and dog walkers on The Strand. If I look to the left I can see all the way down to the Hermosa pier, and to the right, the Manhattan pier, way off in the distance.

I like this spot because I can sit up here and watch everyone live their lives. These rich, full, exciting lives with friends and family and trips to the ocean. Laughter and drinking and playing in the sand. I like this spot because it feels like the only true place I belong in this city.

On the outside, looking in. Observing as everyone else builds and grows and learns and loves and becomes loved by others.

It's a beautiful and tragic place to feel the most comfortable.

When I hear footsteps behind me, I know it's Lucas. Who else would be able to unlock my bedroom door and come up here?

"I locked my door for a reason," I say without looking in his direction, my eyes following a group of friends bringing in their chairs and towels as the sun sets in the distance.

"Well, what would a bedroom lock be without a brother to break it open?"

I can't help the tiny smile that appears, but I'm careful to hide it from him.

"Also, you may have locked *your* bedroom, but you didn't lock the other one. And that one *also* leads out to the balcony." He lifts his shoulders in a shrug and takes a seat next to me, his long legs stretching out in front of him, then bending slightly as he rests his arms on his knees.

I've seen photos of his mom. She's really short, which means he got those legs from our dad.

Maybe Ivy will grow into a pair of long legs, too.

I still haven't processed that part. That I not only have a half-brother, but also a half-sister. An adorable little girl who has done nothing wrong, and yet I can't help but resent just a little bit.

Just a smidge.

But if I'm honest, my care for her outweighs the upset, ten to one.

"I found out about you the day before my fifteenth birthday," he says. "I'd been searching for my dad, trying to find out where he was, why he disappeared years before. So I hired a P.I., and I found out what happened."

My heart pinches, remembering what it was like when I lost them both. My father with his loud laugh and my mother with her quiet smiles and mess of curly hair.

"The P.I. also said there was information about you in that file. A sister. And at first, I was shocked. Until I remembered the one time I met you when we were kids."

My eyes fly to his, an argument on my lips. There's no way we met when we were kids.

But then I see what Lucas has in his hands.

"I looked through this once right after you first moved in. You left it on the dining room table for some reason, and I couldn't help myself. I wanted to see Joshua, wanted to see Henry. So I looked through it all."

He hands the picture book over to me, one of the only possessions I've managed to keep throughout all the years of moving from home to home. Photos of me and Joshua and my parents. It's the most important thing I own.

He sets it into my hands and flips it open, and I can't help but let out a gasp.

It's a picture of me, and Joshua... and Lucas. Sitting on a wall at the pier. A shop I now recognized in the background. We're smiling, our arms around each other.

It never stood out to me because there's no beach in the background. But there it is.

I put a hand over my mouth, the emotions in my chest welling up until they're on the verge of spilling over.

"It makes sense that you wouldn't remember. You were only a toddler."

"I remember," I whisper. My hand drops down to trace over our childhood faces, astonishment surging through my veins. "I kept telling dad that the air smelled like fish. And he took us all to that kid's arcade with the ball pit."

I look over at Lucas, my eyes wide.

"When the investigator gave me all of the information, all I could focus on was the fact I'd never get to know my dad. That all the ideas I had about some fictional relationship we might be able to have someday... that those weren't ever going to come true."

He pauses, and something painful comes over his face. "And then when I did start to think about you, I wondered if the only thing you'd care about was that I had money."

I rear back. "I would *never...*"

"I know that. I *know* that. Now. But Hannah, I was a kid. A teenager. Growing in the surfing circuit. Starting to get fame and interest from other people. And I couldn't help but worry that you wouldn't want to know me, but you'd want what I could provide for you." He sighs. "So I was selfish and cowardly, and I handed that file over to Wyatt and told him to just let me know if anything happened that I needed to know about."

"So you told your friend to stalk me."

But he shakes his head. "No, I know it sounds that way. But mostly it was supposed to be just keeping tabs in case... I don't know. I could do anything? But we both pushed the knowledge of you to the side, moved on with our lives. Not realizing what you were going through all by yourself."

A tear trickles down my face but I bat it away. "It's not your fault that I was in foster care. I'd never set that guilt on you. Ever. I'm not upset you knew about me and didn't contact me until later in life. I am so emotional about this, Lucas, because you literally brought me here and exploited my biggest weaknesses. My biggest fears."

I pause, allowing myself the chance to wipe my tears into my blanket.

"I'm alone in the world. It's just me. And people have used me for most of my life to get something they want for themselves. Have made me feel like my only worth is what they can take from me. To find out that you brought me here and then purposefully pretended to be my friend so you could..."

"I didn't though. I swear it. None of this was pretend. I am so glad I know about you, that you agreed to come here and spend time getting to know me. I want you to be my sister. My friend. The stuff with Ivy was the excuse I used to finally do what I'd been too scared to do.

"Every minute of time we've spent together has been important to me. Maybe it started off the wrong way. But please don't cut me out forever. I just got used to having a sister that I love and want around, and I don't want to lose you because I was too cowardly to be honest."

I don't know how I feel about what he's said, though it does feel like a small weight has lifted off my chest. Even if that doesn't solve the problem.

"I love you, Hannah. I truly do. And if you hate me forever, I'll completely understand. But I want to make sure you know that I love you. And it has nothing to do with Ivy, or anything you can give to anyone. It's just because of who you are."

Another tear trickles down my face.

I feel exhausted. Mentally. Physically. Emotionally. All of my resources have been spent, and all I want to do is curl up and sleep this all away.

But I look at Lucas, who is so focused on me, his expression so earnest, and I feel that tiny little hope fairy in my heart begin to stir.

"I'll think about it," I whisper, tucking myself further into my blanket.

He puts an arm around my shoulders and presses a kiss to my temple. "That's all I can ask."

Chapter Twenty Six
WYATT

It's two whole weeks before I see her again. Ben told me to give it everything I had - getting her back - but I think some of giving everything means I have to fight against my normal response of putting myself in her space, instead choosing to respect what she wants.

And right now, she doesn't want to see me.

Which is why I'm so glad that she's here today. In a space that we're both allowed to inhabit.

I mean, you can't kick someone out of a hospital, right?

We're meeting with Dr. Lyons today. Me, mom, Ivy, Ben, and Hannah.

Lucas was invited, but he said he didn't want to intrude since Ivy still doesn't know he's her brother, so he's waiting in the car to take Hannah home whenever we're done.

I told him to let me drive her home.

He told me to fuck off and that he's working on his own

relationship with her and I should find my own time.

Prick.

But I get where he's coming from, to some degree. I wouldn't let anyone else take away my time with Hannah if she was willing to grant even a few minutes my way.

Right now, she won't even look at me. She's sitting in the corner of the waiting room, signing with Ivy. Smiling and laughing.

Hannah has always been incredibly kind and loving to my sister. More than most people. But I can see the shift, now that she knows Ivy is *her* sister, too.

There's more love in her eyes.

"Hello everyone," Dr. Lyons says, my attention fracturing and heading in her direction as she approaches us.

Then she looks at Ivy.

Ready to come back?

Ivy nods, though that lighthearted happiness she'd had on her face when talking with Hannah quickly dims.

Once we're in Dr. Lyons' office, she closes the door and takes a seat behind her desk.

"A full room today," she teases, her hands moving as she speaks. Then she looks at Ivy. *You have so many fans.*

Ivy giggles.

"The big difference today is that we've brought Hannah with us. She's Ivy's biological sister and is willing to be tested for a bone marrow transplant."

Ivy slips her hand into Hannah's, looking up at her with affection. When we told her about Hannah, she hadn't cared about the logistics or the web of relationships and family. She'd been through the roof. Over the moon excited.

My mom had been... understandably icy when she realized the girl I'd been dating was Henry's daughter, a representative of the family that he wouldn't leave to spend time with Ivy.

But my mom knows how to be the plastic politician when it suits her, so we luckily haven't faced any negative setbacks, because she's keeping her mouth shut.

"How wonderful," Dr. Lyons says, a smile stretching on her face. "We can do blood tests today, if you're up for it?"

Hannah nods. "Absolutely."

Dr. Lyons then launches into a brief but detailed explanation of testing, and what they're looking for in a match.

"You'll have a twenty-five percent chance of having the same HLA as both parents, which is what we're looking for in donors for bone marrow."

Hannah's brow furrows. "We don't have the same mom. Does that impact our percentage."

There's a pause from Doctor Lyons.

"I apologize, I assumed you were a full sibling with Ivy. The current protocol for HLA matching is for identical sets only."

"What does that mean?" I ask, sitting forward on my seat. "You told me a blood relative would be Ivy's best option for bone marrow. I brought you a blood relative."

I can feel Hannah bristling next to me, but I can't focus on her right now.

"Yes, but the likelihood of Hannah's HLA matching Ivy's is significantly lowered because they're not full siblings. We can still do the blood work to see if she's a match, but the likelihood has dropped from twenty-five percent to closer to five percent that she'll be a person who can donate."

A long, painful breath leaves my chest and I slump back in my seat. I can feel the ripple going through the room. My mom's back goes rigid. Ben's looking out the window. Hannah looks on the verge of tears.

Ivy looks around confused, seeming to have only understood part of the information.

Don't worry, I say. *Even if Hannah isn't a match, we'll keep looking for one.*

Then I lock eyes with Hannah over Ivy's head. I'm so saddened by this news, and it's taking everything inside of me to stay calm for my sister so that I don't flip a table or storm out.

It feels like this means I did all of this for nothing. Hannah coming here and getting hurt, raising the hopes of my entire family... it's all a wash.

Hannah stands to leave and go get her blood work done, but drops in front of Ivy and squeezes her hands.

Even if they say our bone marrow doesn't match, I'm still so glad I get to be your sister.

Ivy slides her hands around Hannah's neck, and the two embrace. It's an emotional moment. Something beautiful between the two of them that not even sickness can touch.

Hannah leaves to get her blood drawn, Ivy going with her for her own follow up tests, and I feel like the only light left in all of this is about to get extinguished.

"I'm sorry for the confusion," Dr. Lyons says, speaking to my mom and I, since Ben still looks checked out as he stares out the window. "But we will hope for the best with Hannah, and continue searching for a matching donor in the meantime."

Dr. Lyons asks more questions that my mom and I answer, about Ivy's energy levels, whether or not she's caught any colds since our last visit, but it's all a blur. And before I know it, we've collected Ivy from the lab and we're headed out to the front to go home.

"You guys go on," I say, tucking my hands in my pockets and slowing my walk as we reach the front doors. "I don't want to leave Hannah in there by herself."

Ben gives me a half-hearted smile and Ivy throws herself into a big hug. My mom barely looks at me, just shoving her car keys in Ben's hand and heading out of the automatic doors that lead to the parking lot.

I turn back and return to the lab, taking a seat in the little waiting area.

There's a part of me that wonders if the best thing I could do would be to head off to London. Just get the hell out of here and do my best to help from afar.

Even the idea of that makes my skin crawl. The old Wyatt would have done that. Would have run off and avoided and fled. He really was a coward, trying to avoid the difficulties and emotions and hard jabs that life throws out when you least expect it.

But the new me can't do it.

Funny. I didn't even realize there *was* a new me.

I'm still trying to decide if I like who I am right now.

When the doors open and Hannah appears, she looks exhausted, and I can tell she's been crying.

But her walls come up the minute she sees me. Her shoulders go back and she lifts her jaw. Then she walks right past me and outside.

I follow.

"Go away, Wyatt. I'm only here for Ivy."

"I know, I just... didn't want you to be alone in there."

She spins around, looking at the handful of people scattered outside the hospital.

"Where's Ivy?"

"They went home."

She crosses her arms.

"So you're saying you need a ride?"

I pause, realizing I'm obligating her to spend time with me. But ultimately, I nod.

She huffs and storms off into the parking lot, towards where Lucas' car is parked in the distance.

Instead of following this time, I wait at the curb. I'll go with them if they decide it's okay. If not, I'll Uber. Even if it costs two hundred bucks.

Surprisingly, a few minutes later, Lucas pulls up next to me, and I climb into the backseat.

"Thanks."

Hannah snorts. "If it was up to me, we'd leave you here. Lucas is the one who wanted to give you a ride."

I can hear Lucas rolling his eyes as he says, "That's not at all how the conversation went, but okay, we'll go with your version."

And then we pull out of the parking lot and head in the direction of home.

"Hannah can I talk to you for a minute?"

My question is met with the back of Hannah's head as she walks into the house.

"She hasn't forgiven me either," Lucas says, tucking his sunglasses into his collar. "And I'll be honest, I don't know if she'll ever forget what happened."

I sigh.

The ache in my chest continues to grow.

I should be focusing on my sister.

On my family.

On figuring out what else I can do to help Ivy now that our one little light has been all but extinguished.

But the constant on my mind right now is Hannah.

I'm in love with her and she won't talk to me. Can barely look at me. And the worst part is that I know I completely deserve it.

"I'd argue to give her more time, but I didn't give her any and she at least looks at me." He shrugs. "Maybe get in her face a little more. Make her listen to you?"

I shake my head. "People in her life have been taking away her choices since she was a kid. I can't do that to her now."

To say I'm surprised when my father shows up at the guest house garage the following morning is the understatement of the century.

I'm punching the shit out of my kickboxing bag, trying to exhaust myself and get out all of the pent up emotions that I don't seem to be managing well. And suddenly, Calvin Calloway comes walking around the corner, wearing that same kind of fancy ass suit and tie combo I saw him in at the yacht club.

As much as I hate to admit it, he cares about his image just as much if not more than mom.

I guess they're both plastic.

"What do you want?" I ask, gritting my jaw and refusing to break my concentration from the bag in front of me. What I'd really like to say is *unless it's an emergency, get the fuck out.* But I don't add that part, even though it's taking everything in me to keep my mouth shut.

"You haven't been answering my calls," he says, his voice like nails on a chalkboard.

I hate how he sounds when he speaks. So many people think the patriarch of the Calloway family is charming, handsome, charitable and kind.

If only they knew who he really was underneath that mask he likes to wear.

"Usually when someone doesn't answer your calls, it's because they don't want to talk to you." I keep my voice flat, disinterested. It's the only way I know how to communicate to him just how little I want him here.

But he chuckles instead, the sound testing my nerves.

"Whether you want to talk to me or not isn't really a concern of mine," he replies. "I don't know when over the course of your entire life you've been led to believe that you get to pick and choose if you want to talk to me. But if that has somehow been communicated, let me help clear that up right now."

There's a pause, and I know he's building up the theatrics.

"You. Will. Answer. When. I. Call."

I turn to face him, my chest heaving with the exertion of pummeling my fists into the bag. Resting my gloved hands on my hips, I glare at him.

"Get. To. The. Point."

He smirks. "Such hostility, Wyatt. I thought you would have gotten that temper under control while you were off fucking your way through San Francisco."

"Well, clearly my horrible character flaws were nurture, not nature, then, huh?"

At that, he laughs. Actually laughs, his hands falling by his side and his head tilting back.

"Ah, Wyatt. You've always been my favorite, you know? You're a lot like I was when I was younger. So intense. So full of emotion. Once you learn to stop letting that emotion get the best of you, you'll be able to accomplish so much more."

"Yeah, well, the last thing I ever want to be is anything like you, so I'll happily hold onto my emotions instead."

He licks his lips, and for a split second - a modicum of a moment - I think I've said something that actually hit the intended target.

But his expression changes so quickly, I can't tell.

"Calloway Foundation is christening a new building that will house a local adoption organization," he says, taking a few steps around the garage workout space, examining the different machinery and toeing the medicine ball so it rolls a little bit off to the side.

"I couldn't care less about what Calloway Foundation is doing," I respond, not liking the way he peruses everything.

"I don't remember asking for your opinion," he says, rounding his way back to the garage door that's open to the street, his voice as calm as I've ever heard it. He tucks his hands into his pockets. "You'll be expected to attend, give a little speech, share your own adoption experience and how much it... benefited your life."

"Not a chance in hell."

His head tilts to the side as he assesses me. "Are you telling me no?" he asks, and I do hear a hint of surprise in his voice.

I can't remember the last time I told him no. I might have always been the rebellious one, but I've always shown up where he told me to be, even if I did it gritting my teeth.

But this time? I'm not having it.

I have so many more important things in my life right now, so many other things going on that need my time and attention. I don't plan on giving any of that to a man who treats our family like we're expendable.

"I'm telling you no."

And it feels good, a kind of pressure lifting off my chest that I've never realized was there.

"Well, that's not really an option for you," he says, and I spin away, rip my gloves off my hands.

"Just as a reminder, in case you've forgotten. I'm a fucking adult. You don't get to tell me what to do anymore." Even just saying those words makes me feel like a little kid, like an immature brat screaming *I don't wanna*. But I mean them exactly as they sound.

There's a pause, a heavy one, and I can almost hear my dad shift in that silence. His mind changes course, decides on a new route to get what he wants.

"I've been hearing quite the interesting little rumors floating around town," he says, and I feel like I've been doused with cold water. "Something about Ivy's trashy father having another daughter in town."

I stop moving. Nearly stop breathing. Then I turn around and glare at my father, knowing that whatever is about to come out of his mouth is going to make me want to launch across this room and extract years of anger out on his worthless body.

"Ah. Now I have your attention," he says, crossing his arms, one lifting up to scratch at his chin, like he's some kind of evil dictator thinking over his plans. "Tell me. Is it that blonde I've been seeing around town. The one working at Bennie's and living with Lucas?"

I feel my stomach tilt.

He knows exactly who she is.

My father is a fucking shark. He wouldn't have come here and made a comment like that without having done his own research. Hell, his report on Hannah is probably more thorough than the one currently sitting in my office.

He just shakes his head. "You know, Wyatt, this whole thing is quite a little scandal. And I'm certain that the best way to deal with it is to..." he pauses. Smiles at me. "... deal with the trash?"

"Shut your *fucking* mouth," I bite out.

He grins at me, something insidious weaving its way through his expression.

"Don't tell me you actually care about her. Hannah, right? Is she the one who has been spending time in your bed recently?" He *tsks* at me, a repetitive little sound that echoes in the small space. "She's not like the other girls you've fucked, though I'm assuming her cunt was nice and tight."

In a flash, I'm across the room, faster than I even realize it's happening, my fist connecting with his face.

My father has done and said some truly horrible things throughout the years. Things that have ruined the lives of people I went to school with, that have put my mother in embarrassing positions. He's chalked my brother up as a lost cause and barely even talks to Ivy. And that doesn't even include the things he's said and done to me.

But this.

This is the time that I can't hold back.

Because of Hannah.

I'm a little surprised at my own aggression, my own baser instinct to protect her from the sinister nature in Calvin's bones.

He lays on the ground on his side, spits blood out onto the floor, and I shake out my hand.

I might have wanted to deck him for decades, but I never realized it would fuck with my own fist so much.

Assessing the situation, I know instinctively it was still worth it.

"Don't you *ever* talk about Hannah like that, you worthless piece of horseshit," I say as I stand over him.

He spits out another bit of blood, then raises himself back up to standing. His hand comes up to touch at the spot where I've split his lip.

"Quite the punch you've learned to pack in that fist, son," he says.

"Say one more thing about Hannah, and I won't hesitate to level you again."

"Oh, come on now. Don't think for a second that your threats mean anything to me."

My nostrils flare.

I don't know if I've ever felt this type of rage before. Just the absolute, sheer arrogance in the way he talks. As if what he says is a decree that no one is allowed to confront.

Well, that's not the type of life I've signed up for.

"I don't know if you've picked up on this or not, but I'm done heeling at the sound of your voice. I'm not a dog you can command. I don't need your money or your connections, and I definitely don't plan to help you in your endless endeavor to get more."

My father unbuttons his jacket, slowly slides it from his shoulders, then holds it over an arm while he dusts off the bit of dirt he collected while he was on the floor, not looking at me as he continues to speak.

"I haven't said much while you've been gallivanting off in San Francisco, and working for your friend's little app development startup. But you're working on something different, now. Something important." Then he glances up at me. "Right?"

I furrow my brow, not sure where he's going with this.

"I know you don't need my money and connections. That you can work on this little Elite X project with Otto and Lucas without any help from me."

And then he steps forward, standing just a foot, maybe two, away from me, his eyes menacing.

"But can you do it... *against* me."

I flex a fist, the meaning of his words rolling through my whole body.

"How long do you think this little endeavor will last if I make buckling you at the knees a priority? *No one* in this town will work with any of you if I put the word out."

And then he takes it a step further.

"And do you really think this little... thing you have going on with Henry Morrison's daughter is going to last if I make sure she can't find a job? If I unleash the hounds on her? Make sure every catty bitch in town sees her as a target?"

He shakes his head, and I know I've been well and truly sunk.

I might have knocked my dad onto the ground, left a mark on his face, but I'm the one who feels like I've been sprawled on my ass, my legs swept out from underneath me.

Finding a way to come out on the other side of this when it comes to the Elite X thing? Manageable. Otto and Lucas are resourceful. And they hate my dad as much as I do.

But it was his comments about Hannah that have me ready to throw in a towel. Give him whatever he wants.

"Blow off this speech, and I'll just have to take these little matters into my own hands."

I shake my head, disbelief coursing through my system, even while resignation is threading its way through my very being.

"I'll have my secretary send you the details," he says. Then he gives me a little wave. "See you soon, Wyatt."

I'm left alone then.

Alone to lick my wounds.

Filled with anger and frustration, I do the only thing I can think of.

Without any gloves on, I turn and beat the shit out of the bag, imagining my father's face the entire time.

The following day, two days after our meeting with Dr. Lyons, my mom gets an email that she should call the doctor's office. Ivy and I crowd into the office to listen, and my mom puts it on speaker.

But I can already feel the sense of foreboding.

"Hannah's blood results have come back," she says, her voice echoing in the small space. "I've already spoken with her and she gave me permission to provide the news to you all. Hannah is not a full match with Ivy, so she isn't a good pairing for a bone marrow transplant donation. I'm so sorry."

Ivy can't hear it over the phone, but I sign it to her.

Hannah's not a match.

Her shoulders fall and she leaves the office, her little feet racing up the stairs and probably to her bedroom, where I hear a door slam.

"Thank you, Dr. Lyons," my mom says. "Please keep us posted on the donor match process."

And then she hangs up the phone.

"I have plans with Gigi Forrester. I'll be back late tonight."

My mouth drops open. "You're leaving?"

She looks at me, her mask carefully in place. "I have somewhere I need to be. I said I'll be back later."

I pick up a paperweight off the desk and fling it angrily at a mirror that hangs over the fireplace. It shatters, pieces spraying all over the ground.

My mom shrieks, putting her hands up to protect herself as if the glass is anywhere near her.

"Your daughter is upstairs, probably bawling her eyes out, because she's afraid she's going to fucking die!" I shout at her, blood pumping angrily through my veins. "And you want to run off and pretend life is grand with people you barely care about. At all. What is wrong with you?"

She points a finger at me, her face furious. "Don't get angry with me. I'm the one who has been here dealing with this while you were off doing god knows what and god knows whom. I've been doing it alone! And no one even cares. Your father doesn't and Ben doesn't. You barely did until recently. It's been just me. So excuse me if I need a minute to myself."

"That's not how being a mom fucking works," I shout back. "That's not how this gets to play out. And *bullshit* you've been doing this alone. You've been doing this with Ivy. The one who is scared to fucking death and needs her mom."

Her nostrils flare and her neck flushes red, her tell tail signs of embarrassment and frustration.

"You think you can come in here and solve all of the problems with a few words? That you can show up here with Henry's daughter and save the day? Fix all of the problems that have been choking the life out of us for years? *That* is something that doesn't work, Wyatt. You don't get to come in with your sanctimonious ideas and your broad theories and apply them to my life." She shakes her head. "You don't get to control what happens. You really are a Calloway if you think any differently."

And then she storms out of the room before I can think up anything to say in response.

I stand there alone, looking at the mess I made, feeling like the life I live is starting to crumble and twist and change around me.

I don't know myself.
I don't know what I want or where to go.
No, that's a lie.
I know what I want.
Ivy to find a match.
And Hannah.
That's it.
It doesn't feel like too big of an order.
Those two things should be doable.
Surely I can figure out a way to have both.

I spend the next twenty minutes picking up the shattered glass, slicing my fingers a few times, though it matches nicely with the open cuts on my knuckles from when I socked my dad in the face yesterday afternoon and then beat the shit out of the bag without any gloves on.

I'll be feeling those cuts for a few days to come.

Eventually, I manage to get everything picked up, then vacuum for good measure.

When I'm turning off the machine, I hear a beep in my pocket.

Pulling out my phone I glance at the screen, my blood running cold when I see the message.

Lucas: Get over here. Hannah's leaving.

I immediately dial his number, and he picks up on the third ring.

"What do you mean she's leaving," I ask, my voice hoarse.

"I mean she's leaving. She found out she's not a match for Ivy." He pauses, lets out a sigh. "I'm *so* sorry about that. God, I really thought it would happen. That she'd be..."

"Focus, Lucas!" I bark into the phone. I know he cares deeply about my sister - *our* sister - but now isn't the time for his emotion. I need to know what's going on with Hannah.

"Sorry. She's going back to Phoenix. She already bought her ticket. Her bus leaves tonight."

Pacing the room I try to figure out what to do.

"I can't come over right now. I have to spend time with Ivy. She's a mess over this. Can you stall her? Talk her in to doing a bus tomorrow instead?"

He sighs. "Maybe. I'll try."

Then he hangs up and I squeeze my phone in my hand, pressing a fist to my forehead.

Everything is moving so fast.

Too fast.

I just want it to slow down so I can think. I can barely think.

I take a deep breath, then let it out.

After doing that a few more times, I head upstairs. In this moment, right now, I need to focus on Ivy. On my younger sister who is still just a girl, feeling alone and scared.

Taking the stairs two at a time, I get up to her room and open the door just a smidge, expecting to find my sister crying on her bed.

But it's still made, her bedroom lights off.

Pushing the door all the way open, I flick the lights and glance around.

She's not here.

I blow through her room to her bathroom. Then I check all of the other bedrooms. I've never resented my sister being deaf until this moment, when I can't call out to her when I need to find her.

And after checking every room of the house like a crazy person, my worst fears are confirmed.

Ivy is gone.

Chapter Twenty Seven
HANNAH

A small part of me hopes Wyatt will come to say goodbye. A little voice that wants me to forgive him and move on so I can spend every night in his arms.

But I've been telling that bitch to keep quiet, because I'm busy brooding.

So when there's a knock at the front door, I can't help but be a little happy about it.

Though I'm surprised to see Ivy when I answer the front door.

She rushes me, wrapping her arms around my middle and giving me a tight squeeze.

Hey sweet stuff, I say, once she's finally let go of me so I can speak to her. *What are you doing here?*

I glance behind her, out to the courtyard, wondering if I'll be seeing Wyatt round the corner. But there isn't anyone there, so I look back to Ivy.

No, I'm here by myself.

I furrow my brow. *Are you allowed to be here by yourself?*

I know she's just turned thirteen, and I try to remember my own freedom at that age. My situation might not have been common, but I can only imagine that my parents wouldn't have let me wander off on my own at so young.

Tack on Ivy's red eyes, and the fact she came on foot? I'm gonna guess this is some sort of runaway situation.

Now *that* I am incredibly familiar with.

Ivy rolls her eyes at my question, walking past me and into the house. Then she spins around to look at me. *I'm definitely old enough to be here. Now, I want to try some alcohol. Where does Lucas keep that?*

I laugh, but sober myself when I realize she's serious. *Well, as much as I'd love to help you, I don't think your family would be happy about me giving alcohol to a minor.*

She glares at me, and I can see the look of determination in her eyes.

I'm going to die, so they'll get over it, she says, matter-of-factly.

My eyes widen.

Apparently Dr. Lyons has given them the news. It should have occurred to me the minute she showed up at the door with tears drying on her cheeks.

Honey, that is not true at all. You have to know that you're going to be okay.

"Don't lie to me!" she shouts, her facial expression turning angry, her jaw gritting and her eyes welling with tears. "I'm sick of everyone lying to me!"

I've never heard Ivy verbalize before, and the sound of it breaks my heart. Because it isn't the sound of a happy, gleeful young lady with her whole life ahead of her. It's a painful sound, full of anger and laced with fear.

She paces in front of me, her hands gripped in fists. And then she spins and looks right at me.

The doctors lied and said I was fine. And then everyone lied about me having a sister. Ben lies about why he wants to stay away and Wyatt lies about not wanting to leave. They're still lying about Lucas, like I don't know he's my brother too. Like I don't know that my dad isn't really my dad.

I stand frozen as Ivy has an absolutely deserved meltdown,

her emotions pouring out from her.

I'm going to die soon. I know it. Everyone pretends all the time, and I'm sick of it. I just want the truth.

And then she crumples onto the couch, her body wracked with sobs.

I rush to her side, sliding in next to her.

Her little frame wraps around mine, her body shuddering as she tries to deal with the emotional storm in her body, all of the fears coming to a head and exploding on the closest person.

Me.

So I run my hand through her hair, rocking her slightly, singing to her even though I know she can't hear me.

Lissy always used to say that she liked 'hearing' me sing after I tucked her in on the nights I babysat, because she could feel my body rumbling. She didn't know the words or the songs or the beat, but she liked that little bit of vibration.

So I do the same for Ivy, and her sobs slowly start to pull back. Before I know it, she's fallen asleep on me, pooped out from the hard work of carrying the weight of everyone's problems.

I hold her for a moment longer, feeling so thankful that, in rest, her anxious and upset face has given way to something calm. All I can hope is that sleeping gives her a moment's reprieve.

I give her a soft kiss at the crown of her hair, then move as slowly as I can to shift her so she is sleeping against the couch pillows. Once I cover her with a blanket, tucking some of her hair behind her ear, I get out my phone and give Wyatt a call.

As much as I don't want to talk to him, I can't just not let him know that his sister is here.

It rings a few times before he answers.

"Hannah I really want to talk to you but Ivy is missing," he says, the panic in his voice slicing through me.

"She's here," I say, not wanting to beat around the bush at all. "She showed up and started crying and now she's asleep on the couch. She got here about ten minutes ago."

"Oh my god," he says, his voice coming out in a rush. "Gimme a second."

There's a pause on the other end of the line, and I try to picture what he's doing. Maybe he's slumped against a wall in relief, or he's clenching his phone in anger. But if I know Wyatt at all, which is up for debate, he's standing with his hands on his hips, forcing himself to breathe slowly.

"Thanks for calling me," he says a moment later, once he's collected himself enough to talk again. "I was a mess."

"I can tell," I say, the little chuckle coming out unintentionally. "I'm sorry you were so worried. But she's okay."

There's a pause.

"Lucas said you're leaving."

I sigh.

The idea of leaving without anyone knowing was a decision I made as soon as I got off the phone with Dr. Lyons. I opened up a greyhound app and found a ticket for tonight at midnight leaving from Union Station.

It just seemed easier. Leaving all of this behind, since I can't be of use to anyone anyway.

"Yeah. We're leaving for the bus station at ten."

"That's only a few hours from now," he rushes out. "Hannah, you can't just... *leave.*"

I shake my head. "I can. And it's probably for the best."

"You're wrong. There's so much here for you."

And I can't help myself when the next words pour from my lips. "Like what? A brother who tricked me into coming here, a bunch of rich people I don't fit in with, a city too expensive for me to live in, and a boy who got to *use me in plenty of ways*," I say, my voice cracking at the end as emotion floods me.

"Hannah," his voice is tortured. "Please let me explain. I didn't mean that. I swear. I said it in anger, not because I..."

"Wyatt, you promised you never wanted to hurt me. And you said it *knowing* you were going to. This is why I wanted you not to make any promises. I told you to promise me nothing, and things would be a lot easier. But instead, you made me believe something. Made me believe *in* something. And then you *stole* it from me."

He starts to protest again but I cut him off.

"I called to tell you about Ivy, not to talk this out. Please come by and get her because we have to leave in a few hours."

And then I hang up the phone, just as I hear footsteps coming down the stairs.

Lucas takes in my facial expression and pauses. But before he can say anything, Ivy stirs on the couch.

She stays asleep, and Lucas comes to my side, glancing down at her. "Is that Ivy?"

I nod. "She knows you're her brother," I say. "And that Calvin isn't her dad."

Lucas' mouth drops open, but I look out the window to the ocean in the distance, though it's hard to see with how dark it is.

"She has a lot going on in that mind of hers. I think she ran away. Or just needed a break from her house."

"Like sister like sister, huh?" Lucas says.

I spin around and look at him.

"What do you mean?"

He lifts a shoulder. "Sometimes, when life hurts, or gets too hard, you need a little space and perspective before you go back and face things."

Then he turns and heads into the kitchen, opening the fridge and pulling out a bottle of water.

I nod. "Like me leaving Phoenix and now going back."

"Or you leaving here." Lucas takes a sip of his water, then recaps it. "Maybe you need space and perspective about what has happened here, so you're running away for a little bit."

"That's not what's happening," I say, crossing my arms.

But he just nods, gives me a little shrug. One that oozes of a confidence I wish I had. "Maybe."

"Definitely."

"Okay."

I stomp a foot - really mature of me - and bark at him. "Stop it. You're twisting this, making it seem like I'm running when I'm not. I don't fit here. I don't belong. I never did."

"According to who?"

His face is soft when he asks me that, and I know he doesn't mean to make me emotional, but I feel this sudden urge to break down in tears.

It's an unwelcome feeling. I've done enough crying recently.

"You've repeated yourself over and over. That you don't belong here. That you don't fit. You said it when you got here, you just said it again now. But *you* are the only one saying that, Hannah."

He sets his water bottle down, and crosses his own arms.

"From what I see, you've found a job, made friends, enjoyed time with family, and fell in love. Sounds to me like you found a place you belong."

I shake my head. "It's not like that. You don't know..."

"You're right. I don't know. I don't know and I never will. And that's my fault. If I had been there, maybe I could have changed how your life turned out. Maybe I could have made it so you weren't afraid of relying on people. Maybe I could have shown you that you can believe some of the promises people make. But I wasn't there to do it then. So all I can do is try and prove it to you now."

He steps forward and puts his hands on my shoulders.

"If you need to go, you can absolutely go. You can go to Phoenix and do whatever you want." He gives me a gentle squeeze. "But I'm asking you to stay, so the people here can prove to you that you deserve a home and a place you feel happy. Because I believe that, for you? This is that place."

He hugs me, pulls me in close and wraps his arms around me. Unlike those first times when he hugged me after I moved here, it doesn't feel uncomfortable or unwanted. I enjoy his affection, his brotherly love and care. And I wrap my arms around him, too.

"I can't make you listen to Wyatt or forgive him, or any of those things. Honestly? I don't want to waste anything on trying to fix things between the two of you because I want to fix things between the two us."

I laugh a little bit.

He pulls back and looks at me.

"But I don't think he wanted to hurt you. At all."

I nod, wipe a tear from my eye. "I know. And if I was in his shoes, I might have done the same thing. But it doesn't take the hurt away to know that."

Lucas gives me a tight smile as I turn away from him and continue what I was doing before Ivy got here.

Collecting my things to pack.

As the clock gets closer and closer to our leave time for the bus station, I wonder where Wyatt is. Why he hasn't shown up yet to collect Ivy, who still lies snoozing on the couch.

Eventually, only twenty minutes before we're supposed to leave, I see his car pull into the drive. I make sure to stay upstairs when he comes, though I know it's the cowardly thing to do.

I try to listen from upstairs as I hear Lucas and Wyatt murmuring about something, but I can't make anything out.

I let out a soft sigh, a mixture of sadness and relief, when I see Wyatt's SUV pull out from where I watch at my bedroom window.

Part of me wanted to be able to say goodbye, but I know it just would have resulted in more tears.

A few minutes after he leaves there's a knock on my door.

"You ready to go?" Lucas asks.

I nod, giving him a confident face that belies my true emotions.

"Ready."

"Tell me this isn't the end," Lucas says, chucking my bag on the ground next to the bus that's going to take me back to Phoenix. "Because I'm pretty sure you're my family now. And family doesn't get to ignore each other."

I laugh, give him a sad nod of my head. "I promise," I say. "This isn't the end."

He hugs me again. "I thought you don't believe in promises. Why should I believe yours?"

I pull back and look at him. "I don't give ones I can't keep."

He smiles, then backs up while I climb onto the bus.

Moving between rows, I find a seat towards the back, hoping there might be some empties so I don't have to deal with another chicken wing lady on a long trip.

Settling in, I rest my backpack in my lap and unzip it to get out my book.

My head jerks back when I see an envelope with my name on it stuffed in at the top.

I glance out the window, finding Lucas still standing at the curb, his hands in his pockets, leaning against a pole. Just watching me.

My eyes turn back to the envelope.

I tear it open, pulling out a thick stack of pages folded together.

The top one takes me by surprise.

Hannah,

I'm sad to hear you're leaving. I had hoped we would get to spend more time together. But I'm sure you miss Phoenix. I care

about you a lot, and I feel so thankful to have found a true friend.
Happy travels.
Love, Eleanor.

My brow furrows.
Eleanor?
That's so sweet, but how did she get this in my bag?
I flip to the next page.

Hannah Banana!
When Lucas told me you were leaving, I had a meltdown.
A full scale, heart attack over here.
Not even kidding.
Okay, maybe I'm kidding a little bit.
But when I say I'm sad to see you go? That's not a joke.
You are such a wonderful person, and it was so great spending some time with you. I hope you come back soon so we can spend more brunchy mornings at Mary's, and so I can keep dolling you up in my clothes because DAMN GIRL DO YOU HAVE SOME AMAZING LEGS.
Okay. I love you. Please come back.
Muah!
Paige.

I giggle at that one, but still feel confused.
I flip through the stack, trying to understand where they came from. Eleanor, Paige, Ivy, Ben, Hamish... even Rebecka and Lennon. Letters from people who have nothing but kind words and praises and requests for me not to leave.
And then I get to the back two. The two that I know instinctively are from Lucas and Wyatt.
I read Lucas' first.

Hannah,
There's nothing I'll be able to say in a letter that I haven't either already said to your face, or that I'm planning to say to you before you go.
You know how I feel.
How much I want you to stay.
But I'll ask just one more time.

Don't go?
Regardless of what happens, thank you for giving me the family I always wanted.
Hopefully I can be a poor substitute for the one that you miss.
Love you,
And miss you already.
Lucas.

I shake my head with a grin, then glance back outside, expecting to see his cocky smirk and mischievous eyes staring back at me.

But Lucas is nowhere to be found. My eyes scan the curb, try and look inside the station to see where he might have wandered off to.

Nothing.

My shoulders slump, and I look back to the papers in my hand, finally pulling Wyatt's out.

It's much longer than the rest, his handwriting bold and masculine.

Hannah,
I'm not good with my words. Never have been. English was always my worst subject in school. I could never seem to say what I felt, the words always feeling like a messy jumble that I couldn't organize correctly.
So when Lucas told me that you've decided to leave, and that it's happening in just a few hours, I really don't know if there's anything I put into words that would ever be convincing enough to get you to stay.
But I think that's my problem right there.
I shouldn't have to convince you.
How I feel about you should be so evident in the way I talk to you, how I treat you, that there isn't ever a need to convince you that it's real.
It should be something you know in your bones. Something you feel etched into your skin.
That's where I think so many people get love wrong. They believe love is a game to be played and won, like the other person is a pawn they need to move around in their own ideal world.
I don't see love as a game. But if I had to use the analogy, I

simply need to communicate that you were never a pawn. You were a queen. The most important, the strongest, and the one with the most power. You are capable of anything.

I won't pretend like what I did was right, and I truly am sorry for how it hurt you. My focus was so entirely on Ivy, on what I could do for her, consequences be damned, that I never stopped to consider that someone else's life was in the balance, too.

Yours.

So all I can do now is beg.

Beg you to let me show you how much I love you.

Beg you to allow me a chance to prove to you with my words and my actions and my heart and my mind and every resource in my arsenal that you are that queen.

You are everything I've never known to hope for in this life.

So please.

I ask this without manipulation, without convincing… I ask this with nothing but love in my heart.

Please stay.

Stay so we can start over, start fresh, with nothing but trust and honesty between us.

Stay so I can show you how beautiful it can be when someone loves you the way you deserve.

Stay so I can show you what it feels like when someone promises you everything. And follows through.

I love you, Hannah.

Wyatt

Chapter Twenty Eight
WYATT

"I'm not even hungry," I tell Lucas, plopping down in the chair next to his at our table at Bennie's the next afternoon.

Really, the fact that he was able to convince me to come out at all today is nothing short of impressive.

I never heard from Hannah last night.

I'd thought maybe I'd get a text, at least. Some sort of acknowledgment that she got the letters. But it was radio silence. I don't think I've ever checked and rechecked my phone so many times. Making sure the sound was on, the vibration, the volume all the way to max.

I was up all night, lying in bed and staring at the ceiling, Ivy snuggled in at my side.

She asked if she could stay with me last night and I couldn't deny her. I can't remember the last time she asked to have a sleepover. If I'm honest, it felt good to be needed. Even if it didn't distract me completely from what was going on with Hannah, it gave me a reason not to break down into an emotional heap.

I was up all night. And it wasn't until I verified that Hannah's bus arrived safely in Phoenix early this morning that I finally allowed myself to doze off.

So now, even though I'm sitting at this table with the only other person who has a fraction of understanding about how I feel, I just wish I was still in bed.

"And coming here is depressing," I add. "I don't even know how you talked me into this. After today, no more Bennie's."

Lucas grins at me but just lifts his menu.

Not sure yet if I'm going to eat, I tilt my face up and glare at the sun, feeling like the weather is betraying me.

Where's a foggy, depressing weekend afternoon when you need it, huh?

Eventually he puts his menu down and glances around. "I'm surprised no one has come over to us yet. Normally they're clamoring to serve our table."

I roll my eyes but say nothing, staring off into the distance instead.

"The reason I dragged you out of your house is because you can't just sit at home and wallow."

I glare at him. "That's not what I was doing."

"You were in bed when I got there at noon. You were wallowing."

"I was *sleeping*. I was up most of the night."

"Wallowing."

"Cut the shit, Lucas." Fuck if he doesn't piss me off like nobody else that I know. I turn my head and look around. I do need that server. Time for a fucking scotch.

Lucas lets out a sigh. "Look, as much as you don't want to accept defeat, Hannah's gone. You should just find someone else."

My mouth drops open and if I wasn't so depressed, or if I didn't care about going to prison, I'd pick up this butter knife and show him what's what.

She hasn't even been gone for one day. It's been like, twelve hours. Maybe less. And I'm already wondering what else I can do to prove to her that I meant what I said.

And I did mean it.

I shouldn't have to convince her. My words aren't going to do anything other than confuse her.

It's actions that she deserves.

Actual steps that show her that everything I've said, everything that I've felt... that it's real.

"This isn't about 'accepting defeat,'" I say. "Hannah isn't some game I'm trying to win."

He just raises an eyebrow and stays silent.

"Do you seriously not believe me when I tell you how I feel about her? Because I'm not kidding. I don't need you to tell me to move on. I need you to help me come up with a plan."

"A plan? What kind of plan?"

I lean back in my chair. "Maybe I can move to Phoenix instead of London. Think Otto will go for a different location for Elite X's new branch?"

Lucas laughs. "Hardly."

"Hey, it could happen," I retort, though I know it's not even a long shot. An international branch doesn't work if I live in the fucking desert. Or *not* internationally.

The waitress finally shows up, a redhead I've never seen before, and my heart clenches when I realize she might be Hannah's replacement.

Lucas puts in an order for a sandwich and fries, and I order a scotch.

"You don't want to have a liquid lunch, Wyatt. Trust me."

I ignore him, sending the waitress off with a tight smile and orders to bring back a heavy pour of Glenlivet.

I lean to the side in my chair, putting all my weight on one elbow and rubbing my face with my hand.

"Be honest with me," I say, watching him closely. "You saw her before she left."

He nods.

"You think I stand a chance? That there's any way I can get her back?"

"Let me answer your question with a question," he replies, and I purse my lips in irritation. He chuckles briefly, but his face sobers and he looks at me, earnest curiosity in his eyes. "Is there anything I could say that would convince you that you're wasting your time?"

I shake my head. "Never."

Lucas lifts a single shoulder, a pleased expression overtaking his face. "Then it doesn't really matter what I think, huh?"

I sigh, reaching into my pocket to pull out my phone when I feel a buzz.

My eyes widen when I see Hannah's name on the screen, and I answer it as quickly as possible.

"Hello?"

I stand quickly and step away from the table, leaving Lucas without explanation, not wanting to have a conversation with her in front of him.

I don't want him to see me beg.

"Hey."

It's the only thing she says. I can barely hear her, but just the sound of her voice has my heart thumping in an erratic beat that only she can seem to elicit.

"Hey. Hold on one second, okay? I'm just... I'm at Bennie's and I'm heading outside. It's pretty noisy in here."

I rush down the stairs and into the main dining room, then towards the front doors, trying to find a place that's quiet so I can really focus on her.

I might also be buying myself a few minutes, trying to figure out what else I can say to her. Anything that will allow me to keep her on the phone as long as possible.

When I finally get outside, I put the phone back to my ear and glance around. "Alright, I'm... are you still there?"

"Yeah. I'm still here."

I nod, though she can't see me. And without my planning, my feet start moving me towards the pier.

"I wish you were here right now," I say, wondering where she is instead. I'm assuming she went to her friend Sienna's, but who knows what she decided to do. "And not just because I wish you were here with me. Though, obviously that's true." I chuckle. "It's just... a really pretty day. Sunny and breezy. Though, I'll be honest. With my mood, I feel like I could use a good thunderstorm over the ocean right now. Something big and loud so I can just be mellow dramatic and stare out a rainy window."

"You don't strike me as the type to like storms," she replies.

"Normally I don't. But today isn't a normal day. It's the first day you're gone, and I feel like the universe should be commiserating with me."

There's a pause.

"Storms scare me," she says.

I nod, approaching the bench I sat at with Hannah just two months ago. "They *can* be scary. If you're dealing with them alone. If all you can do is think about what could go wrong."

She stays silent, though I can hear her breathing.

"But it feels pretty good to deal with a storm with someone you love. You snuggle up in front of a fire, have a few drinks. Maybe kiss in the rain."

"Sounds romantic, but unrealistic," she replies, and there's a thread of sadness in her tone. Something I wish I could extract, but I don't seem to have the right tools.

I take a seat on the bench and look out at all of the happy people on the sand, playing in the water, tanning in the sun.

"It only sounds unrealistic because you've never gotten through a storm with someone by your side before," I reply. "Someone to point out the beautiful sky afterwards. Or to hold your umbrella."

She laughs, a tiny little snicker, and it makes something swoop in my chest.

"And you want to be that person?" she asks.

"Absolutely."

My words come out like a whip, with a quickness even I wasn't expecting. Because it's true. I want to be by her side, facing any shit-storm life is going to throw our way... together.

I feel someone take the seat next to me and I sigh inaudibly, turning to ask them to leave. The last thing I want is someone listening to me as I pour my heart out over the phone, during what might be my only chance to get her forgiveness.

But when I turn, I nearly swallow my tongue.

Sitting next to me, a soft, emotional expression on her face, is the beautiful blonde that I wondered if I'd ever see again.

It's Hannah.

It's Hannah?

I blink, trying to figure out what's going on.

But at the same time, all I can do is focus on the fact that she's here. Sitting next to me. Wearing a pair of yoga pants and a loose grey shirt, her hair up in a ponytail and a sweet smile on her face.

She's not in Phoenix.

What is happening?

I lift a hand and place it on her face, my thumb stroking her cheek in reverence as I try to convince myself that she's really here. Right now. With me.

"I thought you left."

She lifts a shoulder, a little shrug that reminds me of her brother. "I decided to stay."

There's a pulsing in my chest. A throbbing, really. Something that lights my soul on fire and has every nerve-ending on my body standing at attention.

She's here.

She decided to stay.

I can't help but grin, so enamored with her that my body physically can't hold my happiness inside any longer.

She reaches up with her own hand, placing it on my cheek, mirroring my position and allowing her thumb to trace lightly under my eyes.

"You look tired," she whispers. "Did you not get any sleep?"

I press my cheek into her hand, unable to keep this stupid, shit-eating grin off my face.

Because she's here.

She decided to stay.

"I couldn't fall asleep until I knew your bus got to Phoenix," I say. I know it makes me sound like a pussy. But I don't give a shit.

From this moment forward, every single word I utter is going to have the sole focus of making sure she knows how crazy I am for her.

How much she means to me.

How much I want her here.

"You read my letter?" I ask.

A soft expression comes across her face, and I see everything flitter across it that I was hoping for. Most importantly, I see the love shining in her eyes.

"Yeah. I read your letter."

We just stare at each other for a minute, and I still can't wrap my head around it.

That she's here.

That she decided to stay.

"Did my begging work?"

Her softness shifts away and she rolls her eyes, but there's a playfulness to it. A teasing lift that she's given me a few times before.

And I'll take it.

Gladly.

"I figured if you're going to be able to show me all these things you've promised, it would probably help if I was around here to see them."

I shake my head, not knowing how to express myself. Not knowing how to tell her how glad I am that she decided to believe me.

Believe what I said.

What I promised.

There are so many unanswered questions moving forward. So many problems and issues, drama and pain, things on the horizon that I have to deal with because… well, because that's life.

But knowing that she decided to stay?

That she decided we are worth taking a risk on?

It makes all of the shit that makes life complicated seem a lot more manageable.

Hannah is, by far, the most amazing thing to ever happen to me. The best gift life has ever been kind enough to throw my way. And I know I need to work to continue to deserve her.

To deserve her time.

To deserve her smiles.

To deserve her love.

Luckily, she makes me want to be the best version of me.

So working my ass off every damn day to make sure I continue to deserve her doesn't sound like too much of a hardship.

Hannah scoots just a little bit closer, sticks her hand out and gives me a little smile that I know is just for me. "I'm Hannah Morrison. I'm Lucas' sister. And Ivy's sister. And maybe I have some other siblings out there somewhere in this town, but I'll deal with that if it happens."

I grin, unable to keep my love for her off my face.

"I'm Wyatt Calloway," I say, slipping my hand into hers and gently pulling her towards me, into me, so I can press a kiss to the inside of her wrist. I love the way her nose wiggles and her cheeks flush. "It's really, *really* good to meet you, Hannah Morrison."

HANNAH

A few days later, I sit between Wyatt's legs on the rooftop at Lucas' house... *my* house... as we wait for the 4th of July fireworks to shoot into the sky. But this time, I'll actually be *watching* the fireworks. There are a handful of other people up here with us, too.

So I already told Wyatt. No funny business.

He gave me this furrowed brow and told me he would *never* try 'funny business' when we haven't gone on a real date yet.

He wasn't joking when he told me he wants to start over.

Be honest.

About everything.

And I do mean *everything.*

It meant we had a hard conversation the other day.

I talked to him about what happened to me in foster care. All of the horrible shit, from Rob's assault to the year I lived at the shelter, and everything in between.

He cried. Partly because he feels responsible. I don't know if that's ever a weight he'll be able to let go of, even though it isn't something I would ever hold over his head. I took his face in my hands and told him that whatever guilt he feels about it, that I wanted to absolve him of it.

He countered with telling me that he wanted to absolve me of the guilt I feel about how Joshua passed away.

It had been a hard thing to hear. I guess we're both going to have to work on letting things from our past go. Because really, we can't move forward together completely if we're still holding on to past pain.

Talking about Ivy and the transplant and why Lucas brought me to Hermosa in the first place was also a painful conversation. Learning that things were orchestrated around me - like Lucas finding a way for me to 'win' a free MatchLink kit, or the bike getting stolen, and the night at the sand dune - made me feel manipulated and maneuvered in a way that's hard to explain. And hard to get over.

But I have every faith that we can work through it together. And I think that's something that's different about my relationship with Wyatt. Maybe even my relationship with Lucas.

The hard times don't mean we have to quit. I'm not going to get shuffled off to a new house just because I get into an argument. It means we're going to talk. We're going to work through things. We're going to compromise and flex and negotiate.

I've never had that before. Never had someone who stuck around long enough that those things ever came into play. So it's definitely different. But I love it.

We're still figuring everything out for the long-term, like what's going to happen with his job and that move to London, and where I'm going to end up when the summer is over.

But it's something we're going to figure out together.

And Wyatt was right.

Weathering a storm together means I'm not as scared.

"You know, if you decide you don't want to do the speech, I won't let him run me out of town," I tell Wyatt as I sit snuggled in his arms.

He told me about the fight he had with his dad. It made me sick, knowing the depths Calvin would stoop to in order to get what he wanted. But I loved hearing how Wyatt defended me.

"I'm doing the stupid speech," he grumbles. "This shit

between me and my dad… it'll work itself out. Someday. But I'm not letting that prick do anything to hurt you, and if I know anything about him, it's that if he sets his sights on you, he won't stop until he's ruined your life." He places a kiss on my temple, his arms tightening around me just slightly. "There will be other times when I can stand up to him. And I will. But not over this. I won't let him use you. Ever."

I tilt my head up to look at him and give him a soft smile, my love for him seeming to grow and expand in ways I've never known were possible. Then I stretch up and press a kiss to the base of his jaw.

I believe him when he says that. And it feels good to hear, knowing I'm in a relationship with someone who doesn't see me as a pawn in his larger game. That line in his letter really did make me swoon.

But I also don't expect that he's going to be able to keep me safe from every shitty person or horrible situation, from any asshole who might see me as a means to an end.

Instead, I just have to be thankful for the effort he does make, and continue to focus on the good. The good people, the good experiences, the good life.

And it really is a good life.

Sienna is going to come out to visit at the end of the summer. I got a sweet little video message from Melanie a few days ago of her and Lissy saying hello and telling me all about New Mexico. Lissy apparently has a new best friend in the neighborhood they moved into, and she's starting to sign more, feeling a little bit less like she doesn't fit in.

And then there's tonight. Right now. I'm surrounded with people I really like, some of them that I love.

Ivy is in her pajamas, sitting on the actual roof with Ben, who agreed to come if I didn't talk to him, since he's trying to keep 'a healthy work balance' since he's *technically* my boss.

I give that a few weeks before it falls apart.

Lucas is here with Remmy, which is a little bit weird, since I've never seen the two of them together before. Who knows what's happening there, but they both look happy sitting in the hot tub.

Paige and Eleanor are sitting happily together, chatting and alternating between the hot tub and the other loungers on the roof. Those two have gotten pretty close, and I'm so glad they hit it off.

Lennon is here as well, but she seems to be a little down, opting to stay on the loungers and face out to the water instead of getting into the hot tub. Though every time she walks over to get another drink, her eyes look to Lucas and Remmy. It makes me sad for her, but I guess I don't know everything that's happening there.

Lucas' parties are typically a lot larger, with hundreds overflowing to the streets. But tonight, he agreed to do something small and intimate with just close friends and family.

Besides, I don't think he wanted to be shown up.

Apparently all of Hermosa Beach is in a tizzy because the guy with all the dogs decided to do one more 4th of July party before he retires the title as the Hermosa Beach Party King and hands the crown over to Lucas.

I'm not kidding when I say that is a paraphrase of his literal quote when he took out a full-page ad in the local newspaper letting everyone in town know that the party was happening.

Good luck to the cops trying to police *that* party tonight.

It makes me laugh, all of the weird things that make this town so unique.

I don't know if I'll ever understand it. Or if I'll ever *really* feel like I fit.

But I've decided to try.

My decision to stay was definitely about Wyatt. About our connection and the amazing love I feel from him.

But it was also about other things as well.

Reading those letters, the ones Wyatt was able to get put together with just a few hours notice... knowing that the people who wrote those wonderful words actually care about me, want me around, believe in me...

Something inside of me just... clicked.

I finally feel like I deserve that.

That I deserve to be surrounded by people who love me.

That I deserve to find a place that I belong.

Staying in Hermosa Beach isn't as risky of a decision as I originally thought it was going to be. Because when I look at my true options, the paths life has presented to me, the choice is clear.

Head back to a place where I have almost nothing.

Or stay here.

A place that affords me the chance to live near family.

Build friendships.

Find love.

Maybe that's what Frost meant in that poem that I hate so much. About picking the path less travelled.

It isn't about picking the one that's harder. That's filled with branches and limbs and things that will make me trip and fall.

It's about choosing to go a different route than I normally would. Seeking out something better. Something more meaningful.

Because the path I've walked my entire life has been filled with nothing but pain, raw emotion, broken promises and feeling like nothing will ever work out.

This time, I chose the path less travelled by *me*. I've never gone down the road that's filled with love. The one overflowing with people that want to walk the path by my side.

And I don't doubt at all that Wyatt will be one of those people, helping to pull those limbs and branches out of the way when I think I might trip and fall.

It won't always be perfect. I can't assume that I won't get hurt. But I've decided to take that risk.

I'm going to start believing in promises.

And that includes believing Wyatt when he says he wants to promise me everything.

For more in the Hermosa Beach series, make sure to pick up Lucas Pearson's love story...

Be Your Anything is available on Amazon!

Acknowledgments
FROM THE AUTHOR

    I can't imagine ever starting this section without focusing on my husband first. **Danny**, it is because of you that I believe happy endings exist. It is because of you that I know the type of love I write about is possible. Thank you for always encouraging me to go after what I want in life, and supporting me on this journey every way, large and small.
    My beautiful **sister**, I am so glad you've found your own romance hero, and I hope he loves you ten times more than my leading men are ever capable. Your relentless encouragement and regular "you're amazing" comments help push me through.
    Mom and **dad**, your emails and texts and constant praise about my work ethic and drive are so, so, *so* welcome and appreciated. I love how you believe in me!
    Oh, my sweet **J-Crew**, how you've grown recently! Your reviews are priceless. Thank you for helping me catch those final typos that I always seem to miss. And **Kara**, I mixed up the food

this time! I hope you're proud!

The **Kaipii Ohana** is officially my escape, and a much needed one when I feel overwhelmed by work. I'm so blessed to call all of you neighbors and friends, and to be able to giggle and laugh and drink endless wine with each of you. Also, I really do love your kids. So thanks for letting us be a part of their lives.

Dawn, thank you for giving cover feedback and asking questions and being so supportive. I'm so glad we're friends.

To every **blogger** and **reader** who has been willing to read, review, steal, download, tag and like my work - this one or any other - thank you! I love to write, and I love hearing your thoughts on the creative works I put out into the world.

Now, on to the next!

Lots of love, and smooches,
Jillian

About the Author
JILLIAN LIOTA

Jillian Liota is a southern California native currently live in Kailua, Hawaii. She is married to her best friend, has a three-legged pup with endless energy, and acts as a servant to two very temperamental cats. When she isn't writing, she is traveling, reading a good book, or watching Harry Potter.

Always.

To connect with Jillian:

Join her Reader Group
Sign up for her Newsletter
Rate her on Goodreads
Visit her on Facebook
Check out her Website

Send her an Email
Stalk her on Instagram
Add her on Amazon
Follow her on Pinterest

More Titles FROM JILLIAN

The Keeper Series
The Keeper
Keep Away

The Like You Series
Like You Mean It
Like You Want It

Hermosa Beach Series
Promise Me Nothing
Be Your Anything
Give My Everything

Cedar Point Series
The Trouble with Wanting
The Opposite of Falling

All books are available on Amazon, Kindle Unlimited,
and for sale through www.jillianliota.com